A PLUME BOOK

THE SIXTH SURRENDER

HANA SAMEK NORTON holds degrees in history from the University of Western Ontario, London, Ontario, Canada, and the University of New Mexico. Her passion for the Middle Ages dates to a childhood spent exploring the ruins of castles and cloisters in the (now) Czech Republic, where she was born and raised, and where she first learned the difference between a halberd and a hauberk. Norton currently lives in the Southwest, where she is married to an Englishman, teaches part-time, and works as a consultant.

D1532055

THE SIXTH SURRENDER

HANA SAMEK NORTON

A PLUME BOOK

PLUME
Published by Penguin Group
Penguin Group (USA) Inc., 375 Hudson Street, New York, New York 10014, U.S.A.
Penguin Group (Canada), 90 Eglinton Avenue East, Suite 700, Toronto, Ontario,
Canada M4P 2Y3 (a division of Pearson Penguin Canada Inc.)
Penguin Books Ltd., 80 Strand, London WC2R 0RL, England
Penguin Ireland, 25 St. Stephen's Green, Dublin 2, Ireland
(a division of Penguin Books Ltd.)
Penguin Group (Australia), 250 Camberwell Road, Camberwell, Victoria 3124, Australia
(a division of Pearson Australia Group Pty. Ltd.)
Penguin Books India Pvt. Ltd., 11 Community Centre, Panchsheel Park,
New Delhi – 110 017, India
Penguin Books (NZ), 67 Apollo Drive, Rosedale, North Shore 0632, New Zealand
(a division of Pearson New Zealand Ltd.)
Penguin Books (South Africa) (Pty.) Ltd., 24 Sturdee Avenue, Rosebank,
Johannesburg 2196, South Africa

Penguin Books Ltd., Registered Offices: 80 Strand, London WC2R 0RL, England

First published by Plume, a member of Penguin Group (USA) Inc.

First Printing, August 2010
10 9 8 7 6 5 4 3 2 1

 REGISTERED TRADEMARK—MARCA REGISTRADA

CIP data is available.

ISBN 978-0-452-29623-7

Printed in the United States of America
Set in ITC New Baskerville and Goudy Trajan
Designed by Eve L. Kirch

PUBLISHER'S NOTE
This is a work of fiction. Names, characters, places, and incidents are either the product
of the author's imagination or are used fictitiously, and any resemblance to actual persons,
living or dead, business establishments, events, or locales is entirely coincidental.

To my mother, "v kostce"

PROLOGUE

Saumur, Anjou, Spring 1200

The whore shifted cautiously and leaned over him, stealthy as a cat. He sensed in her the anticipation of an obstacle surmounted, a goal reached, a desire satisfied. He had experienced such anticipation himself and watched it unfurl in other men before a battle, before claiming a woman. . . . His hand closed on her wrist, poised above his breastbone. The girl cried out in fright and surprise.

"I didn't mean to steal it, sir. Your friend, he told me to wake you."

He sat up, forcing back the girl's wrist. "Vaudreuil knows I don't fall asleep in a whore's bed. What do they call you?"

"La Belle de Bretagne." The girl gasped in pain. "I told you, melord."

"*My* lord. I don't remember my whores' names. And you lie through your teeth, *ma belle*. Vaudreuil would only call if the roof was on fire." He squeezed the thin bones. "Is it?"

The girl winced, her eyes darting away like a guilty child's. She was a few years past childhood, yet her reaction struck him just the same. Perhaps he was beginning to sober up; perhaps it was finding himself near the place where he had spent the short years of his own childhood. He did not like the reminder and so he buried it, just as he had learned to bury the rest of his life.

"N-no. Please, sir, you're hurting me."

He let her go. The girl sat back, rubbing her wrist. She watched him slip the chain over his head. He held out the pendant. She grabbed for it and he let it drop around her neck. She examined the cross dangling between her breasts, cupidity, not reverence, in her voice. "It's gold, isn't it? What kind of stones are they?"

He leaned back against the lumpy pillows. "Amethysts."

The girl frowned. "Amen . . . ?"

"Amethyst. A stone said to protect knights. And yes, it's gold, so don't even think about sinking your sharp incisors into it."

Belle looked confused.

"Don't bite into it to see, you silly bitch."

Belle did not take offense. She wiggled into a more comfortable position, like a cuffed puppy anxious to rejoin the fray. "Hmph. Amethysts. Didn't help you, did it? Did you steal it?"

"I received it in the Holy Land from the hands of Coeur de Lion. He said his mum gave it to him."

Belle clasped the cross to her and laughed. "You've pinched it! Was it a big fat monk?"

"The fattest," he said.

Belle stopped laughing. "You are lying, aren't you?"

"Usually."

Belle was examining him, her hands over her breasts, a gesture of seduction and modesty so intertwined that it again struck in him that same chord, like the reopening of an old wound. He was sobering up. "You're an odd fish," she said. "What's your name?" And then, as if issuing a challenge: "Don't you have a wife?"

He wound a strand of the girl's hair around his finger and tugged at it. "Interesting questions, Belle." She was prettier than most in her profession, but all he felt was a belly-cramping void that nauseated him. It was either that or the cheap wine. "How long have you been a whore, love?" he heard himself asking, not knowing why.

"A year come this summer, me . . . my lord. Papa was going to sell me for just five years, but Mistress said they'd pay for me a good while longer, don't you think?"

"Indubitably," he said.

Belle frowned. "I don't know what that means either." A sly expression crossed her face. "Are you going to tell Mistress I tried to take it? I never had one that kept such a thing around his neck while he dight me. It's a sack ridge, the priest says."

"Sacrilege." He did not know why he bothered.

She stuck out her chin. "The priest said you must turn a cross wall-ward and you mustn't wear one when you are doing it, even to a wife. If you tell Mistress, I'll tell her you wouldn't take it off when I asked you and that you said you stole it. She'll tell the magisters."

The girl was a shrewd little strumpet. He fought down another wave of nausea along with an urge to pelt her. He tried to keep his tone patient. "You are a whore, Belle. You can't swear out an oath and testify against me."

Belle's teeth sank into her lower lip. He could see that she was contemplating whether or not he was lying, wondering how someone like him would come up with a thing like that.

"Then I'll tell the canon of Saint Florent. He asks for me every fortnight. He'll have you—"

He clamped his hand over her mouth and flung her under him. Breath hissed out of her, terror glazing her eyes. He squinted at her, deliberating. It was laughable to be at the mercy of a newfledged tart. When he had first seen the girl, she had about her the pugnaciousness of those who have little to lose. That, he supposed, was why, even drunk, he had picked her. His sobriety made him realize that behind the cunning, Belle lacked the intelligence he had imagined to find there along with a compliant body. For some reason, it angered him. He did not need an altercation over the cursed cross, not when he was about to return it to its rightful owner.

His hand spanned her throat. "One peep out of you and I'll snap your neck, do you understand?" The whites of the girl's eyes gleamed. She nodded. "Good girl," he said and eased off her.

Belle sat up, clutching her throat, watching her customer. Until then, the man had not used her badly, only with more indifference than the others. When he had first gestured for her with a full cup in his hand and a half dozen in him, he had not seemed that old, but now he appeared to have aged years, and the voice and the look in those eyes . . . Belle of Brittany would be murdered in her bed by a penniless *soudoiier,* of that she was certain. "I wasn't going to tell, sir, I swear it. I wasn't."

He considered her. He might have frightened her, but once he was out of this place, she would tattle on him. Sometimes greed and revenge were more powerful than fear. "Do you know why I didn't take it off?"

Belle shook her head, her elbows flattening her breasts.

"When you wear it, it makes it better." She blinked at him. He reached out so not to startle her and traced the valley between her breasts. This time, he smiled. "I'll show you."

She pursed her lips. "Pffft!"

"If you don't believe me, don't try it. But you have to wear it."

The girl's elbows relaxed and her gaze shifted to the clove-pointed cross. She looked up with a dubious frown. "You said you're a liar."

That made him laugh, though the girl could not tell why. "About everything but that."

The change in him puzzled her. She gave him an uncertain smile. "I never like it nohow."

"Close your eyes."

She tried to jump away from him. "You'll throttle me!"

He took hold of her elbows, leaned over, and kissed her. It was not much of a kiss because she was poised to flee, but it surprised her nevertheless.

"Oomph, no! Mistress said I am not to let anyone kiss me without making them pay first. I—" She did not get further because he did it again. She gave a short gasp when the tip of his tongue traced between her lips. She wanted to push him away, but he had already let go of her. "I am not supposed to—"

He drew back enough to see her face. "Then let's not tell her." He could see that Belle was becoming intrigued. She let him kiss her.

"What am I to do?" she breathed after a while.

"Nothing."

"Truly?"

"On my word of honor," he said, wondering if the joke would be wasted on the girl. It was. He watched doubt fight curiosity on her face. For a whore, Belle was as transparent as vapor. She nodded.

It was hardly an unpleasant thing. That came afterward, when he was buckling his sword belt and Belle reached out to him, her features softened, muttering her assurance to him. He divested her of the cross, his lips brushing her earlobe. "Now you are just as guilty, Belle. You are a good whore, but a bad liar. If you defy me, I'll break your neck."

PART I

TILLIÈRES

CHAPTER 1

Abbey of Fontevraud, Anjou, Spring 1200

Sabine de Nevers floated toward the chapter house in a cloud of perfume, a cloak of the finest Flanders wool, and a gown of the greenest cendal, its fashionably long sleeves trailing on the convent's floors. Not appropriate attire for the house of the hand-maidens of the Lord, but well chosen to keep the chill from her bones, and to show off those famous Nevers eyes and what used to be, in her time, a famous figure.

A countess in her own right, she could afford to flaunt conventions, to turn aside pointed remarks that she had reached an age when she should have long retired to a convent, perhaps joining her only daughter. As the confidant and lady-in-waiting to the queen-duchess Aliénor of Aquitaine, Sabine dealt with these barbed monitions the same way her mistress did—by ignoring them.

She knew that Aliénor had not entered Fontevraud to take the veil either, as the world vainly hoped, but rather to conspire and plot, as the world justly feared. The Duchess of Aquitaine's plots required meticulous planning, and that required time, which was the reason for Sabine being sent to Abbess Mathilde. Beyond the half-opened door, Sabine could hear the abbess's voice, uncharacteristically elevated.

"Are you certain you have unburdened yourself, Sister Eustace?"

"I think so, Mother."

Sabine peeked inside. On the tiled floor, a figure in novice's robes prostrated herself in front of the abbess.

"Your memory must be failing, child. You placed a toad in Sister Emma's night lantern and nearly frightened her to death. Sister Domenica tells me you've asked Father Osbert impertinent questions. Last week, Sister Susanne found you reading a book you took from the armarium without Brother Egremont's permission." Abbess Mathilde paused dramatically. "She told me you had picked the door lock."

"Brother Egremont doesn't mind when I read his books, Mother. I always return them. His eyes are not very good but he doesn't want to relinquish his position. I read to him, and he teaches me and allows me to borrow a book or two."

"And what have you read these days, Daughter?"

The repentant tone gave way to an enthusiastic one. "Saint Augustine and Saint Gregory, and Horace and Ovid. I mean Origen. And Abélard."

"Abélard!"

"And Abbé Bernard's condemnation of him, of course, Mother."

"Of course." Abbess Mathilde sighed. "You may kneel now, Daughter."

Although Sabine disliked disobedience in one's inferiors, she found herself smiling. She was about to take her leave when the abbess called out, no doubt alerted by the movement at the door, "Countess, do join us."

Sabine did as asked because despite her rank and the queen's generous gifts to Fontevraud, their small court was, after all, a guest of the abbey.

Abbess Mathilde, a petite, dignified woman of threescore years, stood under a wooden cross, her hands folded under her scapular. The calamitous Sister Eustace knelt in front of the abbess, her head bowed and hands clasped hard. "You may bring the countess a chair, Daughter," the abbess said.

The girl jumped up and set about the task in a swirl of white veil and robes. Sabine watched her with increasing amusement. Her task completed, Sister Eustace remained standing in front of the abbess, her hands properly inside her sleeves, her head again bowed.

Abbess Mathilde assumed a stern tone. "What would you advise, Countess, that we do with a person who has heeded few of our admonitions?"

Sabine fought to hide a smile. The queen's entourage did not include young demoiselles anymore, as it had long ago at her court at Poitiers. Sabine missed the laughter and the teary, inconsequential crises and spats. "Perhaps that person should be allowed to contemplate the error of her ways and come up with her own suitable penance."

"A most excellent idea. You will retire to the chapel, Sister Eustace, and remain there at prayer until you are called. You may go now."

The girl curtsied to the two women and fled in most unseemly haste, the doors slamming loudly behind her. This time, Sabine laughed. "Sister Eustace seems a little distracted."

Smiling, the abbess sat in her chair. "Sister Eustace, yes. Juliana de Charnais can be quite determined. That child must have read every book in the library. The brothers call her Sister Scholastica. She claims she is not ready for her solemn vows, and I could not agree with her more, but what can I do? She inherited Tillières and thinks one day she will reclaim it. Unfortunately, she has already refused one husband."

"That viscounty of the Norman march? Was the queen informed that one of John's fiefs passed to a female heir?"

"Of course, but I suppose there are more pressing matters."

Indeed, there were. After the death of Richard the Lionheart a year ago, John Plantagenet had become Duke of Normandy as well as King of England in the face of fierce opposition from the supporters of his thirteen-year-old nephew, Arthur of Brittany, son of John's late elder brother Geoffrey. To complicate the dynastic mire, the newly installed king-duke lacked an heir. In fact, he was about to divest himself of his childless marriage to his current wife with no new wife on the horizon. His mother, Aliénor, knew it, and it worried her; hence Sabine's mission. "Her Grace asked me to inform you that she is expecting another visit from the Earl of Pembroke. Please instruct the gate mistress to let the earl and his party pass."

"The earl is always welcome. We pray the queen finds other such worthy champions. It is difficult enough for a female liege to maintain the loyalty of her vassals. Fortunately, we can always rely on the One who sustains us all." The abbess crossed herself.

Sabine joined in the gesture. "Blessedly so. But I would yet hold my faith in the queen."

The way to the queen's apartments took Sabine past the great, single-naved church. Through the open door, she caught sight of Sister Eustace. The kneeling girl appeared to be absorbed, but somehow Sabine doubted it was in prayer. Something about the girl's hunched shoulders compelled Sabine to enter the nave.

High above, four cupolas hovered, miraculously suspended between columns punctuated by slender blades of windows, their panes casting rainbows of colors onto the floor stones. The heavy scent of incense and beeswax filled the air.

"So, have you contemplated the error of your ways, Sister?"

The girl started but quickly composed herself. "For five years, Madame."

The forlorn tone kindled in Sabine mixed emotions. It was nothing more than an impulse, she told herself, that made her say, "Will you walk with me to the gardens?"

The girl hesitated before nodding and they walked around the cloister garth into the high-walled abbey garden. Sabine chose a stone bench underneath a still-bare chestnut and patted the seat next to her. The girl took up the bench edge, hands in her sleeves, eyes downcast. Sabine watched Sister Eustace's gloomy face, with its pouting lower lip and a slight crook in the bridge of the nose, a splash of childhood freckles across it. She was no great beauty, but a handsome enough girl, if thin. "I am told you now wish to attain *status conjugatorum*, after all. But are not chastity and obedience the highest virtues in a woman? Does not Saint Jerome teach that only in our innocent flesh can we near the perfection of angels?"

Sister Eustace's gloom vanished in a burst of scholarly fervor. "But Saint Augustine says that chastity cannot be violated without the consent of one's will. And he says that Adam and Eve's *status conjugatorum* received the blessing of our Lord. And doesn't he say that the lust of another cannot pollute the innocent?"

Sister Scholastica certainly had a knack for drawing others into knotty disputations. "Do we not all in the end put aside worldliness? Isn't that what the Church teaches?"

Juliana winced inwardly and tucked in her chin. Oh Mary, her runaway tongue. Would the countess tell on her to the mistress of novices? But how could she put aside thoughts of worldliness when the scandalous queen-duchess had settled at the abbey, and when her presence drew a steady trickle of visitors? She tried to catch glimpses of them and snippets of their world even if it earned her the penance of scrubbing the floor of the refectory. Her disquietude grew. She feared that one day she would deeply discomfit Father Osbert by screaming at the top of her lungs during the benediction, another mad nun. "Yes, but how am I to renounce this world when I have not experienced any of it?"

"I see. Then you would not know that the queen strives to secure the rights of heirs of faithful vassals?"

"Others know better than I do in these matters, Madame." Juliana thought it better to tame her answer.

Sabine noticed and it drew another smile from her. "Oh, I think you know more than you allow, Sister. I believe Mother would give you leave, provided, of course, the queen agrees to find a master for Tillières loyal to Duke John. Would you like me to speak to her?"

Juliana looked up. The grand lady appeared to her like an angel descending from heaven, offering her the world. "Oh, yes!"

How eager the young were to savor the world, Sabine thought, knowing yet so little of it. The bell announced Vespers, and Sabine crossed herself and rose from the bench. As they took the path toward the garden gate, the girl two paces behind her, Sabine said, "So, are you willing to raise the white flag to a husband this time?"

"Surrender to a worthy foe is not a defeat." Her father used to drum that into his squires' heads, and it was as good an answer as Juliana could conjure.

This time, Sabine laughed. "Then I shall have to ask the queen to find you someone worthy to surrender to!" She grew somber. "Choose carefully, my dear. The queen's utmost concern will be not your wishes, but your viscounty."

Black-robed sisters began to converge on the chapel. Juliana watched them, the long, eternal line of black. "I have chosen. I am the last de Charnais. I want my home."

CHAPTER 2

Saumur, Anjou

Outside his temporary headquarters in the respectable part of Saumur, Sir William Marshal, Earl of Pembroke, dismounted and dismissed his men. He gave Jehan de Vaudreuil, who lingered nervously outside the door, a brief scowl, which Vaudreuil knew was not meant for him. "*Par Dieu,* is he here?"

Vaudreuil saluted smartly. "Yes, Sir William, as you've ordered." Marshal dropped his cloak on his squire. "Is he drunk?"

"No more than usual, my lord." Vaudreuil hoped he sounded convincing. Passing, Marshal cast him the kind of glance usually reserved for a nurse who has failed to do her duty. Vaudreuil rubbed the back of his neck. Bloody hell.

Inside, Marshal strode across the small hall and came around to face the man who stood before the table in stolid expectation. A servant came rushing with a cup and a ewer. Marshal waved him back. "Bring another cup. I'd like to know how all in one morn, my lord Lasalle manages to frighten a harlot out of her wits and return to the queen at Fontevraud a cross belonging to her son."

"Good horses, my lord."

William Marshal snorted in exasperation and shook his finger at his captain. "One of these days that wit of yours is going to bring you trouble you can't handle, son. Sometimes I think that's what you want."

Lasalle smiled at his muddy boots.

The servant brought another goblet. Marshal filled it and pushed it across the table. "When Brother Simon delivered your token to Her Grace, she boxed his ears for not bringing you along. You are to go back and explain."

"No. Tomorrow I'll take my men and head for Marseilles."

"You don't say no to Aliénor, son. God's teeth, I need you here, not in some dusty garrison in *outre-mer*. With John on the throne, she will need all the help she can muster to keep him there. There aren't many we can trust among these backstabbing Poitevins."

Marshal gestured angrily, knowing that the aforementioned predicament was of his own doing, and that everyone knew it. After all, he had lent his considerable reputation in favor of John Plantagenet over Arthur, even though the barons of Anjou, Maine, Touraine, and Brittany had chosen the young prince-duke. The Normans, refusing to be ruled by the Breton Arthur, backed John, but only reluctantly. And John had done nothing to dispel their unease when, at his investiture ceremony in Rouen, he turned to his friends to mock the proceedings and the Lance of Normandy slipped from his grasp, to an audible gasp from the assembly.

While Marshal was in England trying to persuade those barons to choose John as their king, the queen-duchess had ordered Mercadier, the loyal captain of Richard's *routiers*, to march his mercenaries against the rebels of Anjou. Fortune at last smiled on John as well. He razed Le Mans, taking its inhabitants into captivity, and then sailed to England to be crowned its king, proclaiming that he intended to deal with Anjou later. In fact, everyone knew that John lacked the resources, and perhaps the intestinal fortitude, for a protracted fight, and that he would return to buy off his challengers with heiresses, royal favors, and promises. Aliénor and Mercadier finally suppressed the Angevin revolt with the dearly bought help of the barons of Poitou, particularly the ever grasping Angoulêmes and the notorious rebel barons of Lusignan.

But the boy-prince Arthur was not the prime sower of this whirlwind. That role belonged to Philip Augustus, King of the Franks, John's and Aliénor's suzerain. Arthur had grown up at Philip's court, filled with hatred of his uncles and his imperious grandmother. This Frankish king would not brook a powerful Duke of Normandy on his doorstep. Philip wanted Normandy for himself, and he would gain it by fomenting trouble in the most troublesome part of John's patrimony.

Before Lasalle could offer his opinion on the subject of the backstabbing Poitevins, Marshal leaned across the table to jab his finger into the middle of his visitor's scuffed gambeson. "I am conferring with Her Grace tomorrow and I was ordered to bring you. Since neither one of you suffers fools gladly, I am certain you'll get along famously. She ought to find you a mesne somewhere. You won't be young forever, trust me. You've done your share of fighting for the Plantagenets. They ought to reward their true supporters."

Lasalle looked inside his cup. "Then I am in no danger, my lord. They took thirty years to reward you."

Marshal propped his fists against his sides with a bark of a laugh. "Ha! Richard was a two-faced skinflint, but wouldn't you say the lady Isabel was worth the wait? She told me to look after you. She said you are naturally trouble-prone."

His captain smiled a smile that Marshal had seen send the plainest of damsels and the most respectable of matrons primping. Marshal had observed, however, with some amusement, that his wife had a somewhat similar effect on my lord Lasalle.

"The countess is kind."

"Isabel doesn't get her head turned. A man needs a level-headed wife—and a landed one."

Lasalle took a patient breath. "I am in no need of a wife."

Marshal finished his cup. "Nonsense. Every man needs a wife. Whores are nothing but trouble. Out of curiosity, what did you do to this one?"

"She wanted the cross. I told her I'd wring her neck if she caused trouble. Would you like me to tell that to the duchess, sir?"

Heading to the door, Marshal gave Lasalle a friendly cuff. "Save your wit for the duchess and your venom for the Lusignans, my lord. You and your men are not to leave Saumur until I send for you. That is an order."

Bowing with arrant precision, Lasalle did not reply, but Marshal saw his trouble-prone captain's teeth clench underneath the stubble.

CHAPTER 3

Abbey of Fontevraud, Anjou

A frail body and a still agile mind—that was her greatest misfortune. Her resolve as sharp as the old-fashioned quill she grasped in her hand, Aliénor, Duchess of Aquitaine, former Queen of France, Queen of England, Countess of Poitou, surely and swiftly signed her name to the last document. "Is that all of them?"

Curtsying, Juliana placed the new sheets at the queen's elbow. "There are two more, and the letters, Your Grace."

In her youth, Juliana had heard, Aliénor of Aquitaine had been dazzling. She found the queen-duchess dazzling still: a fine-boned face with fragile skin marked by the sun of her native south, blue eyes that commanded even more than her light, brittle voice. Aliénor refused to allow age to bow her, although it had slowed her down. With her women, she moved along the corridors as if in a coronation procession, her head slightly tilted upward, making herself appear tall almost by an act of will, favoring the finest cloth in bright colors, jeweled finger rings, and perfumes that often triumphed over Father Osbert's censer, a woman of temperament and temper.

Aliénor affixed her signature to the documents and indicated a painted leather box. At Sabine's urging, they had availed themselves of the girl's services. Sister Eustace was quick and efficient, if in awe of the legendary queen. "Remember, the dispatches must be ready for the rider by tomorrow. Here, my key, girl, and be careful not to lose it. The wax, Sabine."

The Countess de Nevers set aside her embroidery and dripped the melted seal wax over the parchment fold. "One would think, Your Grace, that you were enjoying this."

Aliénor handed her seal ring to her lady. Among the disarray on her writing table, she found a small wooden casket and removed from it a linen kerchief. "I have enjoyed a number of things in my seventy-eight years, but handing out lands to a pack of quarrelsome barons in exchange for their dubious support of John is not one of them."

"Quarrelsome? Surely not the Normans?"

Aliénor held the bundle in her hand. "My Lusignans are up to something."

"*Your* Lusignans, Your Grace? John is now the Count of Poitou, are they not *his* Lusignans now?"

"John is not paying attention. Why do you think I camp at Fontevraud?"

Juliana looked up from her parchments. The Countess de Nevers did not hide her disdain. "The Lusignans reach above themselves."

Aliénor smiled. "So they do. They stole everything in Poitou that we did not nail down. No wonder they took to *outre-mer* like a duck to water. Guy swived Sybilla and got himself crowned King of Jerusalem, thanks to his brother, who had her mother. And Geoffrey acquired a reputation in the Holy Land second only to Richard's."

The lady Sabine was not distressed by the queen's language. But she gestured to remind her of Juliana. "They are nothing but thoroughbred brigands. Brown Hugh practically extorted La Marche from you."

Juliana tiptoed to her scribe's desk and climbed onto her stool, which was fitted with a brazier to keep her feet warm. Soaking up the warmth and each tidbit of news with her every pore, she pretended to busy herself with her pens.

"So he held us hostage. Hugh always claimed rights to La Marche by marriage, only Aylmer of Angoulême wanted it as well. I had a granddaughter to fetch from Spain; that is why I gave Hugh La Marche. John was furious, so I told him to make Hugh pay homage to him for it. John was still not pleased, but then you can't please that man."

Juliana whittled at her pens. The world she had been so long denied sat in this very room. It was all so strange and wondrous.

"La Marche will not be the end of the Lusignans' ambitions," said Sabine.

"Of course not. Hugh's son is to marry Aylmer's daughter come summer. With lands in Poitou and now La Marche, and soon Angoulême, the Lusignans intend to cut Aquitaine from Normandy."

"Good Lord." Sabine crossed herself. "Surely Philip is behind it all."

"Some of it." Aliénor rubbed her temples. "Thank God for Marshal, but Lord, the *routiers* are costly. At least we are not bound to ransom them."

Sabine pressed the queen's seal into another puddle of seal wax. "Mercenaries are a scourge at war and more so at peace. They ought to be destroyed whenever caught."

Juliana pricked up her ears. The Church outlawed all those who killed for profit. She would have felt sympathy for the *routiers*, but the very word evoked universal terror.

"They'll fight past forty days when our vassals pack up their tents. Give me a dozen *routas* and someone like Mercadier to lead them, and you can have all of my barons with their pride and privileges. I miss that man. He kept the mercenaries on a short leash on our lands."

"You have Marshal and the other captains, my lady." Sabine tried to reassure her mistress.

"Marshal is not getting any younger. I have Brandin, Girard d'Athée, Martin Algais, and half a dozen of these robber captains. They fight as long as we pay them, and they waste our lands when we don't. Our barons hate them."

"And Lupescaire, Your Grace."

The queen tossed aside her sander. "Don't mention that man's name to me. I'd have him cracked on a wheel like the common felon he is."

"The duke favors him." The Countess de Nevers indicated to Juliana the changes to be made on the sheets she had handed her. Juliana took her penknife and commenced to scrape a name from a charter. Some unlucky baron was out of favor with the queen. She carefully polished the parchment's bare patch with the tip of a deer's antler. Her ink did not run, not even after several corrections.

"A king is judged by the company he keeps. Mercadier was loyal on principle, and he got himself murdered for it."

"Murdered?" Sabine turned to her mistress, surprised.

"Murdered. Goaded into a brawl by a man who was not as drunk as he appeared."

"Who was he?"

"Armand de Lusignan's hireling, who else? Now there is a man I'd like to hang, draw, and quarter. Do you think me cruel, girl?"

The question came so unexpectedly that Juliana nearly dropped her deer antler. "N-no, Your Grace."

"I will tell you about cruelty, my child. To be immured by your husband for sixteen years while in the prime of your life and to know him to take women to his bed while he keeps yours cold. To watch your children die before you, your grandchildren despise you, to have your struggle and sacrifice imperiled by your last flighty, indolent, stubborn, unforgiving, and impulsive child. There is nothing I would not do to secure what I have battled for, do you understand, girl?"

"Y-yes, Your Grace."

Tidying the queen's pen case, Sabine tried to guide the conversation to safer ground. "They say that the Lusignans are sprung from Mélusine, a serpent-woman who enticed the son of the King of Brittany to marry her. They say that their progeny appears handsome, but is terribly flawed in spirit. They say—"

"Yes, yes," the queen interrupted. "They say that we are the seed of the Devil. Do you believe it?"

"Of course not, Your Grace!"

"A pity." The queen's humor appeared to be restored. "I'd

rather be thought of as the Devil's daughter than a saint's sister. The Holy Father told King Philip to take Ingeborg back to his bed and imposed an interdict on his lands when he did not jump. That's what kept him occupied and amenable to negotiations with John. What have you heard of Ingeborg, girl?"

Juliana barely saved her inkhorn. "I—"

"You've been eavesdropping and reading my dispatches. Are you learning something, girl? You wish to return to the world. What do you think of it?"

"It seems rather disorderly."

"Disgraceful, I'd say. So, what do you know about Ingeborg?"

"Danish princess, married to King Philip and repudiated—"

"After her wedding night. It took her seven years, but she finally prevailed upon the Holy Father to hear her prayers for reinstatement to Philip's bed and throne, one of which is occupied already by Agnès de Méran. Philip also has a bastard by Agnès, and there are rumors she's full with another one." The queen twisted in her seat. "Well, what do you think of that? Would you climb into the bed of a man who did not want you?"

"No!"

"Neither would I. Fortunately, you don't have to worry. No matter how highborn, a man is nothing without a lawful wife between his sheets. The purpose of marriage is to produce a legitimate heir. That is all. Remember it."

Juliana nodded with what she thought was solemn sagacity. That was a mistake.

"So, what sort of a man do you want between your sheets?"

"I—"

"It is a simple question, girl. A young one, a rich one, a handsome one, a brave one?"

"An honorable one and a kind one, Your Grace, if it pleases you, and a learned one."

The two women looked at each other. The Countess de Nevers smiled. The Duchess of Aquitaine burst out laughing. "So you've thought about it, have you? Holy Mother. For your Tillières, I can find you a husband, girl, not a miracle."

"Someone like the Earl of Pembroke," Juliana tried to explain.

She looked forward to Sir William's visits, and she had even confessed to the Countess de Nevers that she liked the earl greatly. The lady Sabine had looked at her in astonishment and laughingly stated that while she found the earl insufferable, she'd heard that his wife had nothing to complain about.

"Sir William is a rare exception. You have already rejected an elderly suitor, Lady Juliana," the queen said pointedly.

"I was young and silly, Your Grace, and I have pledged to abide by the wisdom of my betters."

"You ought to have learned that sooner," the queen noted without much sympathy.

Juliana's hand flew to her nose. Her father's fist had broken it, and when Sir Antoine Crispin of Boutavant saw her bruised and swollen face, the old man swore and withdrew his suit on the spot—and her father packed her off to Fontevraud. That had been while her two brothers were still alive to inherit Tillières.

Sabine reached for the queen's jewelry box. "Perhaps someone of proven loyalty, Your Grace. Although the lady Juliana's family are Franks, Sir Robert was a great admirer of Duke Richard. He gave Sir Robert the castellancy of Rivefort. The de Charnaises are loyal vassals."

"Now, there's a challenge, Sabine. Finding loyal vassals," the queen-duchess sniffed.

"Surely you will find them, Your Grace."

"I will find them if I have to pay for them."

"And how long would that support last?"

"Until I am dead or until Philip gives them a reason to betray me, or to betray John. Unless John betrays them first." Aliénor held up the clove-pointed gold cross with the four smaller crosses nestled under each arm, and amethysts at the five junctures for the Wounds of Christ. Jerusalem cross, they called it. "They should be here soon. Bring me my coronet and white veil."

CHAPTER 4

Juliana grasped the door ring with both hands to draw the heavy leaf toward her, only to be swept aside by the two men who strode into the queen's room—men bareheaded, tall, loose-knit, bred for a destrier's saddle and the battlefield. They filled the room with their presence and the smell of horses, open country—and liberty.

The Duchess of Aquitaine smiled at the girl's reaction. Watching the two men, Aliénor did not blame her. Wearing long surcoats, their hands on sword hilts, they looked as if they expected to be attacked, even inside this convent's walls. The older man Aliénor knew well—William Marshal, chivalry's nonpareil, and thanks to his marriage, the Earl of Pembroke and Striguil, Lord of Longueville, master of fiefs in Normandy, England, Wales, and Ireland.

Marshal approached first, square shouldered, his narrow face matured into weathered handsomeness, his brown eyes clear and sharp. He was fifty-four, enjoying well-deserved fame as the champion of countless tourneys. Under Aliénor's wing, he had risen from a landless knight-errant to one of the wealthiest men in two kingdoms, grown gray in service to her and her children. In addition to steadfast and loyal, Aliénor knew Marshal to be as tough as nails and utterly pragmatic. She especially appreciated his unwavering hatred of the Lusignans, which dated back to their murder of his uncle and to his own wounding and capture at their hands while defending her person.

The other man, black haired, was someone Aliénor intended to know. He had sent her a simple wooden casket; inside, wrapped in linen, lay a gold cross. Her cross. She had given it to Richard to protect him, her brilliant, restless, impetuous son, when he rallied the Christian host to recover Jerusalem from the Mohammedans.

That had been nine years ago, and now Richard was gone. His mortal remains rested in the crypt of the abbey, at the feet of his father, whom he had betrayed so often—except for his heart, which Richard had bequeathed to Rouen, and his entrails, which he had left to the people of Poitou in remembrance of their many treacheries. Next to him rested his beloved sister Joanna and her dead infant. Fontevraud was becoming a Plantagenet sepulchre.

Marshal dropped on one knee in front of her. Aliénor tapped him on the cheek and presented her ringed fingers, and Marshal kissed them with élan. "My queen, you and the lady Sabine put this beautiful day to shame."

The Duchess of Aquitaine motioned for Marshal to rise. "It seems your flattery increases with my age, my lord. I am not complaining, although I sometimes wonder what you tell your wife. Do remember me to her. John is now at peace with Philip, but nothing lasts forever. I have ordered charters drawn up for fortresses without trustworthy castellans."

"Lady Isabel will be honored to be remembered by you. As for the fortresses"—Marshal pulled out a folded sheet from inside his surcoat—"I have several more names for your consideration." While his mistress examined the names, Marshal shifted uneasily. "Your Grace, the duke will not take kindly to your efforts."

"I won't allow John to piss away his patrimony, not while you and I are alive, Marshal. Excellent. Add these names to the list, girl, and make a copy for the seneschal."

Juliana hurried for the parchment, blushing when Sir William winked at her, as he always did. His attentions had baffled her before she realized that it was just his way of acknowledging her presence, her female presence. He had noticed her, unlike the others who had occasionally appeared before the queen, including the man Marshal brought this time.

Although he was younger than Marshal and hardly homely, he looked much too swart, wary, and world-wise. Despite it—or because of it—she was compelled to grant that most women would find someone like that thoroughly fascinating. And he, no doubt, them. *I would wager,* Juliana thought, fighting a sudden attack of the giggles, *that his wife surely has something to complain about.*

Marshal stepped aside for his companion. "Your Grace, as you ordered, I brought with me the man I hold responsible for Richard's great victory at Gisors."

The younger man snapped his eyes at Marshal, who beamed as if he had pulled off a trick at his expense. Not having much choice, the man genuflected in Marshal's place and bowed his head to the duchess.

Taking the opportunity to size up the younger man, Sabine did so with a growing sense of disquiet. Those eyes . . . it could not be. This was a horrible mistake. "Good heavens. Guérin de Lasalle!"

William Marshal caught his companion's reaction at the same time as the countess did—a sharply raised head, one black eyebrow arched, and on the face of his captain a flash of surprise, plain annoyance, and finally fierce anger, as quickly suppressed as it had appeared. Marshal had seen unruly *routiers* retreat three paces under that glare. Lady Sabine was made of tougher stuff.

The Duchess of Aquitaine lifted her gaze from the man at her feet to her lady-in-waiting. "My dear Countess, don't keep us in suspense."

Sabine gestured in consternation. "I present to you, Your Grace, my . . . my nephew."

"Nephew? I believed there were no other Nevers branches," Aliénor said, annoyed.

Sabine swept around the kneeling man as if he were a venomous insect in the middle of a garden path. "That was my belief as well."

What in the blazes? Marshal felt sorry for his companion. Sabine de Nevers and Aliénor of Aquitaine in concert were a challenge for any man.

Aliénor held out an amethyst-set cross and said, a queen to her subject, "The circumstances of your resurrection, sir, are, I am certain, suitably miraculous. Tell us, how did this come into your possession?"

The question, polite on its face, contained a veiled accusation. The man, for his part, did not appear anxious to enlighten anyone. His head slightly bowed, he remained silent, as if charting a strategy out of his unexpected predicament. When he finally spoke, his voice was naturally low, but also oddly hoarse.

"A favor from your son, Your Grace. At Tyre."

The voice answered in the dialect of her own Poitou, releasing a buried memory of another man, half a century ago in the gardens of Antioch. Suddenly, she was twenty-five again, and beautiful. Blood rose to her cheeks at the vividness of the memory. With an act of will, Aliénor wrenched herself back to her old body and this chamber. "Tyre? What Tyre?"

Marshal tried to end the awkwardness. "The city of Tyre in *outre-mer*, Your Grace. Some of the defenders came from—"

"I wish to hear the answer from this man, Marshal. Surely the cat did not get his tongue? Speak up!" She missed the earl's sharp intake of breath, so when the answer came in a stronger but still gritty voice, Aliénor was not prepared.

"No, Your Grace. A Saracen blade did. At Hattín."

The sound of parchments fluttering to the floor ended the silence. Juliana looked down. Her face ablaze, she slid from her stool, dropped on all fours, and crawled after the scattered pages. In the pause that ensued, the queen-duchess leaned forward and placed her hand on the shoulder of the man kneeling in front of her, placed it where the carelessly cut hair nested thickly.

Juliana looked up to catch Lasalle flinch and then make himself very still. The glint of a small silver hoop through his earlobe took her aback, but that was before she saw what the queen did—a pale scar beginning below it, crossing the slope of the neck and disappearing in the hollow of the throat. It looked like a battle scar—only a knight's ventail would have protected that vulnerable part.

Someone had tried, very clumsily, to decapitate Guérin de Lasalle.

Juliana snatched up the last sheet and retreated to her corner. The distraction gave the queen-duchess time to collect herself.

"You have my apology, my lord. The fault rests not in your voice or my old ears, but in my manners." This time she held out her hand for the man to kiss, making him raise his head to her. *Ray-*

mond. No, it was not he. The resemblance was only superficial, in the age and the frame and the same pitch-black hair and the lines in the corners of the eyes, etched there by the blinding sun of *outre-mer;* but it brought back the memory of walled gardens, swaying palms, snow-cooled wine, and the scent of oranges and musk on a man's skin. She was twenty-five and beautiful.

"Your Grace, are you well?" Alarmed by the queen's sudden pallor, Sabine moved to her side, turning to Marshal. "We've had a tiring day. Tomorrow I am certain the queen will be better able to attend to these matters."

Marshal nodded, and before her mistress could object, Sabine had the visitors out the door, the doors barred, and Sister Eustace kneeling to knead the queen's cold fingers. Sabine tried to force a cup into her mistress's hand. "Drink this, Your Grace; it will steady you."

"I don't need to be steadied. I am not about to faint at the sight of scars. Now, get away, girl! Are you trying to hide some unpleasantness concerning your nephew, Sabine?"

The flash of royal temper sent Sister Eustace scurrying, but did not intimidate the Countess de Nevers. She helped herself to the wine cup. "Unpleasantness? It was an outrage." Noticing Sister Eustace in the corner attempting to look inconspicuous, Sabine paused. "The details of which are not meant for innocent ears."

Aliénor tipped her head back. Her memory contained an archive of her vassals' misbehaviors. One never knew where an opponent's weakness might lie. "He murdered a girl, didn't he? His brother's wife?"

Juliana barely stifled her gasp behind her palm.

Sabine crossed herself. "His brother's betrothed, in truth. Céline de Passeis was her name. She was Armand de Lusignan's ward. He had hoped to make by her an advantageous alliance with our family."

"Did he, now? Do continue before Sister Eustace dies of curiosity."

Reluctantly, Sabine obeyed. "Guérin is the son of my younger sister. Yvetta was such a pretty, headstrong thing. She was married well, but her husband died in a hunting accident inside two years. She was left a childless widow with a flock of suitors, including . . . well, never mind. One of them was Guérin de Lasalle, a landless Norman gadabout with Welsh blood, so that's to be expected. She married him for his looks, and he married her for her estates, before anyone could prevent it."

The Duchess of Aquitaine was examining the crucifix. "A fortunate woman."

"Not for long," Sabine happily contradicted her. "I had not seen her again after that marriage, although she wrote to me when things became difficult. I offered her my advice, but she would take none of it. They had two sons, Geoffrey and Guérin. Even as children, they could not have been more different, Yvetta said. Geoffrey loved the Church, which did not please his father. I suppose young Guérin turned out as headstrong as his mother, but when it suited him, he could charm the birds out of the trees. It worked on everyone, except his father. He must have resented the attention Yvetta gave the boy."

"One could name dozens of families with ungovernable youngsters and resentful fathers. Was he sent to Poitou?"

"To a distant relative, I believe."

"Ah, that's where he acquired that charming patois."

"He remained there until he decided to visit his brother before the wedding. He was told then that Yvetta's entire mesne would go to Geoffrey upon his marriage to Céline. Those were the terms set by Armand. How he managed, I'll never know." Sabine cast a glance at Juliana, who sat riveted by it all. "He decided to trump them all by seducing the girl to marry him instead. I am told he worked to turn the girl's head and abducted her without fuss with the aid of a couple of his friends."

The queen smiled to herself. "Seduction and abduction. A direct if old-fashioned way out of a landless young man's troubles. Usually effective, especially if the girl is willing."

"Only at first. I imagine Céline had second thoughts—defiance of her guardian, marriage to a younger son. Guérin knew that if he forced her, she would have no choice but to consent to the marriage to save herself from disgrace."

The queen-duchess appeared to be absorbed in her thoughts. Sabine crossed herself. "Such a dreadful thing. But even after that, Céline refused to marry him, and in a rage, he killed her. Armand de Lusignan and Geoffrey arrived in time to bury the poor thing. Armand locked up Guérin and his friends at Pont-de-l'Arche. They would have rotted there had the Devil not intervened."

"Oh dear," said the duchess with a heavy note of irony. "I had anticipated divine intervention."

"This intervention also involved the Lusignans," Sabine took pleasure to inform her. "Young Guy needed companions on his journey to the Holy Land, a penance for his part in the Lusignans' rebellion against Richard. Armand must have decided that Guérin and his friends were the sort his nephew could use. Guérin and the others no doubt concluded that the Saracens were a better offer than rotting in the Lusignans' gaol. They knew they would receive absolution as well, so they all pledged themselves to Guy."

"How very loyal of them."

"Loyal enough this time to follow Guy to that slaughter at Hattín. Lord, I can still hear the bells. We thought he had perished with the others. A broken heart killed my sister. Her husband went to Wales, where they buried him, as well."

"And the lands?"

"They ended up in the Lusignans' hands after all, as a recompense. Only a small estate was left, near Fécamp."

"And what of Geoffrey?"

"Poor Geoffrey. I heard he had joined the Benedictines."

The bell broke the silence. Juliana fidgeted. If she were tardy again, Sister Domenica would return her to bread and water. She inched from her stool, catching the queen's attention. This time, Aliénor nodded her dismissal. Juliana dropped a cloth over her writing desk, curtsied, and quietly closed the doors behind her.

Aliénor of Aquitaine stood at the window, watching the twilight encroach upon the garden. "How do you find someone to fight for you? How do you bind them to you even after you are in your grave? How do you find someone to pledge their body and soul to your cause?"

CHAPTER 5

The following day, the queen-duchess received Guérin de Lasalle in her apartments, alone, giving strict instructions not to be disturbed. When the Countess de Nevers was allowed to see her mistress, her odious nephew nowhere in sight, Sabine found the queen strangely renewed, and it worried her. The visit, however, appeared to be soon forgotten.

The Duchess of Aquitaine dispatched William Marshal as her emissary to the Count of Angoulême and to the count's half brother, the Count of Limoges. The aim was to bring together during the coming summer an alliance against the Frankish king consisting of her son the Duke of Normandy, the Angoulêmes—and the slippery Lusignans. But the queen-duchess had more in mind than a round of drunken revels, loud boasting, and skirt-chasing, the kind of affair into which these gatherings inevitably degenerated. She therefore sent a messenger to her son in England, requesting him to visit his ailing mother, and then called for the Countess de Nevers.

Sabine curtsied and folded her hands with the air of a hound about to be sent into the sedges.

"I have decided to secure one of John's fiefs for your nephew," the queen said.

"You can't!"

"Sit down, Countess. I don't want your opinion of my decision. Marshal knows how to twist arms. Lasalle thinks he is in for garrison duty."

"Your Grace, you are handing a fief to a kidnapper, ravisher, and a murderer—"

"If I were to drum out of my service every kidnapper, ravisher, and murderer, I would have no vassals left with the exception of Marshal, and I would not stake my last penny on him, either. Admittedly, your nephew leads a dissolute life, but unlike Lupescaire and the rest that John favors, your nephew is not baseborn. His selection will not ruffle the Normans' feathers as much as my son's usual choices. And I do appreciate ingenuity." The queen's rouged lips puckered. "Especially mine."

"I see. Then my help is not needed after all," the Countess de Nevers said very calmly, her eyes defying her words of capitulation.

Aliénor wanted to tell her lady that in tight corners, she and her nephew looked much alike, but decided to save it for another occasion. She handed Sabine a parchment. "It is. You may inform our Sister Scholastica that she is to take a husband."

Since Sabine could do little about her nephew's undeservedly good fortune, at least that was good news. "Very well." Sabine curtsied, her dignity restored. "Whom shall I tell her she is to marry?" In an instant she knew the answer, even before she saw the smile on the queen's face. "Oh, no! No, Your Grace, that is entirely—"

Aliénor held up her hand. "Lasalle takes Tillières and that girl with it."

"That snip of a girl? He'll have her in her grave and her mesne in his hands before the year is out!"

"Your nephew will hold the viscounty of his wife. He'll forfeit it if anything happens to the girl before she gives him an heir. After that"—Aliénor shrugged—"Tillières belongs to the child. Should it become orphaned, John will claim custody of it and the viscounty."

Sabine rolled out the parchment, a standard-enough document. "That will not guarantee her safety. Madame, you will have that girl on your conscience should anything happen to her."

"Many things are on my conscience. Sister Eustace is the least of them. You may inform her that her choice is Tillières and Lasalle or her lonely little cot at Fontevraud."

Shivering in her felt slippers, a bedcover over her shift, most of her short red curls tucked under her night veil, Sister Eustace arrived in Sabine's room. Sabine settled the girl in her own bed, sat on the edge, and told her that the queen had found a new master for Tillières. The girl looked surprised but not unduly so. Sabine offered her a cup of wine. "Don't you wish to know who your husband will be?"

Juliana shook her head and hugged her jumpy kneecaps. "I wouldn't know him, anyway."

"Oh, but you've met him already." The countess removed the cup from Juliana's hand and enclosed the ink-stained fingers between her own. "The queen has chosen my nephew. You will be my niece-in-law."

The countess Sabine's lips were moving, but the roaring sound in Juliana's head drowned out the last words. That was not possible. How could the queen . . . how could the queen chose someone like . . . like that execrable man? Why *him?* Why couldn't the queen find for her someone honorable and lighthearted like the Earl of Pembroke? "And . . . and if I refuse?"

"You are to take your vows."

Juliana heard those words.

Sabine touched the girl's cheek, trying to assure her as much as herself. "My dear, if you choose . . . the queen seems to think there is nothing to fear."

"F-fear? Nothing to—!" Juliana wanted to scream at the top of her lungs, her thoughts scattering like pigeons. One came back and roosted in her mind and in her breast and in her very marrow. "I will lose Tillières. How can the queen ask me to give up my heart?"

The next day, after the convent retired and the servants went to their beds, Juliana was called unexpectedly to the queen's quarters. From her chair, the Countess de Nevers smiled reassuringly at her. Juliana returned a wan response and bowed her head.

"It appears"—the queen set aside her book—"that you are questioning the marriage I have decided to settle upon you, Lady Juliana."

Juliana cast a frightened look at the Countess de Nevers. "No, Your Grace."

"You are not a good liar, girl. You'll need to acquire that skill. You know we have little choice in whom we marry. Even queens. Particularly queens."

"But he is a murderer."

"We are all murderers. We couch it in bloodlines and privileges, and wattle and daub the rest in courtliness."

"I haven't murdered anyone."

"One day, you will."

Tears, burning and bitter, gathered under Juliana's eyelids. She swallowed, desperation making her bold. "My choice is to remain in a place not of my choosing or to wed a man like . . . him."

The queen tapped her finger on the open page. "A dilemma, isn't it? One does not enter marriage expecting to find love there like a pair of mislaid slippers. You know that a woman's silence is taken as her consent. Remain silent then, if you wish, but do try to give your husband an heir before the next year is out. A man marries a fief. Sometimes he marries for love or passion, but passion can destroy, if you are the object of it. Love can destroy too, if you are subject to it. And one day, both simply vanish."

"And . . . and honor?"

"Honor, like love, comes in many guises. One day you will learn that too, Lady Juliana."

CHAPTER 6

The day had turned pleasant, growing warmer in the afternoon. The queen, the countess, and two young sisters, Mathea and Paulette de Glanville, adjourned to the hostel's garden. The girls were the granddaughters of Rannulf de Glanville, the loyal justiciar of King Henry and the queen's reluctant jail warden during the years when she was her husband's prisoner in England. In a twist of fate, before death claimed him, de Glanville had fallen into poverty and out of favor with John. The queen had accepted custody of the two orphans, bearing no ill will toward a learned and loyal servant of the Crown.

The sisters had brought with them a basket full of kittens, and set about pursuing their new friends among the budding trees. Juliana trailed with her pens and a portable *secrétaire* behind the queen and the countess. She dared not make further reference to her future husband, and the queen offered no more advice. The three of them took over the rose arbor, where the queen and Lady Sabine entertained themselves playing chess.

Juliana had hoped that her work would distract her, but her hand shook so badly that she spent most of the time scraping ink spatters from the vellum. At the abbey bell's toll of Terce, Sister Imene came into the garden to inform the queen that her visitor had arrived.

Lasalle came through the garden gate, his scuffed gambeson reaching to the top of his muddy boots, sword at his side and the thin sheath of a poniard slanted across the small of his back. In the open air he looked invincible, like a man accustomed to carrying the weight of a shield and a fifty-pound hauberk, to handling a lance or a sword with one hand and a plunging warhorse with the other. At least Sir William Marshal was pleasant and companionable. Juliana could discern no sign of kindness or forbearance about Guérin de Lasalle. The new Viscount of Tillières was what he appeared to be—a fighter to his fingertips.

He did not notice her this time, either. That was odd, considering he surely must have known that he was to wed her as the price of his viscounty. Perhaps he did not care. A man marries a fief.

The queen leaned forward. "This is a charter to your seigneury, my lord, with the duty of these estates to your liege."

Lasalle took the charter. Juliana could not see the contents, but she could tell that he was holding it upside down. Good Lord. Guérin de Lasalle did not know his letters!

"And there is one more duty I wish you to fulfill," the queen-duchess said before Lasalle could figure out what to do with his patent. "You will hold the viscounty of Tillières and the fortress of Rivefort of their heiress, who is hereby given to you in marriage."

Juliana clasped her hand over her mouth. Oh Mary!

Lasalle blinked, astonishment plain on his face, but not for long. He folded the patent. "No," he rasped curtly.

Lord in Heaven, bless Lasalle's worthless, black soul. She was so overwhelmed by her misery that she had never considered he would not want to marry her. Landless men of dubious pedigrees did not disdain the grant of a wife with a viscounty. No one expected a husband to be faithful to his wife, and it seemed that every man, including her father, had mistresses. The queen-duchess was right. All a man needed from a wife was a legitimate heir. For that, an unattractive spouse sufficed. Juliana fought a wild impulse to throw her arms around Guérin de Lasalle and kiss him in gratitude, just to see the expression on that haughty face.

"Alas, sir, you have no more choice in the matter than your viscountess does. Besides," Aliénor's tone eased into a teasing note, "you may come to appreciate the lady Juliana's talents."

Nauseating fear engulfed Juliana.

"I don't care for the lady's talents. I don't wish to wed Lady Juliana or any other—plain or beautiful, dull-witted or sage!"

Sabine sat on the edge of her seat. Heavens, if the rogue did not want the girl and she did not want him, either, why the battle? The girl looked as white as her wimple.

"Your objections are noted," the queen said. "Nevertheless, you will wed her."

Lasalle threw the crumpled patent at her feet. "I am not your vassal, woman. You can't command me to marry against my will."

Juliana held her breath. Lasalle had not only defied Aliénor of Aquitaine; he had insulted her as well. But the queen-duchess did not dwell on his impudence. She resumed her seat. "Go and look after those children, Countess. Their delightful laughter is giving me a headache. You think of yourself as no one's vassal, sir. That is against nature and God's order. Sister Eustace, tell my lord Lasalle what this writ states."

Her hands shaking, Juliana broke the seal on a parchment the queen handed her. "Her Grace . . . Her Grace exhorts her barons to destroy a *routa* of mercenaries under the command of one Guérin de Lasalle wherever that band appears, being guilty of pillage and plunder of her lands."

"What the—" Lasalle took a step toward the queen. "You can't do that. Richard pledged safe conduct for his mercenaries provided they kept the peace."

"I am not Richard. My Richard is dead."

His hand on his sword hilt, his teeth a sharp white slash, Lasalle took a half turn toward departure. "Then go ahead. I didn't teach my men to sell their lives for a pared penny. We've fought against worse odds."

"Against Marshal?"

"Oh, Madame!" The parchment dropped from Juliana's fingers. Lasalle whirled back. "What the Devil—"

Aliénor smiled. "How well have you taught your men, my lord? Shall I have Marshal tell me?"

"You wouldn't!"

The queen came to her feet as if she had shed years. "Do not presume to tell me what I would, sir. I have John's inheritance to guard, and if you think to stand in my way, you are a fool!"

Guérin de Lasalle was going to lunge for the queen's throat. Juliana was certain of it. The queen took a step toward him. "Go ahead, boy. I dare you."

Holding his ground, Lasalle glared back. A battle waged between them, silent, yet as palpable as blows. And then he backed away and turned, his fist striking the folly's post. The frame shook. Juliana jumped up, ready to fly for aid, but when Lasalle faced the queen, it was with a deep bow and venomous irony. "I accept your conditions for Tillières, Duchess. You may inform the lady Juliana of her great fortune."

"Well, well." The queen's voice sweetened. "A right choice after all, although I am certain you had the lady worried."

"What?" Seeing the smile on the queen's lips, Lasalle swung his gaze to the only other person left in the folly. Juliana prayed for the ground to open up and swallow her. The Lord did not oblige. "She is a nun!"

"A novice. Lady Juliana cannot reclaim her viscounty without a husband, much as you cannot maintain your men without her mesne. I could not have found two other souls so sure to be dedicated to Tillières's welfare."

"But—"

The queen folded back her sleeves with a gesture of satisfaction. "No need for bans. You'll be wed tomorrow, and I wish you to leave for Tillières immediately. You have many flaws, my lord, some more grievous than others. I am not interested in them. I am informed that, unlike some men, you don't find women repugnant. You've bedded your share, and I don't care how you conduct yourself in your marriage. You may find the bride a bit prickly, the portcullis a little tricky, and the garrison temperamental, but altogether nothing a man of your talents can't handle." She opened her palm. "I believe this belongs to you, Viscount."

Too stunned for words, Lasalle dropped to one knee. The queen looped the chain of Richard's cross around his neck, her fingertips light on the pendant gleaming incongruously against the old chamois. "Defend Tillières for John as well as you defended Tyre."

At the queen's signal, the Countess of Nevers hurried to her mistress's side, her expression apprehensive. "We will leave my lord Lasalle and the lady Juliana to make their acquaintance unattended."

"Oh," the queen added to Lasalle after a few steps. "I have decided to entrust the demoiselles Glanville to your wife's care. I believe they will want to bring their beasts with them. Remember, Lady Juliana, *maritus aut murus.*"

Leaning on Sabine's arm, the queen passed through the garden gate, the young sisters and their feline friends joining them. Lasalle watched them with his back to Juliana, the slant of his shoulders communicating pent-up fury.

Maritus aut murus. Husband or the cloister. She stood there, her fingernails scoring her palms. She had to make a connection with this man and she did not know how. She blinked and he was bounding from the folly, leaving her standing there like Lot's wife.

"My lord," she recovered and called out after him. That was a mistake.

He swung back at her. "Holy Mother's . . . You conniving bitch. You knew! She knew it too, saints' piss. She never intended us to fight Marshal!"

Backing away from him, Juliana crossed herself. She had never heard anyone blaspheme that way, nor call her such a name. "That is not true! The writ is genuine."

He sized her up, his eyes painfully green, a streak of perspiration along his jaw, and then he shoved past her with a flash of his earring. "Then I should have accepted my lot. And so, Sister, should you have."

She picked up her robes, overtook him in three leaps, and barred his way. "I don't enter this marriage of my own volition either, sir, and I will strive to end it as soon as I can!"

She had surprised him, but her triumph was brief. He had the advantage of his height from which to look down his fine-bred nose at her, but he deigned to descend to her eye level by a dip of his knees. "That makes two of us."

CHAPTER 7

To be the wellborn mistress of one wellborn man brought no shame; to be the mistress of many such could cause one to be called a whore, if not to one's face, then behind one's back. Therefore it behooved one to be beautiful, wealthy, widowed, and the vassal of the most powerful woman in Christendom. Several days after the unlamented departure of Sister Eustace, the abbey received a visitor of such standing. The Countess de Valence arrived with her escort, her maids, and eight carts of her barest necessities.

"Lady Anne." The Duchess of Aquitaine looked up from her jewelry casket. "You are prompt as to my request and well prepared, I see."

"I thought I ought to be, Your Grace." Anne lowered her eyelashes, as well as herself at the queen's feet in a curtsy that filled the room with rose-hued silks.

"I have never known you not to be prepared." Aliénor gave the young woman her hand. "Do you know Armand de Lusignan?"

Anne kissed the queen's rings. "We have exchanged pleasantries."

"And how pleasant were they?"

"I have not had Armand de Lusignan in my bed. Not that I would mind." Anne kept a well-trained smile on her lips.

The queen motioned the young woman to rise. "I wouldn't mind either, if I were your age. You are to go to Normandy, seek him out, make yourself irresistible, and keep me informed of what he is up to. I doubt he will be much of a pillow prattler, but try not to sleep too soundly. You will have, as always, whatever you need from my chancellor."

"Normandy." Anne picked up the sander, examining it. "Such a moldy place. I shall need new gowns, of course, and a jewel or two, and the horse livery needs refurbishing. Perhaps I should—"

"Whatever you require, Anne," Aliénor interrupted, knowing that the Countess de Valence's needs and necessities increased with each assignment. "How fares John?"

Anne went about the room, examining the appointments. "When I left him, His Grace was bored and uncertain."

"Indecisive, you mean, surrounding himself with his *routier* friends and harlots—present company excepted, of course." The queen-duchess waved away the last comment.

Facing her mistress with a compressed smile, Anne curtsied. "Shall I leave immediately?"

"As soon as you care to. You are also to make inquiries about the Viscount of Tillières."

"I don't know him," Anne replied with indifference to that part of the assignment.

"Nor should you. He is recently minted. His name is Guérin de Lasalle. And his wife's—"

"His wife!" The sander crashed to the floor, spilling its contents.

The queen shook the sand grains from her hem. "Don't tell me. You have exchanged pleasantries?"

Anne leaned against her chair. "I . . . he's a nobody."

"And how did you come by him?" Curious, the queen poured wine and handed the young woman the cup.

Anne moistened her lips. "I visit Isabel de Clare when she resides at Longueville. Sir William once called his captains there. We've met occasionally since. Sir William keeps him busy."

"And I keep you busy. What do you know of this Lasalle?"

Anne shrugged. "What he has done. What he is. I don't allow men to pry into every corner of my soul and I don't pry into theirs."

"Not when there are much more enticing corners. I don't care if you've been tupping from sunset till sunrise. Your nobody turned out to be Sabine's nephew. I made him marry an earnest little soul here who wanted a man of honor. He'll do anything to get himself out of his marriage, but I want it indissoluble."

"Why?" Anne broke her own rule to remain detached from her mistress's schemes, but unlike the others, this one touched her personally.

"Now, there is a question." The queen smiled over her cup.

"Armand de Lusignan and Lasalle hate each other. Would you like me to bed them both, Your Grace?" Anne asked anyway, intending to dislodge some answer.

"I allow you to bestow your favors on any man you want in exchange for bestowing them occasionally on a man I choose. This time I insist on it."

"As you wish, Your Grace." Anne returned the cup to the table with some force.

The queen-duchess smiled, opened a silver-and-ivory box, and lifted from it a necklace of amber, the beads imprisoned in cages of golden filigree. She placed the beads in the young woman's hands. "I do wish. You can have Lasalle as long as you make certain that he and his wife end up in the same bed, preferably at the same time. I don't care if you indulge your anger or vanity, Anne, but don't be blinded by it. We have a kingdom to save."

CHAPTER 8

Road from Saumur to Normandy

Juliana, are we there yet?"

"Not yet, Mathea. Perhaps in two or three days."

Mathea wrinkled her nose in disappointment and kicked her pony into a trot. Juliana let her mare amble after the child. They had departed from Fontevraud at the beginning of May, three weeks before the marriage of Aliénor of Aquitaine's granddaughter, fifteen-year-old Blanche of Castile, to King Philip's son. The marriage was intended to bring about rapprochement between her uncle John and the French king. Juliana thought about that marriage, also willed by the queen-duchess, knowing that the distant events bore directly on her own marriage. That knowledge sparked a small hope in her.

She twisted her wedding ring. It was too small and had hurt her knuckle when he forced it on. What she needed was a way of removing Lasalle from her life forever. He might think that this marriage had dropped Tillières and Rivefort into his hands, but its location on the Norman march made the viscounty vulnerable to the changing vagaries of French and Norman fortunes.

While Paulette remained secluded in her cart, Mathea rode up and down the plodding convoy on a gentle chestnut mare, introducing herself to Lasalle's murderous *routa* and dashing off to examine rotting corpses on crossroads' gibbets with unabashed curiosity. The sight of those chained wretches was not what had filled Juliana with abject terror. It was her anticipation of the nightfall of that first day—a fear that turned out to be groundless. If Guérin de Lasalle had spent that night with a woman, that woman was not Juliana. His decision spoke either of his aversion to her or of his desire not to shock their company. Looking about her, she concluded that the latter was unlikely.

Lasalle's men traveled under a swallow-tailed standard, its blue dye faded and its tails frayed. Lasalle appeared to have chosen as his own the banner of Saint Martin, a Roman soldier who had transformed his life when he gave half of his cloak to the Beggar Christ. Under his colors Lasalle had gathered a polyglot assembly of skilled cutthroats—some Brabançons, half a dozen Aragonese and Gascons, sundry men-at-arms of various origins, and several young men who appeared to be runaway serfs.

The man in charge of Lasalle's cutthroats was a balding, red-faced Rhinelander by the name of Kadolt, who walked with a limp and sounded unintelligible to everyone but the *routiers*. The others in the company were knighted—Jehan de Vaudreuil, a black-eyed, sober-looking man Lasalle had brought as his marriage witness to the chapel steps; Rannulf de Brissard; Hugon de Metz; someone called Saez; and a couple of others, most of the men older than their master. From the looks of them, the knights did not harbor any more chivalrous impulses than he did. With the squires, grooms, and servants, including several loose women who came along as laundresses, their company numbered nearly six dozen souls, not to mention the carts, saddle and warhorses, and pack mules.

And so here they were, one happy family: herself, Mathea and Paulette, and Mistress Hermine, a short, stout, motherly nurse provided by the Countess de Nevers along with two plain, good-natured maidservants for the girls, who had reconciled themselves to being handed off to another alien household with the equanimity of those who know they live on charity. Juliana had immediately liked Mistress Hermine, a decisive woman of two score and ten with cornflower-blue eyes that had seen much and were surprised by little, dressed in a spotless fustian gown and unimpeachably white wimple.

With the roofs of Fontevraud behind them, Juliana found herself retreating behind a wall of her own making. Mistress Hermine did not mind. She settled herself among the pillows, trunks, and trundles, pulled out her spindle, and set about distracting Juliana. Hermine told that she had been nurse to the Countess de Nevers's daughter, Valentine, that she had delivered the girl into this world and seen her through her brief marriage, and that she had remained with the countess after Valentine had entered a cloister.

"My good lady told me that I was all she had of Valentine," Hermine chattered over the drone of the wheels, "but she said that I would be more useful to you, my lady, knowing how you are, with no family to look after you, no woman's ear to tell your troubles. So I said to myself, there is another poor lamb who needs old Hermine, and so here I am, as long as you need me, my lady."

Hermine's simple kindness hurt. Juliana lowered her head to Hermine's lap and cried, from helplessness and fear and from the dreadful, crushing loneliness she had thought she would leave behind when she rejoined the world. Patting her young mistress's shoulder, Hermine made soothing noises until there were no more tears left.

After three days of hiding in the cart, her stomach so knotted that she could hardly force down a mouthful, Juliana decided that she had to face her fears. Hermine urged her to drink some of her raisin wine, but the heavy, sweet taste did not appeal to Juliana. She would rather face Lasalle sober. *If I don't,* she told herself as she climbed out of the cart one morning, *I may as well take the veil.* Still, she could not bring herself to approach Lasalle, and so she smiled tentatively at one of the servants and asked if there was a palfrey to be had.

The man bowed and called her Madame, and a few moments later a dappel-gray mare was brought by a friendly groom of about sixteen, who introduced the mare as Rosamond and himself as Donat. He told Juliana that he had given up the life of a student for far more exciting prospects in the service of my lord Lasalle.

As she listened to Donat, a tide of panic nearly overwhelmed her. Surely they were all looking at her, at her nun's hair hidden under her wimple, her crooked nose, her gown whose lacing only emphasized her ungenerous figure, her propensity to stammer when anxious, and her conventual manner of lowering her eyes.

Her distress must have been obvious to Donat, who assumed the solicitous attitude of an older brother. "Don't mind these men, my lady; they are not as bad as that. Not even Kadolt, not with a platter of sausages in front of him."

Juliana hid her smile behind her hand and was about to ask Donat about his adventures when a snorting sorrel rounsey bore down on them, foam from its bit spattering her gown. She jumped back to flatten herself against the cart wheel. The mud-splattered, ill-tempered rider sat back in the saddle, his hand to his hip.

"You'll not ride without Donat or out of sight of this company. If you do, I'll have you tied to the tail."

She closed her fists against her skirts. Lasalle addressed Kadolt with more circumspection than he offered Juliana de Charnais. At first she had thought that his voice would be a disadvantage to someone commanding a potentially fractious force, but she soon discovered that he kept it low deliberately, to compel those around him to pay heed. Now he was using the same tactic on her.

"Why?" It was a brave question and foolish in its bravery.

"Because you are my wife."

There, he had said it, the truth of the words steeped in sarcasm. She had to hold her breath to keep back a scream. One did not challenge a man who held dominion over one's life. She belonged to Guérin de Lasalle, along with the fishponds and the buttery. He knew it, and spurred his horse past her.

Juliana exhaled. To hide her mortification, she asked Paulette to accompany them, but the girl declined. Paulette was as sedate as her sister was brash, her figure rounding into a perfection of feminine loveliness, her skin without flaw, eyelashes demure, heavy braids of blond hair reaching to her waist. At fourteen, Paulette possessed a composure nothing seemed to disturb, born of resignation or natural passivity.

Oh Mary, how could she be these girls' mother, adviser, and confidant, when she needed such herself? And there was something else that terrified her: The queen must have known that Juliana could not protect her wards from their guardian any more than she could protect herself. Juliana crossed herself. Thankfully,

Lasalle did not pay attention to any of them, other than occasionally sending his squire, Aumary, to ascertain that they had not
fallen out of the carts and drowned in the mud.

Aumary de Beaudricourt appeared to be about Donat's age,
with dark brown hair, a pleasing, somewhat melancholy face, and
soft brown eyes. Although he had not yet reached his full height,
he had begun to acquire the breadth of shoulder and leanness of
haunch of his kind. He held his master in high esteem and tried
to emulate his demeanor, but lost out to his natural gentleness
and civility. Juliana noticed that Aumary did not mind inquiring
about the welfare of the occupants of the carts, especially the one
carrying Paulette and Mathea.

And so, with Donat accompanying them, Juliana and Mathea
rode past strips of fields sprouted with winter grain, across
dandelion-dotted meadows that reverberated with choirs of bees.
Spring sun had transformed the world into a green-and-yellow
blaze of tender leaves and bursts of pink apple blossoms. And
sometimes, when Juliana looked about her, despite her fears and
aching limbs, she felt joyfully happy.

None of it, of course, lasted very long.

CHAPTER 9

Fortress of Rivefort, Tillières, Normandy

Except for the Perche Hills and a line of forests sweeping
northwest from the Avre, no natural frontier marked the
Norman march. The invisible, mobile line defining Frankish and
Norman territory crossed green plains and several rivers guarded
by white-walled fortresses. In the lush landscape under a pale
sky, generations of Normans and Franks had fought and died to
defend or dominate these outposts. As the Duke of Normandy,

Richard had expended a treasury on constructing and refurbish-
ing these bastions, expecting his castellans to withstand prolonged
sieges in order to sap the French king's forces before they reached
Normandy's principal defenses—Arques, Vaudreuil, Argentan,
Falaise, Caen, Montfort, and the spectacular *château-fort* Gaillard,
Richard's "fair daughter," towering above the Seine at Andelys.

At the edge of the viscounty of Tillières, the fortress of Rivefort
formed a link in the chain of secondary defenses of the Avre. Behind the curtain walls with their drum towers, Rivefort's crenellated
donjon could be seen for miles across the rolling countryside. At
the sound of the horn, the cart mules leaned into the harness, their
hooves thudded on the drawbridge and clattered into the first bailey. Juliana peeked out from behind the cart's cover.

In the bailey, men milled about, kindling torches. Several
knights rushed to greet Lasalle amidst furiously barking dogs and
the confusion of grooms, stableboys, and Rivefort's garrison. Juliana climbed from the cart and into the embraces of Louis Pavilli,
Rivefort's steward, and his tiny, fragile wife, Edith. She had not
expected them to be still alive, but they had been looking for her,
even before acknowledging their new lord, and greeted her like a
long-lost daughter.

"Are we home, Juliana?" Mathea tugged timidly at Juliana's
cloak, Paulette beside her.

Juliana put her arms around her wards. "We are home," she
said with all the assurance she could muster.

Partly illuminated by a fire in the yawning hearth and dripping
torches in wall sconces, the hall's timbered ceiling rose above the
thick walls. Puckered plaster and faded tapestries covered the masonry, and freshly strewn hay blanketed the floor. In the middle of
the hall sat a trestle table flanked by benches, with an imposing
armchair at its head. The place looked as welcoming as a tomb.
Behind Juliana, Mistress Hermine was making critical noises.

Juliana half-expected her father to rise from that chair and
shout for the hound master. Up a long climb of spiraling stairs, a
heavy door guarded the quarters of the women of Rivefort. At the

stair head, Juliana relinquished Mathea and Paulette and their maids to Hermine and one of Edith's women, who escorted them to a room at the lower landing.

For Juliana, another door to another chamber waited. It was smaller than she remembered, her mother's room, but with the luxury of a fireplace—and tallow candles, which provided more light than she welcomed. A high, curtained bed crowded the middle of the room, padded by three mattresses piled with chalk-white pillows and layers of coverlets. The top one, lined with lynx fur, was folded down. The bed looked inviting and wonderfully comfortable—and daunting.

Against the wall stood a trunk, where her mother had kept her gowns and a few pieces of jewelry. A small table, topped with a jug filled with sprigs of apple blossoms, took up the space by the door.

"It's lovely, Edith." Juliana smiled at the steward's wife.

Edith wiped her eyes with her apron. "I had the cook prepare blancmange and galantine pie and I have a warm bath for you and the master, my lady. Soon you will feel like you never left. Your blessed lady mother would be so happy to know that we have you back."

Juliana pushed open a low door on the opposite wall, which led to an adjoining room. Her father had stored the viscounty's accounts there, along with patents, plate, and a coin box. Lined with a sheet for splinters' sake, a wooden tub now occupied the middle of the whitewashed room, wisps of steam rising from it. Juliana twisted the edge of her sleeve. The naked body was sinful. The sisters never disrobed completely, sleeping in their summer or winter shifts. She agonized. Lasalle was with his men somewhere in the bailey below. Perhaps if she hurried . . . and even if he came, it had to be endured sometime. Hermine said it would not take very long.

It was the scent of chamomile and lavender that did it, and the arrival of Hermine to take charge of her mistress. Juliana kissed Edith's hands despite her protestations, and when the old woman had left, she let Hermine unlace her gown. Arms crossed over her breasts, Juliana climbed into the tub; it was so deep that she could immerse herself to the chin. With a sigh, she did.

Oh Mary. No wonder that something this indulgent was sinful.

She tried not to look, but could not ignore the sharp hip bones and the staves of her ribs. *Make no provision for the flesh in its concupiscence*, Saint Augustine said. She closed her eyes. What did concupiscence feel like?

She heard Hermine bustling about the bedchamber, reciting a list of household matters that required Juliana's attention. She had none to spare. The journey and her overwrought emotions had taken their toll. She felt so tired and the bath made her so drowsy that she barely heard Hermine's prattle. When it stopped suddenly, it took her several moments to notice it. She turned in her tub to the strong room's door to see Lasalle in the middle of her bedchamber, his cloak over his shoulder, his sword cradled in his arms, wearing one of his pleasant expressions. Juliana's stomach shriveled.

"Leave," he said to Hermine.

"But I have to help my lady."

Lasalle arched his eyebrow at her. Hermine dropped a curtsy and, casting back a worried glance, closed the door behind her. By then, Juliana had clambered out of the tub and into a drying sheet. Her fresh chemise was laid out on her bed. Their bed. Her heart skipped. She took one step toward the door.

That man paced about the room as if staking out his domain, dropping his sword and poniard on the table and unbuckling his sword belt. He left it on the coffer with his cloak and stained gambeson and picked up the fire tongs to poke at the embers. "If you stand there much longer, you'll freeze."

She ducked behind the door like a scolded two-year-old. The words sounded sensible and not particularly threatening, but considering who had said them, they were enough to make her want to bar herself in the strong room. The problem was that Lasalle would undoubtedly be just as happy if she starved herself in there. She took a deep breath. Surely it could not take as long as starving?

Lasalle turned around. Ah, the bride. Red hair, what was left of it. Freckles. Thin as a rail, but not a child bride after all. Not one he could hand to her nurse and repudiate without as much as a peep out of her, not the Viscountess of Tillières. So that's what the scheming old witch thought she had got him into. Sister Eustace was not going to like what he was about to tell her.

"You know well, Madame, that I don't want this matrimony any more than you do. When I give my fealty and homage to Duke John for Tillières, I'll ask for his aid to have our marriage annulled. I'll see to it that you are properly settled." It was the longest thing he had said to her, and he hoped he would not have to repeat it.

Settled? Of course he would settle her—somewhere behind the high walls of a bleak cloister! Desperation and defiance possessed her. "We do not fall within the prohibited degrees."

One corner of his mouth turned down, and before she could as much as cringe, he had a grip on the sheet, his knuckles grazing her skin. "I was thinking of lack of consummation," he said in that peculiar voice of his, "but I can always come up with some other grounds."

"I-I will not be locked away. If you try to get rid of me, you'll lose Tillières. Your men will be hunted. The queen will see to that!"

He peeled his gaze from her flat front and rewarded her with a row of evenly worn teeth. "Aliénor is old and far away. John's coffers run empty. He pays with his fiefs. He'll be more interested in my *routa* than a feckless heiress."

Feckless? How would he even know such a word? "Your duke quarrels with his suzerain. I'll appeal to Philip. Rivefort can have a French garrison as easily as a Norman one."

He raised his free hand. She cringed this time, expecting a blow.

Instead, feather-light fingertips touched her brow, her cheekbone, gliding along her jaw in a confusing, unsettling mixture of threat and caress. And before she could think on that, they brushed her quivering lower lip. She started with a gasp, wide-eyed. No one had ever done such a thing to her, not ever, and he knew it! Good Lord, that's why he did it. His head bent to her, lashes shading his eyes. Surely he was going to . . .

"Don't threaten me, mouse. You are not Aliénor."

That was a blow that landed without a fist. "I am not th-threatening. You hold Tillières of me."

The grip tightened. "Tillières may be yours, but all I need is an heir. And when I am through with that, you may welcome refuge with the good sisters."

His full meaning almost escaped her—almost. She was dashing past him when his arm hooked around her waist and cast her backward onto the bed. She would have rolled to the other side, but he caught the trailing corner of her sheet and reeled her back, his weight punching the air out of her. A smile, half contempt, half menace, hovered above her. "Surrender, Eustace."

Swept on a crest of panic, she braced her elbows against the mattress to hold him off. Against her palms was a frame of bone packed in solid muscle, but she gave herself enough room to haul up her knee.

"Jeeesu!" He slumped halfway off of her.

Planting a sharp elbow in his ribs, she almost succeeded in dislodging him. He swore, wrenching her back. Whimpering with fear and impotent fury, she thrashed with redoubled effort.

"You do grasp the idea, Sister Eus—"

Her elbow snapped his teeth into his lip. He swore and spat across the bed. "You little bitch!"

His knee cleaved hers apart. His hand, as calloused as a peasant's, slid between them. Juliana sucked in her breath. He had done this before, he had done this—"You said you want an annulment," she sobbed out in retreat.

"Bedded or not, you can be put aside."

"Hermine says a forced woman will not conceive. You need an heir to keep Tillières!"

He laughed. "Old wives' tales, Sister Scholastica. The world is full of war bastards."

She fought a spinning spiral of terror. "Many of them yours?"

"Indubitably. Your willingness is preferred but not prerequisite."

Her mind recorded a disjointed fragment: *prerequi* . . . ? "Neither was Céline's?"

"No!" His hand moved.

The wood in the fireplace burst into leaping red tongues. Her teeth sank into his shoulder. He jerked back with a grunt of pain and surprise. She lashed out at him, fingernails peeling skin.

"Saints' piss, you!"

His hand shoved between her thighs.

It hurt. She choked with the shock of it. In a heartbeat, Guérin de Lasalle had shown her that she was nothing. She mattered as little to him as she did to Aliénor of Aquitaine. She opened her eyes. She wanted to remember the face of the man who would rape her.

In the flames' shifting light, she expected to see lust, gloating, or at least anger, but his expression was wiped blank. When he moved, Juliana whimpered, but he only rolled himself away. From somewhere, she summoned enough strength to draw the sheet to her. She was shaking; her teeth chattered. She prayed fervently to the Virgin to intercede, to throw her cloak over her and make her vanish, from this place, from this earth.

He stepped back from the bed. Between the edges of his shirt glimmered Richard's cross; the rest of the skin was a spider net of sweat. "You can keep your virginity, Madame, for now. I am not desperate enough to bed scrawny nuns. You wanted Tillières? You can have it, between the bailey and the barbican."

CHAPTER 10

With her veil and wimple fastened as if for an inspection by Sister Domenica, Juliana descended the stairs. The hall was a hub of activity, with Hermine directing the trunks, crates, and wicker baskets that had burdened their carts thanks to the Duchess of Aquitaine's generosity.

"Oh, Juliana, you are finally up. Look at these." Mathea was dragging a heavy roll across the floor. Paulette sat by the hearth, a kitten on her lap.

All the faces turned to Juliana. Hermine made her way to her mistress through the half-unpacked piles. "Are you well, my lady?"

she inquired in a tone that was lost on none of the women and only on the youngest of menservants.

Knowing that Hermine would draw her own conclusions from the state of her lady's linen, Juliana nodded, trying to appear composed. Mathea led her amidst the disarray and the curtsies and bows of the servants who crowded around them.

"Welcome home, Lady Juliana." "God bless you, Lady Juliana!" "God be praised you have come home, my lady."

Not knowing where to put her gaze or her hands, Juliana acknowledged the greetings and well-wishing shyly at first, but the outpouring was so sincere that she began to draw confidence from it. She made herself answer their myriad queries, lending a hand in sorting the cups, plates, and platters, beakers carefully wrapped in straw, draperies, tapestries, and sober convent woolens and linens: the loosely woven burel and the everyday serge. But it was the silks that sent the women into flights of joy, over the intricately patterned damask; the deep-hued, shimmering sateen; glossy cendal; and scarlet ciclaton with coin-size golden dots woven into it.

"Oh!" Hermine held up a silk of heliotrope purple bordered with quivering slashes of heavy gold thread. "What a color. This surely belonged to a Saracen princess. It will make a splendid gown for you, my lady."

The cloth was substantial yet sensuous, worthy indeed of a royal court, a place she would not likely see. Juliana handed it to Mathea. "Let's not. A gown like that might cause accidents in the bailey."

Mathea giggled. The women laughed, nudging each other. Juliana smiled with relief and went about the stores, listening to Hermine and the girls with one ear and trying to determine with the other the whereabouts of her miscreant husband.

It appeared that since sunrise he had been holding court in the outer bailey to receive reports on the military readiness of the seigneury. Since the death of the previous lord of Tillières, the garrison had remained in the hands of one Harpín de Peyrac, appointed by King Richard's seneschal. Sir Harpín had anticipated becoming the next castellan, and the arrival of the new lord and his band of *routiers* did not sit well with the garrison men, who refused to swear fealty to Lasalle. There also appeared to be some perennial problem with the portcullis, which sometimes braced in its grooves, but that was not Juliana's concern.

She found her warmest welcome in the kitchen, underneath the casements, where the cook and the kitchen help were surrounded by bubbling pots, sizzling pans, and the blood-drained carcasses of piglets and featherless fowl. Juliana blanched when the cook, Thomas, informed her that it was all on her behalf. Rivefort was preparing a wedding feast.

Glad to postpone that event, she made her way to the garden, her mother's own place. At the gate, Juliana asked Hermine and the girls to allow her a moment of solitude. She missed it, the silence, order, and dignity of the cloister. Perhaps she would find it in the garden.

The garden gate sagged from its post, the arbor leaned precariously under the weight of neglected roses, and the flowerbeds all but disappeared under an assault of weeds. Even the herber, kept alive by Edith, struggled for survival against its more vigorous neighbors. The wattles that used to confine the sweet peas, tansy, and peonies had rotted away, and the turf benches bristled with nettles. The cheerful occupants of the weathered dovecote were long gone.

Juliana sank to her knees, put her head in her hands, and burst into tears.

In the bailey, the throng of servants and Lasalle's *routiers* were already in full merriment, thanks to the kegs. The pipes, a flute, a couple of tambours, and the hurdy-gurdy competed with the revelers. Drunken voices joined in. Inside the hall, dozens of men, well into their cups, leaned across trestle tables, clamoring for more. The servants, bearing heavy platters and overflowing wine ewers, jostled among the guests.

Laced by Mistress Hermine into a gown of Almería silk, its only virtue a modest neckline, Juliana fought a wave of panic at the hall's threshold. She did not want to face that man, not ever, but her presence would force Lasalle to acknowledge their marriage publicly.

"My lady," a voice called out, "a toast to your marriage and to your and the viscount's long life and happiness." Jehan de Vaudreuil was rising from a seat at the high table, his eyes bright and his cup high.

"*Vivat! Vivat!*" The men came to their feet, pounding on the tabletop till the crockery rattled, raising their cups to salute her— all except Guérin de Lasalle, who had installed himself in her father's chair, an empty seat waiting next to him. Juliana was about to pick up her train and run back to her room when Lasalle stood up. The noise died down. Hands clasped behind his back, he crossed the hall toward her. Behind Juliana, Mistress Hermine hissed.

Lasalle's demeanor was what Juliana had expected; his appearance was not. Attempts to get rid of the stubble had not been entirely successful, but for once, his hair was combed. From quarters unknown, he had procured a clean shirt and a black gambeson. His boots were brushed. He stood an arm's length from her.

She wanted to run. Instead, gathering her skirts, she curtsied deeply to leave no doubt that her submission had been exacted. Lasalle repaid her instantly by returning a bow, the studied gravity of its execution a perfect foil. Hoots and laughter broke out around them.

Loathing filled her heart as she felt herself blush. She kept her eyes downcast, a stony smile on her lips. Lasalle extended his hand. Careful not to trip on her hem, she let him lead her to the table.

"Accept your defeat, mouse."

She would have pulled her hand away, but he held it tightly. They moved among the cheers and the noise, Hermine following behind them. Once they were seated, the rest of the company resumed diverting themselves with the serving women.

Loose manners soon gave way to loose morals, with the result that more wine was spilled than poured into the cups. The noise, the smell of flesh boiled, broiled, roasted, and stewed in an abandonment of spices, and the crush of the suffocatingly male company overwhelmed Juliana. Next to her, Lasalle was in deep discussion with Rannulf de Brissard. Mortified, she kept her eyes on her trencher. After years of silent suppers in the refectory, this was Sodom and Gomorrah. The Duchess of Aquitaine was right. The world outside the cloister was vulgar and violent. The din around her receded in her ears, and she sat there unseeing, until a voice startled her out of her refuge.

"Perhaps this will be more to my lady's liking." Jehan de Vaudreuil set a bowl of marzipan soaked in milk in front of Juliana and sat down beside her. "She gave the viscount quite a fright last night."

Juliana cast a suspicious glance at him. Vaudreuil winked at her. He was teasing her. Juliana felt her mouth pulling into a smile. She hid it behind her hand, but her stomach unknotted a little. She picked up her spoon. "Have you served . . . known my . . . my lord Lasalle long?"

When Vaudreuil hesitated, she feared that she had done something wrong, but he nodded. "We were boys together."

Juliana's heart skipped. If that was true, Jehan de Vaudreuil must have been one of the men Lasalle had recruited to abduct Céline de Passeis. Could Vaudreuil have been involved in the harming of a young girl?

"I see. And you've served in the Holy Land with him?" she asked cautiously, noting the small hoop in Vaudreuil's ear.

He fingered it and gave her a crooked smile. "Devotedly and then some. These are a couple of Greek whores' wedding rings. They told us these would bring us good luck. Christ, I didn't mean that."

Too late, Vaudreuil remembered that until recently, the lady Juliana's world had not included men with silver rings through their earlobes and Greek or any other whores. He was therefore considerably relieved when his liege's little nun inquired with academic interest, "Truly? And did it?"

"More than I can say for King Richard. No earring," Vaudreuil attempted in a bit of levity.

"What do you mean?" Juliana asked, not out of any interest in the topic, but because she was afraid Vaudreuil would leave her to her own company.

"Crossbow wound turns bad quickly. By the time the sawbones

cut the quarrel out of Richard, it was too late. And that sawbones was a good one. Those ones keep a wound clean and open and let it knit from the inside." Vaudreuil cupped his hands. "It takes longer to heal because the scab has to be stripped, but it's worth it. It saved your husband's life."

There was no polite way to ignore it. "Did it? At Hattín?"

Vaudreuil scratched his ear. Now the girl was brimming with questions. That was not a good sign. Better for him to answer them than to leave it to her duly wedded husband.

"King Guy marched us to rescue a lady who held a fortress about to fall to Saladín. No harm would have come to her—she would have been ransomed—but Guy was better at wooing than at ruling. Some Lusignans are like that. Most are good at both," Vaudreuil assured her with another lopsided grin.

Juliana forgot about her marzipan. "Did he receive his injury in battle?"

"No. Guérin was trapped at Hattín with the others, all dying of thirst. He was captured with the few Temple knights and the Hospitallers who were still alive. Their courage so enraged Saladín he made King Guy and his principals watch while the mullahs beheaded the rest."

"Mullahs?" Juliana asked thinly.

"Their holy men, all scribes and scholars; they came with the troops. They are not used to handling a sword and hacked some of our men to pieces before they—" Vaudreuil halted with a grimace. "God's teeth, this is a sorry tale for a lady."

"But I asked," Juliana assured him, afraid that she would lose the only conduit to the man who claimed over her the rights of a husband and master.

"Well, I suppose the sword was dull by then and the man's arm tired, so the blade only grazed Guérin. We found him among the corpses."

"And you nursed him back to health?"

Vaudreuil did not answer her, for his gaze was sweeping the hall. She had been so absorbed in his account that she had not noticed the silence that had suddenly fallen over the company.

Rannulf de Brissard was whispering into Lasalle's ear with urgency. Lasalle nodded and stood up; Vaudreuil did as well. "My lord?"

"Kadolt and Peyrac."

The crowd parted, revealing the mercenary Kadolt and Harpín de Peyrac facing each other, swords drawn. Peyrac was younger than Kadolt, with high-cut, fair hair and a scar on his chin. Their confrontation did not look like the result of a wine-induced misunderstanding.

"*Baste.*" Lasalle did not raise his voice when he stepped between them, but all could hear the command in it. Kadolt's sword clattered to the floor. The instant it did, Peyrac charged with a roar of triumph.

She was about to become a widow.

Peyrac's blade slashed into the space occupied by Lasalle, but met no resistance because Lasalle no longer occupied it. He had Peyrac by the scruff of his neck, hurled him against the banquet table as if he were a sack of horse oats, and not satisfied, shoved Peyrac's face into a tripe pie that had survived the initial collision intact. Juliana flinched. The proverbial humble pie seemed too obvious a choice for it to be an accident. The entire encounter unfolded so quickly that none of Peyrac's friends had time to rally to his aid. By the time they tried, Vaudreuil, who had left Juliana's side without her noticing, charged into the hall with the rest of the *routiers* behind him, each armed with a sword, ax, mace, or pike, a few grasping long kettle forks.

Lasalle dropped Peyrac, leaving him to his men, who marched their prisoner to the door. Not a single man made a move to intervene. Ignoring the dagger stares around him, Lasalle snatched someone's napkin to wrap around his bloody palm. With a cresting dread, Juliana watched him return to the high table, moving too determinedly for someone anxious to resume his supper. And indeed, he was not.

CHAPTER 11

She fought him up the two dozen staircase steps without any success, thanks to her gown and his grip, which threatened to separate her shoulder from its socket. Oh Mary, this was not the public acknowledgment of their marriage she'd had in mind.

Her bedchamber shimmered in the light of candles, the fireplace stoked, the covers turned down. He had lied to her! He'd said he wouldn't . . . No, she remembered, he had merely said "for now."

He let go of her. "You look like you've lost a wager, mouse. I wouldn't bet on Peyrac. That man has more brawn than brains. The feast is over. This is our proper wedding night."

She forced her feet to move her backward. If she could reach the strong room . . . Lasalle followed her. "And there is something you possess, my love, that I want more than anything else."

Her back came against the wall. She flattened herself to it, squeezed shut her eyes and stifled a sob, waiting . . . waiting.

After enduring the heart-shriveling torture of anticipation, Juliana forced one eye to open. The curtained bed stood empty. Her other eye popped open. Her bedroom was empty. That man had walked right past her and into the strong room! Holding her breath, she inched toward it as if it were a dragon's lair. There, filled with steaming water, was her tub, and Lasalle next to it, wrestling with his belt. "Sister Eustace, you look disappointed."

She was about to slam the door and run when Lasalle's voice stopped her. "I wouldn't, if we intend to pretend. They all expect us to spend this night together. Don't disappoint them."

Juliana clasped her hands till her knuckles ached. "Are you planning to spend the whole n-night here, my lord?"

"I don't intend to spend it in the stables, love. Vaudreuil snores. Help me with this, woman."

She could not move, but he could, bending his knees again to bring himself to her eye level. He waved his bandaged hand under her nose. "If you don't, I am going to get into your tub in my clothes and ruin Vaudreuil's new gambeson."

He confused her enough that she made the mistake of looking up into his eyes. Specks of brown swirled in a sea of spruce green. She wrenched her gaze away and shoved her hands inside her sleeves. "You have your squire."

"Last time I saw Aumary, two of your wenches had him cornered. He wasn't calling for quarter, so I didn't think it wise to rescue him." Lasalle shrugged out of the gambeson and held out his arms to her. Not having much choice, she took hold of the shirtsleeve and tugged it over the bandage. A shard must have cut him. He caught his breath. "Ah, gently now. I didn't think nuns were so bloodthirsty."

"You haven't witnessed the election of a prioress, sir."

He laughed. Not *at* her this time, she assured herself with a quick glance. He waited for her to ease the fabric over his knuckles. "One would think you've never undressed a man before, mouse."

"Abbess Mathilde did not allow that sort of thing very often."

"Then pretend you are keeping custody of your eyes, Madame."

Mortified, she waited for someone to rescue her. No one came. Better to get it over with. He stood patiently until the knots in the ties of his drawers gave, kicked away the pile at his feet, and headed for her tub. She looked anyway.

From distant childhood memories, she had a dim idea of the male anatomy; her more recent memory was of the sick old men brought to Fontevraud's infirmary to be tended by the brothers and the lay sisters. This one was wearing only that earring and Richard's cross glistening against short, black swirls of hair on his chest, and even though an exacting life had hewn him to the rudiments, she did not ever recall anyone who exuded so much . . . health. Under the rib cage, his belly curved in.

She dropped her gaze monastically, but in an unfortunate direction. He was dark there, too. Something scalded her, from her hair roots to her toes. Lasalle threw back his head and roared with laughter. "Pretend, Sister!"

She ran out of the strong room, her heart louder than a chapter bell.

In the strong room and still laughing, Lasalle was settling himself into her tub. Juliana paced around her bedchamber, wringing her hands, her heart pounding in her throat. That man had absolutely no manners and not a modicum of modesty. In the words of Saint Augustine . . . For all the words of Saint Augustine, she could not recall a single one, but she could recall that clean line of flank and hip, like parts of some strange, finely wrought, living machine.

"Come here, mouse."

She cautiously approached the threshold. "Why?"

Lasalle's feet protruded over the edge of her tub; water had spilled all over the floor. He held out a rag to her and nodded toward his bandaged hand. "If I get this wet it will bleed again."

Holy Mother Mary. She quickly crossed herself and dipped the rag in the soap dish, slapped it against his back, and scrubbed as hard as she could, but he did not seem to mind. In places, the dark skin bore signs of old scars, and marks from their more recent encounter. She finished quickly and doused him with a bucket of water, soaking her skirts and taking him by surprise. "God's mercy, woman, I don't wish to be drowned!"

She took that for her dismissal and fled to her room. He did not call her back. She paced the floorboards, casting apprehensive glances toward the strong room. A platter underneath a napkin on the table caught her attention. Oh dear. The sisters' diet did not include meat, ever, and certainly not such portions of piglet roasted with rosemary and apple rings, goose-liver tartlets, or pears in almond pastry. Next to them was a ewer of wine and two cups. With the first sip, Juliana knew it was Hermine's raisin wine, but after a few more sips the wine did not taste bad at all. Perhaps if she had a couple of bites, her head would not feel so light. . . .

"You ate all of it?"

The tone was accusatory. She whirled about and nearly flattened her nose on Richard's cross. Lasalle was standing there, a
sheet haphazardly wrapped around him, smelling of soap, damp
linen, and something else.

"Christ, where do you put it? You're as skinny as a nun after
Lent's fast. Didn't they feed you at Fontevraud?"

"Sister Domenica is a firm believer in the penance of fasting,
m-my lord."

He combed through the leftovers. "Hmph. I am surprised
there is anything left of you."

Praying that he would not notice, Juliana began to back her
way around him. His hair was longer than hers and dampness
made the ends curl.

Sighing with resignation, Lasalle dropped a piece of well-
scraped pork rind on the platter and winced. Despite his efforts,
the bandage was soaked. He started to unwind it. "Find something
dry to wrap this, will you? Move, Sister."

The tone and his expression silenced Juliana's objections. She
squeezed herself past him and returned with several strips of linen.
He held out his hand to her. Fresh blood oozed from a red line
across the palm. Oh Lord. She covered her mouth.

"You are an amazing shade of green, mouse."

Her stomach tried to lodge in her throat. She turned away. "I
don't like . . . blood."

He took the linen from her. "I don't like it either. Especially
mine." He said it with an odd inflection, and before she could
ponder the meaning of it, he said, "Can you at least tie this?"

She saw that his hand was now firmly bandaged, with no sign
of blood. Despite her unsteady hands, she tied the ends around
his palm. Lasalle handed her his cup. "Here, drink some more of
this."

She swallowed the wine in two gulps.

"I see you could drink Vaudreuil under the table," he said ap-
preciatively and took the cup from her.

"I don't . . . drink." She blinked to clear her vision. "We drank
only watered wine. Once Sister Ignatia and I—" Juliana reached

for the wall to steady herself, but it buckled, along with her knees.

They were lying naked together, but she was not protesting. Her fingers dug into his shoulders. Laughing, he pushed her back. She reached up and pulled his mouth down to hers. Her body ached. He leaned into her. *Let him kiss me with the kiss of his mouth, let him become a spring inside me, welling up. . . .*

"Juliana. Juliana!"

Juliana bolted up with a gasp. It was only a dream, praise be, one of those dreams that meld corporeality and hallucinations. Surely that was not what the saintly Abbot Bernard had in mind when he preached on the subject of a kiss, no—surely not that kind of a kiss? Her head pounded, making her nauseous.

"Juliana?"

Light poured through the open shutters and the sound of voices spiraled up from the bailey. She covered her eyes against the brightness. Her cheeks were wet; her chemise clung to her. The shutters clanked and the room returned to semidarkness.

"That's what happens when you drink all the wine and devour the feast. Doesn't the Church teach that wine, gluttony, and venery combine?"

Lasalle stood next to the bed, fully dressed, the whiteness of his shirt contrasting with the severe black of his gambeson. He reached out to touch her face. She shrank away. Her body ached with a dull, persistent throb. In the half-light, Lasalle's eyes and teeth glinted. "Don't worry, mouse. I like my women sober, not under the influence of poppy concoctions."

"Poppy?" Juliana touched her temples. So that was where those dreams and lascivious nightmares had come from.

Lasalle faced her from the door, his eyes hard. "Tell Hermine next time she doses my wine, I'll hang her as a witch."

CHAPTER 12

Pont-de-l'Arche, Normandy

Lady Anne. I am honored to have you grace us with your, uhmm, delightful presence."

Anne de Valence shoved back a strand of her hair. The storm had been brief but furious, and had left everyone drenched to the skin. Her palfrey's tail, meticulously braided with two dozen cinquefoils of chased silver, looked like a muddy flyswatter. The less said about her own appearance, the better. Anne had a distinct feeling that the Count of Rancon was laughing at her. With a mixture of relief and resentment, she slid from the saddle and into Armand de Lusignan's arms. He kept her there longer than necessary before releasing her.

Anne untied her saturated cloak. "My carts are stranded. Will you have your men help us free them, my lord? De Querci will go with them."

Armand de Lusignan arched one black eyebrow at her. He was clean-shaven, with high cheekbones and lustrous chestnut brown hair, swept back from his brow and cut cleanly at the nape of his neck. The Creator had bestowed upon the Count of Rancon a mind and manners that mesmerized men and women as much as his looks, and he knew it. He bowed and smiled as if she were a wayward child, and Anne resented the man even more for being unmuddied, unruffled, and amused. This was not the grand entrance to Pont-de-l'Arche that she had planned. He took her hand and kissed her wet glove.

"Viart, Richieu, go with the countess's guard captain to rescue the carts. Dame Ermengarde, look after the countess and her women. We shall dine at your pleasure, my lady. I am anxious for news of our duchess. Still the same meddlesome Aliénor, I hope."

Bowing again, the Lusignan left her in the care of a desiccated dowager Anne concluded to be Dame Ermengarde. The woman curtsied to her with impeccable servility—except no one fooled Anne de Valence.

Anne dragged her skirts out of the mud. "Have my cloak dried and brushed, Ermengarde. And bring us something dry to wear. And I shall have some good mulled wine, if such can be had in this sodden patch."

Quarters of more than ordinary comfort were provided, a bath prepared, and a good wine, a very good wine, found as well. Her women brought their mistress several gowns. Anne chose a saffron-colored one with a tasseled silk waist girdle. She added the amber necklace. These things had come into their use. She had her women dry her hair before the fire and brush it with five dozen strokes before she allowed them to tend to themselves, and thus revived, scented, and unaccompanied, she went in search of her host.

She found him in the great hall, examining two birds with his falcon master. One of the birds was a gyrfalcon, as white as snow and as yet untamed; the other, an old make, to teach the young one by example. The young gyrfalcon did not like the company and she crabbed at the old one.

"She is beautiful," Anne said softly.

The falcon master bowed to her and to his lord and withdrew, taking the birds with him. Armand de Lusignan pulled off his gauntlet and held her in a steady gaze. "She is," he said, and Anne knew he was not referring to the bird.

Twisting a strand of her polished hair around her finger, Anne said, "A gyrfalcon is meant for the glove of a king, my lord, especially such a rare one. You may want to keep her out of sight if John visits your Mervant."

He hung his gauntlet on the perch. "I doubt John will be seen in that quarter this summer. My cousin's son is marrying Isabelle d'Angoulême, and the place will be crawling with us Lusignans."

"Crawling?"

"I was using the common reference to our family's perambulations. Do you hunt, Lady Anne? I have several merlins."

Armand de Lusignan was going to be a tough nut to crack, if he ever could be cracked. "Ah, a lady's bird. Do you have several ladies as well?"

He laughed. "You can count them under my counterpane or you can join them if you are curious. I thought you might wish to rest first."

Anne folded her arms. "Are you truly that dexterous, my lord?"

"I don't know. You may wish to inquire of the ladies."

Her eyebrow went up. "Modesty itself, my lord?"

He kissed her hand, his eyes as intent as his bird's. "You don't have to spar with me, Anne. Ask what you will and I will send a messenger to the duchess for you."

So much for spying on Armand de Lusignan. *Et bien.* At least the man was neither boring nor loathsome. On the contrary.

They dined alone except for the sound of a flute. The musician, a spare Saracen in black robes, sat cross-legged on pillows before the fire, unnerving her with his expressionless, blind eyes. But once the winding sounds filled the hall, Anne forgot all about him. The music, the table, the wine, and the company filled her senses.

"Should we not dispense with the unpleasantries so that you are not burdened for the remainder of your stay at Pont-de-l'Arche?" Armand de Lusignan said through the soft notes.

Anne decided to go along. "Aliénor wishes to know what you are up to, my lord."

Armand de Lusignan raised up his cup. "You can tell her that I am going to remove her son from the throne of England."

Anne started, knocking over her goblet. "You are mad!"

"So I've been called. More wine?"

"Y-yes. But why?"

"I hate them," he answered simply, refilling her cup. "The Plantagenets. When I was neither grass nor hay, they ravaged Lusignan, despoiled our lands, dishonored our hostages, and hunted us as outlaws. They tried to alter the course of my family's destiny. And I shall alter theirs."

Armand de Lusignan was insane. No, he was perfectly sane.

Frighteningly sane. He was telling her the truth. The fortunes and misfortunes of the lords of Lusignan under old King Henry and Richard were too well known.

"And who will take John's place?"

"Surely that is not a secret, not to you, my dear."

Anne decided to lay out some of her cards. "Let's see. The Bretons make fickle allies and Arthur is still young. You must have someone in mind who is capable of holding on to a king's throne and keeping a duchy or two from Philip's clutches."

"Do I?" Armand smiled and reached for his cup, leaving her without her answer. For now.

Later, in his bed, Anne had hoped that she would discover more about the man behind that determined intelligence, but she was disappointed. As the Duchess of Aquitaine had predicted, Armand the Lusignan was not a pillow prattler. Her consolation was that she had found him to be not only a skilled lover, but one who let her assert herself. Anne liked to assert herself. Only one other man let her do that, and he was the other reason why she had traveled to this damp patch. Anne sighed, exasperated by the thought.

"I have received sounder accolades," Armand chuckled, drawing her to him. "Does that mean you'll be leaving us soon?"

Anne made herself comfortable against his shoulder. "Not if you don't want me to. I shall send a message to the duchess that you are engaged in a grand conspiracy and that I anticipate learning more. You *are* engaged in a conspiracy, my lord, aren't you? I don't wish to lie to my mistress."

He kissed the part in her hair. "That I vouch on my honor, but you seem to be annoyed at the prospect."

Anne shook her head. "Not in the least—not after such a welcome—but I will have to leave for a few days. I have to make inquiries about the Viscount of Tillières and his new bride. She is coy about her marriage bed and Aliénor wants to make sure that he is not. He certainly was not in mine. His name is Lasalle. I thought you ought to know."

He could have been jealous, or at least disappointed. Instead, Armand de Lusignan slumped against the pillows and began to laugh. That annoyed her greatly, and when he finally stopped laughing, she made him pay for it. He did not seem to mind that in the least either.

CHAPTER 13

Fortress of Rivefort, Normandy, Summer 1200

Juliana's governance of her viscounty had shrunk to the distance between the bailey and the barbican, just as Lasalle had promised. Whenever she crossed the bailey, his men watched her like hawks. She needed a bailiff to oversee her viscounty. *Her* viscounty! She dispatched Louis to inform Lasalle of that fact. He returned with a message that my lord Lasalle would attend to the matter. Of course, he did not. The reason soon became apparent: The new Viscount of Tillières had acquired a mistress.

Her name was Ravenissa, a fitting-enough name, and she was, Hermine told Juliana tactfully before she came to hear it from others, the widow of a blacksmith.

"Is she pretty?" Juliana asked anxiously.

"Pretty enough to turn most men's heads around here even while her husband was alive," Hermine sniffed.

Juliana crossed herself with great relief and went to the chapel to give thanks to the Holy Mother. In the next days, she covertly watched Ravenissa as the girl glided across the bailey, a buxom figure displaying an endearing pout and tiny white teeth whenever she smiled, which lately was often. The servants found that development a source of endless gossip, not because the lord had taken a mistress, but because he had taken her so soon after his wedding. The women felt pity for Juliana, who pretended to bear it all with fortitude. Ravenissa was apparently instructed to stay out of Juliana's way, less, she suspected, out of concern for her feelings than as Lasalle's way of obviating her objections, as if she intended to voice any.

Jehan de Vaudreuil had made his own arrangements, with the grandniece of Edith Pavilli. The girl came to help her aunt and within a few days ended up in Vaudreuil's arms. It did not surprise Juliana. Ersillia was a pretty young woman with honey-colored hair and abundant spirit. Mistress Hermine's liking for Ersillia extended to Vaudreuil, in direct proportion to her dislike of his lord.

With a surge of wickedness, Juliana wondered if Ravenissa and Ersillia ever compared their choices. From a new gown, an embroidered bodice, and a squirrel-lined cloak to a changing display of pins and ribbons, Ravenissa had reaped tangible rewards. Juliana could not figure out if there were any intangible ones, besides the envy of one's competition. And there was competition, Hermine informed Juliana. When Juliana could not imagine why, Hermine enlightened her. "The favor of a manor lord raises a freewoman's rank. And if not hers, then her child's."

"Surely a bastard would have no legal claim to Tillières?"

Hermine shook out Juliana's veil. "A bastard, recognized by his father, conquered England and became its king. You have no family, my lady, no champion to defend your claim."

Juliana sat down. Hermine had omitted the other, more obvious means to securing her claim: a child, an undisputed heir. Her child—and his. Juliana shivered and crossed herself. Best to keep busy.

This proved to be easy. In the absence of a bailiff, Juliana's duties weighed heavily on her, including the welfare of Paulette and Mathea. They did not have much freedom either, but Hermine occupied the girls by teaching them embroidery stitches and providing an endless supply of mending, two of a lady's occupations for which Mathea demonstrated as much tolerance as Juliana. Paulette, on the other hand, did not mind sitting for hours with her mending basket.

Juliana tried to teach the girls letters, but neither of them displayed much scholarly inclination, and the tasks and petty disputes among the servants constantly drew her away. Thanks to Mistress Hermine's efforts, she found Father Cyril, a middle-aged, round-faced priest of Saint Honoré, about two leagues distant from Rivefort. For a few pennies and a ham from the larder, Father Cyril assumed the duties of Rivefort's chaplain.

More than anything, Juliana told Father Cyril, she wanted to visit her mother's crypt in Saint Honoré's chapel. Father Cyril tried to intercede on her behalf with Lasalle, and was told that the lady Juliana could order as many Masses as she wished for her mother's soul and purchase as many candles as she desired, but that her person would stay put. Hearing that verdict, Juliana retired to her garden with her fulminations.

The new Lord of Rivefort slouched in his chair, his stubbly chin cupped in one hand, his knife in the other, gouging lines in the surface of the table. The bandage around his hand was gone, but he looked like a man nursing a fearsome toothache. The onerous duties of the viscounty had finally caught up with my lord Lasalle. He was holding manor court, since he had no bailiff to take on such matters. It turned out to be a thankless task for the knights standing behind his chair to lend dignity to the proceedings. Lasalle intended to be rid of his obligations as quickly as possible, and as a result he delivered decisions uncluttered by the concept of justice let alone mercy. Several mutinous serfs from the manor of Belvoir regarded their new master with glum pessimism. Louis Pavilli stepped in front of them. "Next—who's next in my lord's court?"

Two poachers came next, lean-faced men in dirty tunics. Their eyes, dark with fear, slipped pleadingly from Louis Pavilli to Juliana. They had poached, they tried to explain, because my lord's prospering deer herds had destroyed their fields. Juliana held her breath.

"God's teeth!" Lasalle drove the knife's tip into the tabletop. "Take a hand from one and hang the other. They can draw a lot."

The men's wives shrieked and threw themselves around the men's necks, the children clustering about them.

Juliana stood up. "My lord, surely that is not justice to one or the other? Perhaps—"

"Mind your place, Lady Juliana, or I'll hang both of them."

Aghast at Lasalle's callousness, Juliana sat down. The guards shoved the poachers outside, where a crowd of the curious had gathered.

A young couple followed, at first bashful, then quickly emboldened, hurling insults at each other. "Whoremonger!"

"Whore!"

"You took my dowry and went back to your trulls!" the girl shrieked.

Juliana exchanged an astonished look with Hermine.

Lasalle leaned forward. "What the Devil—"

The groom shook his fist at his bride. "To pay me for bringing up Petit Jacques's bastard!"

The girl raised her fists. "You lecher, you."

The in-laws charged at each other. The scribe dropped his pen and his parchments and got out of the way in time to avoid a combative mother-in-law. The bailey dogs barked, circling the contestants, nipping at their heels. Lasalle stood up, a look of fury and incredulity on his face.

"Silence! Silence in my lord's court!" the guards shouted to no effect.

Several men-at-arms burst into the hall. At their appearance, Juliana and Hermine decided to retreat before their nook was overrun. By the time Juliana reached her room, she did not know whether she should laugh or cry. She did both.

CHAPTER 14

You have the advantage of me, Master Thibodeau." Juliana folded the letters of endorsement for one Master Thibodeau from the Abbot of Saint Aubin. She held them out for Hermine to examine. Hermine did, and gave Master Thibodeau a very friendly smile.

The balding, sprucely dressed little man bowed deferentially despite his well-tended middle. "Begging your indulgence, my lady, I was led to believe that you are in need of a bailiff and I was instructed to present myself to you."

"Instructed by whom?"

"Why, by your lord husband, my lady."

Juliana did not hide her astonishment. "And he has engaged you?"

Their visitor shook his head. "That decision he let rest in your hands, Madame."

Even greater astonishment followed. Juliana sat back in her father's chair. If she rejected Master Thibodeau, her estates would continue to wither while she searched for another bailiff. Juliana extended her hand. "I pray, Master Thibodeau, that you will serve Tillières as devotedly as you have served Saint Aubin."

Master Thibodeau kissed Juliana's hand reverently and bowed again, this time to Mistress Hermine as well. Mistress Hermine smiled generously and tidied her wimple.

The herald of the Lord of Dreux brought the news that his master was holding a tourney in honor of the king-duke's return to his continental domains. The announcement sent Rivefort into a dither, from my lord Lasalle to the lowest squire. Juliana secretly shared in the excitement: by the end of the month, she could find herself a tourney widow.

When the end of the month came, Juliana discovered Hermine in her chamber, packing as if for a pilgrimage. She pulled her mantle from Hermine's hands. "Dreux? I am not going to Dreux with that man."

On the morning of their departure she decided to make her stand in her garden, alone. Lasalle found her sitting on an up-turned willow basket among her herb beds. "We are leaving, now. Plant your rump in Rosamond's saddle and don't think of leaving it before I tell you," he said, turning his back on her even before he had finished.

Juliana entwined her fingers around her knees and held her breath. A few steps away, Lasalle noticed her continued immobility. He halted and retraced his steps. She braced herself while he unbuckled his sword. She withered inwardly, conjuring up dreadful images of what he would do to her. He stuck the tip of the scabbard in the middle of her chervil and did nothing more violent than drop to his haunches, his hand on the quillons for balance. Their eyes were disconcertingly level. He smiled pleasantly into hers. "If you want me to tie you to Rosamond's tail, I will."

So he would, and she knew it. What a sight that would make! "But why? Why must I go?" She hated it when he made her sound like a petulant child. "Please. I find it difficult to be in the company of so many . . . people."

The breeze whipped his mane into his eyes. "After Dreux, you'll not have to face any more of us people. You will stay at Rivefort while I am making my pledge to John." He struck his chest with his fist. "On my word of honor."

"Yours, my lord?" There, she had said it, and she expected retaliation.

The corner of his mouth curled up. "Life is full of small disappointments, Eustace. But whatever you think of my honor, I would never lie to you."

Puffed up with indignity, she did not notice him reaching for her and taking hold of her elbows; he pulled her up with him. He stood close and she had to look up at him and he . . . he bent his head, tipped up her chin, and kissed her.

In pure outrage at the ambush, she squawked. That was a mistake, because it merely opened her mouth to him. And so she found herself kissed as she had been kissed once before, only once, when she was thirteen, by a cheeky stableboy whose name was Maurisse. That time she shoved her assailant away and punched him in the nose for good measure, but my lord Lasalle had prepared for that possibility by locking her arms against her sides. He had caught her off guard, as he usually did, but she was not as shocked as she had been the first time, for which she felt a surge of gratitude toward Maurisse. She already knew that this was how men kissed women, how Lasalle kissed Ravenissa and the others. Of course she had none of their experience at it—which was precisely why he did it.

He let her squirm in his grasp before he let her go. She would have ended up in her chervil, but he caught her.

"Why, why?" She tried not to sound so hopelessly out of breath.

His eyebrow shot up. "To satisfy your curiosity, mouse."

"Or yours, my lord?"

He let her slip her hand out of his and when she thought she would be free of him, he caught her wrist between his fingers. The lines along his mouth deepened. He kissed her hand, this time forcing her to meet his eyes. "Get on that mare, Juliana."

She snatched her hand away and took two, three unsteady steps from him, then ran the back of her hand across her lips. It was a futile gesture, and she expected a blow for the offense.

None came, although she thought she saw him flinch. It must have been a sudden gust blowing his hair into his eyes.

"Don't flatter yourself, mouse." He said it without any trace of feeling at all. Prying the scabbard out of her chervil, he turned on his heel and left her, certain that she would follow him.

After contemplating this second mortification, she did. She had no choice. They were halfway to Dreux before she realized that he had not answered her question, either.

CHAPTER 15

Fortress of Dreux, Normandy

They arrived in the open field below the curtain walls to a noisy crowd of jongleurs, acrobats, servants, knights, pages, squires, ladies and their maids, blacksmiths, armorers, pie peddlers, grooms, farriers, beggars, water carriers, prostitutes, pickpockets, footpads, horses, litters, carts, dogs, hunting birds, parrots, bears, and bear keepers, all of them jostling along the avenues between the brightly colored bell tents marked by their owners' standards.

Crushed and suffocating in the rank humanity around her, Juliana was glad to be installed, along with Hermine, in one of the houses that clung to the inside of the town walls. She did not know who had procured it and, still seething about Lasalle, she did not care. His teeth had bruised her lip and his stubble had scratched her cheek.

She fully intended to stay put, even had Lasalle's men-at-arms, led by a Saxon called Bodo, not been posted at the bottom of the stairs. Helplessness feeding her temper, she told Hermine, who walked in with a laver, to take in the festivities by herself.

"But, my lady, I was told to prepare you for the banquet."

"Prepare me? Am I a goose to be basted for company I don't know or care for?"

"I am sorry. Perhaps if I say that you have taken ill, he won't insist."

"He will insist; you know he will." Juliana admitted her defeat with a bitterness she could barely swallow.

❧

The Lord of Dreux, a middle-aged, heavyset man with his hair cut in the old Norman fashion, sat at the high table under a striped *baldaquin* with his indolent-looking young wife beside him, surrounded by his vassals, squires, pages, guests, and contestants. The loud voices, the music, and the sea of colors and patterns numbed Juliana's senses. She was already fretting about spending the entire banquet in Lasalle's company, but as soon as they entered, a squire informed them that the Lady of Dreux had decreed that husbands and wives be seated apart.

Juliana found herself posted between a young knight called John d'Erlée and an elderly one called Sir Baldwin. She immediately worried about keeping up an evening's worth of conversation with these two strangers, but her companions proved well schooled in *courtoisie*. Despite herself, she began to enjoy the evening. She did not know where Lasalle was, and she did not care.

No sooner was his wife out of sight than the Viscount of Tillières ceased enjoying his company. And that was merely the beginning of the evening.

"You are a bastard." The voice was feminine and familiar.

He faced his challenger. "So my father told me. Your servant, my lady."

Anne de Valence took a sip from her cup and snapped her fingers at the little blackamoor page attending her train. "Wine for my lord Lasalle. I believe he'll need it."

He bowed to her. "How hospitable of you, my lady."

Anne held out her hand. "I was thinking of poisoning it. Is that her, boring d'Erlée? What is she? Thirteen?"

He kissed her hand. "I doubt she is boring him."

Paying close heed to what was said and how was a skill Anne de Valence had acquired early. "Noticing a woman's mind? I suppose there is so little else of her."

"Anne, don't," he said quietly, knowing well that the Countess de Valence would not be mollified without an effort. But then, she never was. "The Gorgon of Fontevraud would have turned Marshal on my men if I hadn't agreed to it."

The sound of little bells on his curly-toed slippers announced the return of the diminutive page. Lasalle took the cup. Anne touched the tip of her tongue to the rim of her own. "Now, why didn't I think of that? And there I was, merely offering myself and my lands."

"You would have."

"Is that why you ended up in my sister's bed?"

"Of course," he said without a heartbeat of hesitation.

"What a vile cur you are!"

He caught her hand before she could strike him, and tightened his grip on it until she winced, then kissed it very gently. "Isn't that the attraction?"

Anne smiled at the gawkers whispering to each other. She had always thought that women who reproached their lovers in public demonstrated poor manners. She examined him carefully. He looked as he always did—a solid, animate presence with keen-witted self-possession. And he was right. That *was* the attraction. Her sister, Mahaut, had thought so too. Would his bride have any better luck curing him of his annoying habits? Not from the looks of the child. Anne raised her cup. "Well then, shall we toast to your marriage?"

"No."

"Oh? Have you managed to teach her the sinful pleasures of the marriage bed, but now she is demanding your heart on a platter as well?"

He gave her a crooked smile. "Heart, head, and spleen with basil and onions."

"Ah. Perhaps she and I have something else in common. Introduce us."

"No."

Well, well. Anne noticed that Lasalle kept an eye on the girl, who appeared to be the center of John d'Erlée's attention. She tapped his shoulder. "Don't tell me you are jealous. Is it true that you are keeping her under lock and key at Rivefort?"

"I am."

"Which is it? And don't play obtuse with me, my lord; you do it extremely poorly," Anne snapped, annoyed.

He leaned his shoulder against the wall, and his expression told her not to try him. "I had to wed the girl because Aliénor left me no choice. Hers was no better than mine. I want an annulment and so does she, as soon as she figures out how to get rid of me and hold on to Tillières. I did not bed her and I don't intend to."

Anne ran her finger along his jaw. "Not tempted even a little by all that innocence?"

"No."

"Does that mean you've made other arrangements?" She intended it to sound like an insult. He gave her a smile that told her he knew that. "With some slut of a scullery maid, I imagine," she said. That did not come out any better. She had forgotten how difficult Guérin de Lasalle was to corner, on anything—much like Armand de Lusignan.

"Someone like that."

Anne handed her cup to her page and picked up her train. "I must say that you've surprised me. I am certain you won't mind if I have a surprise for you, as well."

CHAPTER 16

John d'Erlée turned out to be a former squire of the Earl of Pembroke. He had remained in Sir William's service after being dubbed, preferring the wider world of the earl's acquaintance to his own small estate. Juliana passed the evening in an easy conversation with the young man and Sir Baldwin, interrupted periodically by the appearance of the cooks' culinary excesses, which culminated in a parade of peacocks and swans baked, stuffed, and glazed underneath their original plumage. The guests were appropriately overwhelmed.

At the conclusion of the banquet meal, the loquacious gathering gave its attention to the music, the fools, the acrobats, and several young women performing the dance of Herodias's daughter, their master announced. Oh dear. Light-headed, Juliana decided to seek fresh air. Sir Baldwin made his excuses and lumbered off to join his friends, but to her surprise, John d'Erlée showed no intention of abandoning her. He offered her his hand, but she had already tucked hers into her sleeves. They walked side by side into a walled garden. Out of the corner of her eye, she noticed Bodo and two of Lasalle's men-at-arms, but Lasalle himself was nowhere to be seen.

John d'Erlée was a few years older than she was, a finely made young man with an open expression, calm brown eyes, and light brown hair cut short, no doubt to hide the fact that otherwise it would spring into a mass of curls. She liked the way he smiled, even though she was too embarrassed to investigate the matter any further. To hide her confusion, she said, "Have you news of the queen-duchess, my lord?"

"She is waiting for Duke John at Fontevraud to confirm to the Lusignans her grant of La Marche. They are gathering for the Angoulême wedding."

"I don't think the duchess is pleased about either," Juliana offered, feeling on more certain ground.

"None of us is. Sooner or later the war with Philip will resume. You are French, aren't you? And your husband holds Tillières of you, does he not? That ought to make your viscounty secure. If Fortune favors Philip, you could declare for Philip. Others have done so."

So her desperate wedding-night threat about Rivefort having a French garrison as easily as a Norman one was not as ludicrous as she had at first thought. "What would Sir William do? He holds Longueville of Philip, does he not? But his loyalty is to Aliénor and John. If I did as others have done, is that still not treachery?"

"Talk of treachery. How deliciously bold, Lady Juliana." A clear voice rang out behind them.

They turned. Standing there in a richly embroidered tunic was a tall, regal man with dark brown hair and darker blue eyes and the muscular compactness of a well-practiced swordsman. He was one of the most handsome men Juliana had ever seen, but it was the penetrating intelligence in that gaze that left the deepest impression.

Accompanying him was a lady at the height of her considerable beauty, attired in a saffron-colored gown shimmering with gold thread applied by dozens of hands. The cascade of her fair hair reached to her hips, and a small silver mirror on a long cord swung from her hip girdle.

"My lady, may I present Armand de Lusignan, the Count of Rancon, and the Countess Anne de Valence." John d'Erlée bowed to the two very properly.

Juliana curtsied with equal care. The spectacular gentleman helped himself to her hand, lifting it to his lips. His eyes bore into hers. Blood rushed to her head as if she had drunk a beakerful of Hermine's raisin wine.

"You were speaking of serious matters, Lady Juliana. Do continue," Armand de Lusignan said.

"We were discussing the question of loyalty to one's liege," John d'Erlée answered before Juliana could. Armand de Lusignan's gaze slipped to the young man and rested there patiently. Juliana gathered that discussing loyalty with a Lusignan was not the cleverest conversational tactic, but it was too late.

"With such divided loyalties, Lady Juliana's husband will no doubt offer her homage to the duke. After all, possession is nine points of the law." The Count of Rancon gave Juliana a slow smile and released her hand. "Your husband and my family are old acquaintances, you might have heard."

Short on words, Juliana curtsied again. "Y-yes, my lord."

The Countess de Valence's laughter tinkled about them. Armand de Lusignan frowned slightly. "We don't know whether to offer you our congratulations or our sympathies on your marriage, do we, Countess?"

Juliana curtsied again. "Neither, my lord."

"Are you certain, my dear?" Armand touched her chin, a gesture at once forward and innocent. The realization that he was examining the crook in the bridge of her nose overcame Juliana's initial shock at his familiarity. The crook there was not Lasalle's fault, but she had no intention of telling anyone.

Anne de Valence tapped her waist mirror against Armand de Lusignan's sleeve. "Perhaps congratulations should be in order. It appears that my lord Lasalle intends to seek an annulment."

The count released Juliana, his expression one of restraint.

"Does he? In that case, you may be in need of friends and of protection. We have, you see, known your husband far better than you as yet do."

Juliana nodded mutely, perplexed by the turn of events. The Count of Rancon pressed something into her hand. "A proof of my pledge, before which the gates of Pont-de-l'Arche will spring open. Ah—my lord Lasalle. How good of you to join us."

Armand de Lusignan's fingers closed around her fist with gentle firmness, leaving something behind. It was a ring. She hid her hand in her skirts, worried that Guérin de Lasalle had noticed.

Lasalle's attention, however, was fixed on the Count of Rancon. They were the same height and stature, but the count was an urbane man, wearing his attire with the natural grace of one used to luxury. Even in his new surcoat, Guérin de Lasalle had the air of a man who had stumbled in from a battlefield—or intended to head off to one. Anne de Valence's berry-ripe lips were smiling, but it was Armand who spoke, in the disdainful tone of a well-bred southerner. "I didn't know whether to pity your wife or to congratulate her on her marriage to you, Viscount. She tells us neither is necessary. Have you then truly banished all secrets from your marriage bed?"

"And have you banished them from yours, sir?"

Armand de Lusignan smiled at Lasalle's feeble parry. "Not entirely. But I assure you before these witnesses that in your absence, I offer my protection to your wife. And I will as eagerly anticipate news of your annulment as I am certain you do, Lady Juliana. You'll remember my pledge to you?"

Dazed, Juliana nodded. Armand de Lusignan bowed to them all and he and the Countess de Valence took their leave.

"God's blood, what would that man know of loyalty or friendship? He and his family have caused more trouble than all the Poitevins put together!" John d'Erlée's outburst was meant to break the spell that Armand de Lusignan's presence had cast over everyone except Lasalle.

Sword half drawn, Lasalle set after the Count of Rancon as if in pursuit of a mortal enemy. Had he reached him, Juliana was certain, he would have cut Armand de Lusignan down, but Jehan de Vaudreuil appeared out of nowhere with Rivefort's men-at-arms. He placed himself squarely in Lasalle's path, his hand on Lasalle's sword arm. "Guérin, don't. That's what he wants."

"Move or I'll kill you!"

Vaudreuil did not yield, which indicated either his courage or his foolhardiness. "No!" he shook Lasalle roughly, speaking rapidly in what Juliana thought must be the Saracens' tongue. Lasalle blinked, his eyes coming to focus on the man in front of him. Vaudreuil let him go. Lasalle shoved his sword into the scabbard and in the same move took Juliana out of John d'Erlée's presence.

It was not until she was locked in her room with guards stationed outside the door that she noticed she was still in possession of Armand de Lusignan's pledge of protection.

CHAPTER 17

He came to her late into the night, but he came, as she had known he would. She had instructed her guard captain to let him in and then to retire. My lord Lasalle would let himself out. He always did. She waited, her hair unbound, in the middle of her chamber, which was furnished with her carpets, her bed and drapery, her trunks and travel chairs.

He laid aside his sword and poniard, followed by his surcoat, and came to her. Anne sank to the carpets, taking him with her. He leaned over her. She untied his shirt laces and tracked her fingertips along the scar, pale against the dark skin. His pulse ran as fast as her own. Anne smiled to herself. Her hand slid inside his shirt, found the chain of Richard's cross, and drew him to her. She closed her eyes in anticipation, but just before his lips touched hers, he said, "Why didn't you tell me about Armand?"

Her eyes snapped open. "It would have spoiled the surprise."

He held himself away. He was angry, which gave her a thrill of victory, but that unfortunately paled in comparison to what she wanted from him.

When Armand de Lusignan had suggested that they travel together to Dreux, where, he assured her, the new Viscount of Tillières would surely be found, the idea had lent itself to her plans for revenge, for finding him in the arms of her sister, and now for his other surprise, all wide eyes, bony shoulders, freckles, and painful shyness.

"Your quarrel is with me, not with Juliana." His voice had that edge in it. She had heard it before, but never aimed at her. It excited her. He excited her; he always did.

"Is that what you came to tell me?"

"Yes."

"Then I expect you'll be leaving." She shoved him away and stood up. He followed her, spinning her around and flattening her to him. His kiss was an assault; he carried her to the bed. There he touched the side of her face as if to remind himself of the shape of it. It seemed like a truce offer.

"I will, but since you went to so much trouble, I don't want to leave you disappointed."

"You hardly ever disappoint me, my lord," Anne conceded magnanimously.

"Hardly ever?" He raised his eyebrow in one of his quizzical expressions. She liked it when he did that. Anne smiled and let him lift her shift over her head, then stretched out and watched while he took off his own clothes, dropping them by the bedside. She liked to watch him, marveling that she could possess something so alive, something with such a potential for destruction.

He returned to her, deliberate and determined. He knew her, and he wanted to remind her of that. She knew that he did, and she disliked the calculation of it. She let him work to sway her, to remind him that she demanded more than a haystack tumble. She mused on it even as she moved her hips against him. After a while, she did not muse on anything at all.

Catching her breath after the last throes of exhilaration, Anne slipped her fingers into Lasalle's mane and pulled his head up. "I

can tell you haven't been spending all your time in the service of
the duke. Who's had the benefit of your practice since we saw you
last, heading off to rescue the Holy Sepulchre?"

Ribs heaving, he gave her a feigned grimace of pain. "Several
demoiselles, Madame, but none as beautiful as you."

"You are a bloody liar." She pushed back his damp hair and
kissed him without any inhibition. The hunger in him for her was
still there, as much as hers for him.

"And I can tell that Armand has been neglecting you. Perhaps
he prefers someone younger than—ah!"

Anne sank her nails into his flank and he evaded her and rolled
off. "Christ, that's one thing you have in common with my wife."
He gave her a playful slap across her buttocks and hoisted her on
top of him.

Anne liked that; she could kiss him without straining her neck.
"You said you did not bed her." He closed his eyes, but she let him
drift only for a moment. "Guérin!"

"Uhmm." He laced his fingers through her hair. It was long
enough to cover them both and he liked to touch it. "I didn't.
Anne, if you tell the duchess what a cur I am, she might not oppose
my annulment. I'll give Juliana enough to buy herself out of John's
wardship. Why do you think we are here? She can then marry
whomever she fancies, but I need Tillières to keep my men."

The candle's light caught a green glint under his eyelashes. So
my lord Lasalle possessed his share of predatory instincts; he
merely did not reveal them very often. He had returned to her
bed not to appease her, but because he wanted something. She
ran her finger from his temple to the angle of his cheekbone. "You
truly don't want the girl?"

He kissed her palm. "No. Anne, I meant it. You can quarrel
with me all you want, but leave Juliana out of it."

"All I want?" She pressed her palms against the flat pan of his
belly. He held on to her hips, rejoining them slowly as if in a wordless pledge. She bent to kiss him, her hair veiling them, her nails
splayed along his ribs, at first lightly. He closed his eyes and this
time he held still, even when she drew blood.

CHAPTER 18

Fontevraud Abbey, Anjou

h ow filial of you to visit your aged mother, John," the Duchess of Aquitaine said to the man who knelt before her perfunctorily and kissed her hand even more so.

"I was summoned by you, Madame." The King of the English, Duke of Normandy and soon-to-be of Aquitaine, Count of Anjou and Poitou, came to his feet in ill humor, although he had only just arrived. His lady mother gestured him into a chair. They were alone.

"I had to. You were in the vicinity with your army and nary a thought for your mother."

The queen-duchess made a small gesture of helplessness, which her son had learned to despise because he knew it meant she was about to get her way. "You told me to make my presence felt in the south, Mother. I've spent five months at Vernon, contending with Philip over the marriage portion of my niece. It was like arguing with a priest."

"Is that why he walked away with your twenty thousand marks of silver? England is in an uproar."

The king of that realm was about to lose his temper. "What of it? Philip conceded my lordship over Brittany and Anjou, you have Blanche wedded to Louis, I have Arthur's homage, and I am rid of that Gloucester cow at last."

"Don't raise your voice to me, darling. I am not deaf. You are ready to rest on your laurels when there are a number of thorns among them, namely, your wife."

"You are deaf, Mother. I no longer have a wife."

"Precisely." Aliénor of Aquitaine slapped her son's wrist. "Leave that."

John dropped the parchment he had picked up from his mother's table, and slumped moodily into his chair. He scratched his chin; his recently sprouted beard was itching and his mother's company seemed to aggravate it. "The ink is just dry on my annulment. May I not be allowed some respite before I climb into another cow's bed?"

"No. You are thirty-two. And don't refer to women as cows. It shows terrible manners and disrespect for your mother. England and the rest needs an heir. Besides, I found you a wife. Aylmer d'Angoulême's daughter."

His mother had become senile after all. "She is betrothed to Brown Hugh's son! You know that pledge is as binding as marriage. You've insisted that I make allies with the Lusignans. I've been to Mervant already, trying to win Hugh and Aylmer and the others to my side. Why do you think I've brought this army? I am not an imbecile."

"I know well what you are. I've changed my mind about the Lusignans. Aylmer is your vassal; you can annul any alliance he contracts for his daughter without your consent. He only conceded La Marche to Hugh as a condition of this marriage; otherwise they'd still be at swords' points over it. Did you see Isabelle at Mervant?"

"No. And I am not in the mood for some pinch-faced heiress and her coterie of hungry relatives."

"A pity. I am told she is a beauty. That's why they kept her away from you."

His mother's words punctured John's simmering temper. He sat up. "Aylmer would never agree. If he couldn't take La Marche from the Lusignans by the sword, he'll have it by his daughter's marriage bed."

"Of course Aylmer will agree. Tell him his daughter will wear the crowns of Normandy, Aquitaine, and England. After all, her mother is the granddaughter of the last Louis."

John tugged at his lower lip. The idea was preposterous. And bold. Boldness had seldom served him; his advantage resided in patience and subterfuge. His mother, on the other hand, was daring itself. Perhaps too daring.

"And what should I give them as recompense? More fiefs in

Normandy? Speaking of fiefs, the seneschal informed me that while I was dickering with Philip, you'd found a viscount for me as well, for Tillières. I am of mind to deal with him and give the place to Hugh."

"Leave Lasalle alone. I have use for him and so will you. And grant the Lusignans nothing. When you take Isabelle, Aylmer will help you wrest La Marche from the Lusignans. Let him have it; you'll reclaim it by right of your wife when Aylmer dies, and the Angoumois as well."

John twisted the end of his mustache. Bold. Devious, true— but bold. "Ralph de Lusignan has custody of her. How am I to persuade him to hand her to me without making the Lusignans suspicious?"

"You don't. The wedding is to take place in three weeks' time. Go to Aylmer now with your offer and tell him to ask Ralph to send Isabelle to visit her family before the wedding. Aylmer is to renew his homage to you, is he not? What better reason for a family gathering? I suggest you ride to Angoulême and see her for yourself."

"Good Lord, Mother—you want me to marry another Isabelle? How old is she?"

"She is just past twelve."

John let out a hoot of laughter. "Mother, I am shocked. You've chastised me enough for my choice of bedmates. How long do you expect me to wait?"

Aliénor dipped her pen into her inkhorn. "She is marriageable."

John stopped laughing. "You are in earnest, aren't you, Mother?"

Aliénor pored over her parchments. "So should you be unless you'd like to see the Angoulêmes and the Lusignans become in-laws and cut Aquitaine from Normandy. Time to pull their fangs."

John Plantagenet went to the window. "The girl is a beauty?"

Aliénor smiled. Men were such perfect fools.

CHAPTER 19

Fortress of Dreux, Normandy

The tourney commenced later than usual, no doubt to give the contestants a chance to recover from the festivities. Next to Lasalle's tent, his destrier pawed the ground while the grooms tried to curry a checkerboard pattern on his rump. Already mounted, Jehan de Vaudreuil trotted up to them. "My lady; Mistress Hermine. Have you come to wish us good luck? The Bretons are here, and the Franks, and the Flemings in force, of course. Don't worry, Lady Juliana, your husband knows how to take care of himself."

She was not worried. Lasalle, he could go to the Devil, but even though he had spent weeks running Vaudreuil, Peyrac, Saez, Metz, and the rest of the Rivefort knights around Rivefort's lists, here his men faced seasoned competitors who in the heat of the moment had no compunction about maiming or killing their opponents.

"Then may Fortune be with you, sir." Juliana curtsied, turned, and ran straight into Lasalle's charger in high-strung lather, tossing about his grooms. She caught herself on the stallion's shoulder, which was hot and damp, and she backed into a resilient wall of metal links under a plain surcoat.

"Oh!" She tried to find an escape. "My, he is not as tall as Rosamond, is he? What I meant . . ." She gave up.

"Destriers aren't bred for height, Eustace; you'd need a ladder to get on one." Lasalle was squinting past her, helmet under his arm. "Holy Mother."

From behind the tent, attired in the colors of the Virgin, Anne de Valence advanced upon them like an army of one, accompanied by her three maids, and six men-at-arms. "My lord, you left so abruptly last night, I had not had the chance to— Oh, I did not see you. Justinia, isn't it?"

Juliana opened her mouth, but the countess had already dismissed her from her cognizance, smiling at Lasalle with that little knowing smile Ersillia and Ravenissa wore around Rivefort. Blessed Lord in Heaven. Having disposed of his wife under a lock and key, Guérin de Lasalle had visited the Countess de Valence, and not for the purposes of polite conversation. This was fascinating. Justinia indeed!

Eyes chastely downcast, and borrowing the countess's lilt, Juliana gave Lasalle a very prim curtsy. "Oooh, my lord, it seems you've received your well wishes already," she said, and made it out of his reach before he could do a thing.

The battlements had already been claimed by the female residents of Dreux, including the lord's wife, who sat with her women on cushioned seats under an awning, all chattering like magpies. The men of Juliana's guard had stationed themselves at a short distance. Below, the tourneyers faced one another in two groups of riders, each half a dozen deep. Judging from the number of those on the field, the lure of captured horses, armor, weapons—and the payment of a hefty ransom from a high-ranked participant—outweighed the threat of eternal damnation. The contest could go on for a couple of days or longer, until no one challenged the last knight.

The impatient crowd began to cheer. Juliana searched for Lasalle's blue banner, but could not make it out among the cloth of the field. The Lord of Dreux's herald, carrying his master's standard and accompanied by drummers, reined in his caparisoned horse at the edge of the field. The lord took his seat next to his wife. Juliana gripped the edge of the parapet. Knowing that Sir William Marshal made his reputation in such undertakings posed something of an awkward problem, but Sir William's motivation was surely pure, for the glory of his patrons.

The drums drowned out the crowd. The herald held the standard aloft, and the wind caught it. Juliana cringed and shut her eyes as the thunder of hooves merged with a roar from the battlements. When she opened her eyes, the first equine and human casualties littered the field. The contestants broke into groups pitted against one another; in the ensuing free-for-all, it was impossible to distinguish any single man.

"An exciting sight, don't you agree, Lady Juliana?"

John d'Erlée stood there, well turned out and smiling. Glad of the distraction and the unexpected company, Juliana gave him a chipper greeting. "Oh, my lord, aren't you going to join the tourney?" Dear Lord, did she sound like Anne de Valence? D'Erlée did not seem to notice.

"I am under orders from my lord Marshal. The earl now thinks that these games are too dangerous for his messenger." John d'Erlée bowed to Mistress Hermine, but his eyes were on Juliana. "I am to inform the viscount and the others that they are to join the duke without delay."

Juliana kept her eyes on the field below, but felt as giddy as when William Marshal winked at her. The remaining riders began to spread into the countryside, with the pursuers spurring after them. They would dodge and clash until darkness halted the chase. Squires and grooms of the unhorsed men tried to conduct their masters to safety through the cavorting horseflesh and ringing steel. Blood stained trampled standards. *Dear Lord, let me not pray for—*

She crossed herself and stepped back, her escort springing to attention. "I am not . . . I don't feel well. I must return to our lodging."

John d'Erlée touched her sleeve, coming very close, and Mistress Hermine appeared oddly unconcerned about the preservation of proprieties. Juliana looked up at him. He kissed her hand. "Will you allow me, my lady, the honor of escorting you and Mistress Hermine?"

Juliana swallowed, dumbstruck. Mistress Hermine's smile was not exactly disapproving.

CHAPTER 20

Fortress of Angoulême, Angoumois, August 1200

Three days before her wedding to Hugh de Lusignan's seventeen-year-old son, Isabelle d'Angoulême was informed that she was to marry instead a man nearly thrice her age. That man, whom she was about to meet, would make her the Duchess of Normandy and the Queen of England. With her father, mother, and her two ladies accompanying her, Isabelle curtsied and offered her greetings to the visitors in a sweet, childish voice. As if in a trance, John Plantagenet reached out for the girl's hand. He let her up, but forgot to let her go.

Whatever his irreproachable wife might have thought, Lasalle had never considered twelve-year-old girls worth a second glance. This one was—and John Plantagenet thought so too. Guérin de Lasalle was witnessing the King of England falling in love with Isabelle d'Angoulême right before his eyes.

Lasalle cleared his throat, and loudly. John dropped the girl's hand. Count Aylmer and Countess Alice surrounded their daughter and her husband-to-be. Lasalle thought it best to wait out the rest of that episode in the inner bailey. He wished he had never heard of Aliénor of Aquitaine, Juliana de Charnais, or Tillières. He wished he was in *outre-mer,* facing the entire Saracen army. He wished he was not sharing a mistress with the King of England— and Armand de Lusignan.

A fortnight ago, after their return from Dreux, he and his men had left behind Rivefort and its lady, the latter fighting tears of joy. They were brought on as much by her husband's departure as by his announcement that she was free to move about the viscounty.

The news rendered Sister Eustace speechless, a condition into which he had not maneuvered her very often. Juliana de Charnais would probably talk a lot in bed, too. They left at dawn with the girl at the hall's door, armored in her nun's wimple and a pair of garden clogs, heralding to the world her determination to reclaim her post as the mistress of Rivefort. That was why he had put Rannulf de Brissard in charge of it: Unlike Peyrac, Brissard was loyal and unlikely to be swayed by female tantrums.

The only soul sorry to see them leave was Mathea, who had slipped out of her bed and past Mistress Hermine. Lasalle bent down carefully on account of his bound-up ribs, a memento of Dreux, for Mathea to give him a peck on the cheek. But demoiselle Mathea reserved her tears for Jehan de Vaudreuil, who patted her head and promised to bring her and her sister a gift. The lady Paulette apparently slept very soundly and therefore missed their departure.

Several leagues short of Fontevraud, Aliénor of Aquitaine's messenger had intercepted them with an order to wait in camp. They did, and soon found themselves hosts of the king-duke and his company of young gallants.

John of the English looked nothing like his famous brother, standing a head shorter than the Lionheart—and Lasalle. The king-duke seemed to resent that. He stomped around the camp, the chape of his scabbard scraping the ground. His manners made men and horses nervous, and he knew it. Lasalle did notice, however, that John resembled his mother. That was not a good sign. And then there was Anne.

She came up behind him and tapped her riding crop on his shoulder, a smile of victory on her lips. He touched the string of gold droplets adorning Anne's ear as if she were offering them up for pawn.

Anne knocked his hand away, her smile vanishing. "You peasant. He is a king, and you are—"

Before Anne could think of another insult, John's equerry interrupted their reunion. Lasalle kissed Anne's hand and took his leave to find John by the horses. He bowed. John frowned in displeasure and set off through the camp, talking rapidly, expecting Lasalle to follow as if he were one of the royal hounds. He obliged and quickly learned that John Plantagenet seemed to know everything there was to know about Lasalle's immediate past—courtesy, he suspected, of John's mother and Anne de Valence. John informed him that he bore no grudge for Tillières; in fact, he was anxious to receive Lasalle's fealty and homage for it. It had all become worrisome.

And so, in front of his tent and the duke's companions, Lasalle gave his oaths to John Plantagenet for the viscounty of Tillières, the castellancy of Rivefort, and the wife who brought them to him. Anne sat there smiling, rosary beads trickling through her fingers. Lasalle expected that Anne had little time to pray since she had joined John's entourage. After exchanging a vassal's promise of loyalty and a liege's pledge of protection along with the requisite kiss of peace, John beckoned Lasalle to follow him. Inside the tent, the true reason for John's insistence to receive his pledge became clear.

John Plantagenet sought the Viscount of Tillières's aid in absconding with the Count d'Angoulême's daughter, who was affianced to the young Hugh de Lusignan, for the purposes of marrying the girl himself.

Lasalle must have looked perfectly stupefied. When John stopped laughing, he settled himself in a camp chair and rattled off a plan. Somewhere in the middle, Lasalle was assured that as his reward he would receive royal support for the annulment of his marriage.

"Well, Viscount," John demanded impatiently, "what do you think of it?"

Lasalle's ribs throbbed mercilessly. As a result, he did not handle himself well. "I commit my own crimes, sire. I don't commit them on someone else's behalf."

John Plantagenet stood up. "I find your moral qualms surprising, Viscount."

"As you wish, my lord." Lasalle thought it prudent to bow, and did.

"By the holy rood," John began menacingly, "you are too clever by half. Mother told me you might balk, but she said that you would obey in the end. Or are you going to force me to order something appropriately painful and lingering for you?" John paused. "Like a protracted spell in your matrimony. I heard that she is ugly and old!" Pleased with himself, John laughed uproariously.

This was a battle Lasalle could not hope to win, no more than he could have won it against John Plantagenet's mother. After all, it was Aliénor of Aquitaine he was fighting.

"Well, what do you have to say for yourself, Viscount?"

"I am your faithful vassal, sire," Lasalle said and bowed. In truth, he contemplated regicide.

CHAPTER 21

Fortress of La Roche Foucauld, Angoumois

Anne could not find Lasalle anywhere. Not even Vaudreuil knew Lasalle's whereabouts when she called him to her in the garden of the small fortress where John had taken up residence to wait out, very impatiently, his impending nuptials. Or if Vaudreuil did know, he was not about to tell her. Tired of the heat, Anne was wandering the narrow corridors toward her chamber when she was accosted by a man who staggered out of a dark alcove. She reached for her dagger, and then came the voice.

"The love-ly lady Anne. Shall we cel-celebrate early and keep the duke waiting in v-vain?" Unsteady on his feet, he held out a ewer, which slipped from his fingers before she took hold of it. He swore at the sound of broken pottery. "Bloody . . . Do you think the s-steward will let us have another?"

"I think you've had your share already," Anne coldly informed him. "Where have you been?"

He studied the inside of his cup, shrugged, and dropped it as well. Anne cringed at the sound. "I agree. Shall we pro-pro . . . go on?"

"Don't be a fool. John could see us."

"Ah." Lasalle tapped the side of his nose. "I thought that was the i-dea."

Anne stated the obvious. "You are drunk."

He drew her to him. "Un-fortunately, not enough."

She tried to free herself. "John will—"

"John is swiving a couple of kitchen maids."

His mouth came down on hers, his free hand reaching to her thigh to ruck up her gown. But she was not some trollop to be taken standing up in a passageway. She struck him across the face, a sharp, loud crack. His head rocked back; his hand flew to his cheek as if he could not believe it. Anne tried to make it to the door. With one not very sure-footed move, he blocked her way. Anne jumped back. Where on earth were the guards? She had her dagger, but not an inclination to use it.

She thought that she knew Guérin de Lasalle better than his other women did, but she had to acknowledge that she did not know him as well as she had believed. Not wanting to tempt fate, Anne turned on her heel and fled down the corridor. She reached the stairwell—only to collide with someone who was coming up the last tread. Ironically, Anne's next thought was for Guérin de Lasalle. The duke was possessive about his mistresses and not likely to share her with his recently minted viscount.

It was Vaudreuil. He staggered but managed to catch her anyway, surprised yet possessing the presence of mind to consider her pursuer. Seeing Anne in Vaudreuil's arms, Lasalle leaned against the wall and slid down to all fours, half-laughing, half-groaning. "The Chevalier de Vaudreuil. Always to the lady's rescue. You may keep her."

Vaudreuil grinned and somewhat reluctantly released her. "Are you hurt, my lady?" he asked with utmost politeness.

Anne restored her dislodged veil. "No, but it seems that my lord Lasalle is drunk. Would you remove him and let him sleep it off somewhere? The duke need not know."

"Of course, my lady." Vaudreuil took hold of the nape of La-salle's gambeson and hauled him to his feet. Before Lasalle could object and before his knees buckled again, Vaudreuil folded him across his shoulders. Anne stood aside for Vaudreuil to descend the stairs with Lasalle's head and arms dangling, his doleful moans growing fainter with each receding step. Anne took a deep breath. Tomorrow my lord Lasalle would nurse a stupendous headache and undoubtedly offer amends in some suitable manner.

Instead, she was woken up from her own bed at the break of day by Lasalle, who could have been still drunk but managed never-theless to persuade her to accompany him on some secretive and urgent mission. It turned out to involve a ride in the company of two grooms, one of whom carried a cloth-covered basket. Thus they arrived at Angoulême and were led through the bailey to the garden after Lasalle announced that they came from the duke with a gift for the lady Isabelle.

Lasalle pointed to a spot for the groom to leave the basket. Anne removed her gloves, shook the dust from her gown, and smoothed her hair. Lasalle was insane. From across the garden, followed by a duo of dour ladies-in-waiting, came the lady Isabelle, prayer book in her hands. Lasalle bowed to her. Isabelle looked confused, glanc-ing uncertainly at her women. Lasalle got down on one knee.

"My lady, you will not remember me, but I am Guérin de La-salle, Viscount of Tillières and the duke's most loyal vassal. My lord duke has charged me with the pleasure of bringing you one of his wedding gifts."

"Oh." Isabelle's mouth formed a perfect circle. One of the women whispered something in her ear. "I am honored to receive the duke's gift," Isabelle repeated after her. The woman whispered some more and Isabelle extended her hand, and after Lasalle kissed it, she motioned him to rise.

He remained where he was. "He also asked me to deliver a mes-sage to you only."

"Oh" was all Isabelle managed before the other waiting woman spoke up, regarding Lasalle with unconcealed dislike.

"The lady Isabelle cannot be left alone in your company, sir," she said, no doubt concluding that Lasalle was another of John's tankard companions.

Lasalle stood up and bowed with exquisite politeness. "She is not alone in my company. The lady Isabelle's virtue is guarded by the presence of the Countess de Valence. Or would you, mes-dames, wish me to call my lord Aylmer and tell him that you've questioned the duke's wishes?"

Still not certain what part Lasalle would have her play, Anne decided to look as regal as possible, given the state of her gown. The waiting women looked at each other and together at Lasalle, who had not entirely purged the evidence of the previous night's debauch, but his words had their effect. Capitulating, they whis-pered instructions into Isabelle's ear. The girl nodded diligently with a look of fright and confusion, and at last her guardians re-moved themselves to the corner of the garden.

Lasalle gave Isabelle one of his smiles. "Do you intend to take those two old bats with you to England, my lady?"

The girl looked more confused. "Bats? Oh! I . . . they . . . my mother . . . yes, I have to."

"When you become Duchess of Normandy and Queen of En-gland, you can order their dismissal if you wish. The duke has asked me to tell you to choose your court ladies and companions for your journey."

Anne winced. Lasalle was digging himself into an early grave. Isabelle's eyes grew larger. "He did? I can?"

"Would you like to dismiss them now? Or"—Lasalle turned to Anne—"would you like the Countess de Valence to tell them for you?"

Isabelle looked uncertainly toward her women. "I-I don't know. Mother made them wait on me when I had my first . . . when I was to marry Hugh," she whispered, turning pink. "Is that . . . is that my present?"

"One of them. Now close your eyes and promise not to peek."

Intrigued, Isabelle did as she was told, not minding that she was being treated with a great deal of liberty for one who was to be the Queen of England. Lasalle untied the basket cover, reached inside, and pulled out . . . a rabbit. A very large, gray rabbit.

Stroking the rabbit's ears, he placed it gently in Isabelle's arms. Startled at first, the girl squeaked, her eyes flying open. She clasped the furry creature to her. "Oh! Is he mine?"

"She. Her name is Philomena. I think she likes you already."

"Do you?" Isabelle lowered her cheek to the rabbit's fur. Philomena's nose twitched against the girl's ear. Isabelle laughed.

"It is a great responsibility," Lasalle said solemnly. "You must keep dogs away from her or they will kill her. Your pages will have to look after her while you go about your duties."

"I don't have pages," Isabelle said, absorbed with her gift. "They are Mother's."

"You will. Your husband will give you pages and grooms, and maids and ladies-in-waiting, and knights to protect you, and whatever you like."

Isabelle said nothing, caressing the rabbit. After a while, she put it at her feet. Philomena sniffed about cautiously and hopped off in search of clover and dandelions. Isabelle followed her, with Lasalle and Anne behind.

"My lord Lasalle?" Isabelle glanced back shyly. "What was the duke's message?"

"That he loves you very much and prays that one day you will love him, as well."

Isabelle d'Angoulême hugged herself and did not answer.

"My lord Lasalle?" she spoke up after a while. "What happened to your voice?"

"An injury."

"Oh." Isabelle nodded wisely, threading carefully among the gooseberry bushes. "Are you married, my lord?"

Anne held her breath.

"Yes."

"And do you . . . do you love her?"

"Yes."

Anne had not expected that question, and she expected that

answer even less. There was a long pause before Isabelle spoke again. "And did you love her when you married her?"

"No."

Isabelle paused, wringing her hands. "Is it true, then, that you can learn to love someone?"

For some reason, Anne's heart skipped, but Lasalle answered without hesitation. "Of course. It happens all the time. Especially after you are married. Didn't your ladies tell you?"

Isabelle shook her head. "They told me . . . and Father Urbain told me . . . that it is my duty."

"Would you like the lady Anne to tell you? She knows all about it. I'll put Philomena in her basket before she gnaws through your mother's shrubbery." Lasalle bowed to Isabelle and, with Philomena under his arm and an arched eyebrow at Anne, left them.

Isabelle d'Angoulême regarded Anne with apprehension and anticipation. Anne was not sure if she should kiss or kill Guérin de Lasalle the next time she got her hands on him. Probably a little of both. She held out her hands to the girl and smiled, a genuine smile of affection for all the innocent creatures. "Now then, my dear, where should we begin?"

CHAPTER 22

Fortress of Mervant, Poitou, August 26, 1200

Hugh le Brun, the Count of La Marche, was throttling his brother, Ralph of Exoudun, the Count of Eu, and no one in the gathering of Lusignan kith and kin dared to intervene.

They had all gathered that very day to celebrate the marriage of Hugh's son and namesake to the child heiress of Angoulême. The news that she had been spirited away by her own father into the arms of John Plantagenet from under the nose of her temporary guardian, the very same Ralph de Lusignan, ended the festive mood and replaced it with certain animosity toward the Count of Eu.

"You confounded fool!" Hugh de Lusignan roared into the purple face of his brother, shaking him nearly senseless. "Is it your witlessness or base treachery, Ralph? Tell me or I'll snap your neck!"

"He can't answer, Hugh. You've got your thumbs on his windpipe."

Having watched the Count of La Marche vent his fury for a time, Armand de Lusignan broke the fratricidal hold by applying upward pressure to Hugh's little finger. Hugh dropped his brother and was about to lunge at his new nemesis, but cousin Armand stood his ground, his eyes the only threat. It rendered the Count of La Marche civil. The gathering looked on, shifting from foot to foot.

"The only treachery here is John's." Armand helped the coughing, wheezing Count of Eu to his feet. "Ralph had no reason to suspect Aylmer's request to see his daughter before the wedding."

The calm voice brought reason to the fury. The far-flung clan Lusignan, its vassals, and its allies began to settle down like a flock of froward fowl, in anticipation of an answer to their predicament. Armand had it. "John wants to divide and conquer. Who among you will aid him?"

Hugh and Ralph, the latter still clutching his throat, eyed each other.

"He aims to drive us out of Poitou. If he can pit us against each other, we are lost. Let him have this victory."

"No! No, he must never—"

"Let him have his victory." Armand raised his voice, silencing the dissenters. "He will waste it. Let us use that to our advantage."

Hugh's fist crashed against the tabletop. "Advantage? What advantage comes from losing such an heiress? God's teeth, Lasalle is back, aiding John and laughing at you. This time he has not only bested you; he has bested all of us!"

Dredging up that unpleasant fact in the middle of the current disaster was not the most useful course of action. All eyes turned to the Count of Rancon, who did not seem to mind.

"So he has. Lasalle is no one's concern but my own."

The murmur grew louder.

Geoffrey de Lusignan, of the senior branch, stood up. "That may be, but we can't leave unanswered a Plantagenet insult. We have never done so before."

"Precisely. And it took us years to rally. This time, we wait."

"Wait?"

"Wait." Armand de Lusignan cut short the cries of outrage. "We have all sworn fealty to John in this very hall. Let us stand by it and wait. What will his other vassals do, now that he has broken a solemn betrothal of one of them? Will he snatch their daughters at the altar for his *routier* captains?"

The voices died down.

"We will wait for John to offer us a recompense. He won't; he can't. He has nothing to replace the Angoumois. Then we appeal to Philip for justice. Our cause will become Philip's."

Brown Hugh threw the dregs of his cup onto the rushes. "And what do we do while we wait, cousin? Pick up spindles and take to the loom?"

"No. We will serve John, faithfully." Armand de Lusignan turned to the Count of Eu.

"Faithfully?" The rest of the men came to their feet.

"Faithfully." Armand de Lusignan's tone left no mistake to his meaning. "Ralph, when John takes up his court in London, you will offer yourself wherever he wishes you to serve. Your loyalty will astonish even our most implacable foes. Agreed? Hugh?"

The prospect of such abasement did not appeal to Ralph de Lusignan, but its wisdom could not be denied. He and Hugh eyed each other again. They nodded.

Armand de Lusignan surveyed the faces around him. "Go home. All of you. And wait."

After some discussion, the assembly began to disperse in a shuffle of feet and the rustle of fine silks, in humiliation and defeat, but in its midst, a new determination was born.

"Hugh."

Leaving last and forgotten, the young, brideless groom paused in the doorway. Hands clasped behind his back, Armand approached him. "You are the principal aggrieved party. Your father resents the loss of the Angoumois. What about you?"

Young Hugh looked like his father, dark haired and dark eyed, both conscious and self-conscious of his position as the heir to Lusignan fortunes and misfortunes.

"I—"

"You are relieved."

Hugh would have protested, but his questioner's gaze probed his very soul. He lowered his eyes, hoping he would not blush and wondering how he should reply, knowing well that his formidable relative could hone words into daggers.

Armand de Lusignan smiled instead. "She is beautiful and she frightens you."

Hugh kept his gaze at his feet. "She looked at me like I was a bother. They'll all laugh at me now. What should . . . what should I do?"

"What we all do. Breathe and live and learn and wait."

CHAPTER 23

Fortress of Rivefort, Normandy, Autumn 1200

My lady, there is a messenger for you." Mistress Hermine cupped her hands to call into the scaffolding. She had failed to convince her lady that inspecting the hall's new plaster was better left to the hired men. Juliana looked down.

John d'Erlée stood in the doorway, wearing a muddy cloak. Oh Lord. He was the last person she expected at Rivefort. She shoved a plaster-dusted hair strand under her wimple and climbed down the ladder rungs, to the worried exclamations of Mistress Hermine. D'Erlée regarded her with amused alarm, but gave her an unreserved bow. "I didn't know you had an interest in the plastering trade, my lady."

"Only a temporary one, but it seems to take on a permanent character." She tried, she truly tried, to appear perfectly composed for their visitor.

"May I be allowed to rescue you from your labors for a while?"

No, she did not mind being rescued. Mistress Hermine had the servants follow them to the garden with fresh apple cider, a roasted duckling, bread, pickled onions, and poppy cakes, along with a basin of water and towels. Hermine dismissed the servants and, with her spindle, took up one of the turf benches.

Despite Juliana's embarrassment over the circumstances under which she had last parted from John d'Erlée, their conversation flowed as easily as it had at Dreux. He did not mention the tourney, speaking instead of his return from London, where he had accompanied Sir William, who in turn had followed his royal master and his new bride. On October 8, the Feast of Saint Demetrius, Isabelle d'Angoulême was crowned England's queen, an honor denied to her predecessor of the same name. Juliana twisted her napkin. How dare the duke sunder a pledge, when in the eyes of God Isabelle and Hugh were already wed?

John d'Erlée reached inside his surcoat. "I have a message from the viscount. He also went with the duke. He asked me to send it on to Rivefort since I was returning to Longueville with a message for the Countess de Clare."

Longueville was not around the corner, and John d'Erlée could have used a messenger. It was a pleasantly disturbing thought, and Juliana wished it did not come with a reminder of Lasalle. John d'Erlée's hand touched hers briefly, accidentally. "I should let you go back to your duties."

"No! I mean, you've come all this way. What would it tell Sir William about Rivefort's hospitality?"

John d'Erlée smiled. "I would not wish to disappoint Rivefort."

In her room, Juliana broke open the seal. The first sheet, addressed to her, contained several lines in a schoolboy's painstaking hand. At the bottom of the page was Lasalle's signature in the same hand. So he could write, after a fashion. The message to her said, without any salutation, "These orders to Sir Rannulf. Reply by the same courier. No need for haste. Signed, Guérin de Lasalle, *Sieur* of Rivefort, Viscount of Tillières."

Juliana crumpled the sheet. The nerve of the man. Another sealed parchment fell into her lap. It was addressed to Paulette, in different handwriting. Remembering the way the young squire Aumary looked at her ward, Juliana had a happy suspicion about the identity of its author. She called Paulette's maid to take the letter to the girl. Surely Paulette could make out the letters.

No hurry, Lasalle had said, and so after handing the message to Rannulf de Brissard, Juliana persuaded John d'Erlée to wait for a reply. Since Lasalle allowed her to go about her viscounty, she took advantage of her freedom and John d'Erlée's presence. They rode to Saint-Hilaire to place a wreath of rosehips in the clasped hands of her mother's effigy. John held the candles while Juliana lit them. He knelt with her at the small altar and they prayed in silence.

Over the following days, with Hermine, Donat, and Master Thibodeau, they visited every corner of the viscounty, Mathea and Paulette sometimes riding along. John d'Erlée treated the sisters with his usual courtesy, and even the shy Paulette conversed with him freely, especially when he compared her embroidery with the finest in the duke's household.

Their excursions took them to Belvoir, which sat on a wooded rise, an old, squat, thick-walled tower with a small hall added once the danger of raids from covetous neighbors had abated.

"Look, Juliana. What a wonderful place." Mathea leaned over her pony's neck.

Paulette puckered her brows. "Truly, Mathea, it's falling down."

The place *was* falling down. Lasalle had yet to make a decision about Belvoir's tenant, despite Master Thibodeau's efforts. Juliana sighed. "It may seem an odd name now, but flowers cover the hills in the spring."

They waded into the debris-strewn hall, where wild doves fluttered through the rafters and into the empty kitchen with its long-cold fireplace. Somewhere along the way they lost Mathea, and Juliana had just begun to worry when the girl reappeared, cobwebs in her hair. "Oh, please, Juliana, can I refurbish the place? You can spare some of the men now. It's such a shame for it to be so neglected."

Paulette regarded her sister with something akin to horror. "Don't be ridiculous, Mathea. You cannot possibly mind this place."

"I think the demoiselle Mathea is just what this place needs," John d'Erlée said, siding with Mathea.

Juliana was about to agree with Paulette, but the wistfulness in Mathea's voice silenced her. She understood the yearning for one's own home, for the need to feel useful. Paulette was content with her constrained existence, her embroidery, and the occasional venture outside Rivefort; Mathea wanted more. "Only if you take Ersillia and your maid with you. And don't try anything foolish," Juliana added, smiling at Mathea's eagerness.

A few days after Mathea's victory, John d'Erlée announced his departure. Juliana felt as if she were about to lose a dear friend. That evening, they climbed to the top of the donjon. The air smelled of fall rains; drifts of leaves blanketed the ground. John d'Erlée leaned on the parapet, his face concerned. "What are you going to do, my lady? Your marriage is almost dissolved."

She let out a sob of surprise. "It is?"

John d'Erlée pulled back. "Didn't the letter tell you?"

Juliana shook her head. "No. How do you know, sir?"

D'Erlée looked a little embarrassed. "I do have a Christian name, you know. From a discreet and reliable source. Do you remember the Countess de Valence? She is waiting on Isabelle d'Angoulême, and of course she is . . ." He hesitated and she knew why.

"Lasalle's mistress, and he told her." How could one forget the alluring, condescending countess?

He nodded. "Does that distress you?"

"That she is his mistress or that I am about to be discarded?" Juliana pressed herself against the stones. "I don't care about his mistresses. But if the marriage is annulled, he'll take away Tillières and send me back to a cloister."

"You can stand by your rights."

She faced him, her hands open. "John, look at me. I have no family, no friends, and no great wealth or beauty."

"You have friends."

"Yes. Armand de Lusignan."

"Christ's blood, don't ever trust a Lusignan!" D'Erlée's vehemence eased into a smile. "I was hoping you would see friends closer by."

She did, and the pain of it shriveled her heart. "I am humbled by your kindness, but he would kill you if he found out you were trying to help me."

"He wouldn't." John d'Erlée's face was full of youthful certainty. "I can fight as well as any man." He took her hands in his and rotated her wedding ring between his fingers. "When you take this off, you will be free and you will have friends. Think about the future."

"I don't have one until I have Tillières. What would happen to Mathea and Paulette and the others?"

"Don't worry so. I believe Aumary has set his heart on Paulette. He is not an impoverished squire. Didn't you read his letter?"

"Of course not. How do you know?" The young man was full of surprises.

"Aumary came from Wales with the viscount's message and asked me to take his own."

"Wales? I thought Lasalle was in England, attending the duke."

"He was, but found life in London too dull and the duke

granted him his request to help one of the marcher lords with some Welshmen."

That sounded like Lasalle. She pondered the other bit of news. "Aumary has an inheritance?"

"He is a ward of Saint-Sylvain. He told me that when he is fully fledged, he will take charge of the abbey's lands."

The news stirred Juliana's curiosity. "How did Lasalle come by him? The sisters of Saint-Sylvain are strictly cloistered. Their mother house is in Paris."

D'Erlée shrugged. "Does it matter? Good Heavens, you are shivering. I shouldn't have kept you up here in this cold."

She was indeed shivering, but not from the cold. "You are not keeping me. I came because I wanted to."

"Did you? You didn't answer my question, Juliana. What are you going to do?"

"Marriage or a cloister. I don't suppose I could become another Anne de Valence."

He gave a hoot of laughter. "Not without a lot of practice in breaking men's hearts!"

"No." Juliana felt herself flush. She tucked her chin to hide a swell of tears. "No, no danger of that."

John stopped laughing. "Not all men find women like the countess irresistible."

She blinked up at him through wet eyelashes. He wiped her tears, leaned down, and kissed her. He was so careful not to frighten her that it felt perfectly innocent. At first. After a couple of thunderous heartbeats, her arms went around his neck—and she kissed him back. She liked it. All of it. It was that belated realization that brought her to her senses. She tried to extricate herself, but he would not let her.

"Shhh. It's all right. You will not be punished or burn in Hell, I promise." He smiled and placed a perfectly chaste kiss on her forehead. "With or without Tillières, you are a prize, Juliana."

CHAPTER 24

Fortress of Rivefort, Spring 1201

Saint Martin's Lent had come and gone. Shortly thereafter, Father Cyril had celebrated Christ's Mass. A few weeks later, winter's driving rains and lashing snowstorms had abated, and the Great Lent had arrived with its black colors and meager meatless soups. The reward for the penitence of the faithful was the joy of Easter, which brought the new year. The joy, however, was not shared by everyone.

In February, King Philip of the Franks had traveled northward to Soisson to appear with his lawfully wedded and once-bedded wife before the Church's council. Philip had prayed for a speedy and favorable rendering in favor of his petition for the annulment of his marriage to Ingeborg of Denmark by reasons of consanguinity. He had been disappointed. Stymied by the delaying tactics of Ingeborg's hastily appointed clerical defenders, Philip had left the council still a married man, but mitigated that fact by depositing his wife in the convent at Étampes. While he returned to his mistress, his queen had remained cloistered, an all but invisible reminder of a woman's perseverance and of Pope Innocent's determination to reign supreme over all the beds in Christendom.

The Lusignans, who for months had borne silently the insult to their honor in the expectation of receiving some appropriately magnificent compensation for the loss of Isabelle of Angoulême, were equally disappointed. John Plantagenet not only had not offered them even a paltry recompense; he had added to the outrages. While the Count of Eu served him in England, the king had ordered the seizure of Driencourt, which Ralph held of his Norman wife, and commanded royal officials in that county to do Ralph "all the harm they could." At the same time, John had unleashed mercenaries under Lupescaire upon the lands of Ralph's brother, Count Hugh. To add insult to injury, John had commanded Hugh's vassals to pledge their loyalty to him directly.

By April, the Lusignans had had enough. They renounced their allegiance to John and appealed to Philip for redress, charging John with attacking them without cause and despoiling them of their lands. To make their displeasure palpable, they besieged John's castellans in Poitou. Having watched the duke's dealings with the Lusignans at first with approbation and then with alarm, many of his Poitevin vassals decided to join the Lusignans' standard.

By the end of that month, John of England faced the flames of a fully fledged rebellion. His mother kept him closely informed of the spreading disaster, but as was his habit in times of crisis, John preferred to drag his feet. Isabelle's beauty was rumored to be the cause of his distraction. Left to confront the rebellion alone, the Duchess of Aquitaine worked diligently to secure the support of John's remaining vassals.

At the beginning of May, John finally bestirred himself, collected scutage from his English barons, and with his coffers replenished, dismissed them and used the windfall to hire two hundred mercenaries. He sent them under William Marshal and Roger de Laci to put down the Poitevin rebellion.

Standing at the top of the donjon, looking out across the misty, greening countryside, Juliana dropped a piece of crumbled mortar into the void. Lasalle was returning to Rivefort. The annulment of her marriage should not be long in coming either. At least she had some friends—friends who wanted to become more. John d'Erlée. She blushed every time she thought about that kiss, a kiss that was not inflicted for the sake of her humiliation. And there was more to think upon. After John d'Erlée left, another person had arrived at Rivefort—Lasalle's bastard.

It had come as a shock, but hardly a surprise, a male infant brought by a slightly daft girl who served as its wet nurse, along with a message from the child's mother. Lasalle's little by-blow, sired on Ravenissa, just as Hermine predicted. Shortly after Lasalle had departed, Ravenissa informed Master Thibodeau that she was leaving Tillières because she had accepted an offer of marriage. Juliana barely recalled receiving the news; she had been absorbed by other matters.

The message, pinned to the baby's soiled swaddling, stated simply that Ravenissa's new husband, while forgiving his wife's past trespasses, was unwilling to bring up the evidence of them. Juliana had been at a loss for words. Hermine had not been. "What's his name? Has he been baptized? How old is he?"

"I don't know, ma'am." The wet nurse bounced the babe against her hip while Juliana read out the poorly scratched lines. The child, dirty, tired, and hungry, had howled at the top of his lungs. "I did what my mistress told me, brought him right here, I did."

Hermine had freed the baby from his careless custodian. "That's Ravenissa for you. Not a thought in that pretty head. Well, I suppose that's how she came by this one. You there!"

Calling out to a loitering servant, Hermine had ordered her to take the girl to the kitchen and slipped the child into Juliana's arms. Juliana had held it with some trepidation. The youngest children at Fontevraud had been well-grown toddlers. This babe had squinted at her in a most unfriendly manner. "What am I going to do with him, Hermine?"

"What would you do, my lady, if it was a parish foundling?"

"Keep it, of course. Oh, Hermine, that was not fair."

"I am not saying it was." Giving her mistress a sly smile, Hermine had reclaimed the babe. "The cook's daughter has enough milk for two. I will send for Father Cyril to have this little soul properly baptized. What are you going to call him, my lady?"

"Jourdain. We'll call him Jourdain. Something that came from far away."

By early June, the Avre ran low, the garden wilted, and the cattle congregated in the shade. Rivefort's inhabitants sought shade as well, the men hardly stirring themselves to cross the bailey, remaining annoyingly underfoot. Rannulf de Brissard had taken ill, and Juliana almost wished for Lasalle to return, if only to get the men out of the bailey and onto the tilting field. The Duke of Normandy with his bride and his mercenaries landed at Barfleur, and King Philip, in a conciliatory mood, persuaded the Lusignans to cease their attacks on John's fortresses in Poitou.

Philip had a reason to be conciliatory. His mistress was again with child, and the Holy Father, having compelled Philip to take back his childless, long-suffering queen, was considering legitimizing Philip's bastards. John and Philip therefore adjourned to Fortress Gaillard, to deal with the grievances of the various parties.

Juliana rubbed her itchy jaw with the back of her hand and for the fourth time reprimanded a gaggle of chattering girls who were flitting about the bakery. The baker and his usual complement of knaves had taken ill with summer fever, inconveniently in the middle of a weekly round of baking the villeins' bread. Edith's effort to save the day by calling upon several of the laundress's helpers from the village turned into a disaster, as the girls immediately abandoned their tasks to bask in the admiration of Peyrac's men.

To keep the parties separated, Juliana closed the bakery's iron-grille door. Since the oven made the vaulted room swelter, she, like her help, worked in her shift and apron, her hair tied up in clean rags. The loaves, shining like newly peeled chestnuts, filled the bailey with their smell. She counted her flour scoops, not paying attention to the new arrivals in the bailey. Since the eruption of troubles with the Lusignans, a steady parade of knights, men-at-arms, and mercenaries had passed through Rivefort on their way south. She called out to the girls to stop their squabbling and to mind the oven, but her voice was drowned in the noise of the girls' excitement, accompanied by the sound of the door opening.

"I am Eloisa. You can call on me, my lord. I will be happy to wait on you."

"Don't listen to her, sir; she is a sow."

"Dulcie, you—!" A sharp slap followed, causing Juliana to miscalculate her count. She glanced back to see two men disappear under an avalanche of bare limbs and tangles of loosened tresses. From somewhere underneath the pile, she heard them laughing.

Oh pother. Juliana dusted her hands and took hold of the nearest bare limb. "You two, get up or I'll have you turned out of Rivefort without food or forage!"

The man Dulcie had claimed shoved her away and sat up. Too late, Juliana noticed that she wore as little as her help, but by then her bosom hovered level with the man's nose—and he was taking full advantage of it. She drew the edges of her chemise together with one hand and was about to deliver a chastisement with the other when he raised his eyes. She fell back, her tailbone jarring on the stone floor.

"My dear Sister Eustace," said the voice she had almost forgotten, "you'll have to wait your turn. Ah, I believe your bread is burning."

She stood in the middle of the hall, her stomach knotted, her palms clammy inside her sleeves. Lasalle's sword belt hung on her father's chair, the one she had reclaimed in the last few months, and his boots crushed the hay on the floor. The scent of thyme soaked the air. He wrinkled his nose and paused at the oak partition.

Juliana's heart pounded. "It's a solar," she said, trying to dispel the memory of herself and John d'Erlée at the top of the keep.

He drummed his fingers on the wood. "I see. You've held court?"

"Yes." She had, with Master Thibodeau, Brissard, and Louis Pavilli. Who did he think managed his viscounty—*her* viscounty— while he was Lord only knew where?

"I suppose Petit Jacques's name came up."

Why would Guérin de Lasalle remember something so inconsequential? "No. He left Rivefort."

"Chased out by irate husbands?"

She avoided his eyes. "He wished to go into the hide trade."

Lasalle and the other men resembled half-starved hounds. That included Jehan de Vaudreuil, who at least had had the decency to try to sweep the half-dressed Eloisa and Dulcie behind him while offering Juliana comically contrived apologies. Kadolt, who had remained in the bailey, must have dropped at least a stone. And Aumary, the fourth rider, had acquired a pair of shining spurs: Sir Aumary. No doubt he would be leaving soon to take up his estates. Would he press his suit to Paulette before his departure? "My lord?"

"I said, what happened to your hair?"

Her hand flew to her brow. Lasalle was back, pointing out her imperfections. "It grew. What happened to yours?" It came out before she could check herself. She nearly stomped her foot.

Lasalle ran his fingers through his hair, now almost as short as Vaudreuil's, which accounted for the fact that she at first had not recognized him. "Lice."

She looked away, biting her lip. She had not done that for months and she was once again at a loss as to how to deal with this—male. "I see."

She wanted to ask about the state of their annulment, but if it had been granted, surely he would have been the first one to mention it. She curtsied and was fleeing to the door when it opened to Hermine with swaddled Jourdain in her arms. Oh Mary, not now! Not having much choice in the matter, Juliana scooped the boy from Hermine and placed herself in front of Lasalle. "This is—"

"Let me guess. Ravenissa's?" Lasalle picked the babe out of her arms and tossed it in the air as if it were a bread loaf. "What's his name?"

"Gently, please!" She tried to rescue the boy, but Lasalle caught him and settled him into the crook of his arm. The babe squalled and then quieted. Juliana stepped back, her hands sinking, empty. "Jourdain."

"Jourdain." Lasalle seemed surprised. "Did you pay Ravenissa for him?"

"No. I thought you might want to keep him. For the love of Christ, he is your son."

Lasalle held up the babe. Jourdain drooled with delight. "It pains me to deprive you of your pious deeds of charity, love, but he isn't. Just as well. If he were, I'd drown him."

Mistress Hermine crossed herself. "Lord in Heaven!"

Juliana dove for the boy. "Give him to me! How can you say such a horrible thing? He is just an innocent babe, even though he is yours."

Lasalle kept the boy out of her reach. "Interestingly put, but your mummy already had you in the oven when I came to Rivefort, didn't she, you little bastard?"

"Give him to me!" This time Juliana wrested the boy away. "Take Jourdain to my room, Hermine," she said more sharply than she intended, anxious to remove the child from that man's vicinity.

"Yes, my lady." Hermine curtsied and Lasalle, his hand on his heart, bowed to her as if she were a duchess. Responding to that one with a *humph,* Hermine carried the boy away.

"You don't believe me," Lasalle said, and noting that Juliana had slipped her hands into her sleeves, he shrugged. "Nevertheless, it's true. He isn't mine. I would never lie to you, love."

"Then what do you suggest that I do with him, my lord?" It was not a challenge, only a simple question.

Lasalle picked up his sword. "I could drown him for you."

He had her flying after Hermine as fast as she could. How could he say such a vile thing? That man must have left bastards in many a copse and camp—he said it himself—and did not appear to care. What possible difference would one babe make to a man like that? But there was something in the very utterance of those words that Juliana could not dismiss, and she resolved to keep Jourdain out of Lasalle's sight.

She was thus spared finding out until the next morning that my lord Lasalle was that night accompanied to his room high in the donjon by a young woman whose name was Gwenllian.

"To Paris?"

He had startled her, as usual. She was in her garden, humming to herself a catchy ditty she had overheard in the market the last time she visited it with John d'Erlée. Now it all seemed ages ago. Since Lasalle's return and without an explanation, her domain had once again shrunk to the distance between the bailey and the barbican. "Why?"

"John's orders. Philip invited him to Paris to grease a reconciliation. You are coming along."

Juliana picked up her bucket. She liked to come out in the evening and water the rosebushes she had received from the Countess
de Nevers along with a kind note. She had received nothing
from Lasalle upon his return except that exhibition at the bakery
and the presence of his new mistress. It was the talk of Rivefort and
Tillières. Gwenllian did not say much, the servants reported—at
least not in understandable French. There were whispers about the
bailey that the girl was a witch.

"Did you hear me, mouse?"

"I can't leave Jourdain. He thinks I am his mother."

"You're not his mother."

The words stabbed, rendering her breathless. Swallowing tears,
Juliana busied herself watering the rest of her roses.

"You have servants; you are not a peasant. Why do this?" Lasalle's tone had changed to undisguised annoyance.

"I garden. You . . . travel." He would not make her cry.

He flung a mud ball against the battlement. "And now you,
too, can travel. Pack up your folderol and frippery, Juliana. John
wants to see us craven all, down to the last vassal and wife."

CHAPTER 25

Paris, June 1201

Approached from the right bank of the Seine by the Grand-
Pont, the palace of the Capetian kings rose at the west end
of Île de la Cité, a maze of corridors and halls behind stone walls,
where chilly air hovered under the barreled vaulting despite the
blazing braziers and the odd fireplace. At the east end of the isle,
joined to the left bank by the Petit-Pont, resided the Lord-Bishop

THE SIXTH SURRENDER   115

of Paris, busily overseeing the construction of the new church of Our Lady. The Lord-King of Paris had graciously vacated his capital and retired to Poissy. There, Philip awaited the birth of his second child by Agnès de Méran.

The palace and Paris might have been placed by Philip at the disposal of the King of England, but only days into his visit the Parisians decided that John Plantagenet and his pack had overstayed their welcome. Fights between the swaggering visitors and the populace broke out daily, fueled by July's heat, tuns of wine, and raw tempers. Several brawlers on each side were badly injured and the burghers brought their complaints to John. He ignored them. The complaints had no effect on John's retainers, either, occupied as they were with other matters.

At that moment, some of them were casting curious glances in Juliana's direction. She wavered between returning a look of haughty hostility and turning on her heel and running away. Earlier, Lasalle had gathered her, and at her insistence Mistress Hermine as well, from a small, well-fortified house called the Three Dwarfs, nested among the houses of wealthy wine merchants, a stone's throw from the Church of Saint Gervais. After that, Lasalle disappeared. She had not seen him until he brought her to this occasion.

"I think we should leave." Juliana handed Hermine her cup. Kadolt had drawn Lasalle away, whispering something into his ear. Lasalle's decision to bring Kadolt to the duke's reconciliation with Philip struck her as singularly odd, especially since a perplexed Vaudreuil had been left at Rivefort. Juliana had compounded his bewilderment by asking him to look after Mathea and Paulette since there was not a single man of Lasalle's she thought she could trust with her wards.

"You cannot leave, dear; the festivities are about to begin." The ravishing young woman standing there needed no introduction, but she said, nevertheless, "I doubt you will remember me. I am—"

"Countess de Valence." Juliana almost curtsied, but decided against it.

The countess's fingertips brushed Juliana's cheek. "Ah, how sweet. A memory for names."

Juliana flinched at the unanticipated gesture. Lasalle's matchless mistress had something of his ability to meld insult and compliment. From the whispers and titters about them, the company was enjoying the sight of the Countess de Valence conversing, excruciatingly publicly, with the wife of her lover. Juliana had no doubt how she fared in that gossip.

Against the dictates of propriety and fashion, Anne de Valence's hair spilled loose in a shimmering fall over her gown of *graine*. With reluctant fascination, Juliana noted the source of its gleam came from specks of powdered gold. A simple black silk cord circled the lady's brow, traces of antimony touched her eyelids, and pigment tinged her lips, swollen as if from a lover's kisses. Her complexion, no doubt like the rest of her, was as translucent as alabaster, and her every move liberated the scent of lilies. The countess returned a smile of those who were addressed by their inferiors. "Do you mind if I join you? You see, I, too, am left unescorted. At least you've brought your maid. I wish I had thought of that."

Behind Juliana, Hermine huffed. Swallowing what would have been a lame retort, Juliana reached for Hermine. Those standing closest parted, their voices rising in thrilled whispers. The mistress was routing the wife.

"Stay! Lady Juliana, please." The first was an order; the second, a request. Juliana paused.

"My lady, don't let that woman humiliate you," Hermine hissed while Anne de Valence moved toward them, with dismissive glances for those about her.

Anne did not know why she had behaved like that. The girl looked as if she was surprised not so much by Anne's treatment of her as by the fact that she had bothered. She lowered her voice. "Will you accept my apology, Lady Juliana? It was prudent of you to bring a chaperone. Prudence, you see, is not a virtue one encounters in this company."

Juliana took Hermine's elbow. "You mean, Madame, it is usually confined to the provincials."

"Please." Anne reached out. "Forgive me and come, let us give them a cause for gossip. It was not right of your husband to leave you alone in this place. You must speak to him about it." The girl's expression made Anne laugh. "Very well. If you wish, I will speak to him. You see, we do have something in common after all, and to prove it, do call me Anne. Let us take a seat by the fire. In truth, if I could, I'd wear all my woolen gowns and wrap myself in my cloak."

Despite her misgivings, Juliana let herself be led to the fireplace. The whispers about them grew. Juliana did her best to ignore them. Anne snapped her fingers and the little blackamoor appeared, carrying a tray with a ewer and two cups. Anne poured for Juliana. "We can either pretend the other one of us does not exist or we can become friends. I prefer the latter, if you allow. Alas, I am afraid that merely being seen with me will ruin your reputation."

Juliana saw Hermine take to a bench nearby and pull her spindle out of her waist purse. "I don't have a reputation to ruin."

"I wager you'll find several here who would not mind ruining it for you." Now there was an answer to one's prayers. Anne held out her hand to a young man heading for them through the crowd. "My lord d'Erlée."

"Countess." John d'Erlée kissed her hand, but his eyes were on the girl, Anne noted.

"We were only now speaking of you. The lady Juliana tells me she preferred you to all the other gallants. Since that leaves me a much depleted field, you'll have to allow me my escape," Anne said, and she swept the room with her smile and herself across the hall.

Juliana wished she, too, could disappear, but since she could not, she stammered instead, "I am sorry, I did not mean . . . I meant I did not say . . . I meant the countess—"

John laughed. "Never mind; the lady Anne likes to shock. There, you see"—he inclined his head toward the crowd—"she has fended off several propositions and is contemplating the proposals."

Juliana could not help but giggle; surely it was the wine. John d'Erlée was in a jovial mood. She was glad to see him, but remained apprehensive about his safety.

"I saw my lord Lasalle ride away with that man of his," John d'Erlée answered her unspoken question. "I was worried I'd never find you in this crush. I came with my lord Marshal. He brought the lady Isabel with him. You must meet her; she has been asking me about you. Lady Anne is her closest friend, did you know that?"

Juliana listened to the words, but it was John's smile that kept her attention. She wanted John to kiss her again, kiss her in front of all these strangers. Surely it was the wine. Festive horns sounded and the crowd around them began to file into the adjoining hall. D'Erlée offered Juliana his arm. "If you don't mind."

She placed her hand on the young man's sleeve. No, she did not mind at all.

CHAPTER 26

Amazing, isn't it?"

It was. A snorting, muscular white bull pranced through a sea swell with a naked, somewhat pleased-looking figure on its back.

"Zeus abducting Europa," said the woman at the top of the stairs, pointing to the fresco. She appeared to be in her late twenties. A single, thick braid of glossy brown hair intertwined with silver ribbons reached to her waist. She wore a costly robe and well-bred gentility. "He revealed his true nature to her and she gave birth to three sons, although for the world I can't remember their names."

"Minos, Rhadamanthus, and Sarpedon," Juliana blurted out.

The dark-haired woman smiled at her. "You must be Sister Scholastica. I am Isabel de Clare."

"Sister Scholastica indeed. Do you ever wonder, Isabel, how someone in the chaste confines of a convent learned about the fate of poor Europa?" Anne embraced Juliana playfully.

Juliana turned as scarlet as the new gown she wore, courtesy of Anne de Valence's needlewomen and the countess's generosity and persuasiveness. A loan of a girdle with an enameled clasp complemented it. In such a gown, she did not resemble anyone who had spent time in the confines of a convent. That, Juliana suspected, was what Anne's needlewomen had been instructed to accomplish, despite Juliana's protestations to her new, and quite unexpected, friend.

Isabel de Clare descended the stairs and kissed Anne's cheeks. "You are making our guest uncomfortable. Come, we will dine in the garden." She turned to Juliana. "I am told that some years ago this house belonged to the Lusignans. The house is gloomy, but the garden is lovely."

It was. The servants ushered them to a damask-covered table underneath a rose trellis. At Isabel's directions, Anne and Juliana seated themselves on pillowed chairs. Torches were lit and the platters and tureens began to appear.

"Try the *gravé* of quails, Lady Juliana. Anne, I had your favorite prepared—capon with currants."

Juliana nibbled the saffron bread, relieved to put something in her mouth, besides her foot. Between the courses, the two countesses chatted about mutual acquaintances and the latest court gossip, drawing Juliana into their conversation, and soon had her laughing and imitating Sister Domenica, Father Osbert, and Abbess Mathilde. That life seemed so very long ago. The wine helped too.

"I heard you are expecting the annulment of your marriage, Lady Juliana." Isabel de Clare motioned back the attentive servants, who brought them cheese and gooseberry pies.

"Armand de Lusignan has also been asking about the annulment," Anne added, but Isabel only smiled at her friend's eagerness to launch her plan.

Juliana swallowed a mouthful. Armand de Lusignan? Isabel de

Clare dismissed her servants with a nod. "I don't envy any woman whose wardship John would hold. Would it not be simpler to remain married to your current husband?"

Juliana steadied her cup with both hands. Bringing up Lasalle had the usual effect on her, but then she had drunk two—or was it three?—cups. "He is a murderer, isn't he? He said that he would kill me if I did not give up Tillières to him."

"Wasn't that naughty of him? Have you considered that he might change his mind and have his rights instead?" Anne de Valence said.

"Yes, but Hermine assu . . . assu . . . " Juliana gave up on that word. "Swore it would not take too long."

Anne coughed and hid her face behind her napkin. Juliana took another swallow. This was a wonderful wine. "He . . . he was going to ra-ravish me." She held to the edge of the table. It kept moving away from her. There, she said it. Anne leaned toward her. Or was it the lady Isabel?

"Was he, now? Was he very drunk?"

"Drunk? I don't think so. He even kissed me. Once. Twice. No, that was John, wasn't it?"

"Did he, now? What did you think of it, dear?"

"I liked it when John kissed me. I felt like a dab of butter, slowly . . . melting. . . ."

"No, dear, your husband."

"Who?"

"Guérin de Lasalle!"

Why were they laughing? She wished they would not talk about Lasalle. They were spoiling a perfectly lovely evening. "Oh, he always looks at me with those eyes like sooo. . . ." She hoped she imitated Lasalle's squint adequately. "He thinks he'll have Tillières, but he never will, not ever." She moved aside her cup with great care and rested her heavy head on her folded arms. She sighed deeply. "I hate him."

The lady Juliana's snores drowned out the trill of a nightingale. Anne and Isabel stood over their guest. "Well, what do you think?" Anne pressed her friend.

Isabel smiled. "I think you can't return her to the Three Dwarfs like that. You may as well stay too. William won't be coming back tonight. I don't like to sleep alone in this place."

She clapped and her steward appeared with a couple of servants, who carried the lady Juliana to her room. Since Anne and Isabel had in the past dealt with inebriated guests, they had Juliana de Charnais disrobed and tucked under the covers without difficulty.

Anne picked up Juliana's gown and shoes. "You see how I need your help? Aliénor wants this marriage to stand, and I am to make certain of it."

"I can't be of much use to you," Isabel de Clare demurred, reluctant to be drawn into Anne's—or rather the Duchess of Aquitaine's—plots.

"You can. You knew him before I came to Longueville. Please, hear me out. You are the Countess of Pembroke. You are William Marshal's wife, your station is unassailable, your reputation beyond reproach. You have nothing to risk by asking him."

"No one's station is unassailable. I am the daughter of an Irish usurper's daughter and a Norman adventurer," Isabel corrected her. "Would you not rather see their marriage dissolved?"

Anne pressed her palms to her brow. "Oh, Isabel, I have been assigned a duty. I play my part and others must play theirs." She nodded toward the blissfully oblivious Lady Juliana. "The bishops won't grant them an annulment; they are still angry about John's marriage to the Angoulême girl. Guérin could not have chosen a worse time for his petition."

Isabel crossed herself. "Good heavens. She doesn't know it's been rejected? Does Guérin?"

"He does. John handed him the decree personally. I think John enjoyed it too, the bastard."

Isabel de Clare shielded the candle flame. "Why hasn't he told her?"

Anne drew the bed curtains. "Why not indeed."

It was a house at the end of the appropriately named Rue Puteyne. Lasalle remembered the place, which in the intervening years had acquired a new story and a new owner. Beyond that, he did not wish to venture. He hoped he had brought with him enough coin and that his information was not wrong. It had seemed rather odd receiving it, along with a sack of silver, from Fontevraud's Brother Simon. Behind him, Kadolt muttered.

He dropped the sack into Kadolt's hands and tugged at the bell cord. "Even if you had spared yourself yesterday, Heinrich, it would still be in vain. Neither you nor I can afford the queen of whores' hospitality."

The queen of whores had a name—Madame Violaine. She greeted them personally in a plain room with a table, chair, and hearth. The firelight illuminated a sallow-faced figure of uncertain years, attired with the severity of a spinster who had taken holy vows but could not bring herself to give up the rest of the world. Madame Violaine's expression revealed nothing, but the lashless black eyes followed their every move. Keeping close to his lord's back, Kadolt noticed that Madame wore a crucifix on a thong that reached to her loins. She held out her hand.

Lasalle kissed it. "You are kind to receive us, Madame."

Madame's gaze moved to Kadolt and returned to the man in front of her. They were almost the same height. "You have brought—"

Lasalle reached for the coin bag and placed it on the table. Kadolt sighed. A fortune.

"They were here and are likely to return. What is it you wish?" Madame Violaine spoke in a breathy voice whose undertone, Kadolt thought, sounded oddly masculine.

"When they do, send a messenger to me at the residence of the Countess de Valence. Someone discreet," Lasalle said.

Madame Violaine glanced at the table. "You are willing to pay generously, my lord. Surely the information is worth much more to you."

Kadolt held his breath, but his master remained unconcerned. "There are others who will accept less. In time, they will have the same information."

Madame's fingers flexed like cat's claws. She smiled. "No need to seek elsewhere, my lord. You will be informed promptly.

Perhaps your friend would like to sample while we discuss these matters?"

Lasalle nodded. "You are kind, Madame. I wish to speak to those who entertained your guests."

Madame Violaine rang a bell. Two willowy figures entered and Heinrich Kadolt, the murderous mercenary, was confronted by twin gazes of kohl-lined eyes and two pairs of moist, wine-red lips. One pair of the lips smiled at him.

"Ziya"—Madame Violaine's hand swept toward Kadolt—"see to our guest."

A small, warm, feminine hand extended to Kadolt. He seized it. Trapped in the wake of heady perfume, he wondered if my lord Lasalle was amused or angered by his luck, but by then he truly did not care. With those silver marks, my lord Lasalle could afford the whole place, including Madame.

When the doors closed behind Kadolt, Madame Violaine indicated the remaining figure. "This," she said, "is Equitan. Equitan, you are to do whatever my lord Lasalle wishes."

Equitan held the door to another room open for him. Lasalle glanced about it quickly. The room was lit by several candles, with a bed furnished for obvious purposes. On the table waited a ewer of wine.

Moving silently on bare feet, Equitan stood very close to him, dressed in an unlaced shirt under surcoat of Palermo silk. The scent of perfume came from its folds. Dark, almond eyes looked up at him, invitation in them. The candlelight made curls of the short, rust-colored hair look even deeper red than they were. Lasalle did not flinch, only because he expected it when the boy's narrow hand touched his cheek. "Tell me what would please you for me to do, my lord."

He smiled and kissed the cold, white fingers. "It would please me, Equitan, if you would share some of Madame's undoubtedly excellent wine and tell me about your recent patron."

❧

Juliana woke with a start born of the realization that she was not where she was supposed to be, and why. Heavens, what must the

Countess of Pembroke think of her? And Anne! Lead-headed, she threw back the covers. Lasalle was right. She should drink only well-watered wine. A voice came from behind the door.

"Madame, are you awake? I am Davidina, the lady Isabel's maid." Davidina opened the door cautiously and, seeing Juliana, curtsied. "The Countess de Valence and my mistress went to the market. They ask you to wait for them, Madame."

Once Davidina had helped Juliana into her gown, tamed her hair, and brought her porridge, Juliana thought to look about the house. The door on the upper story led her to an open gallery overlooking the city. Below, smoke from kitchen fires shrouded the tiled rooftops and fine-fretted spires of churches. So many people in one place; no doubt so many wonders concealed in those streets, like threads of an untidy skein. It looked like the stone balustrade had been repaired at one time. Good thing she did not suffer from vertigo. The house was a gloomy place, resistant to all efforts to make it appear anything else than an imposing monument to someone's bottomless purse. She decided to cheer herself up by exploring the garden.

This time, glorious morning sun bathed beds of roses and peonies sprinkled among the lavender and heliotrope. The gardener, a spry, well-spoken sexagenarian, bowed to her, eager to share his kingdom. Juliana admired the garden shed, built of half-timbered walls with a thickly thatched roof. She stepped into the doorway to see the inside.

"Take care, my lady!" The gardener held Juliana back with a torrent of apologies. At her feet, an open trapdoor led into black depths. "I am dreadfully sorry, my lady. I usually keep it locked, but I was airing it today. We keep roots there. This spot doesn't flood like the rest of the cellars. I am told they go a distance under there, part of an old aqueduct."

Juliana backed away. The shaft smelled of age-old mold and dampness. She thanked the old man, leaving him to mumble and fuss. On her own, she made a round of the garden that ended at the gate; she was drawn there by the sounds beyond it.

The gate stood half open. Juliana hesitated. Surely there could be no harm to look into the street? A crowd of merrymakers filled the narrow passage, jostling, shouting, laughing. Was today a saint's day she had forgotten?

She took another step.

CHAPTER 27

She took precisely three steps from the protection of Isabel de Clare's gate and found herself captive of a boisterous circle of young people. Four or five girls, painted and dressed in the yellow colors of their profession with loose hair and bared arms, and several youths in students' cloaks and berets laughed and cavorted around her. A girl with crimped blond hair dropped her bryony wreath around Juliana's brow. "Crown the Queen of Misrule!" she called out to the others.

"To the Queen of Misrule!" Two young men swept up Juliana, one of them planting a sloppy, wet kiss on her mouth, tearing away before she could retaliate. They were all mad!

They whirled her around and around until she lost her sense of direction, but instead of being alarmed, she burst out laughing. She had not felt this carefree for years—they did not know who she was and they did not care. The girl who had crowned her held on to her hand and pulled her alongside. The raucous pack barreled past angry housewives and staid burghers, upsetting peddlers' carts and merchants' stalls. Window shutters flew open; residents leaned out, curious, cursing, some emptying chamber pots and others hurling rotting vegetables, crockery, and imaginative obscenities. A turnip Juliana flung back overhand found its mark, to the delight of her companions. They swept down the street like a mad storm. She did not know how far they had traveled when another stream of revelers collided with them. The collision knocked Juliana's hand from the girl's grasp.

The girl reached for her, a flash of fear on her face, but caught only Juliana's girdle. The clasp broke. Juliana cried out in alarm, the crowd swallowing her in the next moment to carry her into another street. The deluge thickened. She sobbed, afraid to slow down, afraid of being dragged under. She lost one of her shoes, and her sleeve was nearly torn off. She started to flounder, to panic. Suddenly, the pressure of the bodies around her eased. The human wave had spilled into a square, unsettling those ahead of it. She took a deep breath. If she could regain her bearing . . .

A blood-freezing scream tore the air. The crowd surged forward, nearly knocking her down.

The square was a place of execution, well under way.

Oh Lord. Juliana shut her eyes, but not quickly enough. Her stomach heaved. Her knees buckled. She commenced to slide under the feet of the throng. A hard hand gripped her shoulder, wrenching her upward. "Why, Sister Eustace, had I known you enjoy watching men hacked to bits, I would've taken you to Wales."

Another scream rent the air.

"Oh God." It came out as a half-strangled sob. "Please!"

She was buttressed by a solid shoulder. "Don't faint on me and don't get sick. These people would take offense, trust me."

The hilt of his poniard dug into her wrist. She held on for dear life. The Parisians were not intimidated by one of the duke's followers rudely elbowing through their midst with a numb girl in his arms. It was like running a gauntlet, although she was shielded from the worst of it.

The crowd's noise did not drown out the next scream. Lasalle recoiled. The sound of it struck her like a bolt as well. It was more than the sound of someone in pure agony; it was someone in the soul-killing aloneness of it.

Oh dear Lord, why didn't Lasalle move? Perhaps the crowd was too thick; she sensed it all around, the unwashed bodies, the raw bloodlust. Their backs were against a crumbling wall, the platform ahead of them. Lasalle was staring at it. Her stomach in her mouth, Juliana followed his gaze.

There was blood. Blood all over the platform, dripping into the sawdust spread at the base of it. And there was still enough left in the man to keep him alive. The executioner, in a blood-smeared apron, had the man shackled to a beam for the whole crowd to see, his clothes—his last earthly possession and already the property of the headsman—carefully folded to the side to avoid soiling. The sight of the neat pile struck Juliana with the stupefying absurdity of it all. And then across the distance the man's eyes caught hers. They were wide open in shock, and they were staring at her.

From among the assortment of blood-encrusted instruments spread on a trestle, the hooded headsman selected a curved knife. The blade glinted in the sun. It descended. The crowd howled. Gagging, Juliana lurched forward. "Oh dear Lord!"

Lasalle's body blocked the platform and its screaming, writhing wretch. He shook her so hard, her teeth rattled. "Not here. Come on!"

He forced their way through the crowd until they were free of it and in a maze of streets so narrow that she could have spanned them with her outstretched arms. The passages stank of mud, offal, and urine.

"Wait!" Juliana gasped out.

He did not, but took a sharp turn that brought them into a small square with a covered fount. A boy sat on the edge of it, swinging his feet, holding the reins of a rounsey. Lasalle let her go. Juliana leaned against the well, trying to find her breath and some appropriate curse to hurl at him.

"What happened to your shoe?" Lasalle towered over her, his fists to his hips.

"I don't know. You drag me along like a bloated goat. Oh no. My girdle! I have to find my girdle. It's enameled with a lion's-head clasp. It's not mine."

Lasalle tossed her up into the saddle and thrust his finger into her face. "Stay there or I'll tie you to the tail."

She stayed.

He snatched her remaining slipper and, not knowing what to

do with it, flung it into the gutter. Then he shoved his foot into
the stirrup and settled behind the saddle. Dropping a penny to the
boy, Lasalle pointed the horse down another maze of streets, scattering mud, dogs, and beggars. They traveled in silence for some
time, Juliana too frightened to say a word. They reached a bridge
and crossed the Seine. The smell of the river, the discards from
the *cité*, and smoke from cooking fires mingled with the happy
sound of the water mills and the shouts of watermen. At the quay,
low-riding barges swayed, heavy with wine casks; cheese wheels
bedded in straw; sacks of grain; dried peas; cabbages; cages
of pullets, ducks, and geese; and penned pigs. They picked their
way around the merchants, servants, housewives, beggars, cut-
purses, fishmongers, prostitutes, and dirty, nimble-fingered street
urchins. When they had left the noisy wharf behind them, Lasalle
slackened the reins and the horse continued a steady pace along a
grassy bank.

Juliana squirmed. "My side hurts sitting like this. Can I walk?"

"You are barefoot."

"I like barefoot."

Lasalle drew a breath of irritation, reined in, and dismounted.
Reaching up for her, he swung her down, her breasts pressed briefly
against him. He let her go. Embarrassed, Juliana shook out her
skirts. It felt good to walk. Lasalle followed her, thumbs hooked on
his belt, reins looped on his elbow. He wore the same shirt he had
worn at Dreux, and his battered gambeson. The horse stretched his
neck toward the water. Lasalle let it go to the bank. Juliana waited,
hugging herself. "Did you know that man, my lord?"

Lasalle watched the rounsey drink in long sips. "Reigner de
Bec. Used to be one of my men."

Juliana crossed herself. She should never ask questions of
Guérin de Lasalle. "What happened?"

He threw a flat pebble, watching it skip across the surface. "He
struck out on his own, robbed a couple of convents for a nest egg,
and got a price on his head. His woman turned him in for it and
went away with a lister."

"Oh, how could—"

"—she go away with a lister? Perhaps she preferred one to the other."

"Perhaps she saw no life for herself with one; that is why she preferred the other. He could have done something honorable, like—"

"Plundering the infidel instead?"

"Yes. No! He chose . . . Oh pother!" Juliana stomped her foot.

"Chose?" Lasalle flung away the last pebble. "Hell, Sister, Aliénor would have us all declared brigands."

Lasalle brought the rounsey around. Juliana climbed into the saddle without his help and they rode the rest of the way in silence. The houses began to look familiar. Juliana felt an inexplicable urge to say something, and did. "I am sorry about your friend."

She felt Lasalle shrug. "We all have to die, though I wouldn't relish being trussed up for it."

She shuddered and looked over her shoulder. "You came so that de Bec would not die alone. You wanted him to see you, and I botched it."

"What an astonishing thought, Sister Eustace."

They were in the courtyard of the Three Dwarfs. Perhaps she could engage in a last moment's honesty when nothing else was expected. "You did, didn't you?"

She caught a fleeting tilt of his eyebrow. "If truth be told, I was returning from a particularly exhausting excursion to one of this fair city's costliest brothels."

CHAPTER 28

Juliana, if you make me accompany you to one more cloister or cathedral, I swear I shall take the veil myself."

Juliana wrung her hands. "Only one more, please."

Anne dismissed her maid. "Very well. The last one, promise?"

Juliana nodded eagerly. She did not wish to upset the Countess de Valence. Anne had come to the Three Dwarfs a few days after Juliana's escapade and discovered her locked up in her room, guarded by Lasalle's morose men-at-arms. To Juliana's delight, her husband's mistress was not at all intimidated by him. Juliana and Hermine listened at the door while Anne and Lasalle exchanged heated words in the kitchen below. When Anne emerged, they heard a horse sprinting from the courtyard, followed by Anne proudly announcing that Juliana was free of Lasalle's locks and shackles as long as she remained in Anne's close custody.

After that, Anne had not allowed her to remain at the Three Dwarfs. Following their visit to the churches, the markets, and the merchants' stalls, they returned to Anne's residence, a hired house within a stone's throw of the royal palais, built around an old Roman colonnade that enclosed a garden. Juliana had her own room, larger and brighter than her room at the Three Dwarfs.

Anne made herself at home on Juliana's bed, inspecting herself in her mirror. "And which is it going to be this time? The convent of Perpetual Spleen? The abbey boasting the Knee of Saint Agatha?"

Juliana crossed herself. "Anne, you are blaspheming!"

Anne laughed and stretched among the pillows. "We Aquitanians live to love and laugh, and worry about the hereafter only on our deathbeds. Well then, where to this time?"

The cloister of Saint-Sylvain stood at the corner of Rue d'Orléans and Rue de Garland, almost at the confluence of the Seine and the Bièvre. It presented a forbidding facade, guarded by a double-timbered door.

Anne adjusted her wimple with a gesture of aggravation. "It looks like a fortress. You couldn't sneak a cat in there, let alone a lover."

Juliana smiled and reached for the bell. The sound died with no sign of life behind the gate. Juliana tried again. And again. Fi-

nally, the wicket window opened slightly. "I am Juliana de Charnais, Sister. I wish to make a request regarding one of your
vassals—"

"You may speak to our bailiff. Our house does not concern itself with worldly matters, and we do not admit visitors." The window started to close.

"Wait!" Juliana grabbed the bars. "I came on behalf of Aumary
de Beaudricourt. He wishes to wed my ward. I want to obtain Saint-
Sylvain's permission, please."

After a moment of silence, the voice said, "Wait."

They did. At last, the door opened with a creak and a groan; it
indeed did not often admit the outside world. The gate mistress
motioned them to keep silent and to follow her.

The Abbess of Saint-Sylvain received them seated in the middle
of the chapter room, two senior sisters attending her—and she
was a beauty. Under her thin-arched black brows, the abbess's gray
eyes regarded them without a hint of self-effacement. The line
of her jaw and chin, emphasized by the *barbette*, was perfection
itself.

"I am Mother Nicola. I am told you have an inquiry regarding
Aumary de Beaudricourt, Lady Juliana." The abbess addressed
them without any pretense of hospitality, her fingers knotted
around a heavy gold cross.

The two sisters drew up chairs for their unwelcome guests. Juliana looked around. All chapter rooms looked alike. She sighed
silently, sat on the chair's edge, and delivered her plea on Aumary's behalf. "Aumary is my husband's squire, and he was recently knighted. I am told that he is an orphan, as is my ward, and
that he holds some lands of Saint-Sylvain."

The expression on Abbess Nicola's face changed, but not for
the reason Juliana expected. "Your . . . your husband?"

"The Viscount of Tillières. His name is Guérin de Lasalle." Juliana gave Lasalle his purloined title and hurried to change the
subject. "Reverend Mother, I am certain Aumary—"

"Has he been brought up properly by his lord?"

Next to Juliana, Anne did not bother to stifle a titter. Juliana

rushed to intervene. "Aumary's qualities, Reverend Mother, are
the result of his own character."

"You've been cloistered, Lady Juliana."

It was not a question. Juliana felt blood rise to her cheeks. "Yes,
Reverend Mother."

"I see." The abbess's tone notched up in hostility. "Your husband must have been settled upon you by your liege."

"More the opposite, Reverend Mother." Juliana tried to fathom
the reason for this turn in the conversation.

Abbess Nicola's eyebrows sprang up. "Not a choice to your
liking?"

"Nor I to his, but—" Juliana wanted to steer the conversation
from that subject.

"Why?" The abbess's tone was of someone who knew it.

"I-I—"

It was Anne who snatched up the gauntlet. "The Viscount of
Tillières is a ravisher, a murderer, and a mountebank. He is more
deceitful than the Serpent, an incorrigible liar, and an all-round
opportunist. He has not seen the inside of a chapel in years, flaunts
the Church's ban by hiring out his mercenaries, wastes his life
in the stews, keeps mistresses under his wife's roof and sires bastards by them. The miracle is that he has not taken to his bed either one, or both, of the lady's wards. Yet." Anne gave the abbess
a warm smile and, as was the fashion, draped her veil over her left
arm with punctilious care. "I ought to know. I am one of the mistresses the chevalier keeps."

The sisters crossed themselves as if they had caught a whiff of
the Devil's sulfur. Juliana tucked in her chin, wishing she could
disappear.

"I see," the abbess said, her tone elongated.

"Reverend Mother." Juliana tried to salvage something out of
that disaster. "Please, Aumary is nothing like his lord. If he were, I
would never speak for this union."

"Then it seems we have two miracles, Lady Juliana."

Juliana crossed herself. "Yes, Reverend Mother."

The abbess inclined her head toward the two sisters, her voice sharp with impatience. "This matter will be addressed in chapter. You will receive our answer at—"

"The Three Dwarfs, Reverend Mother. Thank you, Reverend Mother." Juliana took that to be their dismissal. The abbess did not rise and the two nuns bowed their heads only slightly.

"What a thoroughly unpleasant woman!" Anne exclaimed once they were outside the cloister's gate. She stepped on her groom's back and into her saddle.

With Donat's help, Juliana climbed into Rosamond's. "She had the right to ask about Aumary. I only hope that we did not spoil Paulette's chances."

That night he came to her. His timing was fortuitous, since Juliana had insisted on returning to the Three Dwarfs in case a message came from Saint-Sylvain. Anne had tried to assure her that such would be unlikely, but the girl could not be dissuaded. Anne was relieved to see Lasalle; his absences were suspicious.

He poked his head in the door. "Are you prepared, Countess, for a night of gluttony and lust?"

Anne returned her attention to her book. "I thought it was lust and gluttony."

He kicked the doors shut behind him. "First gluttony, then lust." He settled himself cross-legged on the floor, his back against the wall, on his knees a platter of pig's ribs, leek-and-egg tarts, and braised turnips he had finagled out of Anne's cook, along with a ewer of wine.

From her pillowed oriel, Anne gave his overflowing platter a nod. "You will not be up to the latter after the former."

"Ye of little faith. For that, you are not allowed to share."

Anne threw down her book and picked up her brush. This was as good a time as any. "When do you intend to inform your child bride of the failure of your petition?"

Lasalle paused over a turnip. "Ah. At some inappropriate moment, I am certain."

Well, well. Had my lord Lasalle intended to tell the girl the day of her misadventure and used it to avoid telling her? "You don't have any other choice but to bed that girl after all. You are not a freebooter anymore. Your viscounty needs an heir."

He gestured at her with a half-picked bone. "Besides aiding and abetting in a wife's disobedience of her husband, what else have you been up to?"

"Trying to remove years of Father Osbert from Juliana's head. It is not easy."

"Not for my benefit, I hope. I don't intend to oblige her anyway. Any candidates?"

"John d'Erlée, among others, although I suspect you already suspect. He is very fond of Juliana and I believe the feelings are returned."

Lasalle wiped his fingers on her Limoges carpet. "Tell d'Erlée to hurry up before my saintly mother abbess starts planting turnips in the middle of my bailey. I was afraid it would be Peyrac."

Perhaps skirmishing should proceed to direct assault. "Or Armand."

He poked at the egg tart. "Pray, do tell."

With unhurried strokes, Anne drew the brush through her hair. "Why not? He is better looking than you, wealthy, and he needs an heir too. He is intrigued by your little wife. He asked me about your annulment. He is in Paris, did you know?"

"I do, to spoil your surprise."

She left her oriel. "I have others."

He grinned at her. "So do I. I learned one from a couple of whores at Fat Margo's."

Anne sat by him and rapped the brush across his knuckles. "Don't change the subject, you graceless knave. I doubt those whores could teach you much."

"Coming from you, Anne, what a lovely compliment." He held her arms to her sides. His mouth tasted of wine and plain lust. When he let her go, Anne touched her bruised lips. He sat there, cup in hand, smiling a challenge.

Anne swept her hair over her shoulder, but did not back away. "To you, that's all there is, isn't it? You'd make a good whore, my lord Lasalle."

"Truce, Anne. We are all whores, to somebody."

"And Juliana isn't. Is that what this is all about?"

"We all have our predilections. Virtue and chastity are such tiresome things."

"That girl deserves a normal life."

"With a freebooter and whore?"

He had surprised her again. She touched the back of her hand to his cheek. What had made Céline de Passeis refuse to marry him? A sudden bout of virtue? He stood up, pulled off his gambeson, and went to the laver. He splashed the water on his face and took the towel she handed him. "Is there a point to this?"

"Unlike the rest of us, Juliana still has illusions of a grand amour. And, I think, so does d'Erlée. Why encourage a heartbreak?"

He dropped the towel and took her hips in his hands. "I am not. I intend for them to have what they both desire, although only one of them as yet knows it."

What on earth was that man after? "Dear God, you are a bastard! A cunning, lecherous bastard. Juliana isn't a whore. Yet. Is that what this is all about?"

He laughed. "What a wonderfully depraved mind you have, Countess. I told you, I don't want her. You forget that no bishop would champion an adulterous wife's claim against an aggrieved husband."

"What?" She pushed him away. "Good Lord! I've never heard of a husband encouraging—no, *arranging* for his wife to commit adultery. It's horrible. Disgusting! Besides, the Church doesn't allow adulterers to marry; she could never marry d'Erlée. You may as well sell her to Fat Margo or send her back to Fontevraud. And you get to keep Tillières!"

"Don't be so naive. You can always find a softhearted priest to marry the star-crossed lovers, and if the bishops ever get around to it, there will be half a dozen redheaded little d'Erlées running about someplace. Do you think the Church would set aside that marriage to return her to me?"

"What about the duke? John may not allow her to marry d'Erlée."

"I said I'll give her enough to buy her wardship from John. The duke needs money to hire mercenaries. Then he can hire mine and I'll have my viscounty, without its viscountess."

It was as if she were seeing Guérin de Lasalle for the first time. "You are a monster. The Devil could not have devised this any better."

He reached for her. "Ah, my lovely Anne. Another compliment."

She evaded him. "You are always very certain of yourself, aren't you, my lord?"

This time he shoved her toward the bed. "I am certain that if you don't shut up I'll leave you with your indignation and find myself a more accommodating whore."

"Whore?" Anne wrenched herself free.

Lasalle did not pursue her. "Bloody hell. I didn't mean—"

"No, that's exactly what you meant." Anne flung her coin purse at him. "Here's a denier; that ought to be enough for what you seek!"

He dodged the small missile and knocked her backward onto her bed. Taking a deep breath, Anne treated him to a string of obscenities. He let her, all the while working up her gown and chemise. Anne clamped her knees together. Just let him try. "Is this how you've treated Juliana? No wonder she can't bear your touch."

Lasalle did not move. After a while, he relaxed his weight and dropped his forehead to hers. "Anne? Truce?"

Anne tried to master her anger. "Don't ever call me a whore."

He drew back a little. "I told you, leave Juliana out of this."

"Or what?"

His hand encircled her throat. She had not expected it. She grabbed for his wrist, but by then his hand had slipped down and was parting the fabric of her chemise, molding the shape of her breast. He smiled. The possibilities dawned on her. "You are trying to buy my silence."

His teeth nibbled her. "How very clever of you."

Anne sank her fingers into his hair and wrenched his head up. "Very well. On my terms. You do whatever I want. Your pledge."

He shrugged, returning to his objective. "I usually do, love."

Anne kicked at him. "I said, your pledge."

"You have it." His voice rang raw with frustrated lust. "For Christ's sake, shut your mouth and open your legs."

"No. I don't want your harlots' tricks. I wish to be wooed, like a maid."

He propped himself on his elbows with a hoot. "Ha. You're about as much a maid as Messalina."

"Are you reneging on your pledge already, my lord?"

He swore, words she did not understand, and got out of the bed. Belting his gambeson, he gave her a backward glance of simmering fury.

Anne raised her voice. "If you leave, I'll tell Juliana that you are trying to trick her into committing adultery in order to get yourself an annulment. You've put d'Erlée up to it, haven't you?"

Her words caught him at the door. "You are a bitch, woman."

Anne crooked her finger at him. "My chivalrous lover. If that is how you woo virtuous maidens, no wonder you end up with whores."

He came back to her. "You are trying to elevate our perfectly satisfactory rut to love."

She could not let him get away with that one. "I am surprised you know the difference."

"And I am surprised you do." The words chilled the air. They both knew it, and knowing it, he took her hand, and this time the regret and contrition were there. "Hell, Anne. Life is full of small disappointments."

"Then I want the illusion."

He shook his head. "I don't. Not while I am with you."

Something hitched in her heart and at that moment, Anne regretted allowing herself to be used in Aliénor of Aquitaine's schemes, regretted befriending a dark-eyed, guileless girl, and most of all, she regretted allowing her passion to draw her to this perplexing man. She struggled to find her voice. "Then we must strive beyond it. You may kiss me."

He did, but she remained virginally passive. "Anne, the idea on these occasions is for you to collude; otherwise this will be a long night. Damn it, you are not new to this!"

"What you want is a lie."

"Right now, I'll settle for it."

"No. *You* pretend that I am your mother abbess."

For that, a few moments later, the Countess de Valence was left alone with the dying flames of her fireplace and her own unsated ardor for company, as the sound of my lord Lasalle's boots faded from her threshold.

Anne wrapped her cloak about her, poured herself the dregs of his wine, and watched the flames sink into embers. Well, well. So that's the way it would be. Why not, then, let the very clever Viscount of Tillières reap the consequences of his own cunning?

CHAPTER 29

The king had drowned himself in jewels, his blue tunic edged with gold, his cloak of scarlet blinding to the eyes, and still he could not eclipse his queen-consort. She was a golden-haired apparition in a robin's-egg gown trimmed with a tide of pearls, clinging to her husband, whose arm encircled her waist. The guards accompanying the king and his bride struggled to keep the guests from swamping the royal couple. Like everyone else's, Juliana's gaze followed the young queen-duchess.

"Look at them," Anne yawned. "Our valiant champions. A third of them would murder to have John's place for one night, a third are scandalized, and the rest are wondering what will be served for supper. How do you think Guérin would rank?"

Juliana shot Anne a startled look and pretended to be engrossed in the proceedings. Anne sighed. Grand banquets were so tedious.

"Lady Anne, Lady Juliana. What a delightful vision you two present."

They turned. And stared. They were perused by Armand de Lusignan's midnight-blue eyes, the rest of him leaning negligently against a pillar. Anne mouthed a word that Juliana did not catch. Armand de Lusignan did, and smiled. He wore a black tunic embroidered with silver silk, his gaze resting on Juliana. "My dear child, you look lovely. I pray you are keeping well?"

"Thank you, my lord." In fact, Juliana felt especially self-conscious in a gown Anne's needlewomen had fashioned, and when Anne had finished with her jars and powders, Juliana had not recognized the face in the mirror as her own. And now Armand de Lusignan was examining it. She expected him to burst out laughing. He did not. Neither did he laugh at the scents in which Anne had drenched her.

"I am glad," Armand de Lusignan said, moving forward, "that you had no cause to avail yourself of my pledge to you. It has, of course, not been revoked." He shifted his attention to Anne. "And how fares our liege lady—still ensconced at Fontevraud?"

"The duchess travels these days, I am told," Anne answered lightly.

"And my lord Lasalle? Neglecting both of you ladies at once, I see."

"I believe John keeps him occupied," Anne answered for Juliana.

"Of course. John was considering the viscount to replace our unfortunate Mercadier before he settled on Lupescaire to govern his mercenaries," the Count of Rancon said with a tone of regret.

Anne and Juliana looked at each other. Lasalle was spending most of his time in the company of Duke John's circle of loyal supporters—his Flemish justiciar, Hugh de Bourgh; William des Roches, the Seneschal of Anjou; the Earl of Pembroke; Roger de Laci; and the querulous de Briouze. To the embarrassment of Philip, his host and liege lord, John had concocted a plan to grant the Lusignans justice by charging them with treason against his late brother and against himself. He then invited them to prove their innocence not before a court of their peers, but by fighting a judicial duel against his hired champions.

It was an audacious reply to the charges brought against him by the Lusignans. Hiring champions was not unheard of, except that no one of import had availed himself of it for years—and no one had challenged at the same time the entire sword side of a family famous for its turbulence. Deeply stung by their latest humiliation, the far-flung clan Lusignan refused to abase itself against hired swords. Instead, to protest this latest insult, the Lusignans had dispatched the Count of Rancon as their emissary to John of England and Philip of France.

Standing amidst his enemies, Armand de Lusignan did not appear to have a care in the world. "Of course, I favored my lord Lasalle. Lupescaire is a mere butcher. My lord Lasalle knows how to turn butchery into an art. Richard gave him that magnificent crucifix for it at Acre. He still keeps it, I believe?"

"It was at Tyre, my lord," Juliana ventured to correct the information, uncertain what to make of the rest of it.

"Did he tell you that? Astonishing." Armand de Lusignan tsk-tsked. "But then your husband lies even when he lies. Acre was a great victory for Richard. They say he wept with joy. One day you must ask your husband to tell you the truth of it."

Not caring to be ignored, Anne decided to cast her line. "And you, my lord? What will the Lusignans do?"

"Appeal to Philip to compel John to grant us justice, once Agnès de Méran is safely delivered. Hiring duelists to defend one's honor defeats the whole proposition, don't you agree, Lady Juliana? Except in the case of a lady."

Juliana nodded. "Only . . . only it seems ironic that it is men who can both compromise and redeem a woman's honor."

Armand de Lusignan kissed her hand. "Spoken like a true scholar. If virtue and learning were sufficient weapons, I would gladly put my fate into your hands. Ah, may I suggest that you step away? I believe your husband is about to commit another folly."

Oh Lord. There was Lasalle, sword already drawn. She would have moved, but her knees would not obey her. It was Anne who swept her behind the nearest pillar. The two men matched each other in height and breadth of shoulder, and no one in the hall doubted that the count knew how to face an opponent with a sword in hand—only he did not draw his.

"Enough! There will be none of that here tonight, my lords!"
The accented voice belonged to a corpulent figure in magisterial
black backed by a dozen guards.

"My lord de Bourgh!" Anne abandoned Juliana and rushed to
the man. "No harm was intended, I assure you."

The elderly Fleming crossed the hall with a flat step. "I am glad
to hear it." De Bourgh glowered from one man to the other. "We
are here to serve the duke, my lords, not to gut each other in the
presence of our liege lady."

Deprived so suddenly of his opponent, Lasalle looked foolish,
standing there with a naked sword in his hand. He rammed it
into the scabbard and gave de Bourgh a stiff bow. De Bourgh
took himself and his men after the Count of Rancon, who, open-
handed, had backed away from his opponent, a slight smile on
his lips.

The night wore on, the parade of trays and tureens seemed endless, the air became stifling and the company unruly. At last, the
revelers made room for the musicians, acrobats, and jongleurs.
Two bear tamers poked and teased their animals to dance to the
tune of a flute and the beat of a tambourine. Some of the guests
became impatient and urged on the bears by flinging hot embers
from the braziers under their feet. Growling and snarling with
pain, the bears became entangled in each other's leads and a fight
erupted in the middle of the hall, sending the acrobats fleeing.
Isabelle d'Angoulême did not appear to enjoy the spectacle, but
her husband laughed and the audience hooted and threw leftovers and crockery at the keepers, who tried desperately to sort
out their animals while avoiding the embers, the swiping claws,
and the gnashing teeth.

The fanfare sounded. The young queen-duchess was taking
her leave. Her husband accompanied her to the door, where he
kissed her possessively for all to see before handing her to her
women. Embarrassed, Juliana lowered her eyes and waited for the
queen's departure to make her own escape.

Someone spoke to her, several times. Juliana looked up. John Plantagenet stood there in the company of his men, Lasalle among them. Next to her, the Countess de Valence was already in a graceful curtsy. With hardly a semblance of similar grace, Juliana curtsied as well. The king glanced at her with annoyance. A courtier whispered something into his ear. The annoyance changed to curiosity.

"The Viscountess of Tillières?" The ruby and garnet finger rings aimed at her.

Juliana kissed the rings as if they belonged to Abbess Mathilde. Over her head, the duke spoke to Lasalle with irritation. "It appears that we have been misled, my lord. You had us believe your wife was ill-favored."

"I did not know Your Grace favored bone and gristle."

The hall plunged into silence until someone in the crowd laughed; then others did. John Plantagenet guffawed, his eyes scrutinizing Juliana, his hand stroking his whiskers.

"Bone and gristle, ha! Well, well, Viscount, since your petition for annulment was denied, you will have to reconcile yourself to your matrimony after all!" John Plantagenet gave Lasalle a grin, bowed to Juliana, and rejoined his court. Juliana remained rooted to the spot only a moment longer. And then she ran.

She ran as if pursued by the Furies into a maze of passages echoing with the sound of her disorderly flight. She stumbled and fell, and staggered into a hall lit by wall tapers and empty of furnishings except for a long table in the middle of it and a single high-backed chair.

She collapsed next to the chair, her fists pounding the stones. "No! No! Dear God, I wish I were dead! Dead, dead!"

"*Doucement, doucement,* my dear, please." Armand de Lusignan was kneeling next to her. She threw herself into his arms. "Gently; you are much too distressed. Do not agitate yourself so."

She could not be comforted. Nothing would comfort her. "The annulment. He . . . he never told me. All this time he knew; he knew! Oh Lord, what am I going to do?"

"Hush, please." Anne's robes spread around her like the leaf of a water lily. "You have friends; you are not alone." Under Anne's and the Count of Rancon's entreaties, Juliana's sobs eased. Anne dabbed Juliana's cheeks with her veil. "There, that's better."

With Armand de Lusignan's help, Juliana got herself to her feet. "I am sorry. Thank you, thank you—"

"Let go of her!"

As ominous as Lucifer at the gates of Hell, Lasalle stood under the door arch, the light of the torches behind him. Anne charged toward him. "Dear God! Haven't you done enough?"

Lasalle sidestepped her as if she were an armed attacker and crossed the floor, his sword swept clear of the scabbard. The empty scabbard skittered across the flagstones.

A woman screamed. Juliana's knees turned to wet straw; her fingers locked onto Armand de Lusignan's arm, rendering him defenseless. Lasalle knew it. The tip of his sword blade rested at the base of Armand's throat, where his life's pulse fluttered wildly. Scarlet drops welled up under the steel.

"No!"

She felt no pain until blood splattered her gown and the count's tunic, but her move had deflected the sword blade and given Armand a chance to escape. This time, his own sword rang out of the scabbard.

"Stop it, you fools!" Anne de Valence threw herself between the two men. "Look at her hands!"

Juliana stood frozen, hands spread, blood dripping from her palms as if from a stigmata. Neither of the two men paid any attention. Lasalle passed her, his blow aimed at Armand de Lusignan's flank. The count's sword rolled away the blade, and before Lasalle could strike again, Hugh de Bourgh's men filled the room. They separated the opponents, jostling Juliana and Anne out of the way. Anne quickly tore in half Juliana's veil to tend to her hands. Juliana swallowed. She was going to be sick. She turned away from the sight of her own blood to see Hugh de Bourgh come up behind Lasalle, whose attention never wavered from the Count of Rancon.

"I said, yield, sir!" the old *routier* huffed, his sword point nudging Lasalle between the shoulder blades.

The moment it did, Lasalle half-turned, dropping on one knee in what looked to everyone like a gesture of surrender. It was not.

One of de Bourgh's men yelled a warning; de Bourgh heeded it fast enough to save himself from being cut in half by a slashing backhand stroke. De Bourgh's men charged.

They knew their business, and in the end their superior force prevailed. Lasalle emerged from the scuffle without his sword, pinned between two guards, winded, eyes livid. The men wrestled him to where de Bourgh stood, waiting.

Hugh de Bourgh worked his fingers into his gauntlet. "That was a damnably clever thing, my lord, but I am not your enemy and I'll have you mind that I don't care being your mark."

And without any further ado, de Bourgh's fist landed against the side of Lasalle's face.

Juliana cringed. The blow was meant to bring down an opponent, and it did. The crowd murmured in approbation. The guards let go of Lasalle and he folded onto the flagstones like a child's discarded puppet, his head coming to rest on his forearm. A ribbon of blood soaked the crushed fabric.

Hugh de Bourgh nudged Lasalle's inert body with his boot toe. "Lock him up. Tomorrow let him go and give him back his sword." To Armand de Lusignan he said, "Next time, Count, I'll not stand in this one's way. Take them away."

With Armand de Lusignan escorted by the guards and the spectators drifting after them, de Bourgh motioned to the remaining men to cart away Lasalle. Anne and Juliana were moving out of their way when a woman's voice came from the door. "My lord de Bourgh, perhaps you would allow me to take custody of this person?"

The voice belonged to the Countess of Pembroke, serene and elegant, standing in the archway with the men of her guard behind her. Hugh de Bourgh bowed. "But my lady—"

Isabel de Clare smiled at him. "I have my husband's chambers at my disposal. I will keep the viscount secured until morning and his wife can be looked after by the Countess de Valence. It would please me very much."

De Bourgh growled, scowled, and capitulated. The men of the Countess of Pembroke's guard picked up their prisoner, and with him sagging between them, they followed their mistress.

Left by themselves, Anne helped Juliana into the solitary chair. Juliana's palms burned with lancing pain. Anne knelt by her, tearing the lining of her own sleeve to fashion a more secure bandage. "Let me see that. What a brave and foolish thing to do. Now you have Armand in your debt; you've surely saved his life. Oh dear, look at your hands."

The pain of the flesh was nothing to the pain of the soul. "They . . . they won't grant the annulment."

Anne sniffed. "So they won't."

"What am I going to do? John d'Erlée . . . if Lasalle finds out—"

Anne wound the silk around Juliana's hands. "Guérin knows all about d'Erlée. I suspect he knew that his petition would be denied. He may have paid John to court you or at least encouraged him to do so; I don't know. But I know he counts that sooner or later you'll compromise yourself so that he can charge you with adultery and repudiate you. He wants Tillières, Juliana."

Her ears lied to her. Surely they lied to her? Even for Lasalle, the deviousness was monstrous. "He has no honor so he would take mine, and my home. And now John d'Erlée too!"

Anne shook her gently. "You can still save your home, Juliana, if you are willing to fight him. Are you willing to fight him?"

"How can I fight someone like that? I have nothing to fight with."

Anne took Juliana's face between her hands. "But you do. You have your marriage and your marriage is your weapon."

The girl was looking at her with fear and disbelief. And yet, somewhere in the depths of Sister Eustace's tear-filled eyes, Anne saw a gleam. It was the gleam of a sword blade being forged.

"Will you . . . will you tell me how?"

Anne drew Juliana de Charnais into her arms. There was more than one way for a woman to avenge herself on a man. "Oh, yes," she whispered. "Oh, yes."

CHAPTER 30

Thirty feet if not more. He had already tested the door, expecting it to be bolted from the outside. It was. He drew back from the window with a queasy stomach and a spinning head. No rope and not enough bedsheets. Besides, he was afraid of heights— more particularly, of falling from them. He had a good idea where he was, but not why. He probed his sore jaw. Still, there were worse places to wake up. Pondering his predicament, he wandered through the apartments and found the garderobe, a basin with a pitcher of water, and towels.

That left only himself and a flute for company. Since he cared little for his own company, he reached for the flute. Two flutes, in fact. He discovered them on the table in an embroidered pouch, one of reed, the other embossed with gold ivy leaves.

The door opened and Isabel de Clare walked in, a gathering of flowering agrimony in her arms. "I see you have chosen the plain one," she said and set her flowers on the table. Her Welsh guard captain closed the door behind her, leaving her alone with her prisoner

My lord Lasalle leaned against the wall, affecting a composed exterior. "I was afraid that I would have to play for my upkeep. I was about to lower a basket to the tone-deaf for alms." He touched the side of his face. "Thank you for rescuing me, Countess."

Isabel filled the vase with water from the pitcher. "As I told my husband, rescuing you may become someone's life calling, my lord. Play some more for me."

He put the flute on the table. "No. My lack of skill makes a mockery of it."

"Like it does of your marriage?"

This time he smiled disarmingly at her. "You have been talking to Anne."

Isabel reached for her scissors and trimmed the end of a stem. "Anne has her own fish to fry."

"And I am one of her fish. I don't wish to trespass on your kindness," he said, wariness in his voice.

"Don't you? What a shame. I planned to tear off my gown and throw myself into your arms. What do you think would happen?"

"I'd be minced by your men."

"Precisely. And why do you think that is?"

Loose-limbed, Lasalle sagged against the wall. His shirtfront bore stains from his nosebleed, and dark stubble partly concealed the contusion on his cheek. He picked up the flute, blowing a couple of outrageously false notes before he answered. "I see. It's a game. Because my reputation precedes me?"

Isabel selected another stem. "You play games very well, my lord. It must become tiresome. How old are you?"

She wanted to see his reaction. He knew it, hesitated, and told her. Isabel remained silent.

"Are you proposing to tell your husband to dismiss me on account of my youth and inexperience, Countess?"

Isabel suddenly wished that she had not asked, because she had the disturbing feeling that this time my lord Lasalle had told her the truth. "No. I don't think inexperience is your problem, but it might be your wife's."

He touched his jaw. "I should hope so. But that is no longer my concern."

"It is if she is to remain married to you."

"She won't, and you *have* been talking to Anne."

Isabel was not going to allow him to lead her. "I understand you've spent some time in Poitou. Your family has connections there?"

"Had. I hated all that Normandy rain," Lasalle informed her cheerfully, but Isabel watched his fingers on the reed.

She wiped her scissors and snapped them into their sheath. He waited, expecting further questions. She would have to disappoint him. "I apologize for detaining you. There are people anxious for your welfare, including a fearsome foreign gentleman below, threatening de Bourgh's men."

Guérin de Lasalle hesitated, then rocked himself to his feet and laid the flute on the table. Isabel opened the door and called out. Her guard captain came in with Lasalle's sword, eyeing her guest coldly. Isabel held out the flute. "It would please me for you to keep it. I've had it ever since I was a child, but William gave me a new one as a gift and I don't wish to hurt his feelings." She knew that he was about to decline and so she smiled and said, "I found that a patient player can coax the sweetest sound out of the plainest reed."

He took the flute. "How extraordinary. I thought that a judicious thrashing of the player was the proper inducement."

This time, Isabel did not smile. "That was a wrong lesson," she said. He gave her a look telling her that with that remark she had come close to a part of him few were allowed near. "One more thing," Isabel added. His face went blank. "My husband has a great deal of faith in you, my lord. It may come to it that many lives will depend upon you and you won't be able to save them all."

She expected Guérin de Lasalle at least to say something reassuring, but he bowed very deeply, and steadying himself against the wall, followed her guard captain down the corridor like a man negotiating a treacherous stretch of ice. And for all Isabel knew of the Viscount of Tillières, that was exactly what he was doing.

John d'Erlée. So it had all been a pretense, a part of Lasalle's schemes. Even the kiss.

Juliana stabbed her needle into the cloth. She was a fool ever to trust anyone. While her hands had healed, the dull ache in the pit of her stomach remained.

The thread snagged and she was pulling angrily at it when something caught her eye—an outlandish creature sitting on the half-crumbled wall of Anne's garden. Juliana blinked. The apparition did not disappear. "Who are you?"

Red-tinted nails fluttered in her direction. "I am Equitan. Who are you?"

Insolence from one's servants was one thing. Insolence from something that looked and smelled far better than oneself was another. "I am Juliana."

"Oh, you are Juliana." Equitan's dewy gaze examined the garden's corners. "I am looking for lord Guérin. I don't suppose you would know where he is."

Equitan did not look particularly dangerous. "Is he expecting you?"

Equitan sneezed as if the very air was too much for him. A small satchel dangled from his fingers. "I am to deliver this to the viscount. I shall have to wait."

Juliana picked up her sewing basket and was about to leave Equitan to the company of the flowerpots when Anne came through the garden gate. At her approach, Equitan stirred alertly. Anne paused to take in the full array of scents and colors. Equitan smiled. Anne smiled back and reached out to caress Equitan's ringlets. But the caressing fingers snagged the curls, wrenching Equitan nose-first to the ground. Anne's bootlet pressed on Equitan's nape. Equitan let out a muffled squeak. The tip of Anne's riding crop caressed the painted cheek. "Pray, tell us more, precious."

"I am only a humble messenger, my lady, fulfilling my mistress's wishes!"

The quirt snapped the rouged cheek. "Your mistress?"

"Madame Violaine."

Anne cast a glance at Juliana, who shrugged. The Countess de Valence returned her attention to Equitan. "What is your message?"

"That he is here!"

Anne gave Equitan a kick. "What?"

Equitan cried out, his eyes swimming in tears. "That is the message, gracious lady. And . . . and this." He held up the satchel.

Anne weighed it in her hand. "What is it?"

"I swear by Saint Anthony, I don't know."

Equitan was lying. Perhaps she should turn him over to her guard captain or make an effort to find Lasalle. Anne decided against both. Sooner or later my lord Lasalle would appear. He always did. "Very well, you've delivered your message. Now get out."

Face paste streaked with a cloudburst of tears, Equitan bolted out of the garden.

"Heliette!" Anne called out just as her waiting woman rushed up with the others, alarmed by their mistress's unexpected appearance. "I want to know how that thing got in here. Tell de Querci to have the guards flogged and dismissed, and tell him that I am very displeased with him." Anne pointed to her bootlets. "And do take these off me!"

Tended to but still testy, Anne settled herself on her pillows. "I hate inattentiveness, don't you? Now, it's high time we had a surprise or two of our own for Guérin. Let's see. Won't he be surprised when I tell him that you've yielded your maidenhead to John d'Erlée?"

"But it's not true!" Juliana crossed herself, horrified. "If he believes it, he'll set me aside. I'll lose Tillières."

Anne's voice grew sweet with speculation. "Not without proof. Unless, of course, you would consider prying your knees far enough apart for him. One thrust, Guérin loses his grounds for annulment and you remain the mistress of Tillières."

"Good God, I couldn't! I wouldn't! He is ruthless and devious and—"

Anne sighed with exasperation. "Now you are being silly. Some men take pleasure in hurting a woman in bed, and if Guérin were one, I would never allow him back in mine. Unfortunately, he won't come near you as long as he thinks you are innocent."

The girl's uncomprehending expression became an incredulous one. Anne clicked her tongue. "I know. You could have knocked me over with a feather too."

Juliana clasped her hands. "Mary be praised. But you can't tell Lasalle such a terrible lie about me—please, Anne."

Anne pretended umbrage. "We are not lying. We are turning the tables on him."

"But that means I shall have to remain married to him!"

"So? Do you think Guérin will cleave only onto you? He is not even faithful to me. Soon he will be spreading misery to some godforsaken corner of the world. You only have to do it once, Juliana. King Philip can't set aside Ingeborg because of that once. A completed marriage will save your Tillières."

Juliana's shoulders sank. The price was too high, all borne by herself. She crossed herself. "Anne? What about Céline?"

CHAPTER 31

Surrounded by her pillows, Anne knew the shadow cast over her garden refuge. She teased one of the lute strings. "We thought you had vanished from the face of the earth, my lord, but I see that you are too brazen to do us all that favor."

Balanced on his heels, Lasalle kissed her hand. "I came to apologize and to finish what I started, if you are still willing."

Anne tamped down a tumult of emotions. She touched the side of his face. The bruise was still there. "You damned . . . where have you been?"

He collapsed on her pillows with a grunt. "Serving out my penance."

"Juliana has yet to see any evidence of it and so she didn't wait—"

He boosted himself on his elbows with a sufferer's grimace. "Very well, woman. I did say penance."

He was back and up to his old tricks. Anne was going to tell him what she intended, but changed her mind. It could wait. She set aside her lute and offered him her hand to lead him to her chamber. There she loosened his shirt ties and got the shirt over his head. A pattern of bruises stood out darker against the dark skin. "Good heavens, is that from de Bourgh's men?"

"Mostly Kadolt. That's part of the lesson."

"What lesson? You've let that dreadful man do this to you?" She pushed him back onto her curtained bed and took the heel of his boot.

"In a half-fair fight, I'd take him, but this was not meant to be one. Lord, I haven't been in a decent bed since . . ."

Anne swore. It looked like Guérin de Lasalle would finally do in her bed the one thing she had never been able to persuade him to do. She threw the covers over him and piled his clothes onto a trunk next to Equitan's satchel. She resisted the temptation to open it. Surely it could wait for my lord Lasalle's personal explanation.

❧

He did not wake until dawn and when he did, it was with such a violent start that he roused her from her uneasy dozing as well. He was shaking, muscles cramped, skin damp. Anne sat up and uncovered the lamp. "Shhh, you were only dreaming."

His voice came to him after several tries. "I know. I ought to try snoring instead. I hope I was not too ungallant."

Anne wrapped her sheet around her and slipped out of the bed. "I wouldn't know," she said lightly. "I thought I heard you dreaming in some strange tongue." She handed him a cup. He took it without looking at her. She tried to put him at ease. "It was very inconvenient. I was hoping to discover your darkest secrets."

He handed her the cup back. "You and Isabel de Clare, you are trying too hard. I said I came to do my penance, but I'll need a little inducement." He drew her to him and peeled back her sheet to kiss her, a light, teasing passage across her skin. Even as Anne shivered at the assault of pleasure, she was thinking of Juliana, considering the girl's plea, and decided to ignore it. No, there could be no going back. "That is very nice," she murmured. "Perhaps you can try that with your wife."

"Anne, if you want three in this bed, I can arrange it. Otherwise, I don't want to hear about that dormouse, Lusignan, or d'Erlée."

"You are not listening, love. I was about to congratulate you on your ruse."

"What are you talking about?" His impatience shaded into irritation.

"Your oafishness. It drove Juliana straight into d'Erlée's arms. She was so upset and he was more than happy to comfort her, in this very bed."

"You are lying," he said after a moment's pause.

"I've even saved the sheets for your evidence. Would you like to see them?"

He kept his face expressionless, but his voice was sardonic. "And I suppose you witnessed it all?"

Anne laughed and knocked his arm from under him. She might as well amuse herself while she had him. "Of course. Don't you want to hear about it?"

He did not answer. Anne twisted the chain of his cross. "I must say," she exhaled between her own tormenting kisses, "you did right, putting d'Erlée up to it. He was so much better at it than you would've been. Guérin, are you listening? Juliana is hardly bone and gristle, as you so quaintly put it. Obviously, you have not seen your wife without a stitch on recently. Why don't you take advantage? But remember she is still a little skittish."

He did not breathe. Her hand went down his belly. "Of course her breasts don't compare to mine, but they fit his hands perfectly. And she does have the loveliest legs, and this wonderful little round rump. D'Erlée certainly did not find her wanting. And when he kissed her, your mother abbess just melted away."

"You are lying." In the dim light, his features were gray. "It won't work."

Anne laughed softly. "I think it has worked already."

His fist tightened in her hair. "You scheming bitch!"

She tried to fend him off, but she was too late. He thrust into her so hard that she cried out, a sound smothered by his mouth. From her first husband Anne had learned that in these situations struggling would be futile, so she shut her eyes and let her body go limp for the rest of it.

When he was done, he got up without a word. Anne watched him dress himself from under her eyelashes. The silence was deafening. Something between them had frayed, perhaps irreparably.

"I almost forgot," Anne said after a while, letting her tone sting

as much as her words. "A message came for you, from Violaine.
Unless you were peddling your talents, I am surprised she let you
past her lintel. "

He shot her a glance, not rising to the bait. "What message?"

"That 'he is here.' Delivered by someone called Equitan a couple of days ago. You were expecting this Equitan?"

"No. I told Violaine to send someone less frilly." He picked up
the satchel from the table. "What is this?"

"I don't know. Equitan brought it for you."

Lasalle moved to the window and opened the shutters. Dawn's
light crossed the floor. He shook the contents into his palm. A
strip of silk knotted around something shiny hit the floor with a
metal clink. Anne came to his side and picked up the silk knot.
"Oh, look, it's the girdle I gave Juliana. How did Equitan . . .
Guérin?"

Guérin de Lasalle was gone, the only evidence of his past presence her soreness and a door flung back so violently that the wall
plaster showered the floor.

Dressed in a lawn shift Mistress Hermine had stitched for her, Juliana sat on a stool by the open window. Below, horse hooves thundered into the courtyard; no doubt one of her guards rushing to
his post after a night of surreptitious leching. Her mind wandered
to Tillières, to Jourdain, to her petition to Saint-Sylvain's. How
much longer should she wait?

And that was how my lord Lasalle found his wife, sitting with
her head bowed, the sunrise behind her, smiling to herself, the
scent of drying lavender and summer dust around her. She sat
there with her bare feet propped on the stool rung, the length of
her shift gathered between her knees, picking absentmindedly at
a loose thread while Hermine brushed her mistress's hair, chiding
her mildly over some small thing.

His bursting through the door caught both women by surprise.
Juliana de Charnais's expression of annoyance at what she expected to be an accidental intrusion fled into one of pure
shock—or guilt. He already knew that she could blush like a peony

at a mere glance from him, but what struck him with the force of de Bourgh's fist was the way her thighs came together when she swept her shift over her knees, causing the fabric to slide from her shoulder.

Anne was right. Sister Eustace came not only with the longest fawn's legs, but with small, taut breasts tipped with pink peaks. The rest came in a torrential tide—the memory of her straining body under him, the scent of her vulnerability, the taste of her. He recalled it all more vividly than he did Anne, for all her rare perfumes, even though he had just come from her bed, and at that moment more than anything else he wanted to go back to it, but with this girl waiting there instead.

Mistress Hermine recovered first, exclaimed, and threw her wimple over Juliana's shoulders, flinging her arms around her mistress. For good measure, she scowled at him.

"Dress her and send her down," he heard himself ordering as if Mistress Hermine were an insubordinate *routier*. He slammed the door behind him and made it down the stairs and across the courtyard. There he dropped the bucket into the well and when he hauled it to the rim, he stuck his head in it and kept it there until the blood pounded in his ears.

No one waited for her in the kitchen. She sat on the edge of the bench, sick with dread. What had she done? Perhaps he had forgotten about her. He had not. He came in, his gambeson untied, his shirtfront soaked. Averting her eyes, Juliana stood up. The fading bruise stamped on his cheekbone in the colors of the rainbow did not allay her apprehension. He faced her down the length of the table and threw something in front of her. "Sit. Do you know this?"

She sat. "It's Anne's girdle, the one I lost at de Bec's execution."

"How did you lose it?"

"I don't remember. There were so many people."

He spread his palms on the table and leaned on them. "You'd better remember."

And for the next couple of hours, she was made to recall her escapade until she was no longer certain what had occurred and what she had imagined. If he did not cease, she would burst into tears or lose her temper, with undoubtedly unfortunate consequences for herself, but then Anne's words rang in her ears. She could not remain afraid of him forever. "I don't remember any more! I don't wish to lie, but if you keep asking, I will. Do you wish me to lie, my lord?"

He regarded her with a sliver-thin glare. "Don't ever try to lie to me, mouse. From now on, you'll not leave this place except in my company. You will not see the Countess de Valence or Isabel de Clare."

"In God's name why not?" She did not think that he would answer her, but he did, his hand on the door latch.

"Because you are my wife."

It was the same answer he had given her on their journey to Rivefort. She did not find it much of an answer then, and she did not think it much of an answer now. "Wait!" She rounded the table. "I wish to see the reason for the denial of your petition."

He opened the door. "The reasons are not important. The bishops denied it."

Hot rage of helplessness engulfed her. "I claim my right to know by what reason I am forced to remain your wife! If you don't let me see the answer, I'll ask Father Cyril to go to the Bishop of Évreux and fetch me a copy, I swear it—or do you intend to imprison him, too?"

He faced her so abruptly that she jumped back, but he only reached inside his gambeson and threw a much-folded piece of parchment on the table. At first, the Latin phrases meant little to her, then the roar in her head lessened and Brother Egremont's tutoring came back. She felt Lasalle's eyes on her. "The Church finds no reason to annul the marriage," he said curtly from the far end of the table.

Juliana inhaled. The bloody bastard. "Yes, that is the general ruling. But do you know why?"

His eyes narrowed to slits.

She held out the parchment to him. "You need to brush up

on your ecclesiastical Latin, sir." Her voice shook with outrage and the hilarious, hideous irony of it. "Having taken into evidence the petitioner's past, the bishops rejected the absence of consummation as sufficient grounds for invalidating the marriage. In plain words, the Church denied your petition on account of your whoring."

A sharp flash of pain went through her. She was shoved against the hearth, his face within inches of hers. "Well then, Madame, perhaps we can obtain an annulment on account of yours."

PART II

Pont-de-l'Arche

CHAPTER 32

For a man who had shown no trouble making up his mind instantly on a number of things, including her purported adultery, my lord Lasalle was taking his blessed time. Along with Rosamond, Bodo, and two more of Lasalle's men, Juliana was left to cool her heels outside Master Chlodio's workshop on the crowded Grand-Pont, reputed to be the best goldsmith's shop in Paris. Inside, haggling with the tenacity of a Venetian, was her husband. A man who could not tell a taille from a tithe, Guérin de Lasalle seemed to know the price of expensive baubles. No doubt they were intended as a gift for one of his mistresses. Or was it to atone for some felony Lasalle had lately committed? Or perhaps both?

It was the first time Lasalle had allowed her to leave the Three Dwarfs since his unexpected intrusion and his horrible accusation. She wished she could ask Anne if Lasalle had submitted a new petition with his new charges, but since that day Anne had not made an appearance at the Three Dwarfs.

Her husband having successfully concluded his daylight robbery, Juliana expected they would return directly to the Three Dwarfs, but Lasalle dismounted at a tavern of exceedingly disreputable appearance. Juliana reluctantly left the saddle when Kadolt appeared at the door, his whiskers bristling with excitement. He acknowledged her with a surprised and disapproving scowl and cupped his hand to Lasalle's ear.

A loud crash and raucous male voices from inside the tavern

interrupted him. Lasalle swore, unbuckled his sword with one hand, and handed it and Juliana to Kadolt. "Take the lady to the Three Dwarfs and don't take your eyes off her," he said and disappeared into the tavern.

Left so suddenly in charge of his mistress, Kadolt set about securing her compliance with coaxing words in atrocious Norman French, all the time pretending not to understand her protestations. She was thus half-cajoled, half-bullied back into the company of Bodo and her other guards, who received instructions regarding her disposal. Bodo was about to try to persuade her to comply when another loud noise and a woman's cry distracted the men. Juliana ducked around them, slipped into the tavern, and squeezed herself behind the door. Bodo and the others rushed in to search for her, but the crowd frustrated them. Thinking that she had given them the slip, they hurried outside. Juliana exhaled and climbed onto a stool to gain vantage over the men's shoulders.

Sprawled at one of the tables, five of the Emperor's men—well dressed, well made, and exceedingly self-confident—entertained themselves noisily at the expense of the crockery and their neighbors. One of the foreign knights was accosting a young serving woman, who struck her tormentor across his face and fled to seek refuge with the discomposed publican.

"*Du Schlampe!*" The foreigner charged toward the petrified girl and the old man.

Juliana cringed. In the next moment, the foreign knight pitched amidst the shards, spilled wine, and wood shavings. The pent-up tension exploded into laughter. More surprised than stunned, the Rhineland knight bounded to his feet, shaking his head, looking about for the culprit who had tripped him. The customers gave him way—all save one.

There stood Lasalle, none too sure on his feet, cup in hand, squinting hard. "*Voilà, Alemanni.* F-find yourselves a willing one." He lurched forward with a smirk. "If you c-can."

The man's hand went to his sword hilt. "Do you know who I am?" he growled in a strong accent. "I am Erhard von Hesse!"

Lasalle slapped his forehead as if he had just received enlightenment. "Ay! A sausage eater!" he declared in an exaggerated accent of a Poitevin bumpkin.

The audience roared with laughter. Erhard of Hesse was not impressed by the man taunting him, considering his opponent's bruised face and lacerated throat—evidence of earlier, luckless encounters—his wine-stained shirt, and his shabby gambeson. Erhard of Hesse grinned, pursed his lips, and, inclining his head toward Lasalle, made an unmistakably obscene gesture. Juliana winced. Lasalle looked crushed. The crowd hooted. Confused, Erhard of Hesse looked around him and while he did, Lasalle took a wobbly step—and planted an enthusiastic kiss right on Hesse's mouth.

The crowd broke into wild cheers and wolf whistles. Hesse recovered to fling away his unlikely admirer and, red with rage, drew his sword. The crowd gasped and fell back.

Juliana clamped her hand to her mouth. Good Lord, what was Lasalle doing? And where was his sword? Hidden behind a row of excited spectators, Kadolt was gripping his master's sword, his eyes popping out of his head. Neither Lasalle nor Kadolt had anticipated this encounter, but it was not an accident.

With clumsy-fingered haste, Lasalle answered with his poniard in his left hand. A poniard against a sword offered an outrageously uneven contest. Encountering only derision in the burst of laughter about him, Hesse sheathed his sword and threw it to his companions. Dagger in hand, he flew over the tabletop at his opponent, the blade opening a crimson trough from Lasalle's shoulder to his elbow. The audience groaned. Juliana gagged behind her palm. Lasalle went crashing backward; soaked in sweat, wine, and each other's blood, the two men tumbled among the benches and kegs, broken crockery, and spilled wine in a battering brawl. Erhard's companions and the patrons each shouted their favorite to victory. Hats and helmets made their round for coins and pledges. Although Lasalle appeared to be the crowd's favorite, Juliana knew that the odds were not in his favor. Everyone could see that he was weakening; most of the blood was his. With each passing moment, the audience became more subdued, except for Hesse's companions, who considered his victory all but assured.

Hesse's dagger caught Lasalle's poniard, forcing it downward against the table, where someone had abandoned his cloak. The poniard clattered onto the floor. The room went perfectly still, even the flies. Juliana forgot to breathe. Lasalle would die right in front of her, thanks to Erhard of Hesse. But Lasalle jerked the cloak from the table and flung it at his adversary—and snatching his own poniard from the floor, he drove it upward through the cloak.

Shocked disbelief froze Hesse's features. His knees buckled. He sagged against Lasalle, his arm flung out as if in a lover's embrace, and slowly, ever so slowly, he slipped to the floor.

Pandemonium broke out. The Emperor's men shouted and charged to reach the contenders. It looked like the foreigners would finish the one left standing, were it not for Kadolt, who threw himself in front of them, his master's sword in hand, heaping invectives in several tongues on their heads and daring anyone to challenge him. Others joined in. Sides were chosen. Finding themselves outnumbered, the Rhinelanders retreated to one corner to confer. The publican emerged from behind a fortress of wine kegs, wringing his hands and tearfully assessing the damage to his establishment. One of the Flemings offered Lasalle a towel and indicated the body on the floor.

"Do you know, sir, that you've killed the champion Duke John hired to challenge the Lusignans?"

Preoccupied with keeping upright, Lasalle wrapped the towel around his bloody sleeve and mopped his face. "Good Lord, Heinrich," he croaked accusingly at Kadolt. "Why didn't you tell me?"

That did it. Juliana fought her way to the door, where she ran into Bodo. This time, she offered no objection to being delivered to the care of Mistress Hermine at the Three Dwarfs. She had no idea what she would do with Lasalle once he got there. She had no experience with wounds inflicted by poniards, daggers, swords, knives, or other sharp instruments of death, and the sight of all that blood made her head spin. Perhaps she could persuade Mistress Hermine to take up the task.

She need not have worried. My lord Lasalle did not return to the Three Dwarfs that night.

Anne de Valence had instructed her guard captain to turn away all callers unless they brought a message from Duke John or Lady Juliana. It was therefore to her displeasure when, at the hour of *couvre-feu,* she was told that my lord Lasalle was at the gate and his man was trying to pound it down.

Anne decided to give Lasalle a piece of her mind, but when the gate opened, the first thing she saw was Kadolt's panic-stricken face, and that he was on foot, holding on to the bridle of his master's horse. Lasalle slouched in the saddle, his cloak about him, a sheen of perspiration on his unshaved lip. The sour smell of wine hit her and she drew back in disgust. "You are drunk."

Kadolt snarled at her and flung back Lasalle's cloak. Anne gasped and crossed herself. "Jesumariajoseph, you're bleeding. Oh Lord, what have you done?"

She repeated those words several times while her guard captain and Kadolt bundled up Lasalle between them and got him into her chamber and onto her bed. She ordered de Querci to take Kadolt to the kitchen and to question him, and then called for Heliette to heat some wine and to bring the apothecary box, laver, and towels.

"You stupid bastard. Are you still sparring with that Kadolt?" She removed the blood-soaked wrapping. "Get rid of him before he cuts your throat."

Lasalle tried a smile. "Too late. Besides"—he held his breath while Anne poked at the gash—"it wasn't Kadolt; it was his brother."

Heliette returned with her medicaments. Anne dismissed her and wound a steaming cloth around his arm. "And procurer of your ditch wives, no doubt. I imagine they will all be disappointed."

Lasalle flinched. "Kadolt's brother is . . . was Hesse."

Anne looked up in disbelief. "Good Lord. John's champion? Have you gone mad? John spent a fortune on that man."

Lasalle struggled to sit up. "Aliénor offered a lot more. Fortunately, Kadolt knew enough of Hesse's tricks to teach me to avoid most of them. They've hated each other for years."

"She paid you?" My lord Lasalle and the Duchess of Aquitaine obviously had an arrangement of which Anne had been left ignorant. Anne did not like that.

"Handsomely. John hiring duelists was not what she had planned for the Lusignans."

Anne threaded her needle. "Do you understand what trouble you are in? Marshal can't protect you. He's already at odds with John over Hesse and the Lusignans."

"Fortunately"—Lasalle held his breath again as her needle pierced his skin—"I still have my *routa*."

Heliette brought wine. Anne poured a cup and added a few drops from a vial in her apothecary chest. He sniffed at it. "What's in it?"

"A little henbane. Drink it."

He returned the cup to her. "No henbane."

Knowing there was no arguing with him, Anne gave him a fresh cup, smeared his arm with betony salve, bandaged it all, and stripped off the rest of his shirt. Something fell to the floor. She picked it up and untied the bloodstained wad. In it was a pair of garnet earrings. Anne held them, her fingers sticky with his blood. "You are a most infuriating man, Guérin de Lasalle."

"They are for you. I am sorry." His hand came around her wrist. "But don't do that again, Anne."

"What is it? Tell me."

He drew her to him. "Just don't. I am sick unto death of plots. Yours, Aliénor's, John's, mine. I killed a man who did nothing to me—for Aliénor, for my own reasons." His fingertips traced her jaw with that slow, deliberate touch, the way he had done the first time they came together. "Sometimes, when you don't have your legs wrapped around me, I think of you as a friend"—he tapped her lips before she could speak—"and I would give up everything else to keep that. But I will not have you plot against me—for anyone—and use Juliana to do it. There is absolutely nothing you, Aliénor, or anyone else can do to make me take that girl to my bed. You can tell that to Aliénor."

~❦~

"It was a fair fight."

"It was a brawl!"

"It was murder, sire, like Mercadier's."

The voices echoed under the vaulting of the Duke of Normandy's borrowed stateroom. Surrounded by his advisers and attendants, each of whom, with the exception of William Marshal, pounded the table, John Plantagenet sat slumped in his chair, twirling his whiskers. The four German knights stood to the side, looking rather uncertain of themselves. From behind a pillar where a chair had been provided for her by one of Hugh de Bourgh's men, Juliana de Charnais listened to it all with rapt attention. Was she under arrest? John Plantagenet's men, who had come for her at the Three Dwarfs, seemed to think so, and even William Marshal gave her a worried look before he quickly smiled at her. Juliana attempted to smile back, but did not think she was very convincing. Having been kept waiting for some time, she dared not squirm in her seat.

The doors swung open and Lasalle walked in, between de Bourgh's men. He wore a clean shirt, someone else's *cotte*, and the expression of a man roused from the warm bed of his mistress. Juliana noticed that he was deprived of his sword and poniard. He bowed smartly to John, ignoring the guards at his side and the four Germans.

The Duke of Normandy stood up and clasped his hands behind his back. "It appears you have caused us considerable inconvenience, my lord Lasalle. You seem to forget that you hold your viscounty at my pleasure. I am told that you picked a quarrel with Hesse in order to aid my enemies. Is it true?"

"No, sire." Lasalle was looking over the duke's head.

"It was a simple brawl, Your Grace," William Marshal interposed, glancing with some embarrassment in Juliana's direction. "I understand it was a fight over a woman."

"Ha!" John jerked his head toward the four knights, who regarded Lasalle with Teutonic hatred. "They say you pretended to be drunk in order to goad Hesse into a fight."

Lasalle looked down his nose at his accusers. "They lie."

The men bounded toward Lasalle, shouting and shaking their fists, entreating John to do something about Lasalle's calumny. John's attendants joined in the denunciations until perfect bedlam reigned. John Plantagenet threw up his hands.

"Enough! All of you!" He charged around the table and dragged Juliana from behind the pillar to the middle of the hall. "It seems we have another witness." He turned to her. "Your virtue and veracity are known to us, Lady Juliana." He held up a crucifix before Juliana's eyes. "Did your husband goad Hesse into a fight?"

John's hand rested on her shoulder, the other holding up the cross. Juliana cast a fearful glance in Lasalle's direction. He was not looking at her; he was looking at John. How could she lie when the duke could know the truth already, and why would she lie for Lasalle's sake? She reached out and kissed the cross. Her answer was whispered, but everyone heard it. "Yes."

John gave a short, sharp laugh and stepped away. "What do you say to that, my lord?"

"I say the lady Juliana would lie to gain your favor, since she is about to be set aside for adultery."

Mary, that man had publicly accused her! Juliana crossed herself. "I swear that the charge is utterly false, Your Grace."

"Indeed?" John rubbed his knuckles against his jaw, examining her minutely. "My congratulations, Viscount. You may obtain release from your marriage yet. However, it appears that you owe me the cost of that man. I am of mind to put you forth against the Lusignans as my champion."

Juliana did not know whether she should take that as good news or bad, and from Lasalle's expression, neither did he.

"Sire." Marshal stepped forward. "I can vouch for this man's sword skill, but he is not a duelist like Hesse."

"He killed Hesse, didn't he?" one of John's young men called out smugly.

"In a brawl, yes." Marshal turned to the young man, anger and frustration in his voice. "He would not have defeated Hesse in a formal contest. What man in his right mind would have challenged Erhard of Hesse?" Marshal bowed to John, his voice earnest. "Your Grace, you cannot consider rescinding another oath of homage because of a tavern brawl. Sire, your barons will not take it kindly."

Pinching his chin between his fingers, John Plantagenet paced about. At last, he stopped in front of Juliana and brought her hand to his lips. Over his shoulder, he said to Lasalle, "Consider yourself exceptionally lucky, sir. I'll leave you in possession of Rivefort and Tillières. In fact, I wish you to return there, and not to leave unless you are called. The viscountess"—John smiled at Juliana—"may remain at court to attend the queen, if she wishes," he added smoothly. "Now, get out of my sight."

Lasalle bowed. Flushed, Juliana liberated her hand. For all her fear of Lasalle, she did not think she would fare any better at this court. Mumbling her gratitude, she curtsied and took two steps back.

"Congratulations, mouse," Lasalle said under his breath as they crossed the hall. "You almost succeeded in throwing me to the wolves. One could end up like Reigner de Bec. You do remember Reigner de Bec, Sister Eustace?"

Lasalle continued down the corridor with the clink of his spurs, paying no mind to her, confident that she would follow him. She did. She had nowhere else to go. By the time she caught up with him, William Marshal appeared, carrying Lasalle's sword. While Lasalle fumbled with the belt frog, Juliana tagged behind, ears pricked. Noting her presence, Marshal hushed his voice.

"There is enough treachery in this world without inviting it to our beds. John is vindictive, vain, and stubborn. He thinks his weaknesses are his strengths. Without proper counsel, he'll bring us all to grief. Take your wife and go home, son. Let her take care of you. Women love it when we are helpless."

And with that, Sir William Marshal, the most chivalrous man in two kingdoms, bowed to them and went back to his liege's chambers to continue to wage his own battles. Juliana did not know what to do with herself. She did not know what to do with this man. "My lord—"

Lasalle tightened his sword belt left-handed. "Forget it, Sister. You'd slip me hemlock instead of henbane and claim it was all an accident."

They rode to the Three Dwarfs in silence. Juliana intended to retreat behind the bolted door of her chamber, but Lasalle's voice arrested her before she crossed the kitchen. "I am not done. Sit down."

She did, at the end of the bench. On the table was a chest strapped with iron and secured by a substantial padlock. Holding the lock awkwardly, Lasalle opened it. Inside the trunk were four pigskin bags. "You'll receive the rest when Aliénor pays up and when you remove yourself from Rivefort and Tillières."

Somehow, Juliana had anticipated the second move but not the first disclosure, so she had the presence of mind to ask, "Aliénor?"

"Don't be so simple, Eustace. Do you think I'd go about picking fights with duelists on any odd day of the week?"

She wiped her palms on her skirts, spine-stiffening resolve filling her. "That is blood money."

"It's all blood money, mouse. You have no choice; you are an adulteress. The duke's favor or not, I can snap your neck or lock you in a nunnery. And if you think to challenge me for Tillières, I'll be forced to do something about Mathea and that sister of hers. How old is she? Fifteen? Sixteen? She has no property, but that would matter little to a jaded suitor. I might even make something on her. Or I'll keep her to replace Ravenissa."

Horrified, Juliana crossed herself. "You wouldn't!"

He came toward her with the smile of those who know they have dominion over others. "What is to prevent me? You? My honor?"

"No! Because . . . because Aumary wishes to marry Paulette, if Saint-Sylvain's allows it."

"What?"

"Saint-Sylvain. Surely you know that Aumary holds lands of the abbey?"

Lasalle stood back, fists to his sides. "Aumary? Haven't you been the busy little bee? Having me all but charged with treachery, arranging the marriage of my ward and squire behind my back, and finding yourself a lover. All that by a perpetual postulant."

"*My* ward. Aliénor entrusted Paulette and Mathea to me."

Lasalle padlocked the trunk and threw the keys to her. "When we return to Rivefort, I'll have you all escorted to my aunt. She'll find you a manor where you can raise radishes and glean the duke's favors."

Juliana's voice shook like rest of her, but fear, and not for herself, drove her on. "Granted, you have power over us. I dare you to use it. Go ahead. I'll tell Sir William. And the Countess of Pembroke. And Anne. And the duke will hear how his own mother paid you to kill Hesse. If you or any of your men come near Paulette or Mathea, I'll see you declared contumacious yet. Do you think John will leave Tillières in the hands of a rebellious vassal?"

Instead of answering, Lasalle moved toward her. That sobered her. She retreated before his advance until her shoulder blades met the wall. Good God, what was he . . . Fingertips touched her jaw. "My, you are troublesome, mouse. Perhaps Marshal is right. I should do something about you. Let's see if d'Erlée taught you to kiss better than Hesse."

She wrenched away and, taking three steps at once, flew up the stairs to her chamber. She slammed the door and leaned against it. Aliénor of Aquitaine had married her to the Devil. Her eyes became accustomed to the gloom. Unaccountably, the shutters were latched. The heat made the room stultifying, the smell of lavender overwhelming—lavender, the flower of deceit.

Someone was lying on her bed, under her covers. A sound sleeper, no doubt. It did not alarm her. Servants usually did not possess a bed with embroidered hangings and rainwater-washed linen, and Juliana understood the lure of beautiful things. Gently, not wishing to cause alarm, she pulled back the sheet.

"Félice?"

The servant Félice did not possess such a face, either; the plucked arch of the brows, the rouged lips, the kohl-lined eyelids and soot-dusted eyelashes. Juliana knew that face and the swirls of red curls framing it. It had stared back at her from Anne de Valence's mirror. She was looking at herself. No, not herself. Her other self.

Equitan was lying in her bed, wearing her gown and an enigmatic smile. The last of the sheet slipped to the floor, the edge dark, wet. And then she saw it—a poniard, buried in Equitan's heart.

Behind her, the door swung open.

CHAPTER 33

Agnès de Méran was not safely delivered. On July 19, anno Domini 1201, the Almighty dissolved the Frankish king's bigamous marriage. But Agnès died giving Philip a son, and in public deference to his suzerain's grief, the Duke of Normandy packed up his court and left Paris for Chinon.

Privately, John worried. Agnès's death restored Philip to the bosom of the Mother Church, which would now declare his children by her legitimate. Aside from young Prince Louis, already married to John's niece, Blanche of Castile, Philip now had another son to secure his succession. Rumor also had it that Philip intended to affiance the infant princess Marie to John's nephew, young Duke Arthur. John was not amused. The Bretons continued to maintain stubbornly that Arthur was the true heir to the Lionheart's possessions, and Arthur's marriage to Marie would place the Breton duchy further within the Frankish king's orbit.

Married to his child bride, John Plantagenet not only lacked an heir, he continued to aggravate the Lusignans. Before he left Paris, John called upon them to present themselves at Chinon for a trial by their peers. Unfortunately, his invitation omitted to include a guarantee of safe conduct. When the Lusignans refused to

budge from their fortresses without it, John charged them with
flouting the authority of their liege. And so it went on, the Plantagenet and Lusignan *estampie.*

Heavily veiled, Madame Violaine arrived with her escort, about
as inconspicuous as a peacock in a barnyard. The Viscount of
Tillières was not impressed by the display, but he had little choice
in the matter. Equitan's body was beginning to announce itself
over the lavender.

Madame Violaine lifted the sheet. "The thought has occurred
to you, my lord, to sink it in the river?"

"Instantly." That was not strictly true. His first thought, after he
had regained consciousness on the floor of his wife's bedroom
with the door bolted from the inside and no sign of his wife, had
been to stagger to the window to see if by chance Juliana de Charnais had met her end by a broken neck at the bottom of the precipitous drop. No such luck. His second thought had been to hang
Bodo, impose ruinous fines on the rest of his men, and dismiss
them in disgrace. Then he had noticed the occupant of the bed.
No wonder the mother abbess had scampered out the window
after knocking him senseless by ramming the edge of the door,
with perspicacious accuracy, into his throbbing arm.

Madame Violaine inspected the wound in Equitan's side. "A
dagger?"

"A poniard. Mine."

Madame Violaine removed the ties from the bed curtains and
secured the covers about the body. She called a couple of her attendants, and the men enfolded the body into the blood-soaked
mattress and carried it away. Madame Violaine closed the door
behind her men. "And there is more."

"As always, Madame."

"Ah. The Queen of Misrule." Madame Violaine's fingernails
traced the carvings of the bed's post. "You wish to know about the
girdle. Very well. What are you willing to pay, my lord? Everyone
has their price."

"No, Madame. *Everything*."

Madame Violaine smiled slightly and nodded toward the chair. "Your wound is bleeding. Sit down before you fall down, my lord."

He did as he was told. At least it would impress the neighbors that the most celebrated courtesan in Paris had called at the House of the Three Dwarfs.

Anne was distracting herself with a game of chess solitaire. That way she was certain to prevail. Otherwise, the Countess de Valence was overtaken by an unpleasant suspicion that she, like the Viscount of Tillières, was being turned into a pawn. Her winning streak ended abruptly with the noisy arrival of the lady Juliana. It took Anne several unsuccessful attempts before she understood what the frenetic girl was trying to tell her. "Juliana, calm yourself. We will figure out what to do."

"I can't stay here! He'll come and take me away!" Juliana ripped off her veil, which had miraculously survived her feats of scaling walls and dashing through the streets of Paris.

That was true, and the thought of her men in a confrontation with Guérin de Lasalle did not appeal to Anne. She handed Juliana a cup of perry. "What do you propose?"

Juliana downed the perry in one gulp. "Armand will grant me sanctuary. I only came here because I thought you would know where he resides in Paris."

"He has returned to Pont-de-l'Arche to wait for the duke's next move. Do you know what you are saying, Juliana?"

"I have to reach him. At least John won't fight the Lusignans with his duelists. Lasalle killed Hesse. Aliénor paid him."

Anne hesitated, uncertain what she should tell the girl. "I know. He told me—"

"Did he tell you that he tried to bribe me with that money? He thought I'd leave Tillières to him." Juliana's voice peaked higher than usual. "He killed Equitan! In my own bed, Anne, in my own gown, looking like me."

That was a part my lord Lasalle had neglected to mention. "Are you certain? I don't think he could have—"

"Don't you see? My only hope is a refuge with someone he can't threaten or influence." Out of her bodice Juliana pulled a gold ring on a cord. "He must not find out for the longest time where I am. Tell him that I took refuge with the Countess de Nevers as he told me to. He would never seek me out there. He'll think I've abandoned Tillières to him. Let him think that. You were right, but I need your help. Look after Paulette and Mathea, please. I can't bear the thought of anything happening to them. And Jourdain and Hermine. Can you look after Hermine?"

The girl's blackthorn eyes pleaded with Anne. The timorous mother abbess had transformed into a woman possessed. Anne had to remind herself that Armand de Lusignan was more than a match for Guérin de Lasalle. Perhaps a few days of his wife's sojourn under the protection of the Count of Rancon would kindle enough jealousy in Lasalle's calculating heart to make him want not only to reclaim her but also to pay her proper attention. "Very well, let me find you some suitable clothes."

"Oh, thank you!"

"I don't know if you ought to thank me yet. You must take care, and never forget that you are entering rarefied ranks."

Juliana nodded earnestly but hesitated a little. "Anne, are you spying on the Lusignans?"

"My dear, I spy on everyone." Anne laughed and opened her trunk to pick through her gowns.

"Anne?" Juliana said, her arms weighed down with the rejected ones. "I don't understand. You seem to like to be with men, but you don't ever seem to become—"

Anne reached the bottom of her trunk and held up the last gown. "I am barren. My first husband was drunk and knocked me down the kitchen stairs when I was almost eight months gone. I lost the babe and nearly died. He did not mind; it was only a girl. The midwives told him I could not carry again and he used to beat me for that, but it did not have the desired effect either. Here, try this."

"I am so sorry." Juliana did not know what else to say. How

could someone of Anne's beauty and poise harbor such a dark tragedy? She wiggled out of her gown and into the wide-skirted one Anne offered her.

"It's all right. He fell down the donjon stairs himself. Cracked his skull, even though it was a thick Norman one. Aliénor made me marry twice more. The others wanted me because I was young, beautiful, and rich. They paid Aliénor dearly for the privilege. Both had children by their other wives. Praise to the saints, they knew more about pleasing a woman than the first one."

"All done." Anne finished the lacings and inspected her protégée. Satisfied, she gave Juliana an embrace and a kiss. "God's speed, my dear."

Heliette ushered him in and closed the door behind her with an ear-deafening bang.

"I didn't know that Equitan found so many admirers in this place," Anne's new visitor said, glancing behind him.

Anne was fully ready for him, in a heavily embroidered imperial, her crucifix adorning her bosom. Lasalle's gaze went from it to her lips, accompanied by one arched brow. Anne found it perfectly infuriating. "Only you could jest about something like that. I am beginning to believe that Juliana was right. You did kill him."

Lasalle looked about the room. "What for? Persistence?" He poked about, opening and closing Anne's trunks and trundles. Underneath Anne's cloak, he found Juliana's veil and held it up. "Tsk, tsk, Madame. Still aiding and abetting wives in disobeying their husbands and masters? Where is she?"

"She is on her way to your aunt's estates. De Querci and four men are with her and one of my women. I must say, is there anything you would not do to get your way?"

Favoring his arm, Lasalle regarded her with brief amusement. "No."

Anne took a deep breath. "You could have been killed."

He gave her a careful shrug. "No great loss to Christendom. I have to return to Tillières; John was adamant about it. Can you ask Isabel de Clare to take in the Glanville chits? Rivefort offers limited prospects for them."

His request surprised her. "It seems the prospects are bright for the older girl. Your squire is coming into substantial property and wishes to marry her."

Lasalle shook his head. "Juliana wastes her matchmaking. Aumary will not marry Paulette. I intend to tell that to Saint-Sylvain."

"Those nuns will not see you."

"They will."

The laconic reply sounded too confident to be merely a boast. "Well then," Anne conceded, "I shall speak to Isabel. I am certain your wards will find a warm welcome." She was not sure what else to do with him, so she said, "You have frightened Juliana."

"I know. It saved me from wringing her neck." He paused and then said, "Anne, when you see d'Erlée, tell him where Juliana is."

Saint-Sylvain's gate mistress started to recite to him the convent's rules in rote, whispered voice. He smiled, shoved her his cross through the gate's aperture, and said with as much charm as he judged decent to use on a woman who had pledged herself to God, "I know, Sister, that your rules and the Reverend Mother's infirmity prevent me from speaking to her, but I believe that she would like to make that decision herself, once she sees this."

He knew that he would have a long wait, but in the end the wicket door opened. The room where the nun left him was dim, empty, and silent. Incense permeated the musty air. A wooden partition with a small, iron-strapped window separated him from the room beyond. There was no chair, so he leaned against the partition.

"This is a breach of our agreement, my lord Lasalle," said a cool voice beyond. "Do you come in regard to your wife or your mistress?"

"I come to ask you to withhold your permission for the marriage of Aumary de Beaudricourt to Paulette de Glanville."

"Do you intend to prevent him from ever marrying?" said the voice, its tone one of dry hostility.

"No, Reverend Mother. I don't wish him to marry this particular demoiselle."

"Saint-Sylvain is inclined to grant our permission. Your wife thinks the two are worthy."

"My opinion ought to weigh at least as much as the fancy of a girl who has spent the last five years of her life cloistered!"

There was no pause this time, only contempt doled out in precise measures. "Do you hold that the opinion of women religious ought to weigh less than the opinion of men who have spent the greater part of their lives in the most profligate manner?"

Mother Nicola did not have to wait for his answer, either. "Yes. They know whereof they speak. I say that the son may yet turn out to be like his sire."

Another silence, and finally an answer. "We withhold our decision. Your cross is returned to you. You are not to use it again at the gates of this house of God, my lord Lasalle."

"Reverend Mother—"

The window clicked shut. Lasalle waited, then he bowed to the wall.

Outside, he dropped his forehead against the damp arch of his rounsey's neck. Bloody hell. He was not having much luck with nuns.

Fortress of Rivefort, Normandy

"Praise saints you are home, my lord. I'm through with cattle tallies, cheese counting, and manor courts. I don't know how the lady Juliana makes head or tail out of it. I'd rather face a dozen Saracens. . . . Where is the lady Juliana?" Jehan de Vaudreuil looked up and down the cavalcade.

Having endured Mistress Hermine's wailing for the entire return journey, Guérin de Lasalle fought a strong urge to stay in the saddle, point his horse's head toward the gate, and ride out of Rivefort and Tillières, never to return. Instead, he dismounted.

"Home?" He was a dozen strides across the bailey, leaving the train to his men and servants. "Home is where we've just bedded down our horses and our latest whores. What the Devil do you know about home?"

Vaudreuil hurried after him. "Passed the time pleasantly in Paris, did you, my lord?"

"Hang it, Jehan. I wouldn't grow too fond of this place. If John has his way, I'll be stripped of my title, undoubtedly with the eager help of Peyrac and my less-than-loyal garrison. Speaking of my garrison, have you kept the men away from the Glanville chits, or vice versa, as the case might be?"

"Kept them away?" Vaudreuil broke his stride. "*Christu*, Guérin, half of them are in love with Paulette, and half of them think she is a saint and watch to make sure the others don't try anything. And the lady appears oblivious to them all."

"And which half do you belong to?" Catching Vaudreuil's expression, Lasalle cut him short. "Tell Hermine to pack them up. They are all going to Longueville, today."

"But—"

My lord Lasalle was scattering the dogs, routing pigs, chickens, and a flock of noisy geese across the bailey. "God's bones! What happened to this place? It looks like a sty!"

Vaudreuil dodged the puddles and the droppings. "I'll put up my sword against any man, but I am not your chatelaine. Your wife keeps after this place. I've had my hands full with the men and the *routiers,* the stables, and the armory."

Vaudreuil expected that my lord Lasalle would have something to say on that, but he merely raised the corner of his lip in an unvoiced snarl. In the hall, they were greeted by Master Thibodeau at the table, surrounded by parchments, inkhorns, pens, and leather-encased volumes, his hand on his heart. Lasalle squinted at his steward. "What are these doing here?"

"They are Tillières's accounts, my lord. I have taken the liberty of assembling them, knowing that the viscountess would wish to see them as soon as she returned."

"Get out."

Master Thibodeau bowed several more times before closing the door behind him. Lasalle unbuckled his sword belt while Vaudreuil shoved back Master Thibodeau's carefully arranged piles, this time abandoning formality. "Guérin? Where is Juliana? What did you do to her?"

They used each other's Christian names only rarely—usually when things did not go well—and Lasalle knew it. "Christ, why does everyone assume I did something to her?"

"Where is she then?"

Lasalle dropped his sword on top of the table and himself into the chair. "At Sabine's, trading stories of my perfidy. Call the men."

This time Vaudreuil held his ground. "Guérin? What happened?"

Lasalle set his elbows on the table, his forehead against his fists, and told him. "I told her I'd have her charged with adultery unless she left Tillières. I gave her all the silver Aliénor paid for Hesse. She refused. She said it was blood money."

Ignoring the rest, Vaudreuil decided to ask what he knew Guérin de Lasalle decidedly did not want to hear. "Do you truly think that Juliana would break her vow?"

"She'd better. But if not and Armand wants to dissolve my marriage for me, I can always raise an army and rout the Lusignans."

Vaudreuil stared at him. *My lord Lasalle has gone mad.* "How do you expect to raise such a force?"

"The Venetians are contending for trade with the Byzantines. They need men, good men, and they are willing to pay, besides offering a portion of any booty. With John and Philip dickering, the men are bored."

"Guérin, if you hire out the *routiers*, we won't have enough men to hold this place when they stop dickering."

"Kadolt has plenty of friends for a siege garrison."

"Men you can't trust. And how do you plan to persuade the others to go?"

"Gold and glory, and a chance to swive the most beautiful women in the world."

Vaudreuil sat back. "If you do raise a force like that, John and Philip will feel threatened. Christ, we could end up facing them both."

Lasalle picked up his sword. "Don't look so glum, Jehan. It won't come to that. In a few weeks, send her the silver. By that time, she'll be tired of living on my aunt's charity. She'll take it."

"But—"

"Enough. Call the men."

Vaudreuil knew when not to argue with my lord Lasalle. He bowed, and this time he got to the door when Lasalle said, "Jehan. He had her followed."

CHAPTER 34

Fortress of Pont-de-l'Arche, Normandy, August 1201

The Count de Rancon's ring had gained Juliana admittance to Pont-de-l'Arche, but little else. Once past the portcullis, she pretended composure in front of gaping servants, attendants, and retainers, praying that Armand de Lusignan would be as chivalrous as he had been at Dreux and in Paris. Somehow, she had expected that she would be greeted with at least some ceremony. Instead, she was told by Pont-de-l'Arche's chatelaine, Dame Ermengarde, a dowager whose lips appeared never to have been tempted into a smile, that the Count of Rancon was not expected before nightfall. Dame Ermengarde granted frostily that if the lady Juliana wished to wait, she could. The lady Juliana wished to wait.

She roused herself out of her exhaustion enough to fret about de Querci's men and Anne's waiting woman, but the guard captain told her bluntly that he was not leaving her side. Formal,

tight-lipped, and dedicated, Peter de Querci reminded Juliana of
Vaudreuil. Trying not to look as worn out as she was, Juliana surreptitiously examined her surroundings.

The great hall's corners, alcoves, and niches bristled with Saracen standards, shields, lances, and swords, evidence of the Lusignans' service in *outre-mer* and their ventures elsewhere, valiant and
violent. Carpets of dizzying designs and colors adorned the rest of
the walls, but it took Juliana little effort to decipher the frescoes:
On one wall was Paris choosing to give Eris's apple of discord to
Aphrodite, who had promised him the love of Helen, the most
beautiful woman in the world. To the side stood the rejected Hera,
who had offered him power, and Athena, who had made her
bid with wisdom and martial success. On the wall above a fireplace large enough to swallow a whole log, she recognized Mélusine, the legendary half-woman, half-serpent who was purported
to be the ancestress of the Lusignans. The sprite was extending her
long-fingered hand toward her unsuspecting husband. Juliana
dabbed her nose. Was this Armand de Lusignan's comment on the
power of love, or of deception?

Juliana's ruminations ended with the noise of dogs, horses,
and riders in the bailey. She smoothed her skirts just as Armand
de Lusignan appeared on the threshold, a wildly barking bristle-
haired wolfhound at his side. A huntsman's dagger in a richly
decorated sheath protruded from behind his belt, and a bloody
smear marred his gauntlet. A pack of lymers and equally cacopho-
nous humans crowded behind him.

Juliana dropped a deep curtsy, was raised up, and had a lingering
kiss bestowed on her hand. "My dear lady." The Count of Rancon's
forehead creased with puzzlement. "Pray, how did you persuade
your husband to release you?"

"I didn't." Juliana's voice squeaked. "I ran away."

Around them, the attendants broke into titters and whispers.
Armand de Lusignan glanced over his shoulder. The company
quieted. "He doesn't know you are here?"

"He thinks I've sought refuge with the Countess de Nevers."

Armand de Lusignan's eyebrow crooked, as if he could not
decide what expression to assume. Juliana's heart sank. And then

he laughed. As if on cue, the rest of the company joined in. Someone said Lasalle's name and was hushed by another voice. This time the Count of Rancon chose to ignore the commotion. He kissed her hand again. "Then we welcome you to Pont-de-l'Arche. Querci, you may inform your lady that you have discharged your duty and that the lady Juliana is under our protection. Dame Ermengarde? Why hasn't the Viscountess of Tillières been attended to?"

Dame Ermengarde curtsied, her mouth pinched. "My lord, I did not know."

"And now you do," Armand de Lusignan said very gently, giving Juliana his smile.

And so, with some commotion but little fanfare, she took up residence at Pont-de-l'Arche, though hardly as the center of its lord's universe. That suited her perfectly well. Far from wanting to vie for Armand de Lusignan's attention, she was more than content to move along the circumference of his rarefied circle.

Her women, provided by Dame Ermengarde, were called Thalia, Erato, and Terpsichore. So they announced to Juliana after bursting into her room like a spring storm. Underneath the painted, plaited, and plucked exteriors, they resembled Rivefort's boisterous bakery help; they loved levity and were eager to provide their share of it. Juliana imagined that the gowns they brought her had at one time belonged to one or more of Armand de Lusignan's mistresses. She also suspected that Thalia, Erato, and Terpsichore might have been the very same. Like Dame Ermengarde, their dour mistress, however, the young women did not gossip, at least not about their master. That was a rare trait among waiting women, and undoubtedly one of the reasons why Armand de Lusignan had kept them at Pont-de-l'Arche.

The Count de Rancon also kept Juliana under the watchful eyes of two men-at-arms, Richieu and Viart, informing her that he had charged them with her safety. Since being trailed by murderous-looking guards was not a new experience to her, Juliana did not much notice them. She did notice, however, another almost-constant presence.

A couple of days after she had arrived, she collided with a tall figure dressed in a striped cloak of a strange cut, embroidered along the extremities in red and green silk. The collision knocked from his hand a walking staff, jangling the small bells that were tied around it. Juliana was stammering apologies and returning the staff to him when she looked up into the man's face.

From a walnut-dark visage, a pair of milky white eyes stared back at her. She cried out, tore herself away, and ran. Erato came looking for her and told her that his name was Dawud; he was a Saracen, the count's favorite musician, and he was blind. Juliana laughed with nervous relief. Mary, she had let herself be frightened by a blind musician!

On later occasions, she sat herself behind the others while Dawud entertained the company, sometimes with other musicians, and she listened, a sewing basket at hand. Some of the melodies she knew. Others were alien yet fascinating, the sinuous sounds of distant lands. They made Juliana catch her breath and listen, forgetting about her mending. At these gatherings, the Count of Rancon's love of poetry and song, ribald and otherwise, revealed itself, and she came to admire the cultured, accomplished side of Armand de Lusignan. Yet there always remained about him an air of aloofness.

The days became shorter and hazier, the nights longer, the air brisk. Since no military threat from the Duke of Normandy had materialized, the residents of Pont-de-l'Arche took to outdoor amusements. Even though Juliana had no passion for hunting, she did not wish to call attention to herself, and so, with a clever little merlin on her wrist, she rode out with the others on a spirited chestnut mare. But the experience gave her nightmares, and she soon begged off further expeditions. She knew that the entire company gossiped about her for it. In turn, she thought them blithe and beautiful and devoid of compassion if it impinged upon their entertainment. In order to avoid falling into such vice, she sent away her trio of Muses and explored Pont-de-l'Arche alone.

One day, she rounded a corner and encountered Dawud, his

sightless eyes like those of a drowned corpse. Juliana shuddered, glad the Saracen could not see her, but Dawud bowed deeply from the waist in her direction. "Lady," he said.

"Oh." Feeling foolish, she said, "I was going to the carp pond. Would you like to come?"

Dawud smiled gravely. "If it pleases you, Lady."

Juliana nodded, and remembering that Dawud could not see her, she said, "Yes, it would."

She took the path between the hedges, keeping an eye on her strange companion. Dawud followed a few steps behind her, his staff sweeping slightly from side to side to the soft sound of bells. They sat themselves on autumn grass under a willow, its drooping branches shimmering with yellow leaves. A few carp rose to the surface, their passage marked by bubbles and rippling circles on the smooth water. Peacefulness and solitude surrounded the pond. Juliana did not wish to break the silence, and Dawud, sensing her reluctance, reached for his flute. At the end of his song, Juliana hugged herself under her cloak. "That was lovely, but so sad. What is it?"

"Lament for a lost love."

Juliana glanced at the man. "I am sorry you have had such pain."

Dawud smiled and lowered the flute. "I was playing for you, Lady."

Juliana pulled back her hood. "Thank you, Dawud," she retorted lightly, "but I have not lost any love."

"Everyone has a lost love."

"Oh dear, then I must be sure to find one and lose it."

"Is there no one you have loved, Lady?"

She thought about that day at the top of Rivefort's keep. "I thought there was someone once, but he only pretended. Being duped is not a subject for troubadours. It is, however, a very effective cure when it comes to love."

"And what about your husband?"

"Well now," Juliana replied roguishly, "you will have to ask him if he has been duped, although I imagine he has duped more than

his share. It's lovely here, but a little chilly. Let's walk around before we return."

When they reached the stables, Dawud went on his way with
the sound of the staff bells. Juliana looked inside the high-vaulted
stalls. The horses, groomed and coddled, raised their heads.

"Lady Juliana?"

Juliana forced a smile to her lips. The young man looked a little
abashed, but friendly. He reminded her of Aumary. "I am Joscelyn
de Cantigny," he said with a bow. "Would you like to see some of
the mares and foals? I would be honored if you would—"

Juliana was about to decline politely when she saw Armand de
Lusignan approach. De Cantigny stood back immediately, bowed,
and departed.

"I believe Joscelyn was about to try to seduce you, Lady Juliana," Armand said.

Not wanting to appear gullible, Juliana tried for humor. "In
that case, he has set himself an impossible goal, my lord."

Armand held out his hand. "Then let me try. You will find that,
unlike Joscelyn, I do not capitulate so easily." -

Somewhere inside her a bell clanked a warning. Torn between
an overwhelming desire to run and a determination not to disgrace herself, Juliana took the proffered hand. The bare fact was
that she had placed herself under this man's protection, and she
had nowhere else to go. As they crossed the hall, Mélusine's enigmatic smile followed them.

"I noticed you find the representation of interest," Armand
observed casually. "I had it painted to depict what others whisper
behind our backs, that we are serpents in human form."

"That is surely the talk of those who envy your family's success."

Her host laughed. "Very diplomatically put. Are you certain
that you are not a Lusignan yourself?"

"Not in a dozen generations," Juliana answered cheerfully.

"Perhaps we can remedy that. Still, you are right. We pursue
our goals with diligence."

She was guided to the stairs and high into the donjon. *Perhaps
we can remedy that,* he had said. Her apprehension mounted with

every step. If she screamed, no one would hear her. And if they heard her, no one would come to her rescue. A sense of resignation, of inevitability, came over her. At the top of the stairs, Armand de Lusignan unlocked a door and pushed it open. Juliana's heart froze—and then leapt.

It was a library.

Scrolls of parchments in tantalizing disarray spilled from tables and filled the trunks. And there were books. Dozens and dozens of them. She touched the binding of one and another, her fingers leaving smears on the dusty tomes—thin ones and thick ones, bound in calfskin with intricately worked clasps, some graced with gold webbing and semiprecious stones that sprang into fiery light when freed from the coating of dust. Ovid, Livy, Saint Augustine, Plato, Abélard, Boethius, Galen, Horace—a veritable treasury. She turned to her host, not understanding.

Arms folded, he was leaning against the doorframe, smiling a smile as enigmatic as Mélusine's. "You can see how they have been neglected. I was hoping you might consent to resurrect them."

"Oh!" Disregarding the dust, Juliana picked up an armful. "I would be delighted. I haven't seen so many books since Fontevraud."

Armand indicated the trunks. "You may call on any of my clerks to assist you. And you may keep whatever books you wish as a sign of my gratitude. It would please me to know that they are in the care of someone who appreciates their wisdom and beauty."

Overcome with excitement, she hardly slept that night. At the crack of dawn, dressed in a warm gown with her hair tied up in a coif and an apron around her, she laid claim to Armand de Lusignan's library. A couple of servants brought her a brazier, and as soon as the glue melted and the velum sheets were pressed flat, she was ready to wage war on the torn and battered covers. Dawud came and sat by the brazier, playing his flute and sometimes helping her with gluing a recalcitrant book spine.

Every day provided a new challenge and a new adventure. Sometimes she sat there and read to Dawud an interesting passage that caught her eye; sometimes she became so absorbed in her work that hours flew by. That was, undoubtedly, her host's intention. He had filled her mind and her hands with the things she loved. Suddenly, she wished she knew more about Armand de Lusignan.

He was a great lord, of course, and certainly one of the handsomest men she had ever known, but he was much more—intelligent, amusing, yet thoroughly and ruthlessly pragmatic, learned and pleasure loving, bold and brave and chivalrous. *Perhaps we can remedy that.* She snapped out of her reverie. This was silly. She must have come under the spell of Dawud's flute.

Surveying her work, Juliana gnawed her lower lip. She did not know which books she would choose; she wanted them all! Giggling at the wickedness of it, she locked the door for the night. The thought that sobered her by the time she returned to her chamber was that until she reclaimed Rivefort, she had no home for her new friends.

Several days later, tired of the company, Armand de Lusignan dismissed from his presence all except Dawud and Juliana. "You don't chatter aimlessly, my dear," he explained when Juliana slowly resumed her seat.

To hide her confusion, she reached for a wolfhound pup that tottered toward her on unsteady legs, watched by its fierce mother. The other dogs dozed near the fire. In the shadows, Dawud's flute sounded a gentle note. Juliana played with the pup, half-listening to the melody. The pup struggled and whined and she set it back on the floor.

"My lord," Juliana spoke up, startling herself with the sound of her own voice.

Armand de Lusignan inclined his head toward her attentively. Taking a deep breath, she decided to plunge ahead. "Can you tell me about Céline?"

"Of course. What do you wish to know?"

The answer came so readily that Juliana did not have the time to feel mortified. "I was wondering—"

"How he killed her? He didn't. She took her own life."

Her goblet hit the floor, splintering in a thousand pieces. The dogs jumped up, growling. Armand snapped his fingers and the hounds sank down with their noses on their paws.

"I am so sorry. But why would everyone say . . . ?" It was a stupid question, she knew instantly. She crossed herself. "The Lord and all His saints preserve us."

Armand de Lusignan reached for the ewer, filled another cup, and offered it to her. "She threw herself from some height. Suicides cannot be buried in consecrated ground. I granted your husband and his friends reprieve on the condition of this deceit. To save Céline's soul."

Juliana took the cup and drank it all in one swallow. Armand de Lusignan waited and then said, "There is his child at Tillières, I believe."

Juliana noted the change in topic, but gave it little significance. "He says Jourdain is not his."

"And you have a reason to believe otherwise?"

"Of course he is. Everyone knows it. And he killed Hesse for Aliénor, and a boy called Equitan. If I hadn't run away, I know he would have killed me, too."

Her host stood up. "Indeed. You would not be the first woman your husband found inconvenient. I am sorry, you look unwell. I shall call your women."

"Yes, yes, thank you for your kindness."

In her room, Thalia, Erato, and Terpsichore rubbed Juliana's temples with lavender oil, hovered about her with hot towels, and brought her drafts. In the morning, she told them to inform the count that she wished to see him.

Armand de Lusignan waited for her in the hall, holding out a piece of raw flesh from a silver bowl to his white gyrfalcon. The bird tore at the meat, her talons sinking into the glove.

Juliana curtsied. "I wish to apologize, my lord."

"It is I who should apologize. Pont-de-l'Arche does not often welcome such tenderhearted company. We will not speak of it again."

Juliana folded her arms into her sleeves and kept her gaze on her toes. No one could take away graciousness and candor from Armand de Lusignan. "I am afraid I am about to sully your image of me."

"I don't think that is possible."

"The Countess de Valence is spying on you, sir."

The falcon bolted the last of the offering. Armand de Lusignan regarded Juliana with an inscrutable expression, his eyes dark like those of the gyrfalcon. He smiled slightly. "Is she, now? For that, how can I be of service to you, Lady Juliana?"

"If you could prevail on King Philip . . . I want Tillières restored to me."

The Count of Rancon said nothing, devoting his attention to the bird. Dear Mary, she was not good at intrigues, not good at all—nowhere in the rank of the Lusignans or the Countess de Valence. Armand placed the bird on her perch and pulled off his gauntlet. Juliana watched him, apprehension gnawing at her. He poured two cups of wine, took one, and handed the other to her. "My dear Lady Juliana. To our alliance against the Duke of Normandy and your husband."

CHAPTER 35

Fortress of Rivefort, Normandy, Autumn 1201

Traveling to Nevers and back with a coffer full of coin sacks did not sit well with Bodo, Hugon de Metz, and the five men-at-arms. They had been ordered by Jehan de Vaudreuil to deliver it to the lady Juliana, who resided, their instructions stated, at the Countess de Nevers's estate. Having found no Lady Juliana in residence, only the estimable Lady Sabine, they rode back to Tillières with their burden and a message from the countess for their liege.

Knowing how it was likely to be received, on the return journey
they had drawn lots to choose who would inform him of the news.
Metz had lost.

"And the lady Sabine said to tell you, my lord," Metz continued
to stammer, "that she was going to tell the duchess that you seem
to have"—Metz searched for aid from his companions, but none
volunteered—"misplaced your wife."

Having delivered the ill tidings, Metz stepped back. My lord
Lasalle had returned from Paris in a foul temper, but since the
news of Erhard of Hesse's fate at the hands of their liege had
reached the viscounty, not a single, solitary man dared as much as
grumble within the Viscount of Tillières's earshot. The result was
that more than half the men were eager to take up his unexpected
offer to serve the Venetians. At that particular moment, however,
the viscount was interested in only one thing.

"Are you telling me, sir, that my wife is not at Nevers and that
she has never been there?"

"Yes, my lord." Metz decided to face his fate like a man. He
withstood a blistering glare before he and his companions were
dismissed.

Vaudreuil arrived in the hall in time to hear the worst of it.
Between the arrival of the new men and his souring relationship
with Ersillia, he had forgotten to send the coffer to the lady Juliana until several weeks later. "Guérin? I've heard. Christ. This is
my fault."

Lasalle wrenched at the trunk's padlock. "Bloody hell! I should
have known. Anne lied to me. God rot her, she lied to me!"

"But where would . . . ? Oh God." Vaudreuil crossed himself.

Fortress of Pont-de-l'Arche

Under the gaze of the sprite Mélusine, Armand de Lusignan
handed Juliana a parchment. She unrolled it. It was a charter

confirming the honor of Tillières to the lady Juliana de Charnais. Attached below the meticulous signature of Philip Augustus, King of the Franks, his seal attested to the document's validity. Juliana could not believe her eyes. "But my lord, I have not done anything to prove my loyalty to the king."

"You will." Armand de Lusignan gave her a confident smile. "You will."

Juliana sighed. "I don't know how I can ever thank you, but I don't imagine my . . . Lasalle will relinquish the viscounty once he sees this."

"You are not going to show it to him. In the spring, Philip and John will go to war. When Philip's army arrives at Rivefort, you will appeal to Lasalle's men. I understand it has received a new garrison of men recently. Their loyalty to your husband is not yet forged." He brushed away a strand of her hair. "You will offer to double their wages. With your bailiff's help that should not be difficult. Why do you think they are called mercenaries?"

The touch, as much as the words, sent shivers through her. She looked away. Armand de Lusignan was right. It could succeed. It had to. "I have to return to Rivefort."

He backed away. "Take as much time as you need, my dear."

Juliana curtsied deeply, tucked her charter into her bodice for comfort and as a reminder, and wrapped herself in her cloak. Outside, Richieu waited for her, ready to resume his duty of guarding her. Richieu was a Norman with a perennial scowl and a gnarl of flesh where his left ear ought to have been. Rumor had it that an opponent had bitten it off in a fight. Other rumors held that Richieu had gouged out the other man's eyes.

Juliana did not care for either one of her guards, but she was glad that Armand had charged them with her safety, because she knew that they would never dare to disobey him. Nothing, however, prevented them from teasing and tormenting Dawud, throwing away his cane and spinning him around in their callous version of blindman's bluff. She had chastised them severely the first time she caught them at it, but she knew that in her absence they would bedevil the Saracen.

The sound of Dawud's flute came from the saddlery, where he must have retreated from the weather. Juliana motioned Richieu to stay put and pushed at the door, squinting into the dark interior of saddle stands and horse trappings. "Dawud? Oh, there you are."

He sat at the far end, cross-legged as he did ordinarily when he played his flute for her, wrapped in his hooded cloak. Juliana had heard that tune before, one of Ventadorn's airs about a love-struck knight's devotion to his fickle lady. Juliana tapped the Saracen's shoulder. "That is an appallingly dreadful song. I can't imagine you picking up such rubbish when—"

The cloak flew away along with the flute. She opened her mouth to scream, only to have a wad of cloth shoved in it and a cord wrapped around her wrists. "Now, why would you take such a silly thing so personally, love?"

The glint of an earring, a flash of white teeth, and eyes the color of peridot.

"Awghhh!"

"Breathe through your nose, mouse."

"My lady?" From the outside came Richieu's voice.

Lasalle grabbed her wrists and swung her toward the door, reaching it just as Richieu crossed the threshold. The sound of a boot against wood was followed by the sound of wood smashing cartilage. Blood sprayed everywhere. Richieu went down.

She would be sick; she would choke—

"I said breathe through your nose." Lasalle shoved her to the floor and dragged Richieu's senseless bulk into the saddlery.

"Lady?" Dawud!

She clawed at the gag, rolling frantically along the floor. The Saracen stepped through the door, his staff catching on Richieu's body, sending him stumbling. Juliana froze, expecting Lasalle to dispatch Dawud next, but when Lasalle turned to him, it was only to retrieve his staff and return it to him. But Dawud shook his head vehemently, urging Lasalle on in rapid, low words she did not understand, pressing the staff back into Lasalle's hand.

Sweet Lord Jesus, Dawud was Lasalle's accomplice! What a fool she had been. Juliana wished Dawud could regain his sight, just for a moment, so that she could look him in the eye. Since Dawud could not, she glared at Lasalle in impotent rage.

Lasalle slung his sword across his back and donned Dawud's cloak. Setting Juliana on her feet, he wrapped her cloak around her, arranging the hood to conceal her face. Grunting furiously, she stomped and struggled to shake it off. Pulling up his own hood, Lasalle jerked her to him. "None of that now. You are coming along."

They stepped into the gray daylight. She would have run, except for Lasalle's hand on her elbow. With horror, she realized that no one would pay them any attention, since it would appear that she was guiding the slightly stooped Dawud through the fall mud, not that she was being steered to where a restive black courser waited.

"My lord viscount, welcome back to Pont-de-l'Arche!"

Lasalle dropped the staff and threw himself and Juliana against the curtain wall. Her hood fell. Above them on the allure stood Armand de Lusignan, smiling a quarter smile. Next to him, a dozen archers aimed their arrows at them. And on the ground in a semicircle, Pont-de-l'Arche's guards drew nigh. Beads of cold perspiration raced between Juliana's shoulder blades.

"Don't be a fool, my lord," Armand de Lusignan called down. "Let the lady Juliana free and surrender your sword."

Lasalle swore, hesitating, his arm around her neck—and then he dropped his cloak and bent his knees to reach into his boot top. A knife's blade flashed before her eyes. Oh Lord! But the blade only slipped between her bound wrists; with one upward stroke, the rope fell away. Juliana backed into the crowd and wrenched away her gag. Thank God for Armand de Lusignan's vigilance!

"Very wise, my lord. Now your sword."

This time Lasalle complied without hesitation, his sword ringing out of its scabbard with that distinct sound of menace. He dropped to one knee and held out the sword to her, flat across his palms. "Perhaps you would care to do the honors, Lady Juliana."

She glared at him, the vile taste of the gag in her mouth. Of course she had been taken in. How was she to know that he could play a flute? A flute! Mary, this time he was not going to humiliate her. Her fingers gripped the corded hilt.

Someone shouted a warning. Alas, unlike Hugh de Bourgh, she did not have the presence of mind to heed it. Lasalle yanked.

It was a childishly simple move, like a fisherman landing his catch. She collided with him as he was rising and was spun around, one of his arms around her rib cage, the long edge of his sword under her chin. Juliana dared not blink. Lasalle looked up at the man on the allure. "Which one of us would want to see the lady Juliana dead, my lord?"

Armand de Lusignan did not reply. He did not move. He was looking over her head at Lasalle and so intently that for an instant Juliana was certain she was not at all the count's prize. And for a fraction of that moment she expected that Armand would let his archers release their arrows—at her. Silence fell over the bailey. After an agonizing pause, Armand gestured the archers to stand down.

The sword blade was removed and she was hauled to the courser and tossed into the saddle, Lasalle behind her. He reined the courser into a backward, stumbling retreat along the curtain wall, then under the raised portcullis. No one challenged them. Once the courser's hooves struck the drawbridge, Lasalle swung the horse around.

CHAPTER 36

Fortress of Rivefort, Normandy, Winter 1201–Spring 1202

Armand de Lusignan was right. In her absence, Rivefort had acquired a new garrison, but little else had changed, other than the absence of Hermine and the girls. Juliana missed them.

She was once again Lasalle's prisoner. He never mentioned Pont-de-l'Arche, but Juliana sensed that Lasalle's hatred of Armand de Lusignan sprang from an association whose exact nature she did not wish to probe. She had more immediate problems to ponder. How long would it take her to learn the mercenaries' vulgar tongue? She had the coin to bribe them—Lasalle's blood money, stored in the strong room. No doubt he had it placed there as a reminder that her return to Rivefort was only temporary. The recalcitrant portcullis was not her problem; her concern was Jourdain, who was growing up, fretful and feverish from his teething—and Gwenllian.

Unlike his dalliance with Ravenissa, Lasalle did not bother to keep his relationship with the Welsh girl private. He treated Gwenllian as if she were the mistress of Tillières rather than his latest fancy, even giving her a palfrey and a groom to look after it. Juliana was surprised that he did not hand Rosamond to Gwenllian. And whenever Gwenllian wished to ride, Lasalle would provide her with a couple of knights, and sometimes he went with the girl, just the two of them.

Juliana noticed that even though Gwenllian was retiring with the others, she was not retiring with Lasalle, nor he with her. He called her Gwen, and laughed when she mispronounced her Norman French, to which she would reply in a torrent of Welsh too rapid for him, chastising him with her spindle. Juliana wished she could find some particular fault with the girl, but in all honesty she could not. Around Gwenllian, Lasalle's temper flared less often, and sometimes he gave in when she pleaded on behalf of some hapless mercenary.

The girl also seemed to care for Jourdain, and Juliana did not wish to afford Rivefort the spectacle of their lord's wife contending with his current mistress over his bastard by his last mistress. When Gwenllian was not with the boy, she busied herself elsewhere. She could spin thread as fine as Juliana had ever seen, and her embroidery far surpassed Juliana's own. It did not take much to recognize that Gwenllian had not been brought up as a common drudge. Perhaps because of that, Rivefort's people gave the girl a wide berth. While some men had tried to gain Ravenissa's favors, none of them bothered Gwenllian. If Juliana had not known better, she would have said that the girl had bewitched Lasalle, as well. What if she bewitched him enough that he would consider replacing his rightful wife with her?

Juliana entered the hall at suppertime wearing a murrey-dyed wool gown and white wimple. The guard at the landing dropped his pike. Every pair of eyes turned to her, hands suspended halfway to mouths, and then the gazes went to the head of the table. Lasalle sat with Gwenllian next to him; their heads were bent together intimately. They looked up. Squaring her shoulders, Juliana picked up her skirts and marched to the high table. Around her, one could hear the proverbial pin drop. Mumbling excuses, Vaudreuil sprang up and offered his chair to her.

Juliana ignored it and gestured to the men to resume their meal. Gwenllian said something to Lasalle and stood up. Lasalle's hand restrained her, but Gwenllian shook her head, withdrawing. It would have been enough for Juliana, but Gwenllian suddenly paused in front of her and curtsied.

The men gaped. The gesture took Juliana aback as well, so much so that she could not find a gracious way to acknowledge it. Fortunately, Vaudreuil took charge of the girl, accompanying her to the door. The men watched it all with the attentiveness of village gossips. Lasalle squinted at them down the table and they buried their noses noisily in their trenchers and wine cups. Juliana took Gwenllian's seat and did not mince words. "I don't care if you sleep with every woman in my viscounty, sir, but I will not vanish while you flaunt them and try to deprive me of my rightful place."

Someone handed her a cup and brought her a fresh trencher. The new men were watching her. She acknowledged one of them. His name was Berolt le Roux, and he came from Cotentin, he had told her. Berolt and Harpín de Peyrac appeared to have struck a fast friendship. Juliana took a sip of her wine. Mayhap she would not have to learn Kadolt's clumsy language after all.

Lasalle leaned back in her father's chair. "*My* viscounty. And didn't Anne tell you? One doesn't sleep with whores. One doesn't kiss them either. It costs more."

"And you are obviously a frugal man. Is there a point to it?"

"One calls for the baring of the body; the other for the baring of the soul. That is more than the encounter warrants."

"I don't know how I could have lived without that knowledge."

"I don't either. Did d'Erlée sleep with you?"

"We've bared our bodies as well as our souls." Since she was becoming accustomed to Lasalle's ambushes, she thought she had handled that one rather well.

The corner of his mouth twitched. "It cost you Tillières."

"I found the experience well worth it."

Lasalle speared himself a stewed pear, missed, and tried again. "Well worth it? You ought to find yourself another lover, mouse."

She took a sip of her wine. "I have."

He missed another try. "Armand?"

She answered him with a smile she hoped would make him truly wonder. "You don't suffer from a paucity of women, my lord. Why would you begrudge me the Count of Rancon?"

Lasalle examined her as if he were facing an opponent of unknown quality. "The count and I have always begrudged each other."

Was that a boast or an admission? "Dear me," she replied, smiling back, "a wolf begrudging a wolfhound? The duchess might have contrived to make you a seigneur, but she could not bestow on you manners, taste, or cultivation."

"Dear me, Sister Eustace. You are taken with him. It must be that pedigree going back to Mélusine."

She ignored his jab at the Lusignans' purported ancestress. "I have learned that one should strive for the highest, not the lowest."

"Your marriage may be to the low, love, but you've still committed adultery."

Her temper began to simmer. "Speaking of which, should we expect the arrival of Jourdain's sister this spring?"

Lasalle looked amused. "I doubt it. Besides, I told you, he is not mine."

"Of course. Your word against Ravenissa's and the entire viscounty's. Even Armand believes it."

"Ah, does he?" He said it very quietly, his hand closing on her wrist. "Then I'd better hurry up negotiations with the sisters at Villedieu. The prioress tells me the chapel needs a new roof. They are most anxious to welcome you. Unless you swear that you are free of trespass against your marriage vows. Are you?"

She wrenched her hand away. Two dozen sisters lived at Villedieu, an isolated priory several hours' ride from Tillières. A former lord of the viscounty had given the nuns a plot of land in atonement for some egregious sin. She tried to fight a delaying action. "I need to settle my affairs."

"Your affairs are settled. Isabel de Clare has your chits and your matchless Mistress Hermine. As for Tillières, I understand Thibodeau is frightfully efficient."

"I want to take Jourdain with me."

"I'll take care of that little brachet."

"The duchess—"

Lasalle stood up, threw down his napkin, and leaned to her ear. She sat there like a hen frozen on a tree branch. "Not even Aliénor can protect you against a charge of adultery."

A few days later Gwenllian and Jourdain disappeared.

Juliana would have suspected Lasalle of carrying out his earlier terrible threat to drown the boy. Excepting their conversation at the supper table, however, Lasalle had not shown the slightest interest in the child. When informed of the news, he did not seem particularly surprised, sending only a couple of men to search. By then, a warm spell had thawed the snowy ground, obliterating any tracks. From Thibodeau, Juliana learned that some tinkers had arrived in Tillières and departed abruptly.

Desperate, she pleaded with Lasalle to let her ride with the men to look for them. He was fond of Gwenllian and surely selfishness, if not pride, would make him want to reclaim her. He left her kneeling in the middle of the bailey. Juliana went to Vaudreuil. Avoiding her eyes, he told her that as much as he regretted Jourdain's disappearance, he had his orders and would never do anything contrary to them. Juliana sought out Ersillia, but the girl told her that she and Vaudreuil had fallen out. Ersillia would not say why.

Desperate, Juliana sent her people to make inquiries behind Lasalle's back, to watch the roads, to buy information. Berolt le Roux came and told her that he and some of the men had ridden out on their own but found nothing. She spent the stormy days curled up in her bed, dry-eyed. Edith wanted to put away Jourdain's toys, but Juliana would not let her.

Several weeks later, news came that the woodcutters had found the remains of a small child under some brambles not far from Rivefort, half-eaten by foxes. There was no sign of anyone else. They brought it in a basket to Father Cyril, wrapped in a piece of sacking. Juliana ran to the chapel to see, but the priest and Louis Pavilli would not let her. She shoved them out of her way and saw a patch of black hair on a child's skull and eyeless sockets, and the tatters of a green tunic, the same tunic she had made for Jourdain from Edith's old gown.

Someone helped her to her room. She sat the entire night in the middle of her bed, unable to form a single thought. Somehow she lasted through Father Cyril's service the next day, attended by the whole of Rivefort except for its master. Whispers had it that he was distracted by a new woman at Master Diceto's stews in Tillières. Juliana had the remains buried with all of Jourdain's toys under the chapel floor, returned to her room, and cried herself blind.

❧

Gaudete, gaudete Christus est natus, ex Maria Virginae, gaudete . . .
    In the holly-and-green-bough-decked chapel, among the other attentive worshipers, Juliana sang with them those words of praise, but to rejoice in the birth of the Holy Child so soon after

Jourdain's death made the season a terrible trial. After Christ's Mass, the weather warmed again, revealing black furrows under the thinning ice crust. In the arbor, her roses' last glory clung to the branches, destroyed by the first frost. Some of the buds had barely opened.

She sat on the bench among the withered roses. She, too, felt her life had been blasted away before it could ever bloom. Had she married Sir Antoine Crispin, the old man her father had chosen for her, she would have been the mistress of her own house; she would have had a doting husband and, if God willed it, even a child of her own. Since she had left Fontevraud, everything she grew attached to was torn away from her, and now Jourdain would never grow up to understand that she had tried to make up for his neglectful mother and indifferent father. She drew Philip's parchment from her apron and unfolded it. She should give up her struggle. Perhaps she should—

"More plots, love?"

She cried out, scrambling for the parchment as he whisked it from under her elbow. He held it up with one hand, keeping her at arm's length with the other, letting her twist and struggle until he was done. She backed away, fists in her skirts. Lasalle shoved the parchment inside his tunic, turned, and strode away.

She picked up her skirts and ran after him. "Wait! What are you going to do?"

"Burn it."

She tried to outpace him. "Very well, you go ahead and burn it! Do you think King Philip will forget who rightly owns Tillières? What are you going to do with me?"

"When the roads dry, you are going to Villedieu."

They reached the bailey just as three riders there were dismounting. Their mule carried a leather trunk, and their horse trappings looked familiar; it was Joscelyn de Cantigny, Armand de Lusignan's helpful young knight. Next thing she knew, she was crushing de Cantigny's hand and whispering, "Tell the count his plan is naught!"

De Cantigny gave her a confused look, but recovered for a

proper bow for Lasalle. "My lord Tillières, my lady Viscountess. I have come on the orders of my liege, the Count of Rancon."

He nodded to the two men to unstrap the trunk. The stable hands passed torches around, lighting one off the other. De Cantigny lifted the trunk lid. The trunk was filled with a dazzle of jeweled hues and gold leaf.

"My books! Oh, sir, my heart's gratitude to the count." Juliana reached to pick up one of the volumes, but Lasalle shoved her aside so hard that she almost fell—and seizing a torch from one of the passing servants, he flung it into the open trunk.

She screamed.

The pitch-soaked taper sprang into ravenous flames. "No!" She would have thrust her hands into the flames to save at least one of the precious works, but Lasalle hooked her around the waist and swung her away. She kicked and screamed and clawed.

The trunk and its contents blazed like a bonfire, thick, sooty smoke spiraling toward Heaven. The flames lit up the bailey and the stunned faces of the visitors and Rivefort's dwellers. They could do no more than watch the flames reduce the books to charred clumps. And above it all, Juliana heard a voice, a madwoman's voice, shrieking into the winter sky.

She was told afterward that it had taken three men to carry her to her room. Edith and Catalena, the blacksmith's daughter who had replaced Hermine, looked after her while her fever climbed and broke several days later, as suddenly as it had come. She was told that Joscelyn de Cantigny and his companions had left Rivefort after exchanging unpleasant words with the Viscount of Tillières. In fact, Vaudreuil and Rannulf de Brissard had had to restrain the young man when he tried to draw on Lasalle.

Her strength returned rapidly, but it was as if all her feelings and emotions had burned away along with the books. She could even think about Jourdain without bursting into tears. The only thing she knew was that she had to reach Pont-de-l'Arche before Lasalle sent her to Villedieu. Rivefort would have to be turned over to King Philip by some other means.

The opportunity for her escape came in the new month when some dozen students stopped at Rivefort. From her window she watched Donat greet the bereted, black-cloaked young men. Surely this was a sign from the Almighty. She raced to the kitchen for her egg basket, but this time instead of going to the hayloft she snuck into Donat's room above the stables. Underneath the window, on the bottom of his trunk, she found what she was looking for: Donat's attire from his student days.

That night she did not sleep a wink. At first light she pulled the beret to her ears, filled the toes of one of the young squire's boots with wool, and tied a coin purse around her waist. Over it all, she threw a cloak one of the knights had left in the stables. When the yawning students came out to claim their horses, Juliana slipped among them with a hammerheaded nag. No one noticed her, even though she was certain that everyone must have heard her galloping heart.

CHAPTER 37

Fortress of Rivefort, Spring 1202

On the still half-frozen field Lasalle knocked le Roux's sword out of his hand in two vicious swipes, and booted him into the mud. Vaudreuil swore under his breath and tried to catch Lasalle's eye. Lasalle removed the sword's point from le Roux's neck. The rest of the men, silent through the whole thing, went to hoist le Roux to his feet. There was no other way around it. "She is gone," Vaudreuil said, blowing on his cold-stiffened hands.

Lasalle swung his gaze toward the battlements. "How in the blazes could she?" He was striding toward the drawbridge, Vaudreuil behind him. "She can't be. Where is the *serjeant*? I'll cut off his ears. Mount up the men and spread out. She'll head for Pont-de-l'Arche."

Vaudreuil halted. "Christ, the horses. I thought it would be a good time to shoe them."

Lasalle gave him one of those looks. "Donat, how many horses are ready?"

Donat sprang to attention. "Five. And Rosamond, my lord."

"Get my saddle on her and saddle everything with shoes on it!"

A few short moments later, wearing cloaks against the drizzling fog, they burst across the drawbridge, Brissard and two men down one path; Lasalle, Vaudreuil, and Saez on the other trail. Rosamond quickly outdistanced the others to reach the slush-filled path into the forest. A tunnel of moss-draped trees swallowed them. Surely the mother abbess could not have got very far?

He heard it before he felt it—the whistling rush and the bone-shattering impact. Rosamond's front legs splayed like a broken hobbyhorse's. She went down and he with her. Something smashed against the side of his face, turning the world red.

"Guérin? Guérin!"

Experience had taught him that surrendering to pain in front of one's men was not a judicious thing to do, so he locked his teeth and tasted blood. He felt it too, spreading under his hauberk. Vaudreuil's face, upside down, looked bleached. He tried to grip Vaudreuil's cloak. "Ju-li . . ."

They caught up with her far enough from Rivefort that she had begun to think she would make it. She could not hope to outrun them on her nag, so she reined in and waited. They surrounded her, Rannulf de Brissard and two men she did not know. Brissard took hold of her reins. "You are coming back, my lady—my lord's orders!"

And back they went, galloping into Rivefort's bailey and into a chaos of running men and servants, barking dogs, shouts from the grooms, and steaming horses without riders, including a bedraggled Rosamond.

"*Sacre Dieu!*" Brissard lifted Juliana from the saddle and pushed her ahead of him. In the doorway she collided with Kadolt. He stepped aside when he recognized his lady in that indecent attire and waved toward her chamber, shouting something at Brissard. She tried to dig in her heels, but the old fighter propelled her ahead of him into her room—a room someone had transformed into a slaughter pen.

The source of all that bloody grime thrashed like a speared eel on what used to be her immaculate bed, against all efforts to restrain it. She saw it all, but it was a half-forgotten vision that caused her to cross herself. Her mother on that bed, a thick red pool spreading under her hips, sweat-heavy hair trailing across her breast. She had seen it before Edith had whisked her away, a sight her eight-year-old eyes did not comprehend until years later. But that was not her mother on that bed.

Her first thought was that a horse had trampled him. And then she saw it: a crossbow quarrel driven into his flank, the blood from the wound soaking her bed linen and ruining her mattress.

"My lady, you are needed here!" Vaudreuil's voice cut through the roar in her ears.

She could not—she would not—move.

"He'll die if we don't stop the bleeding!" It was Vaudreuil again. His voice had an edge she had never heard before. It was fear.

He will die. He will die . . . and she would be free of him. In one morning, the hand of Divine Providence had raised her from a pit of despair and restored her to her rightful position as Rivefort's gubernatrix, the liege lady of that man's stiff-necked garrison. And as such, she would leave to them that mangled thing on her bed.

She took a step backward, and another. Two men held his arms; two others flung themselves across him. It did not work. Pain and shock fueled his strength.

"Get her . . . out!" He nearly wrenched from their grasp. Blood sprayed the headboard. Juliana clamped her hands over her mouth. Lasalle howled.

Hugon de Metz eased his grip. "His arm's broke."

Frigid calm spread through her. Her mother had died like that, just bled to death and no one could stop it.

"You," Vaudreuil shouted at the men, "find more sheets. Bring wine, vinegar, and splints." Juliana opted to make herself scarce along with them, but Vaudreuil snagged her by the scruff of her neck, stuffed a fistful of wadding against Lasalle's side, and slapped her hand on top of it. "You press, hard."

She did. Blood instantly soaked the wadding. The crossbow bolt was as thick as a man's thumb, two hand spans long, the leather flight wings decorated with blue dots. Under her hand, Lasalle quivered like a spooked horse.

Vaudreuil worked fast, unbuckling Lasalle's sword belt and pulling it from under him. "Where are the sheets? Spread those covers on the floor. You," he shouted at the men taking up the doorway, "get him on the floor." They did, with dispatch. The back of Lasalle's head cracked against the planks. "Gently, you oafs. Will you make yourself useful, woman?" he yelled at her.

She tried to keep Lasalle's head from sweeping the floorboards. His hair was stiff with blood. When they lowered him to the floor, she ended up on her knees, trapped by his dead weight. She would have extricated herself, but Vaudreuil shoved her back. "Stay where you are. I don't want him fighting me like that again."

Lasalle stirred, dirty, heavy, and reeking of blood. She kept her hands away from him. "I can't hold him—"

"No need; he'll hold for you." Vaudreuil cut her short, sorting through her unscathed linen.

She wanted to scream. "He won't! *They* couldn't hold him, why would—"

"Our male pride, Lady," Vaudreuil answered her with lashing irony.

"Pride? I know all about your pride. You have your pride; we bear the consequences!" There, she said it in front of a room full of—them.

"You know nothing, Lady." Vaudreuil wrung out a rag and pressed it against Lasalle's oozing cheek. "Guérin? Guérin! Look, Juliana is here. We have to cut out the barb."

Lasalle's teeth clicked in short shivers.

She looked too—at Brissard, for help, for something. He scowled at her. Cowed, Juliana did as told, praying that her revulsion would not show on her face. Good Lord, this was not her fault—none of it.

Lasalle sucked in his breath, his body jammed up against her, rills of blood and sweat coursing down his face and throat, his eyes fastened on her as if she were his salvation. She sat there, holding on to him until her arms went numb. Lasalle did not struggle; except for the labored rasps, he did not make a sound. Somewhere into the ordeal he mercifully lost consciousness, his body slumping from her.

"Done." Vaudreuil exhaled. "The rest of you, out."

The men shuffled out of the room. Vaudreuil mopped the blood that had pooled in the vale of Lasalle's belly, folded more cloth, and pressed it against the gaping wound. Mother of God, surely there was not a drop of blood left in my lord Lasalle? With her numb-fingered assistance they secured the linen with several windings of a torn sheet around their patient's middle.

Juliana got to her feet. Her eyes smarted. Giving her a silent look, Vaudreuil held out something to her. It was a blood-caked quarrel with a wickedly barbed tip still attached. "This is a bodkin arrow. It is meant to kill."

She bit her lip and looked away. Vaudreuil opened the door and called for the servants. They stumbled out with the ruined bedding and brought fresh sheets. Brissard came back with a couple of men, and this time they very carefully replaced their master on her bed. Vaudreuil returned to his usual collected self, sending the men to reassure Rivefort that its lord was still alive and to prepare to leave as soon as the horses were ready.

Juliana supported herself against the bedpost. "Where are you going?"

"Whoever did this is out there, and I intend to find him."

She stood herself upright. "Perhaps it was an accident. Perhaps a poacher . . . or revenge. Or Hesse's friends. Or the Count of Rancon."

"Not Armand, never. It takes a skilled marksman to hit a rider through the trees."

Juliana picked up a bloodstained towel and dropped it again. "He can still be there, waiting."

Vaudreuil chuckled. "No doubt an arrow waits out there for some of us. I told you, remember, what to do with wounds."

"You can't leave me here! I don't know what to do. I won't."

"Now, there is a difference," he said, spacing out each word, "between not knowing what to do and not wanting to do it. And since you are his wife, he's all yours—pride, vice, and warts."

"I am not his wife."

Vaudreuil looked at her with no particular surprise and piled the bedcovers on the unconscious man. "Then it is time you did something about that."

Blood rose to her cheeks. Mary, was there no end to this? First Anne and now Vaudreuil. Their patient whimpered, eyes half open. Vaudreuil ignored him and instructed her how to tie the splints. He stepped back to examine their handiwork. "That should do it. We'll be back in two or three days."

"Days? You won't find anything in this weather. Good Lord, he didn't search that long for Gwenllian and Jourdain. He could have. You all could have! I am not going to—"

"Clean him up. When the wound scabs, soak a towel in hot wine and keep it on the scab until it loosens, then wash it with more wine. Don't let the wound close over. If it starts to bleed, press hard until it stops, like you did before. Give him some broth when he wakes up. Force him if you have to. If it gets bad, tie him down or get him drunk, but don't dose him with anything. And be careful about that arm. The rest you can figure out yourself."

"He will die, surely, with all the blood he's lost."

Vaudreuil's hands came on her shoulders, hard, drawing her closer, his eyes as black as the Devil's. He was not teasing her. "If you don't do exactly as I tell you, your husband's wound will fester and he'll die. And if I come back and see you've let it happen, I swear that I will hang you from the donjon for all of Tillières to see, and then I will let the *routiers* have their run of this place till there is not enough left to wall up a privy. I'm leaving Brissard here. He has orders not to let you set foot outside this room. Do you understand, Juliana?"

She nodded. She understood perfectly.

"Excellent," Vaudreuil said, and left his lady in the middle of her wrecked bedchamber.

In the bailey, confused and glum-faced men waited for him. Behind them, the servants pressed in a silent circle. Peyrac brought Vaudreuil's horse. Vaudreuil swung up and lowered his voice. "Take le Roux and find the Countess de Valence. Tell her to hurry to Rivefort and to wear something fetching. She is coming to a funeral."

Juliana's first thought was that men in the knightly ranks seldom lived to a ripe old age. Lasalle could have died in a tourney, a bor-der raid in Wales or Scotland, in Poitou or Normandy, in a brawl over a toothsome tavern wench, or he could have become the ca-sualty of a broken saddle girth. Of course, the man had other ideas, which was characteristic of his bloody-mindedness. He had decided to die right here, in her bed. And if he did so because she had failed to succor him, they would murder her and waste her viscounty. The irony of it did not escape her.

In what followed, at least Lasalle was cooperative. And even that, Juliana noted bitterly, was not his doing. He was barely con-scious, and far too weak to resist. After a few timid dabs she discov-ered that congealed blood and mud acquire all the properties of horse glue. Concluding that more forceful means were necessary, she brought her soap bowl from her strong room and, teeth set, proceeded to scrub Lasalle's inert, grimy body as if it were already a corpse. It helped to think of it that way.

By the evening, with the candles flickering, she unwrapped the bandage and, wincing, pulled off the wadding. She did exactly as Vaudreuil had told her, pressing a rag soaked in heated wine against the wound. The scab dissolved and the bleeding resumed. She stanched it with more wadding, to her unutterable relief. He was still too lost in a fog of pain to give her trouble, but by the morning that had changed.

She attempted to get some wine into her delirious patient, and worrying that he would break open the wound, she called Cata-

lena to find her mother, who was known for her nursing and mid-
wifery. Goodwife Margaret arrived with Rannulf de Brissard. They
held Lasalle while Juliana sacrificed another sheet and, with a
ruthlessness that would have made him proud, tied him down.
After they were done, Goodwife Margaret brushed back Lasalle's
wet, matted hair with a gesture more tender than Juliana would
have expected. Brissard peered over Margaret's shoulder, his
mouth in a grim line. Catalena was wiping her nose on her apron.
They looked like the three Fates.

Goodwife Margaret curtsied to Juliana. "I don't wish to meddle,
my lady, but if he goes on like this he will wear himself to death; I
am certain of it. I've nursed enough men as bad as this." She
sought confirmation from Rannulf de Brissard.

The old knight nodded with another accusing scowl at Juliana.
"I say call the priest."

Juliana looked wildly at the portentous faces. "He can't die!
I swear by the Virgin that I have done everything Sir Jehan
told me."

Margaret picked up a towel and patted Lasalle's streaming
face. "We can try, my lady. Sleep heals. I have my own recipe; it will
have his lordship sleeping like a babe. Jourdain used to—" She
crossed herself. "Well, it is in the hands of the Almighty."

It took some effort to get Goodwife Margaret's recipe into Lasalle, but they did. Pleased with the results, she assured everyone
that the dose would put the entire garrison to sleep. When they
left, Juliana dragged her chair to the bed and rested her head on
her folded arms. She ached as if she had been stretched on the
rack.

Although it seemed only an instant later, she was awakened in
the middle of the night by a raving maniac in her bed fighting against the restraints as if possessed by a demon. Good Lord,
she had forgotten! Vaudreuil had told her not to dose him with
anything.

"Oh God, Céline? Don't . . . don't . . . don't!"

Jourdain had sounded like that once, lost and terrified, when
she left him alone for a moment. She could not imagine Guérin

de Lasalle as a child. To her, he had sprung fully grown, like Pegasus from Medusa's severed head. She drew closer. "Shhh. I am here."

"He'll be back. . . . He'll be back. . . . Céline? Céline!"

She touched his cheek to comfort him. With a sob of terror, he jerked away as far as the bonds allowed. Something was very wrong. She did not try again, but she could not resist asking, "Who will be back?"

Much like her previous questions to him, this one went unanswered. But raging fever and a brew of poppy, henbane, belladonna, and Lord only knew what else had undermined the carefully built bastions of lies and deceit. By dawn his voice had worn down to a barely audible whisper, for which Juliana was eternally grateful. Still afraid that he would remain floundering in a world of phantoms and macabre hallucinations, she searched Hermine's stores, found her cache of raisin wine, and made him swallow a good deal of it.

Guérin de Lasalle spent four days tossing in a sweat-drenched delirium, and Juliana spent them in sheer panic. She kept everyone away until the effects of Goodwife Margaret's nostrum wore off, then gratefully accepted assistance in looking after her patient, but firmly turned down offers of more of Margaret's recipe.

Vaudreuil and his men returned, without their quarry. Vaudreuil was in a foul mood. Wringing her hands, Juliana backed into a corner and prepared herself for the verdict. "Sweet Jesus." Vaudreuil wrinkled his nose. "He smells like the inside of a tun. What did you give him?"

"Raisin wine. Is he going to die? I did everything you told me, I truly did!"

"Die?" Vaudreuil wiped something from his eyes. "He is not going to die. Not now, anyway. The wound drains clear. Cheer up, Lady Juliana. Your husband will be back on his feet in a score and you'll wish you could keep him strapped down and soused." He pointed to the window. "Look there, Peyrac found new troops."

In the bailey below, a fair-haired lady in a fox-trimmed riding cloak was dismounting from a white palfrey with the entire Rivefort garrison surrounding her, all agog. A moment later, she held Juliana in a perfumed embrace. After that, she cast a quick glance at Jehan de Vaudreuil, who returned a soldierly bow, and turned her attention to the black-stubbled, hollow-cheeked occupant of the bed.

Lasalle opened his eyes. When he could focus them, two faces greeted him. On one side of the bed stood Juliana de Charnais, hands clasped to her flat front, fear, relief, and resentment on her thin, sallow face. On the other side were the snowflake-dusted, pink cheeks of the Countess de Valence. He closed his eyes. Dear God, he had died and gone to Hell after all.

CHAPTER 38

Fortress of Rivefort, Normandy, Spring 1202

L ent came and went and the weather remained bitterly cold. At night, lean and ravenous wolves stole into the villages to raid the sheep pens. Their howls made the hair stand up on the back of men's necks. Vaudreuil and the men spent the short days following the bloody tracks, sometimes returning with a carcass or two of the great gray animals. They impaled the grinning heads on pikes outside the gate, where swooping crows picked them clean.

Soon, equally lean and ravenous villeins straggled to Rivefort to beg for food. Juliana provided whatever she could, gathering castoffs, dishing out lentils, pea porridge, and bread, but her charity crossed the limits of the men's compassion, and Jehan de Vaudreuil was elected to speak to her about it.

"My lady," Vaudreuil began, "you can't feed every starving beggar at the gate."

"They were not beggars when they brought in the harvest. If

my lord hadn't plundered their stores to fill Rivefort's, they wouldn't be starving." She faced Vaudreuil in the bakery, where he had made his appearance to remonstrate with her. "If I could, I'd have those good-for-nothings he brought to Tillières on siege rations!"

Taken aback by her outburst, Vaudreuil spread his hands. "Lady, Rivefort's stores must be filled if we are to hold against Philip's attack!"

"Ha!" Juliana brandished the bread peel under Vaudreuil's nose. "A likely story. The way John, Philip, and the Lusignans carry on, they could dance around one another till the crack of doom."

That much was true. The Lusignans continued to clamor for justice, still delayed and denied to them by their duke. Nearing the end of his patience with the maneuvers of his fickle vassal, King Philip had demanded of John Plantagenet as sureties Falaise, Arques, and Château Gaillard. Since the three constituted the most important fortresses in Normandy, John naturally refused, sending instead across the stormy December seas Archbishop Hubert Walter of Canterbury to plead his cause to Philip.

News had just reached Rivefort that the good archbishop had calmed the waters enough for John to travel unmolested to Aquitaine, where he concluded a treaty offensive and defensive with the King of Navarre. With John Plantagenet's latest coup, it was extremely unlikely that Philip would undertake anything as hazardous as attacking Normandy. In fact, Philip's reply to John's thumbing his nose at him was to call another meeting, at Boutavant. Sir Antoine Crispin would be hosting two crowned heads.

With Vaudreuil routed, Juliana pounded the dough, burning with indignation at how she had been treated by Lasalle's loyal guard. Undoubtedly, Vaudreuil also told on her to Lasalle.

Juliana had been more than happy to hand over that man to the Countess de Valence as soon as she arrived. The arrangement caused no end of gossip, but Anne de Valence was neither the merry widow Ravenissa nor the Welsh witch Gwenllian, and as a result, the speculations soon shifted from the health of the Viscount of Tillières to the future of the Viscountess. Oddly enough,

Lasalle's misfortune harbored a silver lining. Anne would have to help her see a way out of her muddle. After all, she was in it largely thanks to Anne's schemes.

My lord Lasalle's temper returned well ahead of his strength, driving Anne's women from the chamber in tears. Summoned by their distress to Lasalle's bedside, Anne shoved him back, straightened the covers, fluffed up the pillows, and informed him that if he did not behave, she would have him tied down. Watching it all through a cracked door with a basket of fresh laundry under her arm, Juliana smiled to herself. Unfortunately, Anne noticed her presence and pulled her into the room.

"There you are. I believe the patient could use some distraction. Would you mind taking a turn? Perhaps a round or two of dice would help pass the time." The patient and his newly recruited nurse must have had the same expression because the Countess de Valence laughed, and, dropping the dice in Juliana's hands, she exited.

Anne had had the fireplace stoked and lavender sprigs tucked about the bed. Tidied and comfortably warm, the chamber no longer smelled like an infirmary.

"I don't suppose Anne left you anything for stakes," Lasalle snapped with the tone of someone who regretted he could not order the hanging of both of his nurses.

"No." Juliana took her seat with that comforting thought. "We could just play."

Favoring his forearm, Lasalle sat himself up. "That is very boring and I am already bored to tears." He pointed his nose at a tray. "For your wimple. Don't worry about losing it; you look remarkably like Hermine in it." He motioned toward the headboard. "Hand me my sword."

She did. He pressed the scabbard to him with his splinted arm and appraised the length of the blade. "On second thought, I doubt you have the proper appreciation for the value of it."

They could compel her to save that man's life, but no one could make her entertain him.

"The pommel is base metal; the grip bone, likely horse shank threaded with twine—none worth more than a half a mark, but the blade is Saragossa."

Lasalle gave a rusty whistle. "Ah, Sister Scholastica. How did you know?"

"I can tell a piece of bone and a string. Father said Saragossa forges the best blades. I imagine," she continued in flagrant disregard of all her resolutions, "that you've saved up for it by refraining from kissing harlots."

He snapped the sword back into the scabbard. "In truth, mouse, my father gave it to me and made sure I knew how to use it, and the whores too. Pour me more wine, will you?"

In truth! Uncertain, as usual, what to make of him, she picked up the dice and proceeded to win not only Lasalle's scabbard and sword but also his hauberk, his shield, his charger with all trappings, and the entire *routa*. She credited her extraordinary streak of luck to Lasalle's increasing inebriation and his tightly bandaged wrist. She staked Rosamond against Lasalle's wager of Jehan de Vaudreuil—and won! Now how was she going to tell the Chevalier de Vaudreuil?

"You have nothing else left to wager, my lord," she told him happily. Until this silly game, she had not been able to best Lasalle at anything.

He helped himself to another cup and saluted her with it. "I do. Til-Tillières. In exchange, you'll wager one night of passionate ab-abandon in my arms, once this bloody splint comes off, but feel free to imagine that I am d'Erlée or Armand or—"

She shoved the tray away. The nerve of the man! "You know you already own all that is mine, sir. You've had your distraction. I must go to my duties."

"*Sacre.* I'll settle for an hour. I'll even give you my pledge for this place if it means so much to you!"

This time, she failed to mind her temper. "I should have known. Nobody loses six wagers in a row. You would cheat, wouldn't you, even when you have nothing to lose? Never mind. You've had your distraction for the afternoon."

He pushed himself up, defensiveness crowding out hilarity. "I swear on the True Cross, I wasn't cheating. It's my father's fault. He couldn't win at games of chance either. Christ, you're the only sore winner I've ever known, Sister Eus—"

She slammed the door behind her. After that, she avoided him on every occasion. He had Anne to fill his arms, splint or not, for an hour or a night.

Spring sun had thawed the snow, but not the frost between the Duke of Normandy and the King of the Franks. At the end of March, John appeared at Boutavant, but King Philip refused to enter Normandy. The king and the duke met at Gouleton instead, with John the one to venture into French territory. No agreement of substance followed, and Philip ordered John to appear at Paris after Easter before an assembly of French barons to answer the Lusignans' charges against him.

John demurred, claiming that as the Duke of Normandy he was obliged to attend Philip's court only when it met on the frontier between the two lands. Philip replied that John was being summoned not as the Duke of Normandy but as Philip's vassal, the Duke of Aquitaine, the Count of Anjou and Poitou. It was a clever legal maneuver on Philip's part, and after much deliberation, John's advisers persuaded him to submit to the summons rather than risk the forfeiture of his lands to his aggravated suzerain. As surety for John's appearance on the appointed day, Philip demanded—and this time received—two lesser pledges. John chose Boutavant—and Tillières. And now Tillières was at the mercy of the fickle John Plantagenet, a man many had begun to call John Softsword.

The bellicose preparations contrasted jarringly with the burst of spring. Larks trilled above the greening fields, ewes nursed their lambs, goose and duck hatchlings waded in the puddles, and snowdrops, primroses, and violets overwhelmed Rivefort's garden. Donat had asked for permission to marry Catalena after the harvest, and Juliana gladly gave it. She wished she would hear from Saint-Sylvain. Aumary had been moping since Paulette's departure, and not even the men's rough teasing could rouse him.

Now that Lasalle did not require their care, Anne devoted her attention to Juliana. She persuaded Lasalle to allow them outside the bailey, and so on a breezy day, they walked to the edge of the lists, making themselves comfortable on pillows and quilts.

Juliana had brought her sewing basket, and set to work on her embroidery. From their vantage, they watched Lasalle and a handful of men try to break to saddle a dozen horses milling about an enclosure. Despite his still splinted forearm, Lasalle was in the middle of it. Anne tossed the pincushion at Juliana. "Guérin's hale and hardy, you can see. I shall leave in a few days. What are you going to do with him?"

Juliana nearly pricked her finger. "Do with him?" She had several thoughts on that subject.

"You said that he was going to send you to Villedieu before all of this. Do you think he'll change his mind now? You know what you have to do."

Threading her needle, Juliana tried to keep her hands from shaking. "I can't. Besides," she said, offering an irrefutable defense, "he doesn't show the least interest in me in that way."

Her husband's mistress laughed. "Kiss him, silly!"

The needle went into Juliana's finger. "Merciful Mary."

"I hope you are praying to Mary Magdalene. Our Holy Mother has little to offer your problem."

Juliana crossed herself. "Please, don't jest about such a thing."

Anne sat up and brushed the shining waterfall of her hair over her shoulder. "All you have to do is hold still for him, and you only have to do it once. If you wish, think of John d'Erlée or Armand or anyone else. Good Lord, that's how I managed my matrimonial duties with my first husband. Get him alone and drunk enough, and kiss him as if you mean it."

How ironic that Anne would offer the same solution as Lasalle. So this was what marriages were all about. "He . . . he'd just laugh at me."

"Don't be ridiculous." Anne assumed the tone of a master instructing a misguided pupil. "He's been without a woman for one day too many, and about now he'd bed your Goodwife Margaret."

"But I thought—"

Anne raised her brows. "I have yet to entice a husband to commit adultery under his wife's roof. Just remember, Guérin can't abide bashful virgins."

Juliana winced. "But he will know, won't he?"

"By the time he figures out you are one, you won't be. Smile, don't panic, and pretend you've done it all a thousand times. Guérin hardly needs directions. As for you, I'll tell you what to do. And I do hope you are not a giggler, like the Angoulême girl."

Anne de Valence was a fount of knowledge about men in general and Guérin de Lasalle in particular. Mistress Hermine's instructions paled in comparison. Listening with burning ears, Juliana found her mind wandering, but she did conclude one thing: Lasalle would need to be inebriated practically into insensibility to accept a substitute of herself for the astonishingly accomplished Countess de Valence and the legions of his other women.

A few days later, much to the distress of the Viscount and Viscountess of Tillières, the Countess de Valence departed from Rivefort with her carts, her maids, and her men. With their departure, Lasalle unleashed his latest round of destruction on Tillières. He had the villeins called up and sent them and the mercenaries to ax and burn the mature trees in the vicinity of Rivefort and along the Avre. Whatever did not burn, the men carted into the spring current. At the end of the day, the mercenaries returned exhausted and cursing, their hands raw, covered with soot and smelling as if they had labored inside the smokehouse.

Everyone was appalled by the wanton ruin, the reason for which no one could fathom. Juliana would have tried to plead with Lasalle, but she knew that these pleas, like all the others, would fall on deaf ears. She kept herself busy, trying to avoid the one decision she knew she could not avoid much longer, not if she wanted to keep Tillières safe from John—or, perhaps, from Philip.

~⦊~

Lasalle found her in the bakery, where she was sweeping the floor, and announced that if she wished, she could accompany him to the horse market at Tillières. The offer came so unexpectedly that Juliana was about to reject it, but she changed her mind. It was impossible to try to seduce that man with everyone at Rivefort watching them avoid each other. There was her room, but since his convalescence, Lasalle never came near it, and moreover, it carried the vivid memory of their first encounter. Lasalle's horse trading could take several days. They could be forced to take lodging in Tillières. Perhaps there . . .

Pondering what had prompted Lasalle to grant her this parole, Juliana filled a wineskin with Hermine's wine, pinned her wimple securely, and dabbed a few drops of Anne's perfume on her temples. She looked at herself in her mirror. Good Lord, it would never work. He would laugh at her, humiliate her thoroughly, and ship her off to Villedieu.

Alas, her plan, like all the others involving that man, failed miserably. By the late afternoon, Lasalle had acquired a dozen horses and several mules. Riding at the rear of the troupe on the return journey, Juliana fell farther and farther back, scarcely believing the destruction Lasalle had wrought on the countryside. With every clip of Rosamond's hooves, she endured half despair, half relief that her plan was once again postponed.

Lasalle reined in next to Rosamond, his voice grating with irritation. "Don't lag, Eustace. You are not stealing away this time."

She kicked Rosamond into a trot. "I am sorry. I am a little tired, that is all."

He took hold of Rosamond's bridle. "Don't sniffle. You shouldn't have come. Very well, we'll rest for a while. Don't move from this spot."

He spurred his horse to catch up with Vaudreuil and cantered back by himself. They walked their horses along the riverbank until they came to an old willow the axes had missed, its branches drooping to the ground. Lasalle went to tie the horses to a crooked piece of driftwood. She took her wineskin and spread her cloak under the green shelter. She loosened her wimple and ran her fingers through her hair. Her hands were shaking.

He returned and threw his cloak next to hers and himself on

it, snapped off a willow twig, and proceeded to grind it between
his teeth, eyes closed. Juliana pulled the stopper from the wineskin and took a sip. *Get him alone and drunk enough.* Perhaps she
should be the one inebriated into insensibility.

"My lord?" she offered timidly.

He opened one eye, spat out the twig, and took the wineskin. In
no time he downed half of it. When he finished, he kept the wineskin and closed his eyes again. She looked away. Much of the flood-
water had receded, leaving a tangle of charred branches piled
against the bank. She gave him another glance. Without opening
his eyes, he took another swallow. He was drinking the skin dry.

She waited and worried herself until she could not bear it anymore. *Kiss him as if you mean it.* Whatever happened, surely it could
not be such a torment? She squirmed herself low on her elbow,
leaned over, and kissed him. No, not truly. Her lips barely brushed
his—and she knew immediately that she had failed to follow
Anne's instructions.

He did not move. He did not seem to breathe, but then he
opened his eyes. From under his eyelashes, he looked up at her
mouth, as if there was some fascination in it, and from there his
eyes swept her face. Under the bowl of spring leaves, his eyes had
the depth of a sea cove, a treacherous sea cove.

She was withdrawing, crushed in defeat, expecting him to
laugh in her face. Instead, his hand fastened on the nape of her
neck, bending her to him. The edge of the splint grazed her skin.
She flinched even though she had promised herself that she would
not, no matter what. Cursing softly, he eased up and raised himself, holding her captive with his good hand.

"Juliana . . ."

He breathed her name and then his mouth claimed hers. Her
wimple fell. Anne had been right. The hunger in him was that of
a man who has been without a woman one day too many, who
did not care that he was embracing a bone-and-gristle, freckle-
faced Sister Eustace with a kink in the bridge of her nose and
tangled hair of unfashionable color. She could taste the wine and
the bitter bark of the willow.

He kissed her as if he meant to obliterate her, reaching for the laced seam on the back of her gown. The ties gave. He slipped the gown from her shoulders and down her arms and he got to his knees and made her stand up, and he drew the garment past her hips until it dropped around her feet and she stood there shivering in her chemise. She let her fear wash over her, let it drown out all sensation except purposefulness.

She smiled and touched the prickly, marked cheek, and he turned his face against her hand and kissed her palm and the pulse on her wrist, and by the time she thought to take to her heels, his clothes had joined hers, and he pulled her down with him and wrapped them both in his cloak. He wanted to strip her out of her chemise, but she stammered out something about the cold. He grunted in her ear and slipped his hand under it. She submitted. He did know what he was doing, although providentially the splinted arm made it awkward for him, which made her own novice clumsiness less glaring. She tolerated this outrageous intimacy only for Jourdain, for Tillières, for . . .

Kiss him as if you mean it, Juliana. She closed her eyes and intertwined her fingers in his hair, which curled in the lee of his neck and shoulder, and kissed him as if she meant it. With an agonized groan, he gave in to her. Slick and hot, he weighted her down. Her hands went along his flanks. He sucked in his breath, holding back. She did not want him to hold back. She wanted it over with. The amethysts of Richard's cross scored her breast. They should not be doing this while he was wearing it; she should not let him. . . . Her knees came up.

"Holy Mother," he ground out between his teeth.

The memory of that first night deluged her. She could not surrender like this, not to him. She had prepared herself to yield willingly, honorably, to someone who would cherish her and her gift, not to someone who would use her as thoughtlessly as a beast. She opened her eyes to plead and saw that had she stuck his poniard in him, he would not have cared. With equal parts desperation, rage, and revulsion, she squeezed her eyes shut and heaved up against him.

He went into her like a sword.

Pain sliced through her. She bit down and tasted blood, but received no quarter, so she held for him, as Anne had told her. It did not take long either, just as Hermine had said. And when he finally collapsed on her with a spent sigh, she was too dazed and battered to move. Holy Mother, this was far more brutal than she had imagined.

After a while his breathing leveled and he raised his head and gave her a languid kiss that went through her, again. This time she made a sound against it, no more than a whimper, but he drew back, leaving her. His eyes flew open—and she knew that she had betrayed herself after all.

His pupils narrowed. "Jees—" He shifted, his hand probing between her thighs. She cried out and tried to evade him. His face turned the color of chalk. "Holy Mother!"

She shoved at him and he rolled off her as if boneless. The effort sapped the last of her strength. She wished she could become an anchoress, sealed off from the world. Rid of her burden, she stared through the green canopy at a patch of the sky. Why did blood and pain mark the passages of women's lives? For Eve's sin, of course. But for all of Anne's instructions, the answer she wanted at that moment was why women put up with it. If they were reputed to enjoy this, there had to be something Anne had neglected to tell her, or they were all different from herself. Yes, that must be it. But it was done. Thank God she would not have to do it again. She ought to make herself proper. It had been not only a painful but also a rather grubby experience, but she had survived it.

She sat up and pulled down her shift. Oh dear. She should get the stains out. No reason to alarm Catalena. The river. She would say that he threw her in. They would believe that. The man next to her remained supine, the cloak twisted around him, arms flung out. He did not say a word, which was just as well. She got to her feet, gathered her flimsy attire, and limped toward the bank.

The Avre's icy waters brought her rudely to her senses. She stood on a sand spit, her teeth chattering. She dipped the stained fabric into the water and rubbed it together. The water diluted the bloodstains, turning them into mud stains. She nearly burst into tears. Infuriated at herself, she scooped up a handful of sand and waded deeper into the stream.

"Juliana, don't!" A vise grip seized her elbow, hauling her back.

She cried out and whirled about. He was standing there, stark naked except for Richard's cross and that annoying earring.

"No!" She shoved him with a force that took both of them by surprise. He flapped his arms ridiculously to retain balance, failed, and went backward in a geyser that drenched her from head to foot.

"Oh!" She tried to cover herself. "Look what you've done! What do you think I was going to do? Drown myself? Good Lord, do you think I would damn my soul forever over that? It was nothing, it was hardly worth—"

"Jul—" He spewed out a mouthful of water, the current swirling around him. He reached for her and she swayed back, nearly losing her own balance.

"Don't touch me!" She caught the fabric billowing around her thighs. Dear God, she might as well have been naked. After all she had allowed him, this was the last straw. "I can manage. I am not helpless, you know."

Fighting the current, she waded to the bank as fast as she could. Once there, she wrung a dirty stream from her chemise. It was hopeless. Her fingers were numb. All of her was numb. She found her shoes, tugged on her gown, and made an effort to tie the laces. It did not work. She flung her mud-and-grass-stained cloak over her gown, untied Rosamond, and, gritting her teeth, wiggled into the saddle.

The mare took toward Rivefort at full gallop, nearly running off the road a worried-looking Jehan de Vaudreuil, who was riding in the opposite direction. His rounsey shied and Vaudreuil hollered at her, but Juliana did not stop. He would soon find out that she had done what he and Anne had told her to do. That ought to make the two of them happy.

CHAPTER 39

In the loft above the stables, where she had retreated from the rain, Juliana set down her egg basket, sat on the hay pile, and hugged her knees. A week had passed. The sun rose, the birds chirped, rains came and went, and everyone carried on, oblivious to the monumental event that Sister Eustace had surrendered her maidenhood to her own dissolute husband—and at her own instigation.

Since then, she had walked around Rivefort in a fog and would burst into tears when no one was about. It had to stop. Nothing that had happened to her would have been any different under any other man. She had to do it only once. Just let him try to put her aside now.

She had not seen him since that day. She wished she could say that he avoided her for chivalrous reasons, but that was far from the truth. According to bailey gossip, everyone had concluded that the master, in the absence of his mistress, had decided to enforce his long-neglected matrimonial rights to his wife and apparently overcame her objections by giving her a thorough thrashing, either before or after, in which the Avre somehow played a part.

Juliana gathered that not a few of Lasalle's men heartily endorsed his methods, no doubt anticipating that he would divert some of his more onerous attentions from them to her. Rivefort's wives offered more diffident opinions. Such speculations aside, the gossip proved to be correct on one account: After an unpleasant exchange with Jehan de Vaudreuil, Lasalle had ridden that very afternoon back to Tillières, where he took up residence in Diceto's stews, got drunk like a Fleming, and remained so for an entire week. Now he was back at Rivefort. Perhaps she could hide out in the hayloft for the rest of her life.

Outside, the rain ceased pelting the roof and the sun broke through the clouds. Idleness is the enemy of the soul, Saint Benedict said. Juliana tucked up her skirts, climbed down the ladder, handed her basket to one of the servants, and told him that she could be found in her garden.

No sooner had she reached the flowerbeds than he found her about as welcome in her sanctuary as the plagues of Egypt. Bleary-eyed and bristle chinned, Lasalle lowered himself onto an over-turned bucket, his elbows on his knees, his head between his fists. "Disciplining weeds, Sister?"

Keeping a safe distance from him, she shoved the tip of the spade under a dandelion. "You ride, fight, and hunt, sir. I garden."

He took a deep breath, no doubt in place of something he truly wanted to say, and said instead, "Juliana, we have to speak of this. I am seldom entranced by lust and drink at the same time." He raked his fingers through his hair. The splint was gone, but his voice was bound with anger. "Yours was a stupid idea, but it was my fault. Next time you'll not find me that distracted."

Her foot slipped from the spade. "Next time?"

"Of course next time. You've made me make a botch of it the first time!"

One would think that the quarrel had struck my lord Lasalle in the head. "You've done all that is required. As you've said, once is all that is necessary. I'll fight your petition and the bishops will sustain me, like they sustained Queen Ingeborg when Philip tried to cast her aside. In her case, once was all that was necessary as well."

Lasalle had her by her shoulders, spinning her to face him. "You don't know what you have done, woman! And whose idea was it? Yours? Anne's? Aliénor's?"

Juliana broke his grip. "What does it matter? You can't undo what you've done. Any midwife will testify to that."

He took a step back, stumbling over her wattles to sit back on her bucket. She tried not to pay him further mind. That proved to be difficult. "Since you are so clever, what will happen to your precious Tillières if you find yourself with child?"

The question was as sarcastic as the questioner. She shoved the debris into a pile. "That is impossible. Everyone knows that the woman has to enjoy the congress to conceive."

Lasalle hooted in derision. "Ha! That again? All that vast knowledge from a nun."

Blessed martyrs, the man was a pest. She should have let him die. Lasalle shook his head in exasperation. "It becomes better the more you try."

That was surely the silliest thing she had ever heard. She went back to her flowerbed. "I see. Like burning one's hand and coming back for more? Are you speaking from personal experience, my lord?"

"I am told," Lasalle snapped back. "Christ, girl, you may as well learn to enjoy the windfall of your determination."

"Enjoy? It was awkward and embarrassing and . . . and it hurt. I won't do it again. Ever!"

"You silly, ignorant chit." He tried to keep his temper. "I am telling you, it doesn't have to be that way. Anne said you kept me alive. Why, then?"

"Vaudreuil," she reminded him.

"Vaudreuil?"

Oh Lord. She was certain that Jehan de Vaudreuil had told him of his threat, and now there was no way out of it. "He said that if I didn't, he would raze Rivefort and hang me from the keep."

He squinted at her. "And you believed him?"

"Of course. He would do it too. He is just like . . . like you!"

"You saved my life because of this"—he waved his arm toward the curtain walls—"this pile of rocks?"

"Why else would I?"

"Christian charity, good works. Hell, you'd show more compassion to a goat with gout!"

Of all the ungrateful things to say. She wished she could strike this arrogant, deceitful man. "Compassion? That is something I can ill afford. Don't preach to me about compassion. When have you ever shown compassion to anyone?"

He was looking at her as if she were a madwoman, and she did not care. "Do you think it was easy for me to come to you as I did? It wasn't. I was afraid. You can't ever imagine how afraid I was. But I did it, for this pile of rocks!" The words came in a heedless rush. "You took Jourdain from me. You never cared about him, but you took him from me just because you could. For that, I'll never let you have Tillières. Never! You'll have to kill me—aaah!"

He was shaking her. "Stop it, damn you, stop it!"

"You let go of my lady, you wicked blackguard!" Someone barreled between them. It was Edith, a bundle of fury in a black gown.

He released Juliana. She collapsed onto her basil.

Edith stayed, comforting her sobbing mistress well after her master had stormed out of the garden, having wrenched the new gate from its post.

CHAPTER 40

hat . . . what are you doing here?"

She backed away from the door she had unbolted. From the soft sound on the other side, Juliana had expected Catalena.

Lasalle shut the door behind him, shoved the bolt in place, and unbuckled his sword belt. "A wife is subject to her husband, and since you've so cleverly bestowed that honor on me, love, go ahead—screech, scratch, and run, but I'll drag you back." He nodded toward the window. "I have my reputation to uphold. There are hefty wagers on whether I can swive you without beating you."

Before her horrified eyes he left Richard's cross on the table and got himself out of the rest of his clothes, strewing them about her room, transforming it, much as he had her life, into chaos. She noted that he was back in fighting shape—long-legged, lean-flanked. She flushed and fastened her gaze on her toes.

Taking her by the elbows, he drew her to him. Her body went wooden. He untied her nightcap, pausing to remark how hideous it was. She took a breath. "You can't—umph—"

He silenced her with a deeply drawn kiss, his free hand under her buttocks, scooping her to him. "I can't now, woman, but give a man a little time. Hmm, now that's better."

Furious, she wedged her palms against the curve of his ribs where the belly caved in. He looked down and grinned. Her face burning, she quickly dropped her hands. "I meant it's Wednesday. The Church says in matrimony we must practice continence—"

"Wednesdays, Fridays, Saturdays, Sundays, saints' days, fast days, penance days, Lent, Christ's Mass. Let's pretend it's Monday and we are not married."

"We'd be committing a sin!"

He reached for her shift's ribbon. "Let's make it something memorable for Father Cyril the next time you confess, love. You've been burdening the poor man lately. Must be sinful thoughts. I had no warning you were such a wicked creature, Sister Eustace."

Her hand flew to stave him off. "No, please. We must not reveal each other to each other. I-I am cold." She tried both arguments, hoping one would dissuade him.

He chucked her under the chin as if she were an insufferably precocious two-year-old. "All right, but for saints' sake, Juliana, don't be so frightened."

"I am not!" That sounded childish and, considering her frozen joints, hardly credible.

He smiled and bent his head to her. She shut her eyes tightly and held her breath. He did not kiss her, not truly, but the light brush of his lips over hers was an unnerving distraction. "Then I presume you are all aquiver with anticipation."

She jumped back, striking at him. "You are doing this to humiliate me!"

He parried her with one hand and turned her chin up with the other. "No, and don't play the ravished virgin. You've had your way with me and I intend to reciprocate. I don't want to leave the wrong impression on women who find themselves in my bed, whether by invitation, design, or accident."

"Good Lord, it's not me at all, is it? It's Céline. Was she not all aquiver with anticipation? Do you think this some sort of penance for driving an innocent girl to take her own life?"

"Juliana—"

"Let me assure you, sir, I have no sinful thoughts after . . . after that. I know how she felt. It was disgusting, degrading, humiliating, and—"

"Christ." Ignoring her, Lasalle pulled the fur cover from her bed and wrapped himself in it, shivering. "You were not as degraded or humiliated as you could have been, trust me, and I am speaking from personal experience." He hunched down by the hearth and added a handful of kindling to the embers. "You'd be surprised how biddable I can be, *midons*. You can ask Anne."

Midons. He must have picked up that one in Poitou. She was not his patroness and he was not her lover, and she could imagine Lasalle biddable only when strapped down securely and in a sottish stupor. None of it was working out the way she had planned, the way Anne had said it would. He was supposed to go back to his whores; he was not supposed to be in her room trying to seduce her. He had to have a reason. "Why? Why the concern, my lord?"

"Because, love, I am done with ditch wives, whores, and courtesans, brothels and barrelhouses, and like Bucephalus, I am willing to submit to the matrimonial curb and bit."

He was talking nonsense. "You must be referring to Bellerophon, sir. And even that is by the mark. He had rejected the advances of Queen Ante and she accused him of attempting to seduce her, and her husband sent him to King Iobates, the King of Lycia."

Lasalle slid forward, his forehead against the skirting of her fireplace. His shoulders shook. He was laughing. At her.

She folded her arms. "I fail to see the jest."

Lasalle looked up, the lines around his eyes deeper. "I know. What I am telling you in my oafish way, Sister Scholastica, is that I've fallen helplessly in love with you, and that I want to teach you to revel in the jousts of Venus as much as others do."

He said it with such precise formality that he surely intended to taunt her. He thought he could make her desirous of the . . .

the act. Holy Mother. He wanted her compliant to get a child on her! He must have overheard her confession to Father Cyril, her ache for something of her own now that Jourdain was gone. Or Anne had told him. And she hated Guérin de Lasalle even more for probing her vulnerabilities, for using them to his advantage.

In her bed furs, he looked like a wild creature drawn to the flames of a human hearth. She felt the tension in him; it was in her as well, a heart-pounding fear and exhilaration, a sense of something seesawing between them. And she reached out with deliberation, as she had at the river when she came to him, terrified and desperate. Her fingertip followed the path of a single drop of perspiration from his temple to the place where the scar began. "But of course." She let her voice dip the way the Countess de Valence's did. "What a silly, ignorant chit I am. That must be why you paid John d'Erlée to seduce me."

He went still, like a thief caught in plain sight. "Ah," he said so softly that she barely heard him over the crackle of the surging flames, "I did not pay him. I thought you might like him. He knows how to woo the virtuous."

Lies came to this man as naturally as breathing. "A pure motivation indeed. I am surprised you'd lack that particular skill, my lord."

This time he smiled, a carnivore's smile, like one of the wolf heads at Rivefort's gate. "You know I do. Anne told you." And before she could answer, he stood up. "Enough. Get in that bed, Juliana. I hate women with cold feet."

She considered fighting him. Her resistance would give her at least a moral victory, but with Lasalle that would count for little. Very well, she had survived it once. It would not take very long and it would gain him nothing. Soon he would tire of her and go to his whores, and they would resume their jousting, as he had so pithily put it, on a more level plain. She gave him a frigid smile. "Go ahead, then."

"Do restrain your ardor, my love. You can confess to Father Cyril that you've sacrificed your marriage bed to forestall my fornications and lecherous desires."

"I don't think any marriage bed would keep you from fornications, sir, not unless filled with a dozen houris with loins of gazelles, bells on their toes, and rubies pasted in their navels. At least I think they were pasted."

Lasalle's eyebrow shot up. "What?"

"Your lecherous desires. I think the poppy in Goodwife Margaret's brew helped."

"Ah." He leaned away. "You are wrong, mouse. Bells on their ankles."

"Wherever."

He laughed, as lighthearted a laugh as she had ever heard from him, and picked her up to drop her on the feather bed. "Shall we paste a ruby in your navel and see?"

She squealed in fury and embarrassment and lashed out at him, but the covers hindered her. He grabbed her ankle and proceeded to give her feet a vigorous rubbing, as if they were his rounsey's fetlocks, his hands creeping ever higher. He was a lithe play of muscles, effortless and gleeful, as if they were children romping feloniously in their parents' bed, as if what he intended to do to her in the end was not such a painful, degrading thing. He assailed her like a hound worrying a hedgehog, and when he had her sprawled under him he sighed with accomplishment and concentrated on her shift's ribbon. The fabric parted. She gripped the mattress. Heat and cold assaulted her. His lips traveled from her earlobe to her collarbone, along the slope of her breast.

"I-I can't. I don't . . . I don't like the light."

He raised his head. "After the last time? You looked like you could do it on the Feast of Ascension."

"Oooh, you!"

"Very well, don't work yourself into a twist, mouse." He braced himself on her knee and flung his shirt over the candle. "There."

The casualness of the gesture jolted her as much as a wayward thought did, just before the candle flame went out. Her mother used to scold her brothers when they visited Rivefort for dousing their chamber candles like that, saying that it was evidence of base manners, learned from frequenting Master Diceto's stews. Juliana had learned to sew by mending those little burn marks, and she had counted them, wondering what prompted them and who Diceto was. And now she knew. How many mended burns were there on Lasalle's shirts, and who had mended them? That woman in Tillières, no doubt, a resident of the very same stews.

He brushed a strand of hair from her eyes. "I can put out the fire as well, but I don't think you'd appreciate it."

"Oooh, that's disgusting!"

"You find most of life disgusting, my love. You ought to try to find some joy in it while you can. There is not much else beyond that."

Good Lord, the man was a pagan. "There is—Heaven!"

He smiled down at her. "So I hear. But sometimes, if you are very fortunate, you can find a bit of it here too, if only for a little while. And sometimes, it is right under your fingernails."

She dropped her hands. The only thing under them was him, and this time she refused to use them. She gave him a skeptical sniffle instead and was about to voice her objections to his latest blasphemy when he cut her short in his usual manner. This time he did not let her distract him. This time she knew what was coming and so she held her breath. *Jourdain, Jourdain . . .*

"Sweet . . ."

He was losing himself in her. Fury choked her. Intent on his purpose, he did not notice. He moved. She flinched.

"Christ, does it still hurt?"

She turned away to bury her face into the pillows. Only a man could ask such an asinine question. What did he think? He was accustomed to consorts as well versed in this as he was, but in and out of bed, she and he were disastrously mismatched, so it hurt about as much as it had the first time, which, if what Anne had told her was the truth, did not make sense. Maybe she ought to ask Anne about it. Maybe she ought to ask those two to show her. Lasalle would undoubtedly like that.

In her absurd position, the thought was more absurd still. She clenched her teeth to stifle a fit of laughter from emotions as raw as a flayed nerve, a laughter that brought tears under her eyelashes.

"Juliana, look at me." Fingertips touched her eyelids. "If you'd only collaborate, it would be better—"

She glared at him. "For whom?"

"Both of us, damn it."

"All that vast knowledge. From one of your whores, my lord?"

"Don't do this." Something flickered under that frown of frustration, but she did not heed it.

"You have my submission. What more do you want?"

Lasalle considered his wife's squared chin, matched by that mother-abbess look in her eyes. He had seen it before, when she had dressed down Peyrac for going after the kitchen maids. Peyrac had skulked away. No doubt the girl hoped it would have the same effect on him, but what he wanted were those fawn's legs around him like they were a moment ago, her nails scoring his back, making those little noises Anne always made when she was about to . . . but the way things were going, he did not hold out much chance of that.

"I don't want your numb submission. And I don't care what Anne or Hermine told you, or what Father Osbert taught you, or what Saint Augustine says or what Saint Jerome says, or whatever else you've read in those silly books of yours . . . bloody hell!" He dropped his forehead against her shoulder, teeth grinding. "I knew you'd do this."

Confused, Juliana raised her head. "What?"

"Talk a man to death!"

He startled her, but his tone almost made her laugh. "I am sorry," she heard herself saying. A moment ago, she had wanted to drive his poniard between his ribs had he kept it close.

"Now you are sorry. It's too late. Next time, ask Anne not just how to lure a man into your bed, but if you must talk, what to say to make him useful there."

He climbed over her and stumbled about, fighting his way into his clothes. "This time you got off easy, woman. Next time, I'll gag you. Bolt the door."

And as suddenly as he had filled her room, he made it empty.
She backed against the headboard. The sheets were still warm
from their bodies. She wrapped the covers around her and stared
into the embers. Now he had everything and wanted more. And
no one could make Guérin de Lasalle biddable, faithful, or for-
bearing, least of all herself, not even if she wanted to.

PART III

MIREBEAU

CHAPTER 41

The sound of their skirmish carried down the corridors of the old fortress, but Eleanor of Brittany did not care.

"Arthur, give it back this instant, you—"

"It's a love rhyme!" Arthur's voice rose and broke in the imitation of a lovelorn poet. "To the Pearl of Brittany, a most excellent lady, the lady of my heart."

Eleanor tore the sheet from her brother's hand. "You horrid little pustule. You've picked up disgraceful manners at Philip's court. Mother will have you whipped."

The boy, strong and tall for his age, tried to twist away. "She will not. Philip promised I shall be the King of England, and no one dares to lay a hand on a king!"

"You are not the king yet, little brother." Eleanor cuffed the boy on the side of his head.

Prince Arthur yelped and tore away. "For that, sister, you'll remain an old maid as long as it pleases me—a shriveled old maid!" He stuck out his tongue and skipped backward toward the open door.

With the parchment in her fist and murder in her eyes, the Pearl of Brittany picked up her skirts and set after him. "You little monster, how dare you?"

They burst into the garden, and in their haste and hurly they did not see the man who stepped into the sunlight. They caught each other short of tumbling at his feet while he regarded them with forbearance, and when he bowed imperturbably and smiled, the sun seemed brighter.

"My lord Arthur. Lady Eleanor."

Eleanor brushed her skirts. Arthur commenced to straighten his tabard before he thought better of it. "Who are you?" he demanded with the belligerence of the young and the wellborn.

"I am Armand de Lusignan," the man said, and this time he did not bow.

Armand de Lusignan announced himself as if no other explanations were necessary. His surcoat, the same dark sapphire color as his eyes, bore the slashes of three silver chevrons. He wore no adornment other than his family's colors, his striking masculine looks, and a simple sword belt with a plain-hilted sword in a black lacquered scabbard. He waited out their astonishment.

"My lord Rancon." Arthur stepped forward and declared loudly as if he had just mastered his lesson in heraldry. "Where are our guards?"

"I sent them away so that we are not disturbed by prying ears."

The voice was clear and resonant and, much like the speaker, instantly captivating. Arthur squared his shoulders. "By what authority have you sent our guards away, Count?"

Armand de Lusignan showed them a row of even white teeth in what looked like a smile. "By the authority of your mother's Council, my lord."

"I don't—"

Eleanor laid her hand on her brother's forearm. "Prying in on what?"

Armand de Lusignan transferred his gaze to her, and Eleanor felt as if she were being examined by a pernickety horse trader. "Why, on our plans to place the rightful king on the throne of England, Lady Eleanor."

Arthur gave her a triumphant grin. "You see, Lenore?"

But Eleanor decided to be forthright about it. "Britain already has a king. I doubt he will vacate the throne for the asking."

Armand de Lusignan laughed, but she had the feeling that he often found amusement at someone's expense. Was she to be the one this time? No, it appeared she was not. "Well put, Lady Eleanor," he said. "We will have to ask him with an army at our back, won't we, my lord?"

The shifting of the Count of Rancon's attention to Arthur took him aback. "See, I told you, Lenore" was all he managed in response.

Eleanor, intrigued but cautious, slipped her parchment poet into her waist purse. "You hold fiefs in Normandy. I have seen you, at Rennes. You brought mother a palfrey as a gift."

Armand de Lusignan bowed. "Your lady mother is a keen horsewoman. I was honored to provide her with a mount worthy of her. I grieve that she is not in the best of health."

Brother and sister looked at each other. Duchess Constance was dying of leprosy. Few knew it, but if the Count of Rancon did, neither one of them would have been surprised. After an awkward pause, Arthur said, "You raise horses, Count?"

This time the Count of Rancon gave the young prince his full attention. "I do. I brought you a destrier I bred and trained myself. Would you like to see him?"

Arthur gripped Eleanor's elbow, his kingdom forgotten. "Did you hear that? Where is he, Count?"

"In the bailey, waiting for you with a new hauberk and shield."

The Duke of Brittany tore himself from his sister's hand and raced toward the garden gate like any fifteen-year-old. "I have to see them, Lenore!"

The Count of Rancon watched with a smile that was neither paternal nor beneficent, and he did not even bother to hide it. Eleanor crossed her arms. "That was unfair."

"Wasn't it? They can be pests at that age. That is why we have them fostered, I suppose."

The Lusignan was certainly a fascinating man, and his family's reputation made him doubly so to her. Nevertheless, she thought she ought to take charge of the situation. "You don't have the Council's permission, do you, my lord?"

"Do you doubt my word, Lady?"

Armand de Lusignan did not look like a man who liked to have his word doubted. Beyond the effect his looks had on her, Eleanor found his self-assurance irritating, the way he had sent off Arthur as if he were a bellows boy; but still, she could not prevent herself from blushing. It was a capitulation, and Armand de Lusignan accepted it graciously. He extended his hand to her and she took it, allowing him to lead her into the garden.

"Your mother is a remarkable woman who has your interests at heart, Lady Eleanor, but you resemble your grandmother, did anyone tell you?"

"No. Mother does not care for Grand-mère and any resemblance to her would not be a point of pride to me, either," she replied coldly.

"It should be. Your grandmother became the queen of two kingdoms and she still rules Aquitaine. No woman can boast more—as yet."

Eleanor halted and pulled her hand away. "What is your purpose in Brittany, Count?"

Armand de Lusignan laughed. "Spoken like the true Aliénor." He grew serious. "I came to inform you that you are about to enter upon your destiny."

"Destiny? My destiny is to live at the beck of a brother who can marry me to his current favorite, his current enemy, or order me to take the veil. Our mother is dying and I am left ignored and ignorant of what is to be my fate. I am an oddity, like a two-faced calf, eighteen summers and still unwed, with no one's thought for my future. My mother has kept away everyone who might have dared to ask. I want someone to heed me!" She stomped her foot, her temper gaining the better of her. Her Plantagenet temper, they said.

The Count of Rancon was not surprised by her outburst. "A husband has already been found for you."

The announcement, as much as the familiarity of the count's address, rendered her breathless. "He . . . he has? What rank? What is his name?"

Armand de Lusignan took her hand to resume their stroll. Eleanor did not object. "That will have to remain a secret until the appropriate moment."

The answer did not please her in the least. "And when is that moment to arrive?"

"When I tell you. I have taken a great risk already in telling you as much as I have. Arthur doesn't know and must not know, do you understand?"

Eleanor stopped, alarm and excitement seizing her. "Would it not be simpler to inform me one day that I shall be wed the next?"

"You are not a common heiress. You carry the blood of Aliénor of Aquitaine and of a valiant ancestry. Your children will rule lands greater than the Plantagenet empire. It will be a Breton one."

"You forget Arthur, my lord," she said to that.

"I forget nothing. Arthur is a healthy youth, but healthier ones have fallen to mischance, like your uncle, young Henry, dead in his prime and no heir left in his pretty French wife's belly."

The stark statement held her back. Armand de Lusignan's expression gave no hint of how she should receive that bald fact. And then she realized that it was left to her. She was, after all, the namesake and the granddaughter of Aliénor of Aquitaine.

Inhaling deeply, Eleanor closed her eyes. Primroses, snow-drops, cowslips, and heady violets had reclaimed the flowerbeds and begun to crowd the lilies of the valley—Our Lady's Tears. It was going to be a wonderful spring. She exhaled. "Tell me about my . . . my husband. Is he handsome?"

"Your women will turn green with envy."

Eleanor opened her eyes, astonished and made once again self-conscious. "Oh!" She laughed, trying to compose herself by falling back on feminine resources. "You presume to know what women favor, sir."

"I do."

The Count of Rancon answered with such casual confidence that she knew it was not a boast. She decided to proceed boldly, like her *grand-mère*. "Are you wed yourself, my lord?"

"No."

"Oh." Perhaps Armand de Lusignan knew more about her husband-to-be than he let on. "Since my women will turn green with envy, will he take advantage?"

"Not if you grant him his due as your husband."

"And I, what shall I receive in return?"

"Your due as his wife."

That answer, nakedly direct, sent blood to her cheeks. She tried to conceal it. "Hmm. No more?"

"As much as a woman, a wife, and a queen is entitled to."

A queen. Her heart skipped. "He sounds like a paragon of *chevalerie.*"

"He isn't."

Eleanor traced a line in the damp earth with her toe. "You seem to know him well."

Armand de Lusignan held a snowdrop in his hand. She expected him to present it to her on his knee as *courtoisie* dictated, but he slipped the stem into the dark plaits of her hair above her brow. "Well enough."

The Pearl of Brittany should have been outraged. She should have sent the Count of Rancon and whatever else he was lord of packing. Instead, she stood there like a scullery maid suddenly transformed into a queen, a true queen. She spoke up like one. "The plan carries certain risk, you've said. Who will protect me?"

He moved ahead of her. "I will see to it that you are protected."

She followed him. Armand de Lusignan had extended to Eleanor of Brittany his assurances, and she believed him. It was all so very odd to encounter someone who would take such liberties, who would speak so obliquely yet so boldly, someone who could even be a candidate for her hand. She laughed lightly to put aside such momentous thoughts, her next question intended to be innocently coquettish, to draw out this man. "And who will protect me from you, good sir?"

He stopped dead in his tracks and faced her. A smile curled the corners of his mouth. Eleanor was staring at it, but before she could complete her speculations, he touched her brow as he had before, gently drawing the snowdrop from her hair. He held it delicately between his fingers—and then slowly rubbed them together. The fragile petals became a crushed smear.

"The Lord Almighty could not protect you from me, Lady."

CHAPTER 42

Fortress of Rivefort, Normandy

he did say next time, and kept his promise. Considering Rivefort's preparations for the chimeric war with Philip, it was a
wonder that my lord Lasalle found the time. But when he invaded
Juliana's chamber a few days later, she was forced to tell him, with
a mixture of triumph and mortification, that her monthly flow
had come.

For the occasion, she put on the nightcap he detested, her
usual shift, her bed wrap, and a pair of socks provided by Goodwife Margaret. She did not want to deal with him. Her back ached
and she felt the cold especially badly. Usually, Hermine or Catalena brought heated bricks, mulled wine, and sympathy. Juliana
considered Lasalle a poor substitute. Upon hearing her news, he
smiled, kissed her fist, and left her alone. But not for long.

His sudden attentions only confirmed her suspicion of him,
but since he had not demanded of her anything particularly alarm-
ing, she had submitted without raising a futile fuss. Only one flaw
marred her reasoning about Lasalle's motives: He was not trying
to get a child on her. He had told her that plainly when she recoiled with shock at what he had done, her ire forgotten. He had
used a vulgar word for this sin against nature, and even supplied
the Latin equivalent. She did not know where he had picked that
one up, but it sounded just as atrocious.

Yet despite her resolution not to oblige him, she was learning.
She was learning that she could make the whole thing as unpleasant for him as it was for her, with paralyzing simplicity. All she had
to do was—nothing. She suspected that underneath that pretended
patience, Lasalle resented her obtuseness, and she calculated that
it would not take him long to become thoroughly tired of her. Instead, he tried to wheedle her.

One night he came later than usual and woke her up with a buss on the back of her neck. She sat up with a gasp. "You are cold and wet!"

He held her back. "Blame the Avre; my horse slipped. I got a thorough soaking, but my, you are dry"—he took a good whiff of her—"hmm, and smell like linen and lavender."

She tried to free her night shift from under him and to stifle his familiarity. "Linen and lye from the laundry tubs. Please, my back hurts."

He flopped onto the pillows with his arm around her and flipped away her nightcap. "Don't be so, now. I've never bargained on a cross wife. Tonight, I could use a warm one."

"You've never bargained on a wife," she reminded him, trying to wind herself away. She did not succeed; he pulled her onto him.

"Ah." He shivered to prove his distress, and tightened his hold. "Certainly not on such an implacable one. Be still, will you?"

She could do little else. Probing fingers found the knot between her shoulders, and from there worked along her spine. She lowered her cheek against his collarbone. How could a dull ache turn into such bliss?

"Siege, storm, surprise, subterfuge, suborning," whispered the voice next to her ear. "They say there are five means of gaining a well-guarded citadel."

Under her, his skin burned. She tried to slide away but he pulled her higher against him. "There is a sixth one. Do you know what that is, my lady?"

A bolt of alarm went through her. "N-no."

"Surrender."

If she kept him talking, perhaps . . . "Whose?"

"That is the true secret, Sister Scholastica. It doesn't matter."

That was easy for him to say; he was not the one required to surrender. Her resentment flared up, along with her apprehension as he hiked up her shift and drew her knees apart.

"No! It's . . . we are not supposed to—"

He laughed. "Deviate from the monastic position. It is considered particularly unnatural, lustful, and earns one several weeks' penance. If used for the purposes of avoiding conception, the penalty is three years—"

"It's—it's—" She slid away from him and wrestled down her shift, searching for words to her outrage. How did he come up with these things?

"Disgusting?"

"Indecent!"

He grabbed for her. "Ah, headway!"

She blindsided him with a whack of the horsehair bolster, and he fell over in a heap. Something in her snapped, as it had that time in the garden, and she hit him again and again; and when he did not counter, she pummeled him with her pillow until it burst into a blizzard of feathers, and continued to pummel him till it was empty of its contents. Somewhere underneath it all was Lasalle, sneezing and wheezing with laughter.

Exhausted and out of breath, she stopped, appalled by her outburst. Goose down circled around them. She did not understand him. Out there, on the lists and in the bailey, he was as removed from her as the constellations. She could not reconcile that man with the one in her bed, laughing himself into hiccups. Why was he like that? Did he think he could make her like it? She backed up against the headboard, hugging the empty ticking to her. Her mother used to warn her that when childish impulses triumphed over adult admonitions, a thin line separated play and pain.

"Juliana?" Spitting out feathers, Lasalle uncovered his head. Seeing her there, he sat up.

She held herself against the shudders of her frayed emotions. "Why do you want me to do this? I could if you wanted an heir, but you don't. There is nothing I can give you that you haven't taken already."

"Juliana, don't do this. We are not used to each other, that's all."

"I hate it!"

He sat back.

She knew it was not the sort of a thing a woman should hurl at a man, particularly not her husband, especially not in their matrimonial bed. She should pretend; she should show proper submis-

sion. "I mean . . . I meant you come here and then you leave, like
I was a . . . a whore. You ought to toss me a *denier* before you go."

He reached out. "A whore? Christ, girl, you are so inept nobody
would pay a *denier* for you. I know. My whores earn their keep."

"Oooh!" A fine testimonial indeed. She knocked his hands
away. "Then why waste your time on bone and gristle?"

He was looking at her wild-eyed. "That's not what I meant!"

"But it is true. I am not Anne. Or Ravenissa. You have your
women. Why come to me?"

"Juliana—"

Defiance drowned her fear of damnation. "No! I won't. I won't
do it."

Lasalle threw his pillow against the wall. "I can't believe it. I
bloody well can't believe it!" He took a deep breath, his forehead
creased with a black frown, but at the end of it he climbed from
the bed. When he returned fully dressed, she drew away, but he
did not touch her. "You won't have to. I forgot that one's whorings
are best left for whores, and I don't have a *denier* on me."

He bowed to her and he was gone. He did not even slam the
door. Juliana wiped her nose. She had won. Surely she had won
something?

CHAPTER 43

April 1202

"My lady, wake up. Something terrible has happened. You are
to come now."

It was Catalena. Juliana leapt from the bed and unbolted the
door. Had someone truly dispatched Lasalle this time? Whatever
it was, she would face it decently dressed. Once in the bailey, she
found it in full commotion.

"Philip attacked. Boutavant is on fire!"

Good Lord. So John Plantagenet had reneged on his word—and King Philip had destroyed the duke's first surety in retaliation. Lord protect Sir Antoine Crispin. She picked up her skirts and raced to the keep. All that time she had feared that she would lose Tillières to Lasalle, and now Philip, whom she regarded as her protector, threatened to destroy it all. She gained the lookout, crowded with men peering toward where dawn's light broke the skyline.

"There, don't you see it, below the horizon?" Berolt le Roux shouted, pointing.

Everyone bunched together to follow his direction with their eyes. The men exclaimed, correcting one another, some sounding dubious; others, convinced. Standing on her tiptoes, Juliana strained her eyes. She came against the edge of something behind her. It was oak barrels, and not empty. The smell of pitch permeated the air. She hitched up her skirts and climbed onto one of them. Over the men's heads, she saw a glow, like a candlewick in a distant window. She blinked. It would not go away.

"Come down before you break your neck."

She nearly toppled off. She had not noticed Lasalle standing next to the barrels, his back against the keep's wall. He reached up to swing her down, his hands around her waist. She did not protest, her mind swept of everything. "Boutavant is burning," she said stupidly.

"I know," he said, his eyes on the horizon.

"My lord?" Jehan de Vaudreuil came up behind them.

Lasalle let her go. "Assemble the men in the hall and bring the lady Juliana," he ordered, then took a torch and ducked into the doorway.

Vaudreuil touched her elbow. She looked up at him. "Boutavant is burning," she said.

Under the hall's tapers and torches, the men argued loudly. Someone rolled in a wine cask and the bystanders split the lid with blows of their sword pommels. Cups were filled, spilled, and passed around.

This would have been her chance to save Tillières and Rivefort—if she still had her charter. She would have stood on that table and shouted to all those men to raise the portcullis to Philip to save their own lives. But she did not have her charter. Lasalle had burned it. She settled into a chair well away from the men, where Vaudreuil had left her to wait like the others.

They did not wait long. The hall door sprang open. Striding through with a clink of their spurs were Lasalle, Vaudreuil, Brissard, Metz, and Kadolt. The noise died and wine cups vanished behind men's backs. The reason was not only Lasalle's appearance, but his—well, his appearance. Juliana stood up.

The gold and amethysts of Richard's cross shone against a tawny tunic made for my lord Lasalle by a skilled needlewoman indeed. The stubble had been scraped with more attention than usual, and his hair, subjected to a wet comb, was for once kept free of his brow. The earring was there, the boots polished down to the gold spurs, his hand on the hilt of his sword. Not only Juliana was taken aback; the men watched the small procession openmouthed. Those closest parted, revealing the cask.

Lasalle kicked it over in passing, spilling the contents into the rushes. He took his place at the head of the table, threw down several sheets of parchment, and looked over his garrison. "The duke's Capetian honeymoon is over. Philip's barons found John in rebellion against his liege, and they declared Aquitaine, Poitou, and Anjou forfeit. Philip put Boutavant to the sword and Rivefort is next. We are at war."

Perspiration broke out under Juliana's fillet. Mutters rose to the vaulting. Lasalle leaned forward, his palms on the table, his attention on each man. "Philip wants nothing less than Normandy, and Rivefort is one of the keys. I prefer not to hand it to him." The mutter subsided. The men exchanged confused glances. Lasalle waited. "The decision about Rivefort's allegiance is mine, but you have my leave to make yours. I am certain that in time the duke will grant a proper reward to those who hold out and hold on to Normandy for him."

Someone snickered, then another. A few grins popped up, followed by a rumble of laughter. "John . . . rewards . . . ha!"

Berolt le Roux stepped forward, his tone unpersuaded. "I am no coward, sir, but Rivefort is not as well walled as Boutavant." Le Roux looked around, seeking support. From the faces and voices around him, he found it.

Lasalle waited for the rumbling to die down. "Boutavant was not prepared for the attack. We are. Most of you will join William Marshal. The rest will hold Rivefort. We are supplied for six months or more if Philip wants to wait."

The turn of events made Juliana's head spin. Some men nodded; others appeared mired in doubt.

"He can't afford to wait. He'll take us long before that!"

Lasalle sought out the anonymous Cassandra. "To take us, Philip needs siege engines and we've cut down most of what he could use. He'll have to haul logs from a distance, and once it begins to rain, he will bog down. He could try to divert the Avre and take out the moat, but he needs skilled men and timber for weirs or he could find himself in a swamp. We have archers to keep any sappers' heads down. Philip will have to decide whether Rivefort is worth it."

The men listened, now nodding in agreement with their neighbors. The tension in the room eased; some of the men offered obscene suggestions to Philip, ribbing one another.

Lasalle spoke up again. "I am reasonably certain there aren't any hidden entrances. Like most of you, I hate surprises in the middle of the night, unless they are the invited kind."

The men laughed, a few casting curious looks at Juliana. She smiled with her lips, her heart in her throat. With his resplendent appearance and solid arguments, Lasalle had turned these fractious men, uncertain and many no doubt frightened, into a confident, even cocky unit. He had their loyalty, and nothing short of a cataclysm would sunder it.

Lasalle returned his attention to the men. "Sir Hugon has a list of those I want to join Marshal and those I wish to stay. Sir Rannulf is in charge."

"Sounds like a life of leisure, my lord, especially if one finds late-night surprises," someone called out. Others burst into raucous laughter.

Lasalle smiled back. "It does. Except that Philip may decide to wait us out after all, and by then he'll be annoyed enough to hang whoever is still alive."

The hall fell silent. Rivefort would come under siege; Lasalle knew it. He had anticipated it for months, calculating what his chances were for holding out. The lump in Juliana's throat squeezed her breath. Rannulf de Brissard stepped forward. "Gather up to hear your names. If you wish to serve, leave your mark; if not, you will be struck from the rolls and released. Bertín le Marle!"

Their names called up, the men stepped forward. They were subdued, but not a single one questioned Lasalle's decision. Each in turn bowed, then left the hall to go about his new duties. Outside, the darkness faded into morning. Juliana sat motionless until the last name was read and the hall emptied except for Lasalle and herself. He was rolling up his lists, his back to her, when she approached him. "Do you truly think Philip would attack Rivefort?"

The parchments under his arm, Lasalle went to the door. "If he does, you won't be here to egg him on, love. Pack whatever will fit into a saddlebag. I'll send you clothes for the journey."

She followed after him. "Clothes? What journey? Where am I going? To Villedieu?"

He did not look back. "I wouldn't inflict you on just any unsuspecting cloister, Sister. You are going to Fontevraud."

To Fontevraud. He was sending her back to Fontevraud. She folded and folded again the small pile of her clothes Catalena was handing her. A boy of about thirteen appeared at the door with a bundle in his arms and handed it to Catalena with an imitation of a bow. "For the lady Juliana. She is to wear them, and this saddlebag is for her too."

"Thank you . . ."

The boy grinned. "Edward de Bec, Lady."

Good Lord. Where had she heard that name? She shuddered as she remembered the bloody platform in Paris. "Edward, are you . . . ?"

"My lord Lasalle's new squire. He says you are not to dawdle." Edward dropped the saddlebag and bounded out of the room.

In the bailey, Lasalle was giving instructions to le Roux and a couple of other men, already mounted and waiting. He held the reins of a roan jennet and looked her over when she came up. She felt like a fool in her guise of a junior squire. She could not tell what the men were thinking because they withdrew to wait at the portcullis. She never thought that she would be leaving Rivefort with the thunderclouds of war gathered over it.

Suddenly, she wanted to ask Lasalle questions—she wanted to ask him a lot of questions, about Edward de Bec and Céline, and . . . "But what about Rosamond?" was all she said.

Lasalle cupped his hand and boosted her into the saddle. "She stays put. Le Roux and the others have orders to get you to Fontevraud, even if it means—"

"I know, tying me to the tail."

He might have been smiling when he checked the saddle girth, but not when he looked up at her. "Rivefort won't fall. You have my word of honor," he said, placing his fist over his heart as he had that time in the garden, offering her the opportunity for a caustic remark.

She could not summon enough wit for one.

He took hold of the jennet's headstall and led them across the drawbridge. The rest of her escort followed. At the end of the drawbridge, he came to her side. He could die. He could die at the end of a senseless siege, hanged from Rivefort's ramparts for the temerity of defying two masters, and Rivefort would be put to the torch. She wanted to reach out and say something, to do something that would give form to the odd bond that this place had forged between them, but her throat went dry. He looked up at her with a chillingly somber air.

"Juliana, if you find out that you are carrying after all, go to Anne at once. She will know how to get rid of it safely."

And before she could think, before she could answer—if there was an answer—he stepped back and slapped the jennet's rump. The roan snorted and sprang away. By the time she slowed the jennet down and looked back, her tears blurred her last sight of Rivefort.

CHAPTER 44

Nantes, Brittany, May–July 1202

At the very instant that the lady Juliana's fortunes were foundering along with the Duke of Normandy's, the opposite appeared to be true for the Breton princelings. The Almighty had freed Constance of Brittany from her dreadful affliction, and for all their natural grief for their resolute mother, Arthur and Eleanor felt liberated from the constraints of the duchess's court and her advisers. Encouraged by his barons, Arthur sought to become more than a puppet in the latest contest between the Duke of Normandy and King Philip.

Shortly before Constance's death, John Plantagenet had called for Arthur's homage for Brittany. At the same time, Philip had commanded Arthur to appear at his court for the same purpose. Arthur gladly complied with the latter, anxious to please the man who was his guardian as well as his surrogate father. Philip received Arthur's oaths and in return took his armies, along with Arthur, into Normandy. As soon as the Franks won a victory worth boasting about, Philip promised to knight Arthur and to pledge his young daughter to him.

Eleanor of Brittany welcomed the unfolding events with excitement. With her brother's fortunes soaring, she easily flattered him into letting her accompany him. The world around her swirled in the tempest of war, ties and alliances being forged and ruptured.

The Pearl of Brittany would wait no longer. She would insist that Armand de Lusignan reveal the identity of her husband, whoever he might be. With the Lusignans proving such a boon to Philip in the south, surely he would have no objections to any alliance they would propose. She was young and beautiful, and she would not ever again endure being ignored.

All they needed now was a victory.

Abbey of Fontevraud, Anjou

Except for the new faces here and there, nothing had changed at the abbey. Abbess Mathilde greeted Juliana with a blessing and a kiss. "Welcome, back, Daughter," she said as if Juliana had returned from a long visit to one of the sister houses. "We are pleased you are well."

Juliana knelt and kissed the abbess's cross. "I am, Mother," she said and took her leave expeditiously.

Anne de Valence exclaimed in surprise and delight when she saw her, insisting that they share the sisters' guest quarters. The Countess de Nevers also welcomed Juliana warmly, commenting on her misadventures and the paucity of correspondence in recent months. It was true, but since Juliana's abrupt departure from Pont-de-l'Arche, the only safe topics revolved around the viscounty's mundane affairs. Anne had already informed the Countess de Nevers of the more recent developments.

"My dear, I am so sorry." Sabine patted Juliana's hand. "That nephew of mine. I so wish I could have prevented your marriage. And do call me Auntie."

To that, Juliana could only curtsy. It was disconcerting enough to think of the Countess de Nevers as Auntie Sabine without being inspected by those Nevers eyes. In the end, she fooled no one at the abbey, since Father Osbert took it upon himself to preach to a new flock of novices on the perils of worldliness, vanity, and carnal

temptation. Despite Sister Domenica's efforts to maintain deco-
rum in the ranks, Father Osbert's sermons caused them to whisper
to one another whenever they filed past Juliana.

From Juliana's stammers and blushes, Anne quickly deduced
that my lord Lasalle had been lured to his husbandly duty at last.
When Juliana let it slip that he had made several subsequent ventures into that territory, Anne caressed Juliana's cheek, the perfect
arch of her eyebrows slightly elevated. "How odd. You don't suppose Guérin figured out that he can get his own back by giving
Tillières an heir?"

So the Countess de Valence had appraised Lasalle's sudden
interest in much the same way she at first had—and Anne, too, was
wrong. Juliana clasped her hands over her middle, relieved that
she did not have to divulge to Anne his parting words, because a
few days after her arrival, she found out that she did not need to.

Anne de Valence smiled and held up a pair of garnet earrings.
"Dress, my dear, and try not to look like a novice. You are a wife at
last, and your presence is requested by the great Aliénor."

Frail but not fragile in mind or spirit, accompanied by her silks,
jewels, and perfume, the dowager queen gave Juliana one hand to
kiss and handed her a packet of parchments with the other. As
usual, her table overflowed.

"Lady Juliana. Sit. We were told that you had returned. Sent by
your husband to prevent you from flirting with Philip and the
Lusignans, I hear. Don't look so guilty, girl. We forgive you, although we cannot allow you to wander about unattended. Read to
me how my son fares against Philip."

Juliana curtsied, sat in the nearest chair, and unfolded the
sheets.

"I am also told the marriage has been finally consummated,"
the duchess said, dripping melted seal wax on a parchment fold,
"and that having a man between your sheets is not to your liking. I
suggest you set aside your maidenly modesty and moral rectitude,
and consider it your duty not to give your husband any reason for
straying from your bed."

"It's too late, Madame. It has not occurred to him to be faithful to me any more than he is to his mistresses, who do not suffer from modesty or moral rectitude whatsoever. I-I am sorry, Your Grace."

"Well, well." The duchess looked at her with pleased surprise. "The kitten has claws. Your husband has felt them as well?"

Juliana blushed fiercely. "On more than one occasion, I am afraid, Your Grace."

"Don't be afraid, Lady Juliana. The world abhors cowards. Who's the woman this time?"

"I believe she is a prostitute at Master Diceto's stews in Tillières."

"You believe? You must pay attention to your husband's affairs, girl. I knew all about Henry's. One never knows when a mistress might be of use to a wife, the Countess de Valence being an example."

"Yes, Your Grace," Juliana answered with the same tone she once used to answer Sister Domenica's castigations. She wanted to ask why her marriage even merited such attention, but the duchess indicated that she did not wish to pursue the subject any further.

And so Juliana once again became Aliénor of Aquitaine's amanuensis, reporting to her the latest footwork of the Plantagenet and Capetian *estampie*.

Since bursting across Normandy's eastern borders, Philip's armies had taken in rapid succession Lyons, Longchamps, La-Ferté-en-Braye, Orgueil, Aumale, and Eu. By early June, with the countryside shimmering in waves of summer heat, Philip had besieged Radepont, only ten leagues south of Rouen, Normandy's capital. After procrastinating for a week, John moved to raise the siege, but Philip withdrew before his arrival. Much to the chagrin of his captains, John offered no pursuit, reportedly waiting for a more auspicious opportunity to strike back. That opportunity, however, fell victim to John's indecision.

It happened at Gournay. Held for John by Brandin, his *routier* captain, and surrounded by marshes and deep moats, the fortress appeared impregnable until Philip ordered the breaching of a dam upstream on the Epte and flooded out Gournay's walls. Magnanimous in his victory, Philip allowed Brandin and the defenders to remove themselves from the soggy ruins. Seizing the occasion along with the fortress, Philip called forth Arthur to receive his reward.

With Arthur's sister and a handful of Breton barons as witnesses, Philip knighted Arthur and invested him with his uncle's forfeited lands—Brittany, Anjou, Maine, Touraine, and Poitou—and formally betrothed little princess Marie to the young prince. Having dubbed, enfeoffed, and affianced his protégé in one swoop, Philip sent him, along with two hundred knights, to claim his inheritance.

The first stop on Arthur's quest was Tours, where he and his small army waited for the arrival of reinforcements from Brittany and Berry, and from the disaffected Poitevins, led by the lords of Lusignan. Eleanor of Brittany was certain that the Count of Rancon would come to Tours, and she intended to be there as well to take her place at her brother's side, resolved not to miss this grand adventure.

The news of Philip's victory at Gournay alarmed Aliénor of Aquitaine, prompting her to launch private negotiations with those Poitevins who would still be persuaded to support her son's cause. Having been dismissed with a ream of missives for the rest of the Duchess of Aquitaine's vassals, Juliana retired to the garden. Amidst the sisters' flourishing flowerbeds, the old folly provided a refuge, and she took possession of it. She sat on the duchess's pillows and looked over the garden where she had tormented herself with longing for the world outside, in the same folly where Lasalle had told her that she should have accepted her fate. A couple of sisters carried water pails to the herb garden. *One of them could have been me. Should I have accepted my fate, knowing what I know now? And what do I know about that man, anyway, after two years of marriage?*

Juliana wiped her pen, picked up her slippers, and marched barefoot across the garden in search of the truth about Guérin de Lasalle. After all, the great Aliénor had encouraged her to take an interest in her husband's affairs.

Alas, Auntie Sabine only shook her head. "I am sorry, my dear. I truly cannot remember when he was born. Yvetta and I were not very close, and after her impulsive marriage to that worthless man, we never saw each other."

Sitting in a window embrasure, Juliana tried to hide her disappointment. "Do you remember how old he was when he abducted Céline, Auntie?"

"The age for a young man to get himself into trouble is all I recall. Of course, none of it would have happened had Yvetta's first husband lived. That's husbands for you. The good ones never last and the miserable ones live forever."

Juliana could not help smiling. "What happened to Lady Yvetta's first husband?" she asked, in truth not all that curious.

The countess's hands rested on her lap. "The same misfortune that befell poor Richard." She crossed herself. "Slain by a crossbow."

Juliana stared at her. Coincidence. Nothing more than coincidence. "Auntie, I don't wish to upset you, but do you know where Céline is buried?"

"She was buried by the sisters of Saint-Sylvain. Are you well, Juliana? You look like you are about to faint."

CHAPTER 45

Tours, County of Touraine, July 1202

The final destination of the pilgrims who passed through the gates of Tours was Saint-Jacques-de-Campostelle, but they entered the city to pray at the tomb of Saint Martin, bishop of the ancient Gauls. The latest gathering outside the city walls, however, bore no relation to pious pilgrims.

The rainbow hues of tents and the gold-and-silver-threaded standards above them belonged to the Franks and their Lusignan adherents, an army of two hundred knights and their entourage of squires, servants, armorers, farriers, lorimers, laundresses, retainers, and hangers-on. The very fact that the enemies of the Plantagenet house had gathered on its ancestral soil indicated how far the fortunes of that house had fallen. The population of Tours gawked at the spectacle.

Eleanor of Brittany would have gawked too, except that she was among those being gawked at—and relishing every moment of it. At that particular moment, however, she sat in the burghers' hall, relegated to the ranks of observers. Her brother's supporters pressed about the table in a storm of argument.

"But my lords, my uncle is still stinging from Gournay. He will not move against us. The route down the Loire is open," Arthur tried to argue, his voice breaking, partly due to his age, partly due to frustration. He was almost lost among the broad backs and shoulders of war-tried men, despite his new surcoat.

"John has been a fumbler, but that is no prediction that he will continue to be one. Before we venture deeper into Aquitaine, we must wait for reinforcements."

That was Armand de Lusignan, speaking with that steel-under-silk tone that Eleanor found intriguing, though not at that instant. Since his arrival the other evening he had ignored her, sending no word or token acknowledging her presence. With Armand de Lusignan came the others—Geoffrey de Lusignan, the Count of Jaffa and the head of that clan; Hugh of La Marche and Ralph of Eu, and their vassals and allies: André de Chauvigni, Raymond of the ever fickle Thouars, and Savary de Mauléon, a beast of a fighter for all of his troubadour's reputation, as well as brother-in-law to Hugh de Lusignan. The de Cantignys sent their juniors, led by young Joscelyn. They all treated Arthur as if he were a juvenile rather than a prince and a belted knight, and Eleanor as if she were invisible.

Eleanor stood up, her voice as clear as crystal. "It seems, my lords, that what is wanting is not reinforcements of arms, but the courage of men."

Hard faces turned to her, male voices falling silent. Blood surged through her veins, propelling her forward.

"My lady!" Her shocked waiting woman reached for her, but Eleanor brushed by, her voice and head high.

"You are not afraid of my uncle; you are afraid of my grandmother. She has foiled you and defeated you and now you are afraid to fight her. We are not. My brother and I carry the blood of Aliénor of Aquitaine, of a valiant ancestry!"

Out of the corner of her eye, Eleanor caught Armand de Lusignan's expression. Let him see what his own words brought him, for all the good they had done her. "You, my lords, you have suffered your homes to be despoiled by our uncle's mercenaries, but with God's help and with the aid of those who seek justice, my brother and I shall defend our inheritance to our last breath. Who among you will aid us?"

They were staring at her openmouthed; Arthur's face glowed with embarrassment and pride.

"Ha!" Fist to his hip, de Mauléon forced his way through the crowd. He halted an arm's length from her, his shaggy head thrust forward. "So, you can't wait to have us spill our blood for you, can you now, Lady?"

"If I were the man you are reputed to be, sir, I would seize a sword and—"

"Ohoo!" De Mauléon threw his head back, his laughter shaking the rafters. "You have a man's courage, Lady, but for some man's sake, I praise the Lord that you are not one."

He gave her a bow to the laughter of the rest of the barons, his hot, boarlike eyes on her.

Eleanor swept them all with searing contempt, blood singing in her veins. They had noticed her. "You praise the Lord that I am not, sir! Our uncle is somewhere about Maine, our grandmother is at Fontevraud, less than twenty leagues from here, and you dally and dither as if they commanded the armies of Armageddon!"

"Still at Fontevraud?" The questioner was not laughing.

The rest of the noise subsided. Armand de Lusignan tried to seek out the speaker, but de Chauvigni moved forward. "At Fontevraud she is a bird in the bush!"

"Then maybe we can flush her." This time it was Raymond de Thouars, hand on his sword, not laughing at all. He looked about.

The hall was silent. Low voices rejoined, some in puzzlement, others in cautious assent.

"By the holy . . . why not? If we have Aliénor, John will no longer fumble; he'll freeze!" Geoffrey de Lusignan claimed the center. "What do you say, cousin?"

"Seizing Aliénor this time will not help us in Aquitaine. John would prefer her seized," Armand de Lusignan replied drily, looking not at all pleased, but the idea had already taken hold of the rest of the company.

De Mauléon struck his sword hilt. "Let us march and see!"

Eager voices vied with one another, fueled by the Franks' scent of victory, the rabid shouts of the Bretons, and the Poitevins' and their allies' anxiety to be in the forefront of the fray. This time Armand de Lusignan was not going to prevail. Arthur knew it as well. He elbowed his way through the crowd to stand next to his sister. Eleanor placed her hand on his shoulder and together they faced the gathering. She and Arthur presented a compelling sight, Eleanor was certain—Arthur with his tunic of scarlet and its blazon of a golden Brittany lion, her gown mirroring his, her braids as thick as a man's wrists and coiled with gold threads. "My lords, the true King of England stands before you!"

A thicket of swords flashed under the vaulting. "*Vivat rex, vivat rex!*"

Brother and sister looked at each other, each reading triumph in the other's eyes. So this was what power felt like; this was how it felt to stir and to inspire men, to be stirred in return.

"My lords, let us ride to victory!"

The roaring reply engulfed the hall. One might as well have tried to stem a tidal wave, and Armand de Lusignan did not try. He let the crowd spill from the hall after the young duke and his sister. "Ralph," he said, catching the Count of Eu. "Take your men and ride to Philip, now."

"What?" Ralph blinked at him in surprise.

"One of us always keeps well away from Plantagenet paws, remember? I will stay with these fools, but you ride to Philip and don't return to Poitou unless it's securely in our hands."

The Count of Eu spat on the floorboards and looked around the emptying hall. "Why me? John dallies at Le Mans. It will be like plucking a virgin."

"You pluck all the virgins you want. That's how you lost Isabelle," Armand reminded Ralph and left him standing there, knowing that unlike the rest, the Count of Eu would obey him.

❧

Abbey of Fontevraud

"Juliana, wait!"

It would have alarmed the lay brothers had they seen her running along the garden path to the guesthouse with a dusty, begrimed young man at her heels, so after a few steps she stopped, smoothed her skirts and her veil, and faced her pursuer. She even curtsied. "My lord d'Erlée."

John d'Erlée kissed her hand. Juliana wanted to box his ears or bloody his nose. D'Erlée did not notice.

"I am so glad to have found you. I wanted to let you know before I saw the duchess." He inhaled. "Rivefort is in Philip's hands. I am sorry. I didn't know how else to tell you."

Her heart's blood curdled. She would have fallen, but d'Erlée was holding her. She sat on the knee wall. "Are they all dead?"

John wiped his forehead with the back of his hand. "God, no. Lasalle negotiated Rivefort's surrender with Philip's man, Roger de Montier, on a pledge to take himself and his men hors de combat. Of course he reneged on his promise the instant he was free and took his men to the duke's camp. I'm sure Philip regrets that he hasn't had Lasalle hanged or set in irons, but he did order de Montier to spare Rivefort and Tillières."

Juliana crossed herself. Praise be. Philip surely spared her viscounty because of Armand de Lusignan's plea on her behalf, but she could not share that knowledge with d'Erlée.

"But that is not why I am here. Sir William sent me to warn the duchess that Arthur and the Lusignans are heading this way. Sir William wants the duchess to seek a safer place. I am sent to escort her to Poitiers. I have only four men."

Juliana turned on her heel. "Thank you for your message, sir. Don't let me delay you any further."

"Sir? Juliana, what is the matter? Last time you were not so formal." The young man's anxious voice began to attract the attention of the brothers who were tending the garden.

She whirled about as if stung by a bee. "You've conspired with that man to dishonor me! I suppose you both thought it was going to be so easy. Naive little Juliana, the silly, ignorant chit!"

"Holy—" D'Erlée glanced about before going in pursuit of the girl, pulling her into the nearest corner. "Please, it's not what you think. I can explain, but first I must see to the duchess. She will want you to come with her, of course."

Juliana dismissed him with a swish of her skirts. "I don't know what gave you that idea, sir. I am hardly important. Besides, not even the Lusignans would dare to invade this abbey. This place is perfectly safe."

Half an hour later, she bounced on her jennet under a blistering sun in the company of the Duchess of Aquitaine, the Countess de Valence, and John d'Erlée and his four men. Despite her loud protestations, the Countess de Nevers was left behind to mind the rest of her mistress's household. Juliana received no explanation why she should have been chosen to accompany the duchess.

In the afternoon heat, Juliana's anger was melting, replaced by anxiety about the duchess, who had taken to the saddle like a soldier despite their entreaties that she travel in her litter.

Riding by Juliana's side, John d'Erlée pulled closer. "We have seen Philip's treaty with the Bretons. It says, 'The King of the French shall keep what he has already gained and also what it may please God to let him gain in the future.'"

Her throat parched, Juliana tried to find her voice. "Philip wants to seize all of John's lands? Good Lord, does the duchess know?"

"She does. That's why she must not be captured. If she is, John will be compelled to grant Philip concessions. Surely even John would not leave his mother in his enemies' hands."

Juliana held back her jennet to prevent him from running into Anne's mare. D'Erlée had sent one man to watch their rear, and the others, coated in dust, rode silently in their helmets, shields at their sides, lances in hand, hauberks under their surcoats. She stole a glance at d'Erlée's tense, sunburned face. He and his men must surely be exhausted, but most of all she could see that he was worried. The knight who had been trailing behind them came around the road curve at full gallop and reined at d'Erlée's side, sweat tracing paths in the road dust coating his face.

"My lord, we can't hope to outrun them! Their advance is no more than two leagues behind, and gaining. We'll never reach Poitiers."

The duchess halted her palfrey and turned to face them. "I agree. Over that hill is Mirebeau. That place has always been loyal to me. We will seek refuge there and send a message to my son."

Fortress of Mirebeau, Poitou, July 1202

Mirebeau did not look like much of a refuge. The party clattered up to one of the gates of a small, walled town at the foot of an unprepossessing fortress, its moat half-filled with the walls' rubble.

The unannounced appearance of their duchess took the gate guards by surprise, but shouts of recognition quickly roused the population. By the time they entered the town square, a crowd surrounded them. A gray-haired knight in a patched jerkin with a puckered scar across his forehead pushed his way toward them and bowed with great ceremony. "My gracious lady!"

"Ah, Sir Ascletín. We are in good hands, then," the Duchess of Aquitaine declared majestically, allowing Ascletín and a couple of his men to help her dismount. "The Lusignans persuaded my grandson to attempt to seize us. How many men do we have?"

"The Lusignans? *Salauds!* Begging your pardon, my lady, but we can't keep you safe. Mirebeau has no more than a dozen men, and only enough stores for two or three days." Ascletín wrung his hands. "Had we known—"

"One never knows with the Lusignans, sir. Very well. Order the gates closed. When Arthur and his pack arrive, they will not be in a hurry. We will buy time by engaging them in a parlay. I need a place for myself and my women. The Countess de Valence and the Viscountess of Tillières are not accustomed to this much excitement." The Duchess of Aquitaine shook clouds of dust from her cloak, giving Ascletín a sharp look. "Well?"

"Yes, my lady. This way, my lady." Sir Ascletín shouted at the crowd, "You've heard your duchess—move!" From the church steeple, the toll of the tocsin spread through the narrow streets. Sir Ascletín pointed across the emptying square to a small house. "You will be more comfortable there for now, my lady."

The inhabitants of Mirebeau, like those of other towns, had their assigned duties in times of siege or fire, and they raced to assume them. Women whisked away their crying children, dogs trotted after their masters, the merchants' stalls emptied, carts disappeared. The Duchess of Aquitaine ignored the commotion her arrival had caused, carrying on as if being besieged in a small, provincial town by a thousand-man army was an everyday occurrence.

By contrast, Juliana's head pounded, perspiration trickled down her spine, and she anticipated the fall of Mirebeau with highly conflicted emotions.

CHAPTER 46

Juliana waited at the window in the room she was to share with Anne de Valence, wearing someone's else's gown, her hair brushed and braided, her teeth set. She wanted something to happen, and soon.

"Juliana?" Not that soon. John d'Erlée closed the door behind him, helmet under his arm.

A terrible wickedness possessed her. She raised her chin, a smile on her lips, presenting them shamelessly.

"Juliana, don't."

"Why not? You didn't mind kissing me before."

"I am so sorry; no harm was to be done. But now things are different, I mean you are—"

"His wife in more than name? Only because he thought you had become my lover! Did he pay you to seduce me too?"

D'Erlée touched her hair with tentative fingers. "Please, don't be so angry. He did not pay me to seduce you. He said the annulment was assured and that you could use a . . . a friend."

She pushed his hand away. "Friend? And to think I was afraid Lasalle would kill you if you tried to help me. The only man who has ever aided me is Armand de Lusignan. I ought to throw myself on his mercy."

He gave her a good shake. "Don't ever trust a Lusignan, not ever! Your anger at me or at Lasalle is of no consequence now. We are watching a dynasty crumble, and I've got three days' supplies, a dozen men, and an ancient keep to prevent it."

"Perhaps it's God's will then, this," she reminded him primly.

"More the Devil's!" D'Erlée tempered his tone. "I am sorry. There is much more, but . . ."

"What is it?"

He maneuvered her away from the window, keeping his voice

low as if they were not behind a thick door and even thicker walls. "Promise you won't say a word to anyone, not even to Anne. The duchess would have me skinned alive."

Sobered by the young man's demeanor, Juliana nodded.

"The duchess believes that the Count of Rancon has schemed a betrothal between the Lusignans and Arthur's sister."

She clasped her hand over her mouth. This was a piece of news. "But how?"

"Years ago, when old Henry and Richard pressed the Lusignans most sorely, Armand prevailed upon Duchess Constance to pledge her daughter to them. A diabolical plan, if I ever heard one. Constance always detested her mother-in-law. That way, she avenges herself on Aliénor by helping the Lusignans to wind themselves into the Plantagenet fold."

"Count Armand . . . he plans to marry Eleanor of Brittany?"

"I don't know. There are others."

"Of course. Young Hugh. He lost Isabelle to John. What a perfect revenge." Juliana quickly offered an alternative, wanting to put the first possibility out of her mind.

John nodded. "Eleanor of Brittany is Arthur's heir, and John's, too. Think of it. If either of them should die—"

"Eleanor becomes the Duchess of Brittany," Juliana finished for him, another thought already forming. D'Erlée encouraged her to complete it. She did.

"And Eleanor's husband becomes King of England."

As terrible as an army with banners, the Scripture said, and she now understood the words. The besieging army arrived below the walls of Mirebeau to the rumble of drums and the ungodly bleat of Breton bagpipes: an array of well-mounted knights in full mail; pennons stirring in the cloying breeze; late-afternoon rays glinting on lance tips, armor, and horse trappings. In the distance, a cloud of dust announced the approach of the rest of the entourage. Judging from the casual attitude of the besiegers, they knew that those watching them from the broken ramparts were not going

anywhere. It gave the occasion a bizarre air of festivity, like rejoic-
ing at a funeral.

A youthful figure dressed in a scarlet surcoat and mounted on
a spirited white stallion advanced to the edge of the moat. The
drums and bagpipes fell silent. The boy stood up in the stirrups,
impatiently brushing his hair from his eyes. "Grand-mère! It is I,
Arthur, Duke of Brittany, Count of Anjou, Maine, Touraine, and
Poitou!" A loud cheer broke from the ranks of Arthur's supporters. Encouraged, he returned his attention to the battlements.
"Grand-mère! Come out and let us embrace. I only claim what is
mine."

"It is not yours yet, ungrateful little toad—or should I say toady?
Brought with you the ever faithful lords Lusignan, I see. Are they
here to wipe your nose or your behind?"

The Duchess of Aquitaine's voice carried remarkably well, giving rise to a gale of scornful laughter from those crowding the
walls. A barrage of crockery and rotten fruit followed. Arthur's
horse went on his haunches, ears back, and the Duke of Brittany
nearly lost his seat. Hoots from the battlements filled the air.

A rider cantered up to join him, the silver embroidery on the
horse trappings glimmering in the sun. "My liege lady," he called
out, "let us not waste words in recriminations."

The thwarted almost-father-in-law of Isabelle d'Angoulême
sat easily in the saddle of a Danish destrier, hand on his hip, reins
in one hand. This was the Lusignan they called Hugh le Brun,
Juliana realized, a dark-complexioned man in his late thirties.
Across the distance, his teeth cut a white swath across his face. He
was enjoying the moment, though his voice was laced with feigned
regret. "My liege lady. It is hot and we've ridden far. Order the
gates opened. We know you cannot hold out long."

"Longer than you think, Hugh. Your discomfort is not my concern. Arthur? Where is that sister of yours? I would speak to both
of you. Arrange a parlay at the east gate—and no tricks, you little
toad. I have my archers on you. Go!"

Without waiting for an answer, Aliénor of Aquitaine turned
her back on the army spread before her and gestured to John

d'Erlée. "That ought to hold them for a while. I would speak with you now."

Le Mans, Poitou

John d'Erlée sat down in the shade of a wall, exhausted, despairing of his helplessness. On the duchess's instructions, he and two of Ascletín's men had made their way safely out of Mirebeau through an abandoned well, and after a mad ride had arrived at Le Mans. He rubbed his burning eyes and blinked across the bailey. Groups of armed men loitered about, quarreling, arguing, gambling, drinking, bargaining with whores, snoring under equipage carts, and sprawling on hay piles.

"My lord d'Erlée. Such gloom on such a fine day. Care to change your luck?"

There stood Jehan de Vaudreuil, juggling a trio of dice. Fighting dizziness, John got to his feet. Vaudreuil caught the dice and him at the same time. "Too much wine, my lord?"

"Too many leagues in the saddle. Arthur and the Lusignans are about to take Aliénor hostage!" D'Erlée snapped at Vaudreuil because Vaudreuil was there to snap at.

Vaudreuil whistled. "Holy Mother's—does the duke know?"

D'Erlée cast a disgusted look toward the hall. "They are there now, debating what to do. The duke is wasting precious time, for Christ's sake."

Vaudreuil gave him a slap on the back. "Who are we to argue with God's anointed? They will lead us to slaughter soon enough. Care to forget your troubles? You've done your part, my friend."

"I can't. I've sent a man to William de Roches, but without the duke's forces we'll still be outnumbered. And if Arthur's reinforcements from Brittany arrive before we do . . . Can Sir William spare some men?"

Vaudreuil's cheerfulness waned considerably. "Not while Philip is besieging Mortimer at Arques. Marshal, Warren, and Salisbury are trying to harass him from the rear. Marshal can't abandon Mortimer."

"And Sir William can't abandon the duchess. I've done all I can to convince the duke to move out. Good Lord—I almost forgot. I don't know what it means, but she said that if the duke refuses to move, to find Tillières and tell him—"

"What does the nightmare of my waking hours want to offer me this t-time? Another bribe or another b-bride?"

Wineskin under his arm, hip against a cart wheel, Guérin de Lasalle stood there, squinting at him. John d'Erlée promised himself that he would watch his temper. The Viscount of Tillières could be disagreeable at the best of times, and from his appearance, this was not one of them.

"It is a message regarding your current wife, sir," d'Erlée said, and watched with disgust as Lasalle gave him an extravagant bow.

"Of course. The bashful one who tacks to the bedpost lists of sins to shun. One has been keeping such diverting company lately, these things slip one's mind."

Despite d'Erlée's resolution, his hand went to his sword hilt. "*Fils à putain!* The lady Juliana found herself your wife through sheer misfortune. You have no right to speak of her in that fashion!"

Behind him, Vaudreuil drew a short breath. Curious faces gathered around them. Lasalle swayed noticeably. "Sheer misfortune, eh? If you had abandoned that chivalrous claptrap for half an hour, d'Erlée, you could've had the lady, maidenhead and all. What more did you want me to do? Tie her to the bed for you?"

Vaudreuil's hand landed on d'Erlée's sword hilt. Struggling ineffectively to free it, d'Erlée would not give up. "You are a crude and vile man, Lasalle! I don't understand how a lady of such excellent qualities could have ended up with someone as base as you."

Lasalle flung the deflated wineskin aside. "Then next time you visit Fontevraud, you may make up to her for your failure and my baseness."

"Your wife is not at Fontevraud!" d'Erlée shouted after him.

"The duchess wanted you to know. She is at Mirebeau with the duchess, about to be seized by the Lusignans. And so is your mistress!"

He did not know which part of the news produced the next effect, but Lasalle was on him, gripping his surcoat in an iron fist. "What?"

D'Erlée tried to pry off his hand. "If the duke doesn't send relief, Mirebeau will surrender and Aliénor will fall into Lusignan hands—and your women along with her."

Lasalle shoved him aside, snatched a water bucket from under the nose of a startled rounsey, and poured the contents over his own head. He mopped his face with his shirt and reached into the hay wagon for a dirty gambeson, and d'Erlée watched Guérin de Lasalle transform himself from an unpleasant drunkard to a still-disreputable but alarmingly sober man.

"How many Lusignans are at Mirebeau? How many men do they have?"

D'Erlée and Vaudreuil trotted behind him. "All of them, I think. Two hundred knights and the usual rabble."

They reached the door of the hall. The guards eyed them suspiciously, but did not challenge them.

"Jehan, tell Kadolt to have the men ready in half an hour. Forced-march supplies, water, and oats for the horses, no frills."

D'Erlée halted. "You don't have enough men to take on the Lusignans, and Duke John won't use his to aid Aliénor."

The Viscount of Tillières leaned his shoulder against the door. "Then he'll have to be persuaded, won't he?"

Left at the door, d'Erlée looked to Vaudreuil, uncomprehending. "What's got into him? I don't understand that man. What ails him?"

"Nothing you or I can cure, my friend." And with that, Vaudreuil left him.

D'Erlée scratched his scalp. Good Lord, what did he have to lose? He cinched up his sword belt and followed the Viscount of Tillières.

Inside the chamber the debate still raged, the men aligning

themselves into factions: Some argued for dispatching aid to the beleaguered duchess, while others, wishing to find favor with the duke, insisted that it was already too late, and still others remained uncertain. The duke reclined in his chair, allowing the mercenary Lupescaire to say what was unwise to air publicly.

"My lords, consider again the distance. To march in this heat, we'll kill the horses and the men will be in no condition to fight. It is impossible to reach Mirebeau in time."

"It is possible if one is not gloriously inept, Lupescaire."

Lasalle was leaning against the wall, arms folded, squinting at Lupescaire, a man some forty years old with deep-set eyes, closely cropped light brown hair, and a clean-shaved chin. Against his rust-colored jerkin glistened a sword hilt of chased gold.

John d'Erlée shared the rest of the barons' dislike of this man, and he, too, resented the duke's reliance on the lowborn, murderous hireling and men of his ilk. This confrontation between the Viscount of Tillières and Lupescaire promised to be an interesting one—not that there was much difference lately between how those two let their *routiers* run.

Lupescaire met his opponent with a slight bow. "My lord Lasalle. Still envious that His Grace granted me the honor of leading his army? Perhaps if you weren't in the habit of falling from your horse dead drunk, his choice might have been different."

Laughter broke out in the crowd around the duke, but not all joined it, d'Erlée noted.

"Even dead drunk, I can still reach Mirebeau in two days. And since you don't intend to lead the duke's army anywhere, I beg the duke the temporary use of it." Leaving Lupescaire to deal with that challenge, Lasalle gave the Duke of Normandy a prodigious bow. Stillness descended on the hall, all eyes on John Plantagenet.

"As much as we regret our mother's misfortune, my lord Lasalle, I am counseled that it is impossible to cover a hundred leagues in that time without exhausting our forces," John Plantagenet said with a testy sarcasm, nevertheless sitting up in his chair.

Lasalle approached the chair. Bystanders gave way until he stood alone in the empty space before it. "Eighty-some leagues.

And you are not risking your forces, sire. The Lusignans won't be expecting us. We will march through the night and take them at first light."

"We can't march at night. What of the wagons, supplies, servants? We'd lose them all!"

Lasalle ignored the objections, addressing instead the men about him. "Some of you have marched at night with Richard in *outre-mer*. The moon is bright enough. We take no wagons, supplies, or servants. They'll catch up with us."

A murmur rippled through the crowd. It grew louder, the debate more heated. The duke sat in the middle of his supporters, his eyes on Guérin de Lasalle.

Another voice broke through the noise. "The mercenaries will not keep up such a pace. What will you offer them to make them move faster?"

Lasalle sent the anonymous detractor a mirthless smile. "Mirebeau."

CHAPTER 47

Fortress of Mirebeau, Poitou

My lady, there will be no parlay. The Lusignans are storming the gates. You must remove yourself to the keep." Sir Ascletín burst through the door just as Anne and Juliana finished dressing the duchess in a gown scavenged to impress her enemies.

While Ascletín and his men ushered their lady to safety, Juliana crammed the duchess's parchments into her saddlebags. Anne was left to scoop up their clothes. From across the town square came the sound of shattering timbers and the rumble of falling masonry, mingled with the desperate shouts of the defenders and the jubilant roar of the attackers.

The keep's gate was winched high enough to allow the duchess and her escort to pass into the poorly lit interior. They rested frequently on the steps to allow the duchess to recover, because Aliénor of Aquitaine refused to be carried. At the top of the keep they reached a circular room, its walls pierced by arrow loops. Anne and Juliana left their bundles on a table that was one of the few items of furnishings.

Through the arrow loops they heard and then watched a flood of men spilling across the town square, swords drawn, the townsmen scattering ahead of the invasion. The pursuers prodded the terrified residents with the flats of their swords, tripping here and there a tardy burgher and relieving him of whatever worthwhile items he possessed, more in mischief than mayhem.

"My seal ring; I must have my seal ring!" Aliénor cried suddenly, tossing aside her pens and parchments. A frantic search ensued, to no avail.

"It must be at the house." Juliana reached for Anne's hand and squeezed it quickly. "I'll run and see."

She was out of the room before anyone could stop her, dashing past Ascletín's men and under the gate as the guards were lowering it, ignoring their shouts.

She reached the chamber without mishap and spotted the seal ring almost immediately on the floor, resting against the table leg. Relieved, she retrieved it, but when she looked out the window, the square swarmed with men.

Don't ever trust a Lusignan. She backed away from the window. No doubt Arthur of Brittany and the Lusignans would soon take the duchess hostage. Perhaps in the confusion she could blend into the crowd and make her way to Fontevraud, and from there to Rivefort.

She slipped the seal ring onto her sleeve point, knotted the end, and ran to the adjoining room. The room's only window faced the garden. She pulled the back hem of her gown between her legs, tied it to her girdle, and climbed through the opening to the roof. Cautiously, she crawled along it to a nook between two rooftops. She was reasonably comfortable there, and the lengthening shadows provided shade. It would be unlikely for someone to start inspecting Mirebeau's roofs, wouldn't it? Her stomach growled. Juliana hugged herself.

She woke up with a start from the nightmarish dozing in which she had passed the night. The men below had kept up a noisy celebration, some busying themselves walling up one of the town's two gates. They were waiting for daylight to accept the surrender of their duchess. Now, in the dawn hours, all below had fallen quiet. Thirsty, famished, and aching in every limb, Juliana shivered. Perhaps she had acted foolishly. Perhaps she should have confronted the men below and demanded to be taken to the Count of Rancon. She was certain of one thing: Lusignans or not, she was not going to spend another night on the roof. And then she heard it.

Clutching her skirts to her, she inched herself to the roof crest. The street from the one unbarred gate was filled with men running crouched along the walls. These men, with axes, maces, pikes, swords, and falchions in their hands, were not Arthur's baronial levy. Arthur's men slept soundly, sprawled on piles of hay and straw, next to walls, against cart wheels and overturned wine casks, with their shields, hauberks, and swords cast aside, secure in their knowledge that they were safe. And no one guarded the one unbarred gate for an approaching enemy.

"*Aux armes! Aux armes!*"

The rallying cry drowned in the sound of horseshoes on stones. Behind the men on foot, riders burst into the square, filling it with the ring of steel, the dull whump of steel sundering bone and muscle, and cries and screams. The sounds carried along the narrow streets, through which the horsemen and the footmen charged, falling upon the confused and dazed men. Some tried to escape into the streets, only to be driven back. Few offered resistance. With the only other gate sealed, the Duke of Brittany's men were caught in a trap of their own making.

"*Quartier! Quartier!*"

Overwhelmed, Arthur's men threw down their weapons and

threw up their arms in surrender to be trampled, rammed against the walls, crushed, and bloodied. The victorious, exultant attackers proceeded to secure the prisoners in threes and fours and drag the bleeding, bruised men through the gate to an uncertain fate.

Ignoring the chaos around them, other attackers pounded the doors, shattered the locks, pried open bolts, and invaded the houses. Cries, shouts, and protestations rose from the interiors to the crash of furnishings and pottery. Bedding, trunks, and furnishings flew out the windows, raining on those below, who leapt on the loot, tearing at it and quarreling.

A young woman broke away from one of the doorways, two men in pursuit. Like wolves on a doe, they caught her and brought her down. They wrenched her skirts over her head, muffling her cries. Her white legs flashed briefly. One of the men straddled her.

Juliana slid back from the roof ridge as fast as she could, curled up, and stuffed her fingers into her ears. She mouthed the Paternoster and a prayer to every saint she could recall, particularly to Saint Peter ad Vincula, whose day this was.

The sun had broken through the morning haze, and in short course its rays turned the roof into a griddle. Juliana squirmed, her fingers numb from being pressed into her eardrums. She eased up the pressure a little, expecting to hear those horrible sounds that had filled the previous hours. Instead, she heard the sound of horns, sharp and clear, again and again. Gathering her courage and her skirts, she crawled back to the roof ridge.

Below, instead of the voracious mercenaries, knights in full mail, swords drawn, were reclaiming the town. They were not Arthur's baronial levy either. They set upon the mercenaries, beating them off their victims and evicting those still inside the houses. One mercenary stood up to a knight who without as much as a pause split the man's skull. Blood and matter splashed the sun-bleached walls.

Juliana cowered and gagged, yet felt glad that *routier* had met his deserved fate. After that, the rest of the mercenaries came under curb and, shouldering whatever they could, filed out of Mirebeau's gate. She waited until the square was almost empty before she took a step—and slid down the roof as if on a greased slope, ending atop a soft mound, right in the middle of horsemen dismounting in the stable yard below. Her unexpected and violent appearance sent the horses shying in all directions, the men shouting and cursing. Still, a couple of them picked her up from the pile of barn manure before she could catch her breath.

A heavy hand covered her mouth. "What the Devil? Ha! It's a Lusignan spy!" announced one of the men laughingly, standing her roughly on her feet.

"And a dirty and smelly one at that." The rest of the men's anger turned into bawdy merriment at the discovery that their assailant was a female. From behind, a hand groped her breasts for confirmation. "Come on, sweetheart, let's get you washed first!"

She let out a half-strangled screech, fighting to free herself as they dragged her to the horse trough, to be met halfway there by a couple of new riders. The foremost horseman spurred forward. "You've had your orders, curse you. Let her go and get back to camp. There are prisoners to guard!"

The man tightened his proprietary grip on Juliana. "She's ours. We found her. She fell off the roof."

"Let her go, you whoreson!" Reaching down, the rider wrenched Juliana free. She was about to give vent to her injured dignity when her rescuer sat back in the saddle. "Christ in Heaven. Lady Juliana."

The rider dismounted and pried off his helmet. It was Jehan de Vaudreuil. He looked her over as if he could not believe it, then gave her a terribly correct bow, which, considering her appearance, seemed to her as incongruous as anything he could have done.

"We've been searching for you for hours. The duchess offered a hundred marks to anyone who knew of your whereabouts, and your husband promised to hang every Lusignan hireling unless they produced you safe and sound. Bloody hell. Corneille, tell the viscount to save the rope. His wife has been found. My lady, sit down, you've had a nasty fall."

Juliana dropped on a bench by the stable door. She did not comprehend any of it. "Is he . . . is he here?"

Vaudreuil squatted in the dirt by her, looking like a man who had not slept, changed his clothes, or come near a laver for days.

"He is." Vaudreuil's mouth twisted into a mischievous grin. "And John is now crowing like a dung-hill rooster, thanks to your husband. He made John look like a miserable coward, along with that carrion Lupescaire. God's teeth, the Lusignans didn't expect us at all. They say that Geoffrey didn't believe the duke was about to attack and said he was not about to be driven away from his pigeon pie!"

Her head buzzed. "All of them," she said faintly.

Vaudreuil rubbed his campaign-short hair and tugged at his earring. "Ah. Yes. Except the Count of Eu. Still, that ought to put the bee into Philip's bonnet."

The Lusignans' capture signaled her own defeat, but Juliana could not dwell on that calamity now. "The duchess . . . the duchess will be worried about her ring." She stood up. Her knees wobbled.

Vaudreuil steadied her and sat her down again. "Don't move. I'll bring you some wine."

She nodded and closed her eyes. Dear Lord, what more could possibly go wrong? A cup was placed in her hand and guided to her lips. She drank the wine as if it were water, her nausea abating. She opened her eyes to thank Vaudreuil—and dropped the cup, spilling wine all over her lap.

That man was on one knee in front of her, a coat of mail under a torn and bloodstained surcoat, sweat-soaked hair plastered to his forehead, a grimy crust around his mouth, and a madman's eyes in a sun-seared face. He shook her so hard that her teeth nicked her lip. "You stupid bitch! Where have you been? God rot it, I could strangle you!"

The threat hung in the air like the sword of Damocles. Behind Lasalle, the men occupied themselves with horse trappings. Vaudreuil came to her rescue. "It appears the lady Juliana spent the night on the roofs of the good burghers of Mirebeau."

Lasalle assayed her from her tangled hair to her soot-and-manure-besmeared gown and ruined slippers. Juliana squirmed. He was going to say something very unpleasant. Instead, he re-mounted his horse. "Sir Jehan, escort the lady Juliana to the Duchess of Aquitaine and don't let her out of your sight."

Soaked, scrubbed, scented, dressed, coiffed, and repeatedly chas-tised, Juliana sat dutifully with Anne de Valence under a *baldaquin* behind the Duchess of Aquitaine's chair. She wished she were anywhere but where she was, in the middle of the Duke of Nor-mandy's camp, witnessing the formal submission of his nephew and his nephew's supporters. From Mirebeau's walls, the mauled townsmen watched their ravagers-turned-rescuers celebrate their triumph.

Attired for the occasion in a white damask surcoat, a collar of gold lions on his shoulders, and a ducal crown of entwined roses on his brow, John Plantagenet looked both martial and irrepress-ibly gleeful. Despite his mother's disapproving glances, he jumped up from his seat next to her whenever a new prisoner was brought forth. In a chair on the other side of her grandmother sat the Pearl of Brittany, her lips bloodless, her eyes fixed on the scene before her. In front of the dais, piles of torn banners and stan-dards of the Frankish, Breton, and Poitevin barons testified to their defeat. Around them pressed the duke's mercenaries. At an anvil dragged from a smithy for the occasion, the blacksmith was hammering manacles onto Arthur of Brittany's wrists. The Lusi-gnans and the rest of the rebel barons waited by, their hands tied in front of them—and Armand de Lusignan among them.

Juliana experienced an uncomfortable jolt even before his eyes found her. The Count of Rancon gave her a smile and a slight bow, as if in regret. She was not sure for whom. She bit her lip and glanced away into the crowd.

The mercenaries' ferocity had evaporated, and except for their armfuls of wicked weapons, they looked like so many sapped, ragged, and dirty men. Among them she spotted Kadolt, favoring his leg, and next to him, she recognized several of Lasalle's men. Anne pointed out to her William de Roches, sitting at the end of the dais, an imposing-looking man who had joined his forces to the duke's to bring about the downfall of the Duke of Brittany and of the lords Lusignan. Juliana noticed that de Roches did not look particularly happy.

Her eyes wandered farther to find Lasalle at the edge of the crowd with Vaudreuil and a couple of Rivefort knights. Since no danger threatened, they wore only scuffed gambesons over shirts the most zealous laundress would reject. For a man who hated the Count of Rancon with a passion, Guérin de Lasalle did not look happy either. *No doubt nothing short of Armand de Lusignan's death would make my lord Lasalle happy.*

The guards brought their prisoners forward to exchange their ropes for iron fetters. That must have been the reason for William de Roches's darkened brow. No baron worth his salt would submit freely to such a humiliation. But then, the Lusignans had little choice in the matter.

"Will you look at that?" Anne pointed her chin to where the guards held out Armand de Lusignan's wrists for the blacksmith. "There goes enough craftiness, pride, and ambition to bring down two kingdoms."

Juliana averted her eyes. *If John d'Erlée's words were true, Anne had no idea how close to the mark she came.*

Rubbing his hands, Duke John returned to his seat beside his mother. "We've had an excellent hunt, Madame. I've crushed your nest of vipers. Philip will yield to me now."

The Duchess of Aquitaine tended to her borrowed strands of pearls. "I am glad you are pleased that you changed your mind and came to rescue your mother after all, John. Pity my town is despoiled."

"I came as fast as I could. Christ in Heaven, I had to prod the *routiers* with something, but nothing I do meets with your approval." John sprang up and waved to the guards. "Bring them!" The guards were still prodding Arthur and the Poitevins toward the dais when John charged at the prisoners, his finger stabbing toward the ground. "On your knees, knaves! I'll have your submission this time. You'll beg my forgiveness and the forgiveness of your duchess, and perhaps I'll spare your worthless lives."

Even blood-marred, under guard, and in irons, the Lusignans exuded palpable disdain for their captor. Taking his cue from them, Arthur assumed the same mien. None of the prisoners volunteered to kneel, so the guards compelled them with blows.

Armand de Lusignan went last. A trickle of blood slid down his brow, yet he looked up at the Duchess of Aquitaine with only mild annoyance. "My admiration, Your Grace, for arousing such loyalty and dedication among the duke's supporters. Still, one wonders how long the Viscount of Tillières will champion your son's cause? Will you have him rewarded with the command of the duke's armies in poor Lupescaire's stead or grant him the seneschalty of Normandy?"

"You impertinent son of a—" John jumped forward, the back of his hand cracking across the face of the man mocking him. Juliana gasped and so did the onlookers, but Armand de Lusignan hardly flinched. John raised his hand again, then encountered the Count de Rancon's steady gaze. The duke held back his hand—and then lowered it.

"Uncle! I demand justice. I demand to be heard by my one and true liege. I stand by my claim and my investiture!" Arthur broke in shrilly, not to be outdone or forgotten.

Fist high, his uncle spun toward him. "Silence, stripling, or I'll snap your neck!"

"You wouldn't—oh, Uncle, you wouldn't. Grand-mère!" Eleanor of Brittany flew from her seat and threw her arms around her brother, who stood flushed by his own bravery.

At the sight of the Pearl of Brittany's distress, the rest of the prisoners began to stir, shouts of "Shame! Shame!" ringing from their ranks. The guards struggled to restrain them. The voice of the Count of La Marche won over the rest. "You! Normans and all. Behold your liege. The abductor of women and violator of his vassals' beds. Softsword, bah!" Hugh de Lusignan spat on the ground at John Plantagenet's feet.

The Duke of Normandy's sword was halfway drawn when his mother's voice halted it. "Words of spite and impotence, John. Take them away. You, Eleanor, sit down."

At the duchess's crisp command, the guards reclaimed their prisoners and commenced to haul them away, with Hugh le Brun's invective raining upon the duke's head until he was silenced by a blow. Reclaiming his authority, the Duke of Normandy waved his hand toward the remaining guards. "Finish with the others. I want them secured and watched, every one of them!"

The rest of the prisoners were brought forth, but the mood had already soured, the duke's victory tarnished. At the edge of the crowd a further commotion began to detract from the proceedings. Juliana saw that Lasalle and Vaudreuil had mounted up but could not progress against a growing crush around them. Those closest were slapping Lasalle's knee and the horse's rump until the stallion began to fight the bit. The two horsemen had not sought or welcomed the attention, but they had it and it grew. Someone in the crowd picked up a marching drum kept silent during their approach to Mirebeau. Another drum joined it and then others, and from somewhere came a pair of pipes, those dreadful Breton bagpipes, relieved of their former owners. The drummers struck up a measured beat, the steady, deep-hearted beat of an army. And from the cacophony came an unmistakable roar, like a surging sea wave. "Rich-a-a-rd! Rich-a-a-rd! Coeur de Lion! Coeur de Lion!"

Anne de Valence looked at Juliana with delight and disbelief. "Good Lord, do you hear them?"

Juliana heard them and so did those about her. The prisoners forgotten, the duke's attendants gaped, confused, only their mindfulness of the positions they held of their liege restraining them from joining in the spontaneous procession. The rest of the Duke of Normandy's camp was not so restrained. They were cheering. They were cheering Guérin de Lasalle, who had led them to a spectacular victory. Their victory. And through their midst he rode, his gaze fixed ahead, his appearance a glaring contrast to his liege's monarchical splendor. Part of the human wave also swept up William de Roches, chair and all, bearing him aloft and along before the seneschal could make a move.

At first stunned by the spontaneous outpouring, John Plantagenet twisted his head toward his mother, his face convulsed in apoplectic fury. He spat some words at her, but the duchess kept her profile to her son and replied composedly over the noise. Whatever she said, it sent her son to his feet. Gesturing sharply to his attendants, he turned his gaze to Juliana. He paused as if trying to recall who she was, and while her heart sank, he charged toward her and Anne. Pulling Anne from her seat, the Duke of Normandy abandoned the field, dragging the Countess de Valence toward his tent as if she were a camp follower.

The crowd closed behind them. But before it did, Juliana caught a glimpse of the Count of Rancon behind a barrier of lances, shackled and bloody—and looking quite pleased.

CHAPTER 48

"Y ou clumsy sow!"

Juliana fell back, her hand to her cheek, which stung as much from the rebuke as from the blow. The tray lay on the floor along with shattered bowls, wine ewer, and goblets, knocked out of her grip by Eleanor of Brittany. They were in a small room of Mirebeau's keep; Eleanor, her waiting woman, and herself.

Juliana's first instinct was to strike back. She and the Pearl of Brittany were about the same age and almost the same size, except for the Pearl's feminine curves, which her gown displayed to advantage. Eleanor of Brittany's woman tried to calm her mistress, offering Juliana a look of sympathy. Juliana swallowed her words, tucked up her gown and, napkin in hand, knelt to sweep up the shards.

A pair of painted and embroidered boots planted themselves next to the puddle. One of them stomped. "Leave it. That was not fit for the dogs. How dare you serve it to me?"

"That was all the cooks had. They are trying to feed the men."

"You will not speak to me in such manner!" Eleanor of Brittany raised her hand and took a step toward Juliana.

Juliana jumped up, the tray in her hands. "Do that again and I swear you'll wear this."

The waiting woman cupped her hand over her mouth. Juliana's resolve, however, must have been plain to the Pearl.

"You are not a serving girl." Eleanor rushed to the arms of her woman. "Dear Lord, you are here to spy on me!"

Juliana dropped the tray on the table. That was the second time she had been accused of being a spy, and she did not appreciate it. "I am not either, Your Grace. And losing your head while your men are in danger of truly losing theirs is not very helpful, is it?"

"How dare you? Who are you?" Eleanor of Brittany brushed her hair from her brow and examined Juliana suspiciously.

"Nobody. My name is Juliana. I've waited on Her Grace at Fontevraud."

Eleanor's expression relaxed slightly. "Oh, you are one of those," she said, the explanation having exhausted her interest. She turned to her woman, her tone once again aloof. "My comb, Clemence. Find my comb and my veil."

Keeping an eye on the Pearl, Juliana resumed her task while Clemence combed her mistress's hair, murmuring softly. Suddenly, Eleanor of Brittany clasped her hands to her heart and closed her eyes like a child with impossible birthday wishes. "I am the granddaughter of Aliénor of Aquitaine," she whispered as if to reassure herself. "I am the granddaughter of Aliénor of Aquitaine. . . ."

A sense of unease seized Juliana. The fact that Eleanor of Brittany's fate and her own should both be tied to one man struck her with heart-stopping force. She curtsied.

"I shall bring another tray," she said, glancing at Clemence, whose anguish for her mistress was too painful to contemplate. The waiting woman nodded, tears in her eyes. With nothing else to be said, Juliana picked up the tray and called out to the guards to open the door.

❧

That evening Juliana attended the Duchess of Aquitaine alone, Anne de Valence's company being reserved for the Duke of Normandy. After settling the duchess in bed with a cup of wine, Juliana was dismissed.

Exhausted, she backed herself into a couple of knights waiting outside the duchess's quarters. She assumed they were Sir Ascletín's guards, but that was before a hand covered her mouth and she found herself being whisked away between the two of them. They half-dragged, half-carried her to the keep's top, shoved her into a room, and locked the door behind her.

She shouted and pounded the door, then ran to the window and decided that the drop did not deserve serious consideration. Shaking with anger, she paced the room, which appeared to be Sir Ascletín's bedchamber. The door latch rattled. Juliana bounded to the table, and armed with the candleholder, confronted the intruder, her laughable weapon raised. The intruder did not laugh. He stood there with a lamp held high in one hand, wine flagon in the other.

"Bloody hell," he said.

She lowered her arm. "I am sorry. They must have mistaken me for Anne, though I don't know how."

Lasalle looked her up and down. "Neither do I."

She turned away, to hide whatever evidence there was of Eleanor of Brittany's temper, she told herself, and not because of the words, or because of those cheekbones, the combative, stubble-blackened jaw, or the very green half-moon glare. Since their last meeting he had scrubbed sufficiently in some trough, but the temper was still there, encouraged no doubt by the absence of Anne de Valence, the presence of herself, and the contents of that flagon. Resolved not to engage him on this or any other front, Juliana gave up the candleholder and tiptoed toward the door.

Lasalle kicked it shut in her face. "Planning to wander about at night in a place packed to the rafters with drunkenness and lechery, are we?"

The words nailed her to the spot. From beneath the window came snatches of drunken laughter and bawdy shouts to interrupt the refrain of an equally bawdy ditty. Lasalle crossed the room and slammed the shutters against the rest. She flinched, at once apprehensive and relieved, left with a distinct feeling that it was not done to spare her sensibilities.

Lasalle ignored her. He left the lamp on the table, dropped his gambeson on the trunk, and poured water into the laver. The shirt went next. Juliana swallowed, trying to keep her eyes anywhere but on the sinew and muscle rigged so precisely in God's own design of what a man's form ought to be. He glanced back at her, Ascletín's razor in hand. "How fares the Pearl?"

She slipped her hands inside her sleeves with her gaze to the floorboards. "Worried. Afraid . . . alone."

She did not think that was the answer he wanted, but that was the truth. He hesitated, as if he wanted to ask her more before turning to the tarnished mirror to concentrate on maneuvering the razor's edge along his jaw.

Anger and resentment flared up in the pit of her stomach. By what right had this man turned her world upside down, and the world of humble and great families, and even grander dynasties? And how dare he charge through these calamities unscathed? The image of Eleanor of Brittany, of Mirebeau torn apart, the violation of the terrified young woman, doubtless one of many, filled her with cold fury. "You've won a great victory, my lord."

"*Veni, vidi, vici.*" It was the reply of a conqueror who discovers he has nothing left to conquer.

Juliana made a face at his back for that mossy bit of Latin. "*Vincit qui se vincit,*" she retorted before she realized that his irony was aimed, for what reason she could not fathom, at himself.

He wiped off the soap and crooked up his eyebrow in the mirror at her. "Subtle, Eustace. Good old Publius. How did you manage to learn so much, mouse?"

He allowed her a spate of soundless sputters before he faced her, taking advantage of her dumbfounderment. She tried to rally. "'I have . . . I have burned more oil than . . . than—"

"'I have drunk wine'?" he finished for her, a current of amusement in his voice. Something in his manner had changed. A tocsin sounded in her head. He indicated the flagon. "'*In vino veritas*,' they say."

Another challenge, and simple enough, but the wick's flame mirrored in the droplets that meandered along the living planes and ridges occupied all of her attention. He clicked his tongue in disappointment, advancing toward her. "Alcaeus, Sister Scholastica."

"You—you know Greek?" She knew she sounded foolish, utterly foolish.

He flattened his palms against the wall on both sides of her. "I know wine"—his teeth flashed—"and women." He leaned closer, the smell of wine, Ascletín's soap, and that something else on him. "You are losing custody of your eyes, love."

"You are drunk."

Fingertips touched her cheek where the sting from the Pearl of Brittany's hand remained. "Not as much as I could be."

"You ought to be celebrating victory with your friends."

He leaned closer. "To the victor, the spoils."

She gulped, praying for the stones at her back to yield. "You said we wouldn't—"

"'The unwilling Minerva.' So I lie."

"T-Tacitus."

His finger poked through the loop in the neck ribbon of her gown, a simple gown of some petty burgher's daughter. "Horace. I made the same mistake once and I can still hear my ears ringing."

"'*Ira . . . ira furor brevis est.*'" She was losing and badly, and he knew it and smiled.

"Horace again." His lips almost touched hers, his voice a raspy whisper, his eyes half concealed. "Anger, like passion, can be brief, or not."

The words suspended all else around her. She knew what he sought and did not understand why she should be the object of it, beyond her presence in this chamber. And then she understood that was the reason, as much as that young woman was a reason for those men, yet despite it, she said, "But why come to me?"

"'*Docere et delectare.*'"

That was not a mossy bit of market Latin. None of it was. And to think she had assumed he couldn't even read. This revelation spun in her mind, making her for a moment forget all else. That, clearly, had been his intention.

He scooped her under the knees and carried her to the bed, to sit her among the covers, face-to-face with him. Her wimple went undone, and her veil, and the other layers too, her skin covered by his touch and his lips, stake for stake. Behind each carefully wrought move, his determination was there, negotiating the line between his intent and her panic in the face of it. She suffered the touch until she had to free herself, had to save herself from being drawn into the treacherous depths of the Avre, where she would drown and dissolve into nothingness. She pushed him away violently, her nails inadvertently scoring skin.

He went stone still, eyes closed briefly, holding his breath and himself—and she realized that he expected her to use them, not accidentally or in mindless fright, but on purpose, as if it were part of it. His hand slipped from her elbow in anticipation of her recoiling in revulsion. She should have, but Anne's words came to her: *You have your marriage and your marriage is your weapon.* Her fingers relaxed instead, splaying against the hot, taut skin. His eyes met hers, surprise in them.

"*Placet*," she said instead, and this time she smiled, knowing that this surrender was to be his, not hers.

He stretched across the width of the bed. Finding no counterpart, he rolled onto his belly, chin on his forearm, eyes heavy lidded, and watched his wife. She had thrown open the shutters and sat in the window embrasure, the hem of her shift hitched up to reveal a white calf and a line of tapering thigh to remind him why that sight had invaded his dreams. He wished he knew what she was thinking, what she had felt. With the others, he thought he knew.

No sound came from below, only the crowing of a rooster anticipating the dawn. The air was warm, perfumed with honeysuckle
and drying hay. The lamp oil was almost gone.

"What time is it?"

She threw the fabric to her ankles, hugging her knees to her
chin. "Lauds."

He smiled, envying her prim dedication to remaining a child.
But perhaps this time he had managed to pry open her heart,
even if just a little, by seducing that neat, adamant mind. Last
night he had gambled, he knew, revealing too much about himself, but after Mirebeau, none of it would matter. He would not let
it matter. "Come back to bed."

Juliana would not look at him. *So this was what the voice of the
Serpent sounded like, luring Eve with whispered promises of* . . .

He knew how to handle childish petulance. "'I have come
into my garden, I have gathered my myrrh with my spice, I have
drunk my milk and my wine—'"

"'He had threescore queens and fourscore concubines, and
virgins without numbers.'"

His smile froze. She made no move when he came to her and
stood there, shoulders slack. "Juliana, I've only had one. She is my
wife," he said very quietly, no fight in him.

There was in her. "Until you find some other man to try to cor-
rupt her so that you can more conveniently discard her?"

He gripped her arm, hurting her. "Juli—"

She wrenched herself free and away from him. She had her
gown slipped on by the time she reached the door. From there
she looked back at him, with bitter defiance. "To the victor the
spoils, my lord. Now, thanks to you, we are both prisoners, Eleanor
and I."

She did not slam the door. It swung on its hinges, shutting in
his face as he reached it. He could have flung it open; he could
have brought her back and made her give herself to him willingly,
like she had last night. Only she had not been willing; he had let
himself be convinced because he wanted to be, just as he had at
the Avre.

He struck the door's knotty wood until blood streaked his knuckles.

Intending to be at the duchess's side for Matins, Anne left the duke's tent and hurried through the town gate to the keep, where Aliénor and her granddaughter had spent their night. She came around a corner and found herself shoved roughly into a doorway. She drew her dagger, expecting her attacker to be an inebriated *routier*. She was right.

"Let me go, you—! You are drunk."

"Not as much as I ought to be. Damn you, Anne, I told you to leave Juliana out of this. You've used her against me, you—"

Anne sheathed her dagger. "I used her? 'There is absolutely nothing you, or Aliénor, or anyone else can do to make me take that girl to my bed,'" she mimicked his voice. "You canting bastard. You've wanted her ever since they shelled her out of those nun's weeds. You wanted her; she wanted Tillières. You both got what you wanted, all within the bonds of holy matrimony!"

He kept her trapped between his arms. "Aliénor put you up to this, but you went along because of Mahaut, didn't you?"

"Did I?" Anne fluttered her eyelashes. "I might have become your mistress, Guérin, but on my terms. My sister was not part of the bargain. What does it feel like to be made a fool of? You've had your mother abbess, why grouse about it?"

"Because other people bear the consequences of our foibles. You've stuffed that chit's much-too-impressionable mind with my every proclivity, but you've neglected to tell her to cultivate some of her own!"

This was an unexpected twist. "Good God. You're not stewing because I told your little wife how to make you bed her. You are stewing because she does not want you back."

Lasalle considered his mistress with teeth-grinding fury. That smothered the laughter on her lips and he saw the fleeing shadow of fear in her eyes. He therefore said, very calmly, "You and I have indulged in our share of low dalliances, but we've embraced them with our eyes open and we don't drag the innocent down with us. Unlike you, Juliana won't accept the lot she drew. What sort of marriage does that offer her, Anne?"

He was trying to make her feel guilty, the sot, pontificating about *her* morals. Anne pushed him away and put enough distance between them to give him a piece of her mind. "A marriage you've made, sir knight, all by yourself. You want to know how to kindle your wife's passion? Tell her to find herself a better lover!"

CHAPTER 49

The prisoners were shackled and assembled, the oxen yoked, the horses saddled, and the tents struck. The Duke of Normandy was leaving Mirebeau. In the midst of it, the Countess de Nevers arrived with the rest of the duchess's household to escort her mistress to Poitiers. Relieved of her duties, Juliana escaped to the town's walls. High on the allure, breeze stirred the morning air. She took off her wimple and leaned out between the merlons. She needed time to think. Unfortunately, she was soon discovered by a subdued John d'Erlée. She curtsied, largely to avoid his eyes, but he only pointed wearily to the line of carts below.

"Arthur is going to Falaise; the Lusignans, to Caen; Eleanor and the grander Franks, Poitevins, and Bretons, to Corfe. The duke even handed some prisoners to the viscount, none important enough to matter, of course. They've all had quite a set-to, I've heard, about the Lusignans."

Behind them, the purl of silks and the scent of lilac announced the Countess de Valence. Anne gave Juliana a peck on the cheek. "You look peaked, my dear. Anything wrong?"

Juliana shook her head more vehemently than she intended.

Anne smiled at d'Erlée. "A set-to? Nearly came to blows. The duke is boiling mad about being tricked. He's having the Lusignans tied to the oxen's tails for the journey. De Roches took umbrage at such a humiliation of men of rank. De Roches could not get in a word regarding Arthur, either, and now he is threatening to withdraw his support. *Et bien.* My duchess and my duty call. I would have a word alone with Lady Juliana, my lord."

When John d'Erlée bowed and withdrew, Juliana slipped her hands into her sleeves, a feeling of helplessness flooding her along with tears born of strained emotions. "I am not going to Poitiers with the duchess, am I?"

Anne caressed her cheek. "I am sorry. She wants you to return to Tillières with him. Guérin and Aliénor are below arguing about it. Care to guess who is winning?"

Juliana knew that Anne meant to cheer her, but she wanted to throw herself at Anne's feet and tell her everything.

Anne lifted the girl's chin. "I came to tell you that Guérin has been in the cups more than usual lately. He picked a fight with Lupescaire, and Aliénor just kept the duke from taking Tillières away from him. Don't get on Guérin's wrong side, especially when he is drunk. If he comes to you, let him. Bide your time." She embraced Juliana. "Brave face, now. Safe journey and God be with you."

After the tumult in the Countess de Valence's company, her departure cast Juliana into despair and confusion. The one person who could provide her with at least some answers was walking out of her life, perhaps forever.

"Wait!" she called out before Anne reached the end of the allure. She hurried to her. "I have to know. Don't you think there is something odd about the Count of Rancon and Lasalle? They hate each other, but it is as if they once were . . ." Juliana covered her eyes. "Oh Lord, I can't."

A surprised silence was followed by an outburst of laughter from Anne. "Lovers? In this world, anything is possible. Would it matter to you?"

Juliana pressed her palms to her temples. "Heavens, no. It's not as if I wanted Lasalle to choose between the two of us, is it? Would it matter to you?"

Anne slipped on her riding gloves. "No. It is not as if I wanted him to choose between the two of us either, is it?"

And before Juliana could ponder that question, Anne gave her a kiss, swept up her train, and swept out. D'Erlée came to Juliana's side and they watched Anne cross the bailey to her waiting palfrey and her men, grooms, and servants.

"I am a fool." D'Erlée took Juliana's hand and this time drew her to him. "Come with me, Juliana."

She did not resist, and for a moment there was a hopefulness in her eyes, as if they were standing alone at the top of Rivefort's keep—but that had been before she truly became someone else's wife. "I can't, John."

He knew that it was not a rejection; it was a plea. And he also knew that he would honor it, this time, just as she would honor her marriage, where she found neither love nor honor.

The hall's door stood wide open, and she could hear Eleanor of Brittany's voice and the Duke of Normandy's sharp retorts. Juliana had expected to find only Lasalle and the Duchess of Aquitaine, so she slipped herself, as had become her habit, between the wall and the door leaf, uncertain what to do. In the middle of the hall, surrounded by John's attendants, the Pearl of Brittany was contesting her uncle once again, her hair spilling about her, her eyes burning at the indignity of it all. She and the Duke of Brittany were being treated like prisoners, common prisoners! Her voice rose in hysterical disbelief.

John Plantagenet was not pleased either. It seemed that he and his men had arrived in the middle of his mother's lively engagement with the Viscount of Tillières. Seething visibly, Lasalle stepped aside to subordinate the matter of his marital difficulties to the cresting tide of royal tempers. But he had not distanced himself far enough for the duke's pleasure, for John snapped his riding crop against the tabletop. "I do wish you would hasten as speedily out of my way as you had sped away with my army, Viscount!"

Hearing this, Eleanor of Brittany spun about. "You!" she

shouted at Lasalle. "You are that *routier*. You're responsible for my brother's imprisonment. And for those men's deaths. You've hanged helpless prisoners. I spit on you!"

And she did.

Someone gasped and the hall went silent. Juliana clamped her hand over her mouth. Leaning on her cane, the Duchess of Aquitaine stood up, her voice a warning. "Eleanor, dear—"

It was too late. Lasalle wiped the back of his sleeve across his cheek and took a step toward the Pearl of Brittany. Eleanor yielded one step and no more. She was, after all, the granddaughter of Aliénor of Aquitaine, and no man in his right mind would dare . . . But this apparent madman took hold of her as if she were a common strumpet, and when Eleanor opened her rose-petal lips to express her outrage, he twisted a handful of her tresses around his fist, and his mouth claimed hers.

The Duke of Normandy and his entire entourage gawked, jaws slack. Juliana would have staked Tillières that Brittany's precious Pearl had never been kissed like that, and not by someone like that man. A muffled peep acknowledging that fact escaped young Eleanor. She struggled briefly and then she capitulated, just like that. Once released, Eleanor leaned against the table, her lips the color of crushed berries, her eyes wide, abrasions left by stubble blotching her cheeks. Having concluded his assault, Lasalle executed a perfect bow that encompassed the girl, her grandmother, and his liege, and left them all standing in the middle of the hall.

Juliana dove farther behind the door until the sound of Lasalle's spurs faded, to be replaced by an explosion of oaths from Duke John. "Get out! All of you, standing there like poleaxed cattle. Out!" His sword struck the candlesticks from the table. "And take this shameless hussy with you!"

A flight of the duke's supporters followed, taking the slightly tarnished Pearl of Brittany with them. Juliana wished she could flee as well, but did not want to become the next target of the duke's wrath.

"Holy Mother of God!" John Plantagenet raged. "Did you see

that, Madame? That creature of yours practically ravished my niece in broad daylight. The unmitigated gall of that man!"

Aliénor of Aquitaine brushed a piece of wax from her skirts and resumed her seat. "Did you expect him to challenge her to a duel? You've practically ravished his mistress in broad daylight and sent him his peevish wife instead. He was getting his own back."

John slammed his sword on the table. "His own? Who does Lasalle think he is? This is all your fault, Mother. How long must I be humiliated by that whoreson? I'll have him—"

The duchess's cane struck the floor. "You will not. That whoreson has been loyal to you, unlike most of your barons. Don't alienate the others. De Roches wants your ear in councils, your favor, and titles. Give them to him. Lasalle wants nothing more than Tillières, and he won't plot against you."

The Duke of Normandy's jaw worked furiously. "Does Lasalle strike you as a man happy scraping horse shit off his boots for the rest of his life in some border viscounty? Very well, I'll let him go this time. But if I find that he has as much as entertained a thought against me, I'll make an example of him the rest of my Norman numskulls won't forget. As for that girl—"

"Find her a husband to cool that temper of hers. Someone safe and attentive to keep her belly round and her away from Philip's plots. Young d'Erlée, perhaps," his mother said, her fingers rapping on the cane head.

Her son returned a fractured smile. "A husband, Mother? Until Isabelle gives me a son, you know well that Eleanor and that snot-nosed brother of hers are my heirs—some say Richard's true heirs. That was the closest she'll ever get to a man!"

"That's enough, John." The duchess kept her voice dispassionate, but underneath it something had trembled. "That girl is nothing. Arthur is the one to mind."

"Nothing? Do you think I'd allow Eleanor to tempt any number of my barons?"

"John!"

The Duke of Normandy picked up his sword, came to his mother's side, and dutifully touched his lips to the fold of her wimple.

"God's speed to Poitiers, Madame. Isabelle is waiting for me at Caen. Sometimes I think she is the only one who truly cares for me." He turned on his heel and strode from the hall.

"John," Aliénor called with a voice of command. "John!" she repeated, and this time her voice quavered. Her son did not heed, no doubt because he heard it.

Juliana prayed she would vanish, but the duke walked past her hiding place without sighting her. A silence ensued. She counted her heartbeats.

"You can come in now, Lady Juliana."

Juliana not only obeyed; she threw herself at the duchess's feet. "I did not mean to eavesdrop, Your Grace; I truly did not. I was told to take my leave, but they—"

The cane tapped against the tiles. "Enough, girl. You are not about to be raked over hot coals. Sit up."

The duchess leveled her gaze at Juliana as if intending to know her every secret, especially the latest one. Despite her effort, Juliana flushed.

"Well, well." The duchess leaned back. "He's had you, or you've had him, hence the temper. Good. I wish you to keep that husband of yours out of trouble. I won't live forever, you know."

"Your Grace, I can't govern the viscount any more than— than—"

"I can govern my son. I have known that for some time. It is a terrible thing to see the labor of a lifetime imperiled by the one person to whom fate has decided to grant this patrimony."

Juliana was not certain how to acknowledge that fact, and so she said, "I hold no sway over the man you chose for me, Your Grace."

The duchess harrumphed. "Nonsense. A husband's faithfulness is not a requirement for a tolerable union. You've seen my son."

Juliana took a deep breath. "I was told not to expect to find love in marriage and I am not such a fool to expect faithfulness there either, although I am told it is not impossible. Sir William is faithful to the lady Isabel—"

"Sir William is a rare exception and so are my Lusignans," the duchess interrupted impatiently. "Robber barons all, but you won't find many Lusignan bastards running about these parts."

"Yes, Your Grace."

"What, no philosophical rejoinders, Lady Juliana?"

Lady Juliana stuck to territory closer to home. "He killed Hesse for you."

"He was paid well." The glass-fine features and implacable eyes dared to be disputed. "Lasalle has more lives than a cat, and a Lusignan's cunning. If he had not sided with John, I would consider him a troublesome man. I want you to return to Tillières and make him behave like a husband. Husbands become reconciled to their wives faster if they are presented with an heir, need I remind you? Anne must have taught you something."

"Yes, Your Grace." Lacking an answer to that one, Juliana curtsied and hurried to the door. She wished she could slam it behind her.

She charged through the encampment, dodging horses, oxen, mules, men, and piles of camp gear, manure, and debris. She did not notice a thing until a distinct, familiar voice cut through her storm.

"Always in a rush, Lady Juliana?"

She tripped over a discarded kettle. In front of her, ironed to a cart wheel and surrounded by their guards, the three lords of Lusignan awaited their deportation. One of the guards moved forward. He was a raw-boned *routier,* dressed in a patched *broigne* and bristling with eyebrows and whiskers, a pennant lance in his hand. "I am Fulbeck, Lady. Don't come too near; they've got more tricks up their sleeves than a dockside whore. Oh, begging your pardon, my lady." Fulbeck grinned and thrust the butt of his lance into the ribs of one of the reclining prisoners. "Get up, my lord, you have a visitor."

The Count of La Marche sprang to his feet like a wounded boar, only to be brought down by a swift knock behind his knee by his partner in bonds, the Count of Rancon. Before Brown Hugh could retaliate, his cousin levered himself upright against his shoulder and crafted his cracked lips into a careful smile. "How kind of you to visit old friends, Lady Juliana." Armand de Lusignan brought up his manacled wrists. "Do remember us to your husband."

Was that a threat or a warning? Juliana settled for an equally ambiguous curtsy.

"I've heard that you and your husband have reconciled, and that you are expecting a blessed event, Lady Juliana. My congratulations," the count continued, as if they were in the middle of his own hall.

She smiled back with hard-won composure. "Rumors, my lord."

He bowed as much as his irons allowed. "Ah. Regrets, then."

"None required, my lord." They were playing a game, a game whose rules she was not privy to, but of one thing she was certain: The Lusignan was as curious about her relationship with Lasalle as she was about his. And as absurd as it seemed, she had the oddest feeling that she was in fact in competition with Armand de Lusignan.

Decidedly disconcerted, Juliana ended the encounter with another brief curtsy and escaped between the guards, only to run headlong into a man leading a splendidly caparisoned destrier. She was about to stammer her apologies, but she found herself looking into a pair of winter-dead eyes in a cleanly shaved face—not an ugly one, but a memorable one for its lack of any trace of benignity.

"Lady." The man bowed slightly, those eyes on her.

She did not need anyone to tell her who the man was: Lupescaire.

She crossed herself and quickly steered past the infamous mercenary, and actually felt relief to find Lasalle's company, one of the last to decamp. She found that Duke John had indeed given Lasalle the bother of eight Poitevin hostages to guard and feed, none of them of rank high enough to recompense Lasalle with their ransom. To her unease, she recognized among them Joscelyn de Cantigny.

Next to his dismantled tent, Lasalle was saddling his horse, a gray stallion with black nostrils, a high-curved neck, and a braided black mane—one of the splendid coursers bred by the Count of Rancon. Juliana hesitated. Would Lasalle punish her now for last night? She tried to avoid his eyes, but caught his scowl. "Get your rump in that saddle and don't leave it before I say so." He turned to Vaudreuil. "Everyone on the road, move!"

Lasalle might have been anxious to depart, but so was the Duke of Normandy. They had to wait for the duke's party to pass and therefore had the opportunity to witness the proud lords of Lusignan trudge through the choking dust, dung, and flies, secured to the oxen's tails.

Juliana glanced at Lasalle. He sat rigid in the saddle of the Count de Rancon's steed, watching the prisoners with hate in his eyes.

CHAPTER 50

Fortress of Rivefort, Normandy

For the rest of the journey to Tillières, Juliana devoted herself to avoiding Lasalle and easing the lot of his hostages. They were all young—some younger than herself—and dazed at the sudden turn in their fortunes. For some of them, Mirebeau represented their first taste of war—and defeat. She noticed that Kadolt was not among Lasalle's men; he had, it appeared, decided to join Lupescaire's mercenaries, no doubt for better pay.

"I see the viscount has fully recovered from his wounds, my lady." Joscelyn de Cantigny smiled at her when she placed bread and a slice of cheese in his hands. They traveled through territory still crossed by Philip's troops, and Lasalle forbade campfires.

"How do you know about his wounds, sir?" Like the young man, she kept her voice low.

"The count roared like a lion when he heard of it. Everyone at Pont-de-l'Arche dove under the nearest bushel. He sent Viart to Tillières to find out how the viscount fared. He would not calm down until favorable news came."

Not wishing to draw Lasalle's attention to the young man, Juliana smiled blandly and moved on to the next prisoner. She could not imagine the Count of Rancon in a temper. With all the hostages fed, she retreated to her tent and lay down, too worn out to eat anything herself. She had only just closed her eyes when someone shook her. Lasalle squatted next to her pallet, and before Juliana could compose herself, something smooth and round was slipped in her hand. "It's an egg," he said. "Eat it."

The speckled egg looked harmless; its purveyor did not. He wanted her to say something on the subject of last night. She would not—not ever.

"Wear your hat, Juliana. You are beginning to look like that egg."

Fingertips brushed her cheekbone, startling her. She must not allow him to unsettle her. She must pretend composure at all times. "Why did you surrender Rivefort?"

"To see if it accommodates a French garrison as easily as a Norman one."

He stung her with her own words. She expected further verbal combat, but he only shook his head, as if he wanted to commence anew. "Camp fever broke out in Philip's camp. We struck a deal. De Montier could claim he seized Rivefort for Philip, and I got my men out."

There it was. An answer unembellished and simple enough to be the truth. For some reason she felt foolishly brave. "Anne said you've quarreled with the duke about the Lusignans."

"I told him to drop them all into an oubliette and roll a millstone on top of it."

"Including the Count of Rancon?"

"Especially the Count of Rancon."

"He asked about you," she said, her stomach knotting.

"Of course he did. Armand takes great interest in my affairs. And who better to tell him than my wife?"

A hot flush spread over her. "I would not!"

Lasalle looped his sword belt over his shoulder and pushed aside the tent flap. "Of course you would not, love. There is precious little to tell, isn't there?"

Whatever damage the fortress and the viscounty had sustained during its brief occupation by the forces of King Philip, the evidence of it had largely vanished, along with Roger de Montier's men. Like Philip's other captains, de Montier had withdrawn from Normandy upon learning of the disaster at Mirebeau. By the time Juliana returned, the fields glowed with green-gold swathes of wheat and barley, hay copses grew higher in the meadows, and apple-tree branches bowed under the weight of new fruit.

After the luxury of a bath and dreamless sleep in her own bed, Juliana's first concerns were Lasalle's hostages and Master Thibodeau's books. As efficient as ever, Master Thibodeau presented her with a list of damages and the cost of repairs. Master Thibodeau was indeed a gem. The very next day, Lasalle assigned to her the care of the hostages, not neglecting to remind her that if they escaped, the cost of their ransom would be borne by Tillières, together with an explanation to the Duke of Normandy.

Not worried in the least about that possibility but at a loss as to what, exactly, one did with eight young, healthy male prisoners, she brought the men to Jehan de Vaudreuil. Vaudreuil accepted them with as much enthusiasm as if he had been ordered to swallow a trugful of live minnows. After a few days she noticed that they for some reason preferred her company to Vaudreuil's, a development which, Juliana suspected, Vaudreuil encouraged. In the process, she was reminded that what they said about Poitevins was true. Unlike the taciturn Normans, the southerners were well versed in all the graces of *courtoisie*.

With the Poitevins provided for, she wrote to the Abbess of Saint-Sylvain about the state of her petition on behalf of Aumary de Beaudricourt. She also wrote to Isabel de Clare, asking her to return Mathea and Paulette. They were wards of the Viscountess of Tillières and she could not shirk her responsibility for them, though she thus far had not fulfilled it very well. And she wanted Mistress Hermine back.

No reply came from Abbess Nicola, but Hermine and the demoiselles Glanville arrived under an escort of the lady Isabel's men, along with a couple carts of belongings that they had somehow acquired at Longueville. Relieved of his duties for the occasion by William Marshal, Aumary de Beaudricourt headed the procession. The word of their return had spread, and before they had crossed the drawbridge, the entire populace of Rivefort had turned out to greet them.

Despite her grown-up appearance in a lady's gown and smoothly braided hair, Mathea could not restrain herself. She jumped from the saddle of her full-size palfrey and threw herself around Juliana's neck, covering her with kisses. Plumper than before, Mistress Hermine climbed from her mule with the help of two grooms, straightened her wimple, and headed for Juliana.

"God be praised to be home. It was not my doing to leave you like this, my lady. Let me look at you. Oh, my poor lamb, you are as thin as a wraith."

Lost in the confusion, Paulette was waiting patiently for someone to help her from her palfrey when the eight Poitevins spotted her and trampled one another to rescue her. At least Paulette and Mathea would not find the transition from the Countess of Pembroke's elegant household to Rivefort's rustic one too unsettling. Juliana smiled, and then she noticed Lasalle by the stable door, with Edward de Bec strapping on his lord's spurs with lip-chewing concentration. She did not know that Lasalle had returned to Rivefort from Lord only knew where—most likely Master Diceto's establishment.

"I don't recall giving you permission to bring back those two," he said to her without a preamble, presenting his conscientious squire with his other boot.

Juliana curtsied. "I didn't think it necessary to ask you about how I should manage my duties, sir, just as I would not think it proper to interfere with yours."

Lasalle cast a disparaging glance at the Poitevins besieging Paulette. "You make it your business to interfere with mine at every turn, Lady."

"Kept locked up they could have become ill and died. I am to keep you out of trouble." To forestall any misunderstanding, she added, "On the orders of the Duchess of Aquitaine."

Lasalle struck the riding crop against his boot top. "Of course. La Bella Doma. Never too busy to salve the cankers of this world. And how do you propose to do that? Keep me on a leash like one of your swains?"

"I am not keeping them on a leash. They are honorable men who wish to please and amuse of their own volition, nothing more. You can see that their attentions are drawn elsewhere already."

"Then praise God for the return of the demoiselles. Does that mean you'll let me back in your bed?"

He had lured her into an ambush like a yearling into a hunter's sight. "You—you know you have that right."

He clamped her chin in his hand and leaned very close. "I don't need to be reminded of my rights, but some men prefer what is offered rather than what is taken. Didn't Anne tell you?"

If he comes to you, let him. She did not move. He held her for a heartbeat longer, then let her go and cut a gesture to Donat, who rushed up with the black-legged courser. Lasalle mounted and reined the stallion into ever tighter circles around her, forcing her to turn and turn until she dizzied.

"No need to panic, love. One can always pay and take."

CHAPTER 51

Aumary de Beaudricourt appeared to have grown a foot and had acquired a bit of a swagger. He lapsed into it only when he thought he was not being observed, but earned himself merciless teasing anyway, especially when it became apparent that Aumary was completely and helplessly in love with the fair Paulette. In truth, most of the male population of Rivefort was smitten with the girl to various degrees, and she grew even more retiring before the covetous eyes.

Juliana tried to discover Paulette's feelings for Aumary, but the girl merely smiled her gentle, sweet smile and replied that she was honored by the attention. Juliana put it more bluntly. "Of course you are. But what would you say if Aumary asked for your hand in marriage?"

Paulette slipped the silk thread between her fingers. "Whatever you wish me to say, Juliana."

Juliana smiled, caressed Paulette's cheek, and went with Mathea to the garden. They brought scissors and baskets, and snipped the lavender and rosemary to sweeten the floor hay in the winter. "I wish I knew what your sister truly wants."

Mathea sighed wistfully. "I don't think she knows. We've always had others tell us. She had Longueville eating out of her hand, and she did not even notice."

"Paulette may speak her mind. I would never force her into a marriage against her will," Juliana assured the girl.

"I know. But we are not heiresses, are we? Not many men will marry us for our charm and good disposition."

Mathea had not lost all of her impishness, but her figure had rounded out and most of her childish manners had disappeared under the tutelage of the Countess of Pembroke. At times Mathea displayed the wisdom of someone far older. "The status of heir-

esses, sweet pea, is much exaggerated. They are not married for
their charm or good disposition either," Juliana said.

"I know. But it makes it difficult for the man, too, don't you
think? Suppose you are a man who has nothing to offer the lady
he wishes to marry? And suppose she has nothing either?"

"Aumary can marry anyone he wishes. She doesn't have to be
an heiress. And you'll not have nothing, Mathea. We will come up
with something, provided we can find someone who is not too
demanding of a dowry."

A man marries a fief. Juliana thought about the coins Lasalle had
tried to foist on her in Paris, which had later been hidden by Master Thibodeau from de Montier's men. The coins would make
Mathea a handsome dowry—blood money put to good use. And
then there was Belvoir. A modest living, but surely she could find
for Mathea a young man who would prefer a compatible wife with
a small estate to a disagreeable one with a larger dowry.

Mathea dropped a sprig of rosemary into the basket. "I know
all about being married. The lady Isabel told us."

Juliana mouthed a silent thanks to the lady Isabel. "One wedding at a time, please. First Catalena and Donat, then Paulette and
Aumary."

"But Juliana, that could take months. I am almost fifteen. I
have to find someone!"

"Patience is a virtue, child." Juliana laughed, assuming the tone
of Father Osbert. "Besides, we don't have anyone for you to marry
yet. It's easy to find a man to marry. Any stable hand could do." A
thorn tore into her finger. She untangled her hand and knelt next
to the girl. "But you must marry someone who will be your companion, not just your husband. I don't want you to be unhappy,
please understand."

"I understand," Mathea whispered, her eyes filling with tears.
She held Juliana tightly. "Oh, I am so sorry. I did not mean to
cause you worry. I know I am selfish. I don't know what comes over
me. They all fall at Paulette's feet and she doesn't even notice.
Nobody ever notices me. Sometimes I wish I was as beautiful as she
is, and then I'd become a nun, just to show them!"

Juliana kissed the girl's forehead and smoothed her hair. She understood Mathea's pain and frustration at the unfairness of it all. "We'll find someone for you, and to him you'll be the most beautiful lady in Christendom."

Aumary's courtship of the lady Paulette did not escape his liege's notice for very long. Soon the news spread throughout Rivefort that my lord Lasalle had forbidden Aumary de Beaudricourt to pay court to the lady Paulette. Thunderstruck, Aumary complied without question; Juliana could not hide her outrage.

Le Roux told her that Lasalle had ridden out to the carp ponds with his new falcon. She had not known that he owned a falcon, let alone knew what to do with one. No one stopped her or Donat at the portcullis, which Juliana took to mean that Lasalle no longer cared if she ran away—or, more precisely, that with Armand de Lusignan's imprisonment, he knew she had nowhere to run.

She left Rosamond and Donat with Lasalle's gray courser. The marshy ground muffled her footsteps. Lasalle had his back to her, gazing skyward. He wore what he usually did, a threadbare shirt and a gambeson, which hardly distinguished the viscount from the forest reeve; the only addition was a falconer's glove. Above, scythe-shaped wings appeared in the sky and dropped toward the reeds, skimming their tops at the last moment. Talons spread and wings braced, the snow-white gyrfalcon came to Lasalle's glove with a jingle of tail-feather bells and a keening cry. Lasalle fastened the jesses around her feet swiftly and adeptly.

"My lord!" Juliana pitched her voice over the bird's shrill cries. The gyrfalcon leapt up with an alarmed screech, nearly becoming airborne again. Lasalle grabbed the jesses and the bird slipped off the glove, her wings flapping like a market fowl's.

"Christ, woman, stay where you are!"

Mortified, Juliana obeyed. He untangled the bird, perched her back on his glove, and secured her hood ties with the aid of his teeth. "Don't you know anything? She is becoming used to me and I don't need you to frighten her."

Juliana cringed. Not a fortuitous commencement to her petition, but at least Lasalle appeared reasonably sober. "I am sorry. I
didn't know you knew about falcons. That is a gyrfalcon, isn't it,
just like the Count of . . . good God, it *is* the Count of Rancon's!"

Lasalle bent his knees halfway and picked up a sack. He shoved
it at her. "It *was* the Count of Rancon's. There are a thousand
things you don't know about me, mouse. What is it you want?"

A puff of bloody feathers and a jumble of yellow webbed feet
spilled from the sack. The gyrfalcon did her new master's bidding
after all. Juliana knotted the sack's top, trying to keep up with
Lasalle through a field of cow parsley.

"That we share Tillières. Like you share Anne with the duke
and the Count of Rancon." She tried to put in a note of sophistica-
tion. "That is, when the others are not around. To avoid embarrassment. We'll make sure we don't cross each other's path more
than necessary. You'll conduct your life as you wish, and so will I.
We call a truce."

Lasalle slowly faced her, his left eyebrow at an angle. "What is
it that you truly want?"

"That you rescind your orders to Aumary about Paulette."

Keeping the bird balanced, Lasalle mounted up. "No. Go
back to your epistles and keep that sharp nose of yours out of my
affairs."

She went for the reins, bringing the high-stepping stallion to a
halt. "Why not? Aumary loves her and I am certain she is very fond
of him. Doesn't somebody at Rivefort deserve to be happy? Why
must you always make people miserable?"

"Let go, Juliana." His voice had that undertone of threat in it.
She ignored it.

"You have no rights over Aumary. He is of age. I have two
wards and I will make certain they both have kind, honorable
husbands!"

"You think highly of yourself as a matchmaker, Eustace."

She hung on to the reins. "Does that mean you intend to keep
them locked up at Rivefort as well until we are all old and gray?"

Lasalle changed his tactic and short-reined the horse away

from her, the gyrfalcon voicing her discontent. "You are all free to go as you please. Take le Roux, Peyrac, and de Cantigny, or anyone else from our southern guests. Take Vaudreuil."

That was an unexpected offer. There had to be a catch. And indeed there was, for where would she go? "I will not leave Tillières to you. I wish to pay a visit to the sisters at Villedieu!"

He nodded readily. "Will you be visiting long?"

"You'd want me to stay there forever, wouldn't you, but the duchess won't allow it!"

Instead of answering her, he spurred the horse into the white field, leaving her spitting mad with a sack full of dead drakes.

Shaded against the late summer heat by a curve of green hills, Villedieu looked nothing like Juliana recalled from childhood memories. Neither the impressive size of Fontevraud nor a fortress like Saint-Sylvain, the priory actually looked welcoming. Juliana had decided to come here to see the place Lasalle intended to consign her, but once she was inside the stone walls, she winced at the stab of nostalgia for the orderly world behind them. The establishment housed two dozen sisters, four novices, and half a dozen schoolgirls. Still a young woman, the prioress greeted them, smiling and energetic. The new chapel roof was impossible to miss.

"Yes, the viscount has been very generous." With a touch of worldly pride, Prioress Reglindis guided Juliana and the girls through the convent's rows of onions. "He told us you are something of a gardener yourself, Lady Juliana."

"Not on such a grand scale, Reverend Mother." What else had Lasalle told the prioress?

"We all have to begin small and watch things grow," said the prioress, smiling. "We are delighted to welcome you. Would you and your wards like to sing with us at Vespers?"

Juliana gladly agreed. Perhaps Villedieu would not be such a bad place once she saw Paulette and Mathea safely wed. After passing another pleasant day in the company of the sisters, they reluctantly took their leave. Paulette was the last to tear herself from the company of Mother Reglindis. With the rest of the party filing through the gate, the prioress came to Rosamond's side. "Lady Mathea is charming, but Lady Paulette, she has the face and the voice of an angel, does she not? We will pray for all of you, and we look forward to welcoming you again."

Juliana glanced up at the chapel roof. "No doubt very soon, Reverend Mother. I know the viscount has made arrangements for me. At least Villedieu won't be a place of strangers."

The prioress looked puzzled. "He has not attached any condition to his gift, Lady Juliana."

Juliana took up Rosamond's reins. "He will attach it next time."

CHAPTER 52

Autumn 1202

Rivefort threw itself into preparations for Donat and Catalena's wedding, but travelers seeking shelter at Rivefort brought with them disturbing news. Upon his return to Normandy from his southern campaign, Duke John whiled away his days at Caen, savoring his wife and his spectacular coup at Mirebeau. With the Lusignans and their allies locked up in his fortresses, John entrusted the defense of Normandy to Lupescaire, ordering him to have his mercenaries harass the estates of those Normans who had displayed less-than-burning zeal for their duke's cause.

Thus far the news had brought nothing more than faint echoes of the fraying relationship between John and his barons, although Lasalle sent out patrols to follow reports of strange men moving about the edges of the viscounty. The patrols returned, reporting nothing suspicious. No doubt the villeins had drunk too much young wine.

Donat and Catalena's wedding took place after the long days of feverish work to gather the fruits of the season's labors. Juliana bore up under the servants' ribald revelry, which only served to remind her of the emptiness of her own marriage. Donat and Catalena took all the teasing in stride, safe in their own world. That was until, in the middle of everyone's good cheer, a rider on a black-legged courser trotted into the bailey. Cups halted on their way to thirsty lips. The sound of the hurdy-gurdy faded along with the merriment.

Lasalle swung himself out of the saddle and sat down in the empty chair next to Juliana, the smell of wine swirling about him. He helped himself to a drumstick from her trencher and waved it at the musicians, who found a very lively tune.

"You are a very discreet woman, Lady Juliana. That's why you ought to take a lover. How about poor Joscelyn? He's been making calf eyes at you ever since Mirebeau. Or was it Pont-de-l'Arche?"

He was surely drunk, and if not, he was surely mad. "You've already tried that ploy, my lord," she reminded him, keeping the exchange to themselves. "I am not going to take a lover just to please you."

"The idea, mouse, is to take one to please you. You don't have to worry about the consequences. Any child you care to keep will be acknowledged as my own unless you plan to shout to the contrary from the top of the steeple."

"Good Lord, who do you take me for?" Juliana stood up. The music died in the last screech of the hurdy-gurdy. The Poitevins and the rest of the guests craned their necks. Lasalle stood up as well, dropping the bone to the dogs under the table. She faced him, fists at her sides, fury choking her. She wrenched her wedding ring over her knuckle and flung it into the spit's fire. "I will never commit adultery, sir, and I would never conspire to pass off as his own a child not of a lawful husband. Any woman who would is an adulteress and a harlot, and you will not make me either!"

The look in his eyes failed to warn her. The open-handed blow knocked her backward; a blinding explosion blurred her sight and deafened her ears. *My nose is broken again.* That terribly practical thought passed through her mind before she plummeted into blackness.

She woke up in her own bed with the anxious faces of Hermine, Mathea, and Paulette around her. They helped her sit up, washed away the blood, applied a poultice to her cheek, and cosseted her. More concerned about their distress than her own, Juliana at last persuaded her nurses to return to the wedding guests. When they did so, with great reluctance, Juliana saw in her mirror that her nose was not broken again after all, but her swelling lip made her look like a hare. She winced and pressed back the poultice of Solomon's seal, useful for wives who walked into their husbands' fists. She would make a sight when she appeared in the bailey, and she could not even pretend that she had fallen against her trunk, like her mother used to. A black stream of hatred flooded her.

When it abated enough for her hands to stop shaking, she found a piece of parchment. Time for another missive to Abbess Nicola at Saint-Sylvain. Several days later, she surreptitiously passed the letter, along with several silver coins of Lasalle's blood money, to a mendicant friar whom God had sent her way.

After that, she took up the challenge of persuading Aumary de Beaudricourt to disregard his lord's orders and to renew his court of the Lady Fair. That was what Lasalle called the girl, resurrecting Juliana's fears for Paulette's safety. Young Edward de Bec would serve as the perfect intermediary. Worshipful of Paulette already, he would relish his role as a faithful knight selflessly serving his one true love.

The tallies and supervision of stores for the winter kept Juliana busy from dawn to dusk, even with the help of Master Thibodeau and Mathea, and the befuddled assistance of Paulette. Despite the throng of activity, unsettling news brought by travelers and pilgrims reminded everyone of the other events outside Rivefort's walls.

Stunned and frightened by Duke John's iron-fisted response to their rebellion, the barons of Brittany clamored for the release of Arthur and his sister, pinning their hopes, like the Lusignans had done before them, on King Philip. Philip Augustus unfortunately appeared unable or, more alarmingly, unwilling to support their appeals. Suspicious minds believed that he welcomed the crushing of the Bretons and the Poitevins, his potential rivals.

At the same time, the Norman barons, especially those on the borders of Maine, grew restless. Soon, rumors of another rebellion came from all corners of John's domains. The disillusioned and disaffected William de Roches, the travelers hinted overtly, would lead it. Those barons who still remained loyal to John began to vacillate, revisiting and recounting the humiliation of the Bretons and the Poitevins, dragged off in chains and exhibited in towns along the way by their wrathful duke. John's triumph at Mirebeau was turning into a Pyrrhic victory.

An English knight who arrived at Rivefort brought more shocking news: Duke John had starved to death some of his prisoners at Corfe. More shocking still, rumors circulated that at Falaise he had ordered Arthur mutilated to make the boy unfit to ever rule, but that the young prince's gaoler, the dour Hugh de Bourgh, had refused to carry out such a monstrous command.

Huddled on benches around the hall table, Rivefort's hostages received the news in stunned silence. Lasalle's knights were equally taken aback, then started to mutter loudly, some expressing the sentiments that perhaps the time had come for Rivefort to declare itself on de Roches's side. Juliana noticed that Jehan de Vaudreuil did not join these men, though he appeared particularly disgusted, downing another cup. When it came to drinking, Juliana feared, Vaudreuil had begun to match Lasalle.

When Mathea and Paulette heard the dreadful reports, their eyes filled with tears. Juliana kept her gaze on her trencher. Ransomed or not, she would release Joscelyn de Cantigny and his companions at the first chance, before John demanded that they be surrendered to him.

Soon, more ominous news arrived. William de Roches had resigned his custody of Chinon and openly joined the opposition to

John. The rebels had gathered at Angers and nearly captured Queen Isabelle, left there in safekeeping by her husband and suddenly made vulnerable in the formerly loyal town. Only in the nick of time had one of John's faithful knights spirited the terrified girl out of the city and reunited her with her husband at Le Mans.

The duke's fury at William de Roches's betrayal and the near loss of his dearly loved wife exploded. Eyewitnesses brought accounts of the abductions of the wives and daughters of the duke's suspected enemies by his mercenaries. Pillage, rapine, and murder abounded in the burned-out strongholds, towns, and villages. The Duke of Normandy had declared war on his own vassals.

At Rivefort, everyone turned up in the chapel to pray for the safety of the viscounty. Not a single person in the congregation deluded himself that Tillières would remain safe forever from the mercenaries' predations, but thus far the mesne had not suffered any attacks. Juliana did not know whether she should ascribe it to their prayers or to Lasalle's devilish luck. At least these events kept Lasalle and the rest of the men away from Rivefort on a reconnaissance of the viscounty. Aumary rode out with them, but whenever he returned, Juliana arranged for his and Paulette's paths to cross. And so one cold, misty morning, Juliana unlatched the gate to her garden and caught herself in time to prevent an unwelcome trespass.

Aumary and Paulette stood under the arch of the rose arbor, where the last of fall's roses had scattered their petals. Paulette's chin was tilted upward, her eyelashes lowered demurely. Aumary held the girl gently and when Paulette rose on her tiptoes to meet Aumary's reverent kiss, Juliana's heart ached, her eyes watered, and her nose itched. She did an about-face and retreated to her room. Once there, she cried till her apron was soaked.

Finally, some unexpectedly good news reached Rivefort. Saint-Sylvain had granted permission for Aumary de Beaudricourt to wed Paulette de Glanville. Juliana whooped and kissed the messenger-friar on both cheeks; he stammered all the way to the kitchen, to which Juliana ushered him for a meal of his heart's desire. After that, she climbed to the stable loft and gathered straw flowers from the bundles drying in the rafters. At the bottom of the ladder, Louis Pavilli waited for her.

"My lady, we have visitors," the steward said in a hushed voice.

"We always have visitors, Master Louis," she replied cheerfully.

"Not like these." Pavilli indicated the bailey. Juliana peeked around him.

At the horse trough several dismounted riders crowded, red crosses stitched to the white surcoats of three of them—Knights of Solomon's Temple, a holy order of martial monks. The others were sergeants of the order, in black cloaks with red crosses, and several lay-brother servants. The Order's dedication and zeal in fighting in *outre-mer*, along with its military and monetary prowess, had gained it almost a legendary reputation—and the fear and envy of some.

Juliana tugged at the steward's sleeve. "What should I do? Their rules forbid them to look at the face of a woman, even a mother or a sister. I don't wish to offend them."

Louis Pavilli patted her hand. "Don't worry, my lady, I will see to them."

Relieved, Juliana hurried to get to the chapel before the torches went out. Whatever the season, she brought flowers to fill the niche above Jourdain's resting place. She was reaching for the door ring when voices inside the chapel caused her to pause. Someone inside was in the middle of a heated, albeit one-sided, argument. No, not Father Cyril; that was Lasalle's voice.

Good Lord, she did not know he had returned. Through a crack in the door she could see Lasalle pacing the floor, his spurs clinking angrily. Kneeling before the chapel's simple cross was another Templar. Juliana could not see his face, only a shadow of a dark beard and black hair. She could not understand a word of what they were saying because they spoke in the language of the Saracens, but tiring of Lasalle's tirade, the Temple knight crossed himself and stood up, retorting in a calm tone. The reply did not have its intended effect, for Lasalle seized the man's surcoat and shoved him against the wall. She heard the cloth tear.

The Templar was not a man to turn the other cheek. His size

matched Lasalle's, and before his back hit the wall, the edge of his hand struck Lasalle's forearm with such force that Lasalle broke away with a painful gasp. Dropping a sarcastic word or two, he gave the Templar an exaggerated bow and left the chapel to him.

Juliana stepped into the shadows before Lasalle could see her. She had acquired quite a skill in avoiding my lord Lasalle. When she looked in, the Templar had returned to his prayers. She would have left him, as well, but the door hinges gave her away, and there she stood under the fluttering flames of the torches.

"I am sorry, my lord, I did not mean to disturb you. I was just taking some flowers . . ." She hunted for the words, afraid that she was causing the Temple knight to breech his vows by her presence. The man cocked his head to the side.

"You are?" he said in a low voice that nevertheless resonated under the vaulting.

"Juliana. I mean, I am Juliana de Charnais. I live here. I mean, Tillières is my viscounty." Oh dear, that did not come out well at all.

"Does not Tillières belong to the viscount?" the Templar asked, unperturbed, but she thought she heard amusement in his voice.

"It does not! He is only my husband." That came out worse. "I am sorry. Please don't take his manners personally. He is like that with everyone."

"Including Tillières's heiress?" The Templar glanced over his shoulder. "I am sorry. I do not wish to embarrass you, Lady Juliana."

"Oh. I don't suppose it's much of a secret."

"And you seek refuge in this chapel?"

"Oh, no. I mean, I do attend prayers every day, but I only came to leave these flowers. I will not disturb you any further, my lord." She curtsied and hurried to place the flowers in the niche. Behind her, she heard the man rise and move discreetly to the far wall.

"You have a friend here you wish to remember?"

"No. I mean yes. A very small friend. He was taken from me before we could truly become friends."

"I am sorry for your grief, Lady Juliana. You must draw comfort from knowing that your child resides with Our Lord." The Templar crossed himself, his voice sounding genuinely regretful.

Juliana crossed herself as well, but rushed to correct him. "Oh, I do, but Jourdain was not my child. That is, I don't have . . . I never had a child. I mean, I had a child, but not my own. Jourdain was my husband's. What I mean . . ." She gave up. That explanation alone would require days. In the dim light, she tried to make out the man's profile, which he carefully kept from her, and decided it was her turn. "Do you know the viscount, my lord?"

She thought that the man smiled, either at her impertinence or her awkwardness. "We've both served the King of Jerusalem."

"Oh!" She took a step forward, hoping excitement concealed her ambivalence. "Guy de Lusignan?"

The Templar nodded. "You are acquainted with that family, Lady Juliana?"

"No. Yes. Somewhat. Through my husband's . . . connection. But not lately, of course, not since their imprisonment. They say the duke will never release them."

"But the duke already has."

CHAPTER 53

Winter–Spring 1203

The Lusignans set free—all of them.

With his treasury empty, the enemies he had made at Mirebeau besieging loyal fortresses, and a plague of rebellion spreading among his continental vassals, the Duke of Normandy had released the treacherous Poitevins. As a condition of their release, the Lusignans had pledged solemn oaths to cease their hostilities, handed over forts, and surrendered hostages as sureties—and then promptly joined the disaffected barons. The few remaining supporters of Duke John tore out their hair in disbelief, William Marshal foremost among them. After weighing the advantages of shifting their support to Arthur, who was still malleable and unversed in the intrigues of the Franks and the Plantagenets, those lukewarm in their allegiance renewed their demands for the release and restoration of the young Duke of Brittany and his sister.

Juliana did not know whether to laugh or cry. She wondered what the Duchess of Aquitaine might have had to say upon receiving that news. What my lord Lasalle thought of the unexpected turn of his fortune, Juliana could surmise without difficulty. She wished she could have found out more, but her conversation with the Temple knight had ended abruptly when his brother knight came to fetch him. After that, Juliana lit a candle, knelt on the stone floor, and gave thanks to the Almighty. At least Armand de Lusignan was alive and safe, and perhaps willing to resume their alliance. She remained on her knees in the chapel until Hermine came for her with the news that my lord Lasalle had taken his leave of Rivefort after announcing that in the autumn, Aumary de Beaudricourt would return to serve Sir William at Longueville. That did it. She had a few months to persuade Aumary to press his suit for Paulette's hand. Henceforth, Guérin de Lasalle would face war on two fronts.

Autumn 1203

Aumary de Beaudricourt wore his riding cloak over his surcoat, his gold spurs on his heels, and an anguished expression. Juliana pushed the parchment toward him. "No one will suspect. Instead of riding to Longueville, you'll wait at Villedieu until Paulette arrives. Prioress Reglindis will gladly give you shelter and find a priest."

Juliana wished she could ride out with Paulette, but Lasalle had restored his orders for her confinement, fearing no doubt that she would try to seek refuge with the Lusignans.

Aumary picked up the letter and read it again, chewing his lower lip. By now, he ought to have memorized it, Juliana thought with exasperation: Saint-Sylvain's gave permission for its ward and vassal Aumary de Beaudricourt to wed Paulette de Glanville. *These two,* Juliana thought, smiling to herself despite her impatience, *do not wear their hearts on their sleeves, sharing instead a quiet devotion to each other.* Who said that Juliana de Charnais was not a matchmaker?

"You must act now. Edward and Donat will accompany Paulette. She'll wear Catalena's cloak and ride her mother's palfrey. Everyone will think that Catalena and Donat are riding to the market. I'll write a letter for Paulette to take to the prioress," Juliana repeated for the third time.

Aumary sighed deeply. "I am most grateful, Lady Juliana, but I owe my allegiance to my lord Lasalle. I still have much to learn, and if it is his wish that I should not wed Paulette, I can't defy it. I owe him that, and more."

Juliana tapped her fingers on the window embrasure. What a dreadful thing for Aumary to be torn between love and duty to one's lord, especially a lord like Guérin de Lasalle. And she dreaded to face another winter of trunk-splitting cold, prowling wolves, and starving villains—and Lasalle in her bed, this time not a helpless convalescent. Time for a different tactic. Juliana moved toward the young man. "Do you owe him Paulette in his bed, too?"

Aumary's shocked gasp was her answer.

"Ah, you've heard," she said. Nothing remained much of a secret at Rivefort. Someone must have overheard Lasalle's threats against Paulette, delivered that night at the Three Dwarfs. Hermine, perhaps? If Hermine had, she had undoubtedly confided in one or two of her friends.

"He wouldn't!"

Juliana reached for Abbess Nicola's letter. "No, of course not. That is unthinkable."

Aumary de Beaudricourt shifted from one foot to the other, his gaze on the floor. Juliana watched him from under her eyelashes.

Aumary had matured into a fine young man, tall and gentle and honorable, a true knight. He made the servant girls blush and sigh, and if he had taken up with any of them, at least he had the good sense not to flaunt it. He would never hurt Paulette by his actions, and he would love her and cherish her for the rest of their days.

Juliana folded the parchment, praying silently and desperately, and when she could not delay any further, she said, "Then I wish you God's speed on your journey, Sir Aumary. Please take my greetings to the Countess of Pembroke. I am certain she will wish to know how Mathea and Paulette are faring."

She had walked all the way across the hall before Aumary caught up to her, his hand gripping the hilt of his new sword, the boyishness gone from his face.

"I will wait. At Villedieu."

A day after Aumary de Beaudricourt departed, junior squire Edward and the groom Donat with his new bride—the girl all but invisible in her cloak—rode out of Rivefort on their way to Tillières's market.

Standing at her window, Juliana suppressed her excitement until the riders disappeared into the bend of the road. As the chatelaine of Beaudricourt, Paulette would prove woefully inadequate, but perhaps if Master Thibodeau went along for a few weeks, the household of the lord and lady of Beaudricourt would survive its new masters. Rallied by her success, Juliana brought her account book to her table.

"Goodness, my lady, the fire has gone out." Hermine opened the door. "Where is that woodcutter's boy? I swear servants are here to vex us."

Hermine draped her cloak around Juliana's shoulders and waddled off. Juliana shivered. Without a blazing fire, the room had turned frigidly cold. She lit a candle and brought it closer to the pages. The sound of tumbling logs startled her.

"Oh, Hermine? The Belvoir villeins owe us two pigs and forty sheaves? That is impossible. Either my numbers are wrong or Master Thibodeau is feathering his nest."

"Your numbers must be wrong. Master Thibodeau always serves his master with devotion. I mean his mistress."

The inkhorn toppled, and Juliana jumped up to avoid the black trickle racing toward her. Lasalle scooped up the accounts, allowing the ink to drip harmlessly onto the rushes. He examined the book's spine and dropped it on the unaffected portion of the table. When he knelt by the fireplace and added several logs, Juliana inched toward the door, but he knew exactly what she was doing.

"I did not give you leave. A woman who uses a glib tongue against her husband in the presence of his inferiors can't be countenanced, no matter how much she feels aggrieved. Moreover, she is a fool to taunt a man who is not entirely sober unless she first sews him in a bedsheet or nails him in a barrel. I had expected by now for our ways to part permanently if not amicably. My patience is not limitless." He stood up and kicked the embers into the hearth. "Well, what do you have to say?"

Her hand remained on the door latch. "That depends on how sober you are, sir."

The corner of his mouth twitched. "As sober as I'll ever be. You came to me with a truce. I came to negotiate the terms."

Saints save us. There had to be some trick to this. "No terms are offered, my lord."

Lasalle squinted at her. "What? Sister Eustace opens her gates unconditionally?"

"No, sir. I am no longer seeking a truce. I could end up like Roger de Montier."

He gave a snort. "Christ. How do you think wars are waged? One doesn't fight the Lusignans with volumes of Boethius. I'd take them under a truce flag, starting with your favorite count. I did my turn as the royal ratcatcher. Next time, I'll wring their necks myself and hang them by their tails."

She crossed herself. "That is madness."

"We live in a mad world, Sister."

"We must. How else would one explain this marriage?"

He turned to stare into the flames. "How indeed. Marshal is right. We have a marriage, till death do us part. For whatever my word is worth, I will honor it and you and I can take after the wolves, confining our conjugal embrace to twelve times of the year."

That certainly was inventive, but Lasalle's terms were as preposterous as they were unacceptable. He must have thought that she was desperate. She might have been, before Aumary and Paulette, before the Temple knight. "You have nothing to offer, my lord, that I would ever want."

He was on her, his hand around her throat, his head bent to her, soft menace in his voice. "Then tell me, why did you consent to this marriage? You did not want to become a bride of Christ so you became the bride of a man. Only you are not either one, are you? Heaven forfend something disgusting might happen to you. The virtuous Lady Juliana. Saint Juliana of Tillières!"

"You are hurting me!" The words came out in a half-intelligible gurgle. Lasalle shoved her against the door.

"Is that what would make you willing, Juliana? Or is it Sister Eustace?"

She ducked under his arm and backed to the table. Her hands swept the top and grasped her sharpening knife. She retreated toward the strong room, the knife held fast to her.

His voice cajoling, he circled her. "Why all the fuss, love? What makes you so different from the others? None of them ever complained, including Anne, and she's had quite a few pass between her sheets. Didn't Paul tell wives to submit to their husbands? You wouldn't want to dispute the Church's teachings, would you, Eustace?"

Her knees were not shaking; neither was her voice. "This is not a matter for the Church's teachings. You are about as near as one comes in this world to the Devil. You are deceitful, cruel, and arrogant. You dole out crumbs of affection to enthrall the unwary and you destroy their lives. You don't want my body at all. You want my soul. You nearly damned Céline's."

He shot her a look that told her he was aware that knowledge could have come from only one source, but he went to the window, his voice full of scorn. "Another sermon? She . . . women come to me, Lady, and I don't recall one of them worried for her soul before she rolled on her back."

"And you think that exculpates you?"

He struck the wall. "What do you want from me? To fast on bread and water? Become a friar? Would that change anything?"

"No, sir. Repentance must be sincere."

He watched her for a moment, standing there with her penknife in a white-knuckled grip, then presented her with a sweeping bow. "Truce already, Lady Juliana. By the by, where is my pimply shadow?"

"I sent him to Villedieu with Donat and Paulette. By now Paulette and Aumary are husband and wife and on their way to Beaudricourt, and no one will deny them their happiness, not even you."

Lasalle stood there, looking at her as he had just before he struck her. Juliana's heart shriveled and the knife slipped from her fingers, but this time she was not the target. He spun around, knocking down the woodcutter's boy with his precarious burden and, reaching the end of the hallway, he wrenched back a startled guard and flung him toward the stairs. "Find Vaudreuil and get me a couple of coursers and remounts or I'll skin you alive!"

CHAPTER 54

They made it almost to Villedieu, knowing all along that they were too late. Against the naked tree branches no one could miss the fluttering garment, hanging there like a bloody gonfalon of victory.

Vaudreuil reached it first, spurring on his exhausted horse with a desperation he summoned only when his own life was at stake.

He stood in his stirrups and ripped down the gown and dropped from the saddle to his knees. Lasalle leaned his elbow on the saddle bow, sweat stinging his eyes. He wanted to kill Jehan de Vaudreuil. "Christ crucified. You fool. She could have been yours for the asking!"

Vaudreuil held the torn fabric the way he had never held its wearer, remembering the shy smile and the scent of chamomile in her hair. He kept his eyes closed. "No. Juliana would have thought it was your idea. It would have made everything worse."

Lasalle dismounted and shook him with all of his might. "Worse? That woman would take Rivefort apart with her bare hands and salt the ground to make sure I won't get it. I should've walled her up in the tower. I should have . . . oh, bloody, bloody hell."

Vaudreuil swallowed. "Donat and the boy?"

"Maybe they were luckier, but I doubt it. Take the horses with you and go on. I'll search."

Vaudreuil remounted with a shameful sense of gratitude that the decision was made for him.

When Vaudreuil disappeared over the rise, Lasalle spurred his tired courser into an ever widening circle. He crossed the trail on a slope covered by a living blanket of shimmering ravens' wings as if to preserve the modesty of what his eyes could not avoid. The birds flapped away at his approach, returning to settle in the tree branches.

From *outre-mer* to the Welsh border, he had seen enough of such sights when enemy troops or his own friends, in retribution, boredom, or drunkenness, in victory or defeat, had sought a confirmation of their own survival on the nearest available female body, willing or not. He had sought such himself. This one had not been willing, and that was perhaps why there was barely enough evidence left to show that this was a female body. He did not fear an ambush, so he hung his sword belt from the saddle bow and took off his cloak to cover the remains of what had once been a gentle and beautiful young girl.

Usually he did not stare at mutilated corpses any more than he had to, but when he held the cold, still hands to bind the wrists, he glanced at the palms, and what he saw made him sit back. Unless the Lady Fair led a secret life he did not know about, these were not the hands of the lady Paulette. He got to his feet and went to the nearest oak, and struck the massive trunk until pain and exhaustion wore him out, then stood there with his eyes shut, listening to the pounding of his heart.

With its new burden, the horse plodded steadily to Villedieu. The sisters came out with a blanket and helped him lower the body into it. Lasalle handed the reins to an old lay brother who had come out of the stables, then bowed to the prioress. "Reverend Mother, perhaps only the older sisters should—"

The prioress nodded, her hands in her sleeves. "Yes. We know. In the chapel, my lord."

Outside the chapel door, Vaudreuil was waiting for him. Vaudreuil followed the procession with his eyes and wiped his nose with the back of his sleeve. "Aumary's inside. He went looking for her. He found Donat. He is alive, just. The sisters are taking care of him. And Guérin—"

"I know."

Despite the altar candles, the chapel was dark. Aumary turned away from the altar, offering a glimpse of a tear-streaked face. The man who stood with his hand on the young man's shoulder lowered it slowly at Lasalle's approach. Lasalle walked down the middle of the nave, the sound of his spurs fracturing the silence.

"Get away from him."

Armand de Lusignan smiled slightly and stepped back, hands open. "Do you intend to slay me on hallowed ground, my lord? I bring no weapons to this sanctuary."

"The thought has crossed my mind. Aumary."

"She is dead, isn't she?" The boy's voice broke with hopelessness.

"Yes. Go outside and wait with Vaudreuil."

Aumary hesitated, seeking approval from Armand de Lusignan, and when he nodded, Aumary went past Lasalle, wiping his eyes.

The strain of his incarceration had brought out streaks of gray along the Count of Rancon's temples, but the haughty features, superb carriage, and effortless elegance of dress and manner remained. They had not laid eyes on each other since Mirebeau, and Lasalle had not thought that he would ever see Armand de Lusignan in this world again. That had been the plan, at any rate.

"What do you want?"

"Thank you for inquiring after my health, Viscount." Armand de Lusignan's contempt was thorough. "The usual, my dear. The girl for your by-blow. That is your choice."

"The child is dead."

"You disappoint me, Guérin. I am not your wife. I cannot be fooled so easily. The boy and that Welsh whore of yours did not disappear from the face of the earth. I will find them."

"Then find them."

"Tsk, tsk. Let's not aggravate each other." The Count of Rancon pulled on his riding gloves. "You try to trick me one more time and the girl dies."

"She could be dead already. You've killed that other one."

"I certainly did not." Armand de Lusignan raised his eyebrow. "Viart blamed Richieu, of course, and Richieu claimed that she screamed in a most unpleasant manner."

"Who was she?"

"How would I know?" Armand de Lusignan flicked the riding crop impatiently. "I am not here to discuss a worthless peasant. Now, as to your dilemma."

"I have no dilemma. I still have no proof the girl is alive."

"Then you will have to trust me. I thought you'd be in England by now, trying to rectify your egregious blunder. You know as well as I do that you are not going to leave Eleanor as John's prisoner for the rest of her life. From the rumors about her brother, it may be a short one."

"And then?" he said, fully aware of what the question told.

Armand de Lusignan pressed by, their shoulders brushing briefly. "Bring me Eleanor of Brittany or this time, Guérin, I will solve your marital morass for you."

The instant Lasalle and Vaudreuil galloped away across the drawbridge, Juliana had raced past the sprawled woodcutter's boy and an alarmed Mistress Hermine to the hall. Joscelyn de Cantigny met her there with a worried frown, a sheepskin around him for warmth. Juliana took de Cantigny back to the fire, gesturing the other Poitevins to gather closer. "You are all free. Take your swords and horses and leave this place."

De Cantigny shook his head vehemently. "My lady, we all pledged to be your hostages until our ransom is paid. We are not faithless knaves; we will not break our oath."

"You are not breaking your oath. I am releasing you. A messenger from Duke John could ride through the gate at any time and demand that Rivefort surrender you to him. You must leave now!"

The young men looked at one another, and one spoke up. "The viscount is angry enough with you already, my lady. If we leave, he'll be even more so."

The concern of these men for her safety touched Juliana, but she wished they would forsake their chivalry. "If you leave now, I shall have little to fear. But your freedom does have one condition. I should be glad to know that I have friends in Poitou."

More whispers and hesitation followed, but at last, one by one the Poitevins nodded their assent and, bowing to her, filed out of the hall. No one stood guard over the armory or the stables, and Juliana haughtily ordered the grooms to saddle the men's horses, implying with convoluted phrasing that my lord Lasalle had requested his hostages' presence.

Mounted and reunited with their swords and lances and shields, the Poitevins became once again brave and dashing knights. They saluted her as they charged across the bridge with Joscelyn de Cantigny in the lead. Drawing her cloak to her, Juliana dismissed the few curious servants who had ventured out to the bailey. Rannulf de Brissard was not among them, laid low by rhum.

"Juliana?" Mathea came up behind her, bundled up against the cold. "I heard a noise. Did Paulette and Aumary come back?"

Juliana hugged the girl and steered her toward the hall. "They are well on their way to Beaudricourt. Come and help me in the bakery."

Several hours later they were taking stock of the flour stores when a dreadful shriek in the bailey sent them running to the door. They saw Catalena facing Aumary de Beaudricourt, her hands clasped to her mouth. Juliana and Mathea pushed their way through the crowd of onlookers. Aumary held out something to them. It was a bloody, torn gown embroidered with twining silk rosebuds along the sleeves' edges.

Juliana could not tear her eyes away from those perfect stitches. Next to her, Mathea took a step forward and screamed, fell to her knees, and screamed again.

She screamed until horse hooves struck the drawbridge. The crowd parted and Lasalle, his features as hard as frozen ground, rode up with Vaudreuil behind him. Looking to neither side, Lasalle got down from his staggering courser and walked into the crowd, toward Juliana. Her heart sank, but Lasalle ignored her and Aumary and Catalena. He picked up Mathea as if she were a doll, threw her over his shoulder, and headed toward the chapel.

"Get the priest and Brissard. Vaudreuil!"

Shouts produced Father Cyril, tripping over his chasuble, and Rannulf de Brissard, his nose gleaming like a beacon. The appearance of Father Cyril gave Juliana the courage to intercept Lasalle. "Good God, what are you doing, my lord, don't you see . . . ?"

She refused to believe it. It had to be God's terrible test, a trial, surely. She looked helplessly around for some explanation, from someone. Vaudreuil had dismounted and stood there, horse and rider covered in mud.

Lasalle had reached the chapel door, where Father Cyril and Rannulf de Brissard met him. Lasalle looked back. "Vaudreuil!"

Vaudreuil handed the reins to the nearest man and walked past Juliana without a word, like a dog to the summons of his master. Juliana picked up her skirts and ran toward the chapel. Lasalle dropped Mathea on her feet, taking hold of Juliana to shove her at Brissard. "Take this woman to her room and lock her there, then come back. I'll need witnesses."

"No! Oh God, no!" Juliana struggled like a madwoman.

Vaudreuil snapped out of his daze. "My lord, you can't—"

Lasalle turned on him. "You swore to obey me, sir, and by God, you will, or I'll give her to Bodo, for all the poor substitute she is. Father!"

Father Cyril crossed himself. "My lord, this is most irregular."

"And you, priest, will give the Church's blessing or you'll find yourself head down the well."

Father Cyril gripped his crucifix. "My lord, I must protest most strongly!"

"Protest all you want. The Church's blessing or not, I am making this matrimony."

Juliana opened her mouth, but Brissard had a fast hold on her. "Lady, you've heard. Come quietly now."

She did not go quietly and in the end Brissard had to drag the Lady of Rivefort from the chapel door while she screamed at the top of her lungs, "Mathea, you have to say you don't give your consent. You can't remain silent. Mathea! You have to say it!"

In the end, it was all for nothing. The girl stood there, a forlorn figure in what would have been a plain homespun gown, had it not been graced by an exquisite embroidery of rosebuds along the sleeves' edge.

Being thoroughly drunk did have its merits after all.

She did not know what had happened after that travesty on the chapel steps. She did remember that Hermine had tried to console her to no avail, and so Hermine had brought out her raisin wine. After that, at Juliana's pleading, and sobbing into her apron, Hermine returned to the bailey. Lasalle was going to kill her. She wanted him to kill her. Only during the long night, no one came. Now there was not much wine left in the ewer.

The next thing she knew, she was being dunked into the half-

frozen Avre. She shrieked, choking and flailing, to discover that
she was not being dunked in the Avre, but into her own tub, gown
and all.

"You are going to sober up, damn it."

"I am going to be . . . oh God!" She was dragged out of the tub.
Something sharp pricked her nape and then came the sound of
tearing cloth. Her hands were pried from the bedpost and she was
husked out of the sodden thing, and left standing there as naked
as the day she was born.

"You c-c-can't." She shrank away, but her mind and her body
occupied two entirely separate places.

"I can do bloody well anything I please. By the laws of God, I
am your master and will remain so as long as we both reside on
this earth. Your defiance of me caused the death of your ward and
may yet cause the death of others. You will accept your duty as my
wife, and you will never plot against me!"

Her knees wobbled. She did not know if it was due to the raisin
wine or the declaration. Twin mirages of masculine nakedness
swam before her eyes. *Pretend, Sister!* A fiery wave flooded her to
her toes. Before her eyes appeared Father Osbert, pointing at her,
denouncing her willfulness. *If we do not repent, hideous demons will
drag us into the depths of Hell, where we will suffer agonies at their hands
for Eternity!*

Juliana moaned, covering her own nakedness as best she could.
"I repent, Father, I repent."

"The road to Hell is paved with good intentions, Sister
Eustace."

A green-eyed demon from the depths of Hell picked her up
and had her supine on her mattress before she could blink. By the
time her mind could make her body resist his claim of it, he had
claimed it, and after the first heart-withering sensation, her
thought was that it did not hurt as much as it had the other times.
Where, then, was her suffering and her punishment?

She ought to ask—surely a reasonable question to ask a deni-
zen of Hell?—but she could not because he held her face between
his hands, forcing on her his brutally intimate assault. Perhaps

that was her punishment, but before she could think on that, the
demon's hands, calloused by stoking pits of fire, moved to other
parts of her. Oh Mary.

She wanted to fight him. She let go of the mattress and dug
her nails into him. It did not hinder him. The demon was undoubtedly accustomed to resistance from his victims. She sobbed
at the unfairness of it, to be overwhelmed and overpowered, to
have her mind clouded by wine. Soon she would feel the pincers
of her tormentors. Only there were no pincers, and still only one
tormentor.

A flash of anger and disappointment swept over her. She had
prepared herself for dreadful agonies and torments. Wait. She was
experiencing a torment of sorts, a torment that was . . . distracting.
Frustrating, even, and the demon was luring her nearer and
nearer the fiery pit.

She would topple him into the pit as well! She set her heels
into the mattress; a stab of blinding sensation went through her.
Something was terribly wrong. She had been told that those who
lent themselves to such unholy congress found it either devoid of
any feeling or excruciatingly painful. She could swear on the True
Cross that neither was the truth. On the contrary. And this demon
did not have a scaly hide, a boar-bristled hump, or ram's horns
either. Neither did he possess the hairy quarters of a goat. Juliana
frantically assured herself of it, and the demon made no move to
stop her. This could not be. She *was* being tricked.

She broke through the maelstrom of sensations like a surfac-
ing pike. This was not a nightmare of her inebriated imagination.
Her nails were gouging taut, hairless flanks; her knees were yoked
in the most wanton fashion around long-muscled haunches that
most certainly did not belong to a goat. *Mother Mary!* The reason
for this appalling situation came to her in a thunderbolt, and the
wild, ungovernable frenzy that had taken possession of her fled
like Lucifer before the Cross.

The man felt her bolt from him and tried to bring her over the
precipice with him. He would have succeeded had she not resisted
with such a ferocious act of will that it seemed to tear her heart out

of her. That was her punishment, and her atonement, she prayed, and she even briefly gained a sense of superiority when he could not likewise resist.

After a while, all sensations ebbed away into shame and disgust so profound that nausea overwhelmed her. She inched her way from under him, pulled the sheet about her, and limped to the strong room, to the nearest bucket. When she could not retch up anything more, she huddled against the side of her tub, her teeth chattering. It was then that she saw him.

He, too, was down on his haunches, leaning against the door-jamb, wrapped in her lynx cover. She did not know how long he had been watching her with those odd-colored eyes. It did not matter. Juliana squeezed her eyes tight, the sheer weight of it all crushing her. And when she opened them again, he was gone, as if he had been a nightmarish figment of her imagination.

CHAPTER 55

Surely the culprit had been the raisin wine. She would not touch it again, as long as she lived, and wished she could hide herself in the strong room as long. But Rivefort, her Rivefort, awaited the presence of its lady for the burial of the Lady Fair.

I can't face him, Juliana moaned inwardly, leaning on Hermine for every step. And there were others to face in the bailey: kitchen knaves and men-at-arms, mercenaries and knights, crowding outside the chapel door. Men she had thought hard-hearted wept openly, tears rolling down weathered cheeks and stubbled chins. Women sobbed loudly in each other's arms and into their aprons. No tears came to her. Nothing would relieve her anguish. She had caused Paulette's death.

In the chapel, candles burned at the four corners of a bier supporting a plain casket in which a shrouded body rested. Like pure snowdrifts, finely embroidered drapery provided by the sisters of Villedieu embraced it. Next to the casket, Father Cyril dabbed his eyes. Aumary de Beaudricourt was not present, but Lasalle was, his mouth set, brows drawn. His gaze scoured Juliana when she entered the chapel. She faltered, holding on to Hermine. Behind them, the crowd pressed closer. *In nomine Patris, et Filli, et Spiritus Sancti. . . .* Hermine had to nudge her to join with the congregation. *Libera me Domine de morte aeterna. . . .*

Father Cyril swung the thurible. The smoke stung Juliana's eyes; her lungs constricted. Although she had heard such words before, she found that now, in sight of the coffin, these assurances of resurrection sounded hollow. Candles flickered. Father Cyril's voice droned on; whispers, sobs, and sighs rose under the ceiling; hands were clasped; breasts beaten. Juliana could not help but notice that Lasalle's eyes never wavered from the bier. Suddenly, he pushed past it and charged out of the chapel door. Father Cyril looked up and nearly dropped his missal. "Merciful God in Heaven!"

A woman screamed. Those nearest to the coffin tried to draw back, while those behind pushed forward, shouting, pointing, crossing themselves. Pressed closer to the source of their distress, Juliana saw it as well—stains, dark stains, seeping through the shroud like the blooms of some unnatural flower. *A body bleeds in the presence of its murderer.* The words spread. The smell of death oozed from the casket, and the clouds of incense could not obliterate it.

"Back, you oafs—let my lady through! Can't you see what a dreadful time she has had of it?" Mistress Hermine's shrill voice and sharp elbows assaulted those around her without regard to sex or rank.

They made it outside. The sharp air filled Juliana's lungs. Good Lord, it could not be. But the sign surely pointed to the presence of Paulette's murderer in their midst. It could not be otherwise, could it? She had to think, to find some explanation for this. . . . Her garden. She would sit in the garden until she came up with something. But the garden was no longer her refuge.

There, Harpín de Peyrac, backed by Berolt le Roux, faced Lasalle. Most of Rivefort's garrison knights pressed at the gate, the
mercenaries and men-at-arms behind them. Peyrac approached
Lasalle, his hands at his sides. "We declare ourselves absolved of
fealty to you, sir. Your abuse of ladies gently born releases us!"

Lasalle hooked his thumbs on his sword belt. "Ah, Peyrac. You
shouldn't take your defeats so personally."

Peyrac's sword was half drawn when le Roux and a knight
called Malger sprang to him. "No! He wants to pick us off!"

Peyrac spat on the ground, naked enmity in his eyes. "I say let's
just kill him."

Lasalle smiled. "A jolly idea, sir. Murdering one's liege offers
excellent chances of finding another who would put his trust in
such a man, especially with Philip's men prowling about."

"Philip's men? This time of the year? We have nothing to fear
from Philip," Malger countered belligerently.

Lasalle bent up one eyebrow. "Of course. That explains the
tracks we saw at the fording, and all those barns with hay slept in."

The sound of confused men filled the void until someone
called out, hesitatingly, "Then surrender Rivefort to Philip—sir!"

Lasalle included them all in one contemptuous sneer. "Ah.
The casus belli revealed. From chivalry to cowardice."

Le Roux took a step forward. "We are not cowards, and we will
find another liege. The duke is losing and we will not go down
with him."

"Ah. I thought this was too clever for Peyrac."

The crowd went quiet, the only sound the wind in the tree
branches. In the next moment the drum of hooves ended the
silence. Across the lowered drawbridge, riders in helmets and hauberks, shields at their sides, lances in hand, poured into the bailey.
Where was the watchman, the guards in the barbican? And then
everyone saw the reason for their inaction: The bareheaded rider
in the lead was Aumary de Beaudricourt. And behind him Joscelyn de Cantigny and the rest of the Poitevins. And behind them
more men.

Their appearance plunged the Rivefort garrison into confu-

sion. It surprised Lasalle, too, but hardly confused him. The look
he bestowed on Juliana assured her of that. "Well, well, haven't we
been the busy bee?"

One of the riders trotted through the garden gate to halt in
front of Juliana. He gave her a brisk salute. "I am Roger de Montier and I claim Rivefort and Tillières for my lord, King Philip, the
rightful suzerain of all Franks and Normans. Will you acknowledge him as your liege, Lady Juliana?"

Roger de Montier was not old, but he was all business. Hardly
prepared for the appearance of the Franks on top of everything
else, Juliana stammered out, "There is a Viscount of Tillières, sir.
You ought to make your address to him."

De Montier pulled off his helmet, dismounted, and gave her
an official bow. "There isn't. King Philip declared the Duke of
Normandy's lands forfeit. I am to reduce any of the duke's vassals
who defy their suzerain. I am told you hold Tillières of the king.
Present your charter, Madame."

The men shifted, their surprise at the occupation of Rivefort
dissolving into palpable relief when it became obvious that no
harm would come to them. The first tentative gestures and words
exchanged between the occupants and the occupiers signaled the
inescapable fact that Rivefort had simply exchanged a Norman
garrison for a French one.

Juliana performed a shallow curtsy. "I no longer possess my
charter, my lord."

De Montier scratched his ear. "In that case, I'll hold Rivefort
until the king's wishes are known to me."

Juliana's eyes strayed to Lasalle. Standing to the side, he did
not look particularly distressed at being relegated to one of the
lesser roles in this drama. Roger de Montier, however, did not
forget him. "Surrender your sword, my lord. You are in my custody," he ordered Lasalle with some satisfaction.

"No!" Sword in hand, Aumary de Beaudricourt charged past
de Montier. Halting a few feet in front of Lasalle, he raised the
blade's point toward him, his voice thin with emotion. "I, Aumary
de Beaudricourt, challenge you, Guérin de Lasalle. You have ar-

ranged the abduction of Paulette de Glanville to dishonor her and to murder her after disposing of her only protectors, the boy Edward and a groom called Donat."

The crowd at the garden gate buzzed like a broken hive. Joscelyn de Cantigny took his place next to Aumary, the rest of the Poitevins behind him. "Three knights make a tribunal," de Cantigny declared formally. "There are a dozen of us, mayhap others."

From the gathering, shouts joined in. Yes, there were others. Juliana saw it in their faces, heard it in their voices.

"I did not kill her, Aumary." Lasalle's voice was low and weary.

"He lies!" Mistress Hermine forced her way past the men and horses, her chin wobbling, her cheeks flushed, her finger accusing the man she despised. "He schemed to take the lady Paulette to his bed. He said so himself." Hermine crossed herself. "Lord help me, I heard every word, and my lady heard too, and he intends to keep her silent. And one day, mark my words, he'll succeed and our lady will be dead—dead I say, like my innocent lamb!"

Ignoring Hermine, Lasalle bowed slightly to Aumary. "Congratulations. It seems you've learned something after all. Subterfuge and suborning. Or was it the Count of Rancon's idea?"

"Enough!" Aumary threw off his cloak. "Defend yourself if you can."

Lasalle took a step back. "I will not help you commit suicide, Aumary."

Aumary charged. Lasalle nearly went to the ground, scrambling along Juliana's chervil to recover his balance with the aid of an abandoned rake. A puny weapon, but useful enough to snag Aumary's sword. Lasalle saved himself from a renewed attack with a head-over-heels tumble that brought him to the gate, where Aumary's chestnut stomped, reins dragging on the ground. Aumary's sword blade bit into the post of the rose arbor. The structure creaked. The audience groaned.

"We are causing damage to the lady's garden, but I believe she will forgive you. . . ." Lasalle threw himself to the side as Aumary wrenched his blade free. "But the Countess of Pembroke will not, for if you kill me"—Lasalle hooked a basket with his toe and sent it under Aumary's feet, forcing the young man to swerve—"I can't return something I confess I stole from her."

Advancing, Aumary kicked the basket out of his way. "Stole, my lord?"

Retreating, Lasalle wiped the mud from his face. "A small item, fits in a painted leather case. In the donjon."

Trapped between the garden gate and the contenders, Aumary's chestnut tossed his head and snorted. Lasalle groped backhanded to reassure the frightened beast. Appearing to wrestle with the horse, Lasalle let the animal sidle and stomp between Aumary and himself. De Montier's men had removed their helmets and dismounted, leaving their horses in the bailey. An alarm pricked at the back of Juliana's neck.

The courser's reins in hand, Lasalle swung into the saddle.

"Holy Mother's—!" someone shouted.

The Franks closest sprang forward, only to be driven back by the hooves of the rearing animal. The moment the chestnut's hooves struck earth again, Lasalle's sword slashed the man who dared to come nearest. A geyser of blood and matter splattered the trampled ground. The courser, spurs to his flanks, charged toward the garden gate.

"The cullis! Drop the cullis! Drop it, you fools!" Roger de Montier roared, springing forward, naked sword in hand. Panicked, the guards in the barbican opted to obey the command over their better judgment. With a thunderous rumble over the rattle of the ratchet pins, the portcullis plunged from its height. Someone shrieked. Juliana could not tear her eyes away. The horse and rider were going to be smashed; they were going to be impaled by the gate's prongs.

Halfway down, the portcullis hesitated a hair's breadth in its clamorous descent. With its rider flattened to the courser's neck, the chestnut's tail cleared the portcullis as it bucked free and, driven by its massive weight, bore down, its sharpened points biting into the frozen earth.

Roger de Montier kicked his helmet across the bailey. "That whoreson . . . that whoring . . . !" He struck the nearest man. "Get the others and raise up the damn thing, you piss pot. Everyone mount up and after him!"

That was an order more easily issued than carried out. As soon became apparent, the portcullis remained recalcitrantly stuck, and all their heaving would not budge it. A raging Roger de Montier was trapped with his men inside Rivefort by the very man who was supposed to be his prisoner.

"I warned the viscount that the portcullis still braces when it is lowered too quickly," Louis Pavilli said, limping toward Juliana and shaking his cane. "He said he had the men fix—" Louis paused and crossed himself. "Son of the Devil."

It took the greater part of the day and the combined forces of Rivefort's and de Montier's men for the portcullis to creak up. Juliana was in her solar, where Aumary de Beaudricourt arrived exhausted, mud-soaked, and burning with fury and frustration. They faced each other awkwardly.

"I've prayed that I could ease your grief, Sir Aumary. I so blame myself. If I had not insisted, Paulette would be here, safe."

Aumary's face softened. "It's not your fault, my lady. I should have taken her away from here sooner, but I didn't. I wanted to be loyal to him; I truly did."

Much was left unsaid, and they knew that neither of them had the heart to say it.

"What will you do now?" Juliana asked, allowing Aumary's words to somewhat balm her guilt.

"I will return to the lady Isabel whatever it is that man stole from her and tell her . . . tell her what happened. Then I swear that I will bring him to account. I would have killed him, Lady Juliana. I would have killed him, even if he didn't defend himself, so help me God. I brought de Montier here. I saw that de Cantigny and the others had joined up with him. You'd tried to give her to me, and we wanted to give Tillières back to you."

The agony and the despair were there, and the revelation of a desperate, cold calculation forced on a young man who could no longer bear the conflict between love, loyalty, and honor. Juliana was about to lower herself into her chair when Aumary reminded her, "If I may, he probably lied, but do you think you would recognize in his room what belongs to the countess?"

At first glance, nothing in the keep resembled anything that would belong to the Countess of Pembroke. Juliana threw her half-burned taper on the already dead ashes in the brazier. She would order the servants to sweep the place and she would ask Father Cyril to sprinkle holy water about it.

As she began to search, something fell to the floor from among the bedding. She picked it up: a ribbon, red. She wove it between her fingers. Gwenllian's ribbon. It had adorned so well that raven-black hair. Shivering, Juliana flung the ribbon into the brazier and watched the taper flame turn it to ash, then she combed method-ically through the other ashes of Lasalle's existence.

Underneath the books and parchments on the table she found a gaily painted leather pouch. Inside was a parchment roll with a dangling seal, wrapped around something. That something was a wooden flute, but her attention was on the parchment. She smoothed it out, her heart thumping. It was a charter. A charter to the viscounty of Tillières, held of Philip Augustus by Juliana de Charnais. Lasalle had not burned it after all. He had hidden it and used the ruse of the flute for her to find. Juliana crossed herself. Why would Lasalle do that? She did not understand it, but she presented her charter to de Montier.

Roger de Montier's advice to Juliana was that when it was safe, she ought to present herself to Philip to have the charter at-tested in order to secure fully her possession of Tillières. She gave the flute to Aumary and he left Rivefort along with Peyrac, le Roux, and several others. Even Rannulf de Brissard came for his wages.

"Yes, yes of course." Juliana hid her relief as she counted out the coins. "You will not join the king's garrison, Sir Rannulf? I am certain de Montier would welcome a man with your experience."

"I swore fealty to my lord Lasalle. I don't hobnob with his

enemies." Brissard gave her and Hermine his customary scowl and, shoving his coin pouch under his surcoat, walked out on them.

"At least that's the last of that man's pestilent pack," Mistress Hermine sniffed with undisguised pleasure. "God grant we never see any of them again."

Juliana dropped into her chair. "Except Vaudreuil. He will bring Mathea back, won't he? Won't he?" Next thing Juliana knew, she was sobbing into Hermine's maternal bosom. She had Tillières back, but at a terrible price, paid not by herself, not truly, but by others, the helpless and the innocent.

CHAPTER 56

Except for the restoration of the Viscountess of Tillières's personal liberty, life at Rivefort under a French garrison did not turn out to be different from life under a Norman one. Juliana sent letters about the latest events to the Countess de Valence and to Auntie Sabine. Since Donat was still recovering at Villedieu under Catalena's care, Juliana rode out to visit him and saw that his recovery would be a slow one. The sisters were unflaggingly kind.

One after another, days came and went—but not her monthly flow. She had only missed one, or was it two? It meant nothing. She had been under so much strain, so tired, her stomach and breasts so tender, perhaps she was a bit ill, but surely it meant nothing? Pretending to untangle her skein, Juliana listened to the serving women gossip about men. Juliana did not wish to hear about men.

Go to Anne. Nausea claiming her, she dropped her skein. She made a lame excuse about some neglected duty and ran out of the solar—and headlong into Jehan de Vaudreuil's child bride.

Mathea wore her cloak and a rustic gown without a wimple,

along with a surprisingly calm air. "Juliana, I did not mean to startle you!"

Forgetting her own cares, Juliana clasped Mathea to her with all her might, crying and laughing, covering the girl with kisses until Mathea begged for release.

"I am perfectly well, I swear it, Juliana. I am not going to disappear," Mathea reassured her.

"Of course you are not. This time, I won't let it happen. You are not going to leave Rivefort ever again. Where in heavens have you been?"

Mathea untied her cloak, sat on the edge of a bench, and sighed deeply. Juliana sank to her knees in front of her. "Dear Lord, Mathea? What is it?"

"I want to leave Rivefort."

"Yes, yes of course you do. How stupid of me. There are so many sad memories here. I'll arrange for Isabel de Clare to take you back. You must rest first, of course. But I'll write to her this instant." Juliana jumped for her parchment box. "When shall I say you wish to arrive?"

Mathea looked up at her, a hesitant plea in her voice. "I don't want to go to Longueville. I want to return to Belvoir."

"Belvoir?" Juliana turned, surprised. "I know you are fond of the place, but the villeins neglect their duties, Master Thibodeau says. Besides, we need to make arrangements for your annulment."

"But I don't want an annulment. I love him."

"You love whom?" Mathea had experienced a dreadful blow—surely her mind was confused?

Eyes shining and cheeks flushed, Mathea smiled. "Jehan."

"Jehan!"

Mathea stood up, her voice quivering. "I know he doesn't love me, and perhaps he never will, but I will try to be a good wife to him."

The pen snapped in Juliana's hands. "Of course he does not love you. He thinks that he can get his hands on Belvoir through you, and that Lasalle will grant it to him. Only my lord Lasalle is no longer in a position to give away wives or land. Oh, Mathea, do you think Vaudreuil would look at you twice if you did not come sweetened with Belvoir? A man marries a fief. He sent you to get by me. He doesn't have the nerve to do it himself!"

Color drained from Mathea's cheeks, but another voice spoke for her. "I did not send her. And I don't want to get my hands on Belvoir."

The blunt, familiar voice behind her made Juliana spin around. Vaudreuil stood in the door, his riding cloak thrown back, his black eyes burning. And before Juliana could reply, Mathea rushed past her and with a heart-wrenching sob threw herself into Vaudreuil's arms, and he, without hesitation, embraced her. The two so natural gestures of seeking and granting comfort told Juliana that there would be no annulment of this marriage, not on the obvious grounds.

"Dear Lord," she said, very loudly.

Vaudreuil ignored her. He tipped his wife's chin to him, his usually stern face softening. "Mathea, go and gather your things, and say good-bye to Hermine and Father Cyril. And don't forget your cloak. I won't be long."

Blinking back tears, Mathea nodded and, casting a frightened look at Juliana, took her cloak and ran out of the solar. Juliana sat on the bench in her place. Vaudreuil took a step toward her.

"My lady—"

She jumped up, fists balled. "God in Heaven, how could you? You've ruined her! How am I to find her a husband now? I suppose you will abandon her soon enough now that a plain face and scraped knees won't come with a fief!"

"You don't need to concern yourself. Mathea has a husband who will not abandon her, and you are the one who called her plain, not me. Belvoir was Mathea's idea; she said she was happy there. I would not have allowed her to say a word, but your new *serjeant* was anxious to question me. Was that on your orders?"

Jehan de Vaudreuil stood as tall as Lasalle and could look just as fierce, but she had nothing to fear from either one of them anymore. "I have little to say about how Rivefort is guarded. If you have any complaints, sir, take them to de Montier!"

"I came here to ask you. Where is Guérin?"

She could have screamed, but that would only make her appear foolish. "I assure you, sir, he neglected to mention his latest destination. Praise be, I will no longer be subject to his ridicule, his blows, his threats, his plots to dishonor me, his pillage of my estates, his shameless lies, his legions of mistresses!"

Vaudreuil gave her a short bow of capitulation. "Good God, I can see how you'd drive a man to the nearest keg, Lady."

She threw herself in front of the door. "Wait! Where are you taking Mathea? She can't tromp about the countryside without a friend to turn to, without food or shelter or proper clothes like—"

"Your husband, Juliana?"

Oh, the gall of the man. "Your concern for that man is rather belated, sir. I wonder what has detained you? I love Mathea and I am responsible for her happiness. I promised her I would find her a husband, a good husband, someone suitable. Someone who would love her for herself!"

Vaudreuil leaned forward. "And now she has someone not so suitable, but that is all she has. She always lived in the shadow of her sister, did you know that?"

Juliana would not move from her spot. "Everyone lived in Paulette's shadow."

"Then you know that for some time, Mathea had prayed for her sister's death?"

Juliana crossed herself. "Good Lord. I don't believe Mathea would do such a thing."

"Why not? I don't imagine you've ever prayed for someone's death—have you, Juliana?"

Her color answered him for her.

"That was why she became so frantic. I took her to Belvoir. It was close enough for a roof over our heads." Vaudreuil stepped back and struck the wall with his fist. "Good God, woman, do you think I intended to keep her? She threw herself at my feet, shrieking that she had murdered her sister. She said God should have taken her instead of Paulette. She said she was wicked because she had so envied her. She caught fever and I could not leave her. Thank God a couple of villeins came and their women brought us firewood and food and their potions, and they took care of her. When she recovered she begged me to take her to Villedieu."

Juliana did not move; she did not make the slightest sound. But she knew that Vaudreuil's pain was as great as hers and Mathea's, and she did not know why.

"I could not let her go, do you understand? The sisters at Villedieu are kind, but in a few years, I knew she would have become like—"

"Like me." Juliana leaned against the door. Her chest ached.

Vaudreuil glanced away. "I have two spinster sisters. They are not as fine as Isabel de Clare, but they will take care of her. This war is nearly done. We are losing Normandy, piece by piece. The barons despise John, and he won't lift a finger to help them."

"In that case, what is it you intend to do? Rally John's barons for him?"

"No. The man for that is your husband, Juliana. I have to find him. If you would unbar the door."

Despite the weight on her shoulders, Juliana did not unbar anything. "I see. You are willing to sacrifice your wife to your duty to your liege. How long will she have to wait? She is in love with you, do you know that? And she knows you don't love her."

If ever a man looked guilty, it was Jehan de Vaudreuil. "Oh Christ," he said.

"A man can't fool a woman's heart, my lord," she said. She meant it, she supposed, as Vaudreuil's punishment, but she knew that she would forgive him, but never herself or Guérin de Lasalle.

She expected denial or at least contrition, but Vaudreuil looked her straight in the eye. "Then a man must count himself fortunate indeed if she allows him to fool the rest of her."

Color surged to Juliana's cheeks so undeniably that in spite of all, Vaudreuil laughed. She tucked in her chin, feeling like a fool. That was precisely the sort of male conceit with which Lasalle would have settled her. She should have been furious at the Chevalier de Vaudreuil; she should have been scandalized. Instead,

she discovered that behind Jehan de Vaudreuil's austere exterior
and footloose attitude resided what Ersillia, and no doubt many
other women, had already discovered—a perfect charmer. All he
had to do was laugh. And she also discovered why Jehan de Vaudreuil hardly ever did so. The man possessed a spectacular set of
dimples.

"Yes. I see." Juliana bit her lip and fidgeted with her sleeves.
She was the mistress of Tillières and Belvoir and she'd better act
like one. "I am sorry. I have let my disaffections rule me. Mathea
is right. Belvoir is hers, and yours, my lord, if such a small fief is
not beneath your dignity. It seems you've already been able to
cope with the villeins there."

"My lady, yours is a generous offer, but I have a duty."

"Have you thought that he may not wish to be found? How do
any of us know what he might be up to this time? What if de Montier sends someone to follow you? Is it not wiser to wait for his
message?"

Vaudreuil paced about the room, jabbing at the wool bales.
She let him mull it over, not wanting to ruin her case with loose-
tongued eagerness.

"Very well, my lady." Vaudreuil knelt before her, his hands
clasped for hers to enfold. Startled as she was, she did, and Vaudreuil bowed his head to her. "I, Jehan de Vaudreuil, pledge my
body and my sword as your faithful vassal. I pledge to mind your
villeins, to keep the hart out of your crop and the thieves out of
your cowpens, but when I receive your husband's message, I will
leave and commend Mathea to your care."

The unexpected twist of receiving this man's homage instead
of his enmity lightened Juliana's heart for the first time in many
months. Blushing, she gave Vaudreuil a kiss the way her father had
done with his former Belvoir vassal. "And I, Juliana de Charnais,
grant Belvoir for you and your heirs . . . but in exchange, could
you keep an eye on de Montier for a few days?"

CHAPTER 57

Paris

Kneeling in the chamber of the Frankish king was, for Juliana, the culmination of months of praying, plotting, and planning. Yet no drums, fanfares, or heavenly choirs sounded. King Philip Augustus, thirty-eight years old and corpulent, sat hunched in a carved and painted chair, a squirrel-lined robe all but swallowing him, a skullcap hiding his thinning hair. Pits marked the pale skin, and one blind, slightly drooping eye made him appear like a monkish clerk rather than the warrior king who had outlived Coeur de Lion and who was about to seize the duchy of Normandy from the Lionheart's own brother. Even his voice was tremulous. The king's chancellor handled the whole proceeding quickly and efficiently.

"You have an eloquent champion in the Count of Rancon, Lady Juliana. Your rights to Tillières stand confirmed." The king of the Franks released her hands from between his cold ones. "We will have your marriage dissolved and find someone for you and Tillières. Someone without all that endless resourcefulness, no?" Philip Augustus smiled ever so slightly.

Juliana backed away with her attested charter. She was dismissed, but throwing caution to the wind, she dropped her deepest curtsy yet. "Sire."

Already concerned with the next petition, Philip turned his sighted eye to her with a hint of impatience. "Yes, Lady Juliana?"

"I ask not to be compelled into another marriage, sire."

Philip regarded her with melancholy pensiveness. The chancellor bent to his ear, whispering. Juliana kept her eyes downcast. Dismissing the clerk, the king pulled the robe up about his shoulders. "You are young, Lady Juliana. You may wish to marry without our consent."

Strangely, Juliana found the King of the Franks more approachable than the mercurial Duke of Normandy. "I shall never wish that, sire," she assured him with some fervor.

Philip clasped his hands under his chin. "I understand your marriage was arranged by the Duchess of Aquitaine," he said at last, "and that you did not find the matrimony agreeable."

"Yes, sire."

The dry sound that followed was the king's chuckle. "I know all about disagreeable marriages, Lady Juliana. Very well. My chancellor will arrange payment of your fine for the privilege. De Montier will act as my new castellan of Rivefort. God's speed."

Juliana curtsied and walked out of the council chamber with her charter and her head held high. Outside the door to the king's chambers, the porters trotted up with her sedan chair. It had been raining cats and dogs, and she had hired the chair and the three men-at-arms for herself and left her escort of de Montier's endlessly carping men at the Three Dwarfs, the only place she knew in Paris. Shivering and exhausted, she hugged herself under her cloak and winced at the tenderness of her breasts. In the narrow streets, light faded early.

The porters turned another corner and another, and she was about to inquire why it was taking much longer than their original journey when, with a thunk, the men lowered the chair. Juliana rolled up the window flap. A lantern held up to her face blinded her. She blinked, annoyed, aware that beyond the lantern's light rain poured into a courtyard—but not the courtyard she had left that afternoon.

"My dear Lady Juliana." A hooded figure leaned forward and, with a precisely administered pressure on her wrist bones, scooped her out. "Let us step out of this beastly weather. I do dislike this French rain, don't you? Do watch the puddles."

She knew that voice, and she also knew the grand hall they entered, with the prancing white bull on the wall. She shook back her hood and was greeted by the sight of the Count of Rancon handing his own cloak to a servant. Another servant took hers. They were not Isabel de Clare's people.

As if reading her mind, Armand de Lusignan gestured toward

the hall. "I had my agents purchase the place back from the Countess of Pembroke. She was glad to sell it, I understand. I called it the House of Cerberus, after my dogs. Now, let Dame Ermengarde help you, my dear." A snap of his fingers conjured up the woman, as forbidding as Juliana remembered her. "Mulled wine for the lady Juliana, warm towels, and a pair of dry slippers. Do sit by the fire. I see you've secured your charter. Excellent. Philip is not much of a conversationalist, is he? But he does have sharp ears."

A hot, pricking sensation at the nape of her neck replaced the wet chill there. Her only other choice being to create a scene, no doubt to no good purpose, Juliana sat down, spread her skirts to the warmth of the fire, and took the wine cup from her host's hand. She tried very hard to keep her own hand from shaking. "Have I been abducted, my lord?"

Armand de Lusignan's perfectly scored features gave him the appearance of a gyrfalcon. "Abducted? My dear, I am hardly Zeus. Your husband has far more experience in that arena, which is why I require his talents as well as yours. I shall be most generous and grateful."

Don't ever trust a Lusignan. On previous occasions, she had fluttered around this man like a moth drawn to a flame, oblivious to its danger. This time, she was truly frightened. Armand de Lusignan must have known it, but he took no advantage of it. Yet. "I regret that there is nothing I can help you with, my lord. I will gladly swear a solemn oath that I have not seen him since before Christmastide."

"Of course you have not." Armand de Lusignan leaned over reassuringly. "No doubt is cast on your veracity. Besides"—he examined his wine against the flames—"I have him here."

That had her heart jumping, in one loud beat. Juliana placed her cup on the table with great care and dragged her steaming skirts from the hearth. "I see. Then I don't know how I can be of service to you, my lord. But I thank you for your gift and your hospitality. I did not have the chance to do so at Pont-de-l'Arche."

Armand de Lusignan stood up likewise, regarding her with those enigmatic eyes. "Are you not curious about what your husband is doing here?"

Reaching for her cloak, Juliana allowed herself a hint of ill humor. "No. He left behind a number of extremely unhappy Frenchmen at Rivefort. They say he murdered my ward. That was before he gave her sister to one of his men. I shall have to take my leave now."

A firm hand held her back. Juliana decided it would be unwise to object, so she folded her hands with that peculiar gesture of submissiveness and superiority that is the province of all nuns. Her pretense of self-possession held no truck with the Count of Rancon.

"How very distressing for you. However, Roger de Montier was always full of himself. But rest assured that the enchanting Lady Paulette and your squire are alive. And I believe so is our darling little Jourdain."

Juliana took to her chair, her mind a blur. Underneath the layers of her skirts, her knees knocked.

"Of course, I know you will require proof." Armand de Lusignan held out something to her. It was a pair of scissors, delicately wrought, with silver handles shaped like the beaks of mythical beasts. She had seen them before, at Paulette's girdle, but never given them much thought.

"Beautiful work, isn't it? Welsh, you can tell. One wonders how Jehan could have afforded them. It is not as if Guérin is known for his generosity."

"I don't . . . I don't understand."

"It's perfectly simple. Vaudreuil could never hope to marry the girl, and he knew it. You would have objected most strenuously, would you not? You had a handsome young man with a handsome mesne picked out for her. I don't suppose Paulette noticed Jehan was enamored of her either."

Juliana opened her mouth but that was all.

"I apologize; were you thinking about your husband? It's also very simple. He is under a long-standing obligation to me, but he refuses to fulfill it. You know how obdurate Guérin can be. I had no way of compelling him except by regrettable means. You must forgive me."

It was as if the Avre had closed over her head. What had Isabel de Clare said in this very hall? *He revealed his true nature to her.*

Hands clasped behind his back, Armand addressed the fire. "I have come to admire you, Lady Juliana, as a woman of staggeringly common sense. I am offering you a choice. Your ward and squire for persuading your husband to reveal to us sweet Jourdain's whereabouts."

That was a threat delivered as if it were a favor. Her voice almost failed her. "Who, then, is buried at Rivefort?"

Her host crossed himself. "Some poor souls."

She could only stare, and then she asked, "Does he know?"

"About the demoiselle de Glanville? Of course he does. No need to blame Vaudreuil. He didn't know himself. Your husband lies to everyone," Armand de Lusignan informed her avuncularly. "Rest now before supper. Dame Ermengarde, show the lady Juliana to her room."

CHAPTER 58

Madame Violaine's establishment on the Rue Puteyne enjoyed the favors of lords spiritual and temporal, but this man Madame Violaine could not rank. Since he also arrived before Prime, his appearance doubly disconcerted Madame. She had amassed her fortune and her reputation by intuiting her clients' most secret desires and most private of vices and fulfilling them to the fullest at an exorbitant charge, but at more reasonable hours.

This man, wearing a hooded cloak, dropped a coin-heavy sack on her table without being asked, and requested that she call her entire household. She did, compelled by the weight of the satchel and her own curiosity. The visitor folded back the hood and proceeded to examine the array of assembled temptations with the darkest blue eyes, an amused arrogance in them and in the curve of his lips.

Madame Violaine knew that she had encountered those eyes and that curve before, a fact that she found even more disconcerting. On the other hand, she believed in turning every opportunity into an advantage by becoming as flexible as steel.

"We know of no such person, my lord," Madame Violaine answered her guest's single question, trailing after him and dismissing with a flick of her wrist those he had examined and declined. The man paused by the next girl. She curtsied deeply, as tempting as a nymph.

"An excellent choice, my lord. Her name is Ziya. I have paid a Cyprian merchant well for her."

The man reached out, his fingertips parting the silk that did nothing to conceal two perfect globes dusted with gold and tinted with crimson. Suspended on a braided silk cord between them rested a cross with amethysts at the clove-leafed corners. At the sight of it, Madame Violaine experienced an unpleasant jolt. She would have the stupid whore whipped.

"A Cyprian indeed, Madame, but only by trade," said the man, unperturbed.

Madame Violaine gave her guest a shallow smile and a deep curtsy. "We should have anticipated your discernment, my lord."

The man did not answer. Without touching the shimmering skin, he torqued the cord around the girl's neck until she gasped, and he lifted her to her feet. He smiled into the girl's terrified eyes.

"Well, well. Tell me what happened to the rightful owner, Ziya. And if you think to lie, as Madame no doubt told you to do, it is more than likely that one morn very soon, before the cock's crow, this house and all its occupants shall perish in a dreadful conflagration."

Juliana did not care to rest in her former room. She wanted the door to be unlocked and she wanted to confront the Count of Rancon, to tell him, to shout at him. Yet she could do nothing but pace about her room, her mind in a storm, until Dame Ermengarde unlocked the door to bring her a laver and a fresh gown. Juliana pushed past the woman, and was standing in the middle of the grand hall before she noticed that Armand de Lusignan was not the only presence at the lavish table before her.

The other man sat slumped, cup in hand, considerably thinner than the man she remembered, with the sallow pall of someone who spent most of his time in the vicinity of a keg. Was that how he had ended up in the Count of Rancon's custody—found dead drunk in some tavern? Still, he appeared a reasonable facsimile of himself, down to the stubble and the suspicious squint with which he greeted her presence. Juliana chose to ignore him for the moment. Armand smiled at her reaction and escorted her to a seat set midway down the table before taking his place at the head of it.

"You do us great honor by joining us, Lady Juliana," he said, as if she had any choice. "I feel I ought to inform you of what may be of interest to you."

She decided to follow his lead. "What is that, my lord?"

Armand de Lusignan motioned to the servants to begin their round of platters. "Roger de Laci still holds out at Gaillard, but once it is reduced, Philip plans to claim Argentan, Falaise, and Caen. The capital of the Conqueror's own Normandy is soon to be in Philip's hands," he informed her delightedly, and helped himself to a portion of chicken galantine.

Juliana stole a glance at Lasalle. He had not touched his trencher, although a muscle worked along his jaw and she gathered that the servants had been instructed to keep his cup full.

The Count of Rancon noticed the direction of her query. "Oh, your husband knows, but decided to turn wastrel at the worst possible moment—didn't you, Guérin?"

The skill and familiarity with which Armand de Lusignan managed Lasalle unnerved Juliana, all the more for the fact that Lasalle made no effort to strike back, even though she sensed him seething.

"Not that he could do much, mind you. The Normans decided to throw in their lot with Philip. John has not a single baron he trusts, except Marshal and the *routiers*, which is why he handed

Falaise to Lupescaire. The Bretons are furious. They want Arthur back. Some of them have taken the Avranches for Philip. Others have thrown their support behind the Pearl and her husband."

"Eleanor doesn't have a husband," Juliana said, wanting very much to put d'Erlée's revelation out of her mind.

The Count of Rancon smiled at her tolerantly. "Let me assure you that she is about to acquire one soon."

"But John will never allow Eleanor to marry. He said . . ." Oh pother. Why couldn't she keep custody of her tongue?

If he were in the habit of expressing himself so inarticulately, Armand de Lusignan would have sniffed. He accomplished the same effect with impeccable politeness. "You do have a grasp of the dynastic chess game. Of course he won't allow her to marry. But that is only a small detail."

"And the Count of Rancon, like Brutus, is not interested in small details or small lives when kingdoms call, are you, my lord?" Still slumped in his chair, Lasalle gave them a salute with his cup.

Juliana clasped her hands in her lap. Lasalle with drunken wits was worse than Lasalle sober. "Empires, Guérin, not kingdoms— empires," Armand chided him. "If you are well enough for a whore, you only need to ask. Otherwise, you are being disagreeable."

Lasalle stood up unsteadily and flung the rest of his wine into the fireplace. "In that case, send to Madame Violaine for Ziya."

Armand de Lusignan shrugged, as if he wanted Juliana to witness how thoroughly unreasonable Guérin de Lasalle was. "You do have an expensive taste in bawds, Guérin. Oh, very well. Now, sit down. You will lend us your presence and keep a civil tongue. You are discomfiting your wife."

"It doesn't matter." Juliana tried to keep out of the looming collision of those two.

"It does. A man who parades his trollops in his wife's presence is an embarrassment to everyone." Armand de Lusignan's tone softened. "Still, there are a few things your wife ought to know that not even your whores do. Shall I tell her?"

"*Don't!*" Lasalle spun back. The indifference was gone and fear, raw fear, replaced it.

Armand de Lusignan remained seated but something leapt in

his eyes, as if the game had been flushed and the hunt joined. "Don't what? Tell her that you have perfectly sound grounds for an annulment which not even the bishops could countermand, and that you've refused to avail yourself of them?"

This time she could not ignore Lasalle. "Is this true? Why in God's name? You didn't want this marriage any more than I did. You said so yourself!"

"Don't be too harsh with your husband, Lady Juliana." Armand assumed a tone of conciliation. "I am certain he had every intention to rid himself of you. Unfortunately, you are not easily rid of." The eyes of a gyrfalcon dwelled on her. "After a while, it all changed. The reason is frightfully simple. He fell in love with you."

She could only stare at the Lusignan.

"I am certain you've wondered why he came back to you after that unprepossessing performance at the Avre. It is also very simple. He found that you were the first thing that truly belonged to him. You do hold a certain allure to someone who, for his entire life, has had to make do with other men's leavings. Guérin hates that, let me assure you, despite his pretense otherwise."

Lasalle's chair toppled behind him. "That's enough! I'll fulfill my obligations. She means nothing to you and even less to me. This marriage will be dissolved. No one will remember it ever existed."

Armand de Lusignan raised up his cup. "Of course it will be dissolved, love. How is up to you. I will tell her where she will find Paulette and Edward in exchange for you telling us where Jourdain is."

Jourdain. So this was not about herself, Paulette, Céline, or even about Lasalle and Armand de Lusignan, whatever it was that had passed between them. This was about Lasalle's son. She wished that for once in their marriage Lasalle had told her the truth. Or had he?

"He is not"—the look in Lasalle's eyes was that of a man throwing himself on the mercy of his executioner—"going to tell you," she said instead.

Armand de Lusignan circled her. "I see. Has he seduced you after all to abet him? The last of the de Charnaises did not exactly fling herself out the window when he returned to knock at those well-guarded gates, did she? At least I can say that much for Céline."

The accusation was pure, unadulterated contempt. Juliana crossed herself. "You can assail my family's name, sir, but you can't sully it. You hail from an ancestress who was a viper."

Armand took her hand and kissed it, retaining hold on her wrist, his contempt melting into a disappointed, seductive smile. "Ah. Is that your last word on the idea of a matrimonial alliance between the Lusignans and the de Charnaises, Lady Juliana? Then allow me to—"

"*Don't!*" Lasalle lunged toward them. "God's blood, I will tell you where Jourdain is!"

Armand de Lusignan laughed, but not in triumph. "Is that so? Well, well, you've just told me all I needed to know." And taking Juliana's arm he dragged her, despite her stumbling resistance, toward Lasalle. "Now, tell your wife the rest!"

Lasalle was retreating, retreating until he could no more, and he slid down the wall, his head buried against his forearms. It was not a defeat; it was a rout. She tore her hand away from the count's grip. "Tell me what? He may have features of a nature's monster, but you, sir, you are a fully fledged one to transfer your unnatural obsession from him to Jourdain."

"Unnatural?" Armand de Lusignan laughed and gave Lasalle's ankle a sharp kick. "Did you hear that, Guérin? Your wife does possess an imagination after all." His voice rose as if to deliver a *coup de grâce*, "One almost hates to confess that although we Lusignans have engaged in a number of unsanctified practices, we have yet to try for incest."

"I wouldn't put it past you, you—" The words left her mouth before comprehension set in.

They were all liars. Liars versed in subterfuge and devilish deviousness. "That is impossible." She wanted to laugh wildly and hysterically. She wanted to run. "He can't be!" She dropped on her knees next to Lasalle, her hands balled into fists. "You can't be a Lusignan. For the love of God, deny it! It's a lie. You lie about everything. You are in this together. Why? What in Christ's name do you want from me? I am a nobody!"

He did not look at her.

Behind her, Armand de Lusignan inhaled deeply. "It is dreadful to be denied, isn't it? Imagine being denied by your own flesh and blood. Geoffrey and his pious drivel I could at least suffer."

"G-Geoffrey?" She was shivering despite the heat from the hearth.

"My firstborn. Geoffrey is a family name. So is Jourdain. That was my father's name. What an uncanny sense you have. But Guérin is not your husband's true name either. It is the same as mine. The circumstances of my sons' conception were somewhat unorthodox, granted, but since Geoffrey gave up his rights for God, your husband is not only my trueborn son; he is also my heir."

Although the world collapsed around her, the walls stayed plumb. She sat there. She could not give up. "You can't be his father."

Armand de Lusignan clicked his tongue. "I don't know why I need to convince you, my dear. Notice that my son offers nothing to counter it. I was sixteen when I fell in love with the sister of the Countess de Nevers. I was her husband after she became widowed, and I fathered her two sons, not that worthless Welshman she took for her third husband. One does not gain a prime litter from every pairing, but this one whelped true."

Lasalle would not look at her. His eyes were closed, thin-lidded like the eyes of a corpse, and he would not look at her. She could see him only through her own gathering tears. She wiped her cheeks with the back of her hand. "Why—"

"Why Jourdain?" Armand de Lusignan gestured with disgust. "My son decided to strike back at me by depriving me of posterity, and he has been most assiduous about it."

Juliana swallowed. "Dear God. I have to—I must—" She clamped her hand over her mouth, clutched her skirts to her, and ran down the length of the hall, under the light of the half-burned torches, reaching the laver in her room barely in time. When she finished, she collapsed by her bed, burying her face in a towel. She was going to die.

"Well, well," said the ironic voice from the doorway. "My dear, dear Lady Juliana. And what shall we call this little viper?"

CHAPTER 59

She was picked up from the floor as if she were a foundering heifer and deposited on the bed. She huddled there, nauseous and exhausted. Armand de Lusignan did not believe in discreetly withdrawing from the presence of a lady in distress. "My dear Lady Juliana, you look woeful. Have you not shared the happy news with your husband?" When her glance strayed to the door, he said, "Don't worry, my son is busy drowning his defeat in my best wine."

"I am not with child."

"No? Shall I call Dame Ermengarde for confirmation?"

"No! It's not his. I have a lover." Trapped and defeated, Juliana snuffled into the towel, for once wishing she had listened to Lasalle, or whatever his true name was.

Armand de Lusignan laughed. "You do not, girl. You are the emblem of wifely chastity. If you are enceinte, it is certainly my shiftless son's doing."

She forced down a rush of bile with a loud gulp. Armand de Lusignan narrowed his eyes. "I believe my son went to some lengths to avoid getting a child on you. It is your safety as well as my grandchild's that I am concerned about. If the child is a boy, you understand that I will have some interest in his future. If not, you may keep it, but do pretend it is a Parisian foundling you have taken to your bosom. In either case, you can rest assured that your marriage will be dissolved and that yours and my son's paths will never cross again. Do we have an understanding?"

She nodded.

"Excellent," her father-in-law said. "You are a creature of common sense after all. Do rest now. Sweet dreams."

"Wait!" Juliana rallied herself before the door closed. "Tell me where Paulette is. Is she at Pont-de-l'Arche? Tell me!"

"Of course, my dear—how can I be so forgetful? I gave her to Lupescaire."

Despair and fury dogged her days, but at least she did not have to contend with those two vile creatures. Sometimes she almost regretted it, wishing that she could confront them, to shriek at them, to accuse them, to shame them, to . . . Oh, what was the use? She had to think. If she could free herself, she could put wiser heads together and recover Paulette, Edward, and Jourdain. She owed something to the little boy whose parents had so heartlessly discarded him, and with Paulette surrounded by Aumary's love, surely she would recover from her ordeal. As for Lasalle . . .

As usual, she came across him at the most unexpected moment and in the most singular circumstance, at the foot of a staircase to the side courtyard. The knaves carried kitchen ashes there and fed leftovers to the wolfhounds that took over at night. Despite its unwholesome appearance, Juliana took the passage when she wanted to escape into the garden. The voices ought to have warned her, but she was too deep in her thoughts.

"Try again, pig."

The ring of steel striking stone reverberated through the staircase. Juliana halted. Two men faced each other, the thickset one lunging furiously but fruitlessly at his unarmed adversary, who avoided his dagger with hair-raising dodges: Lasalle and Viart, her guard from Pont-de-l'Arche. Juliana stepped back—and onto her hem. She was saved from a stumble by an arm in black samite. "Shh. Don't distract your husband, Lady Juliana. He is enjoying himself."

She could not have budged anyway.

At Viart's next sally, Lasalle threw himself sideways to drive his knee into Viart's belly. It knocked the man backward with a whoosh of pain, but Lasalle also faltered. The count's man recovered, gripping the dagger with renewed confidence.

"Well done, Viart," Armand de Lusignan called out just as Viart was about to resume his assault. "But before you inflict more damage on my ill-mannered son, consider that I'll throw you to the wolfhounds!"

Startled, Viart paused, and Lasalle, seizing upon his opponent's distraction like a market-day brawler, scooped a handful of fresh ashes and flung them into Viart's face. Viart dropped his dagger, clawing furiously at his eyes.

"Have no fear, Viart, it won't be the wolfhounds after all!" Armand de Lusignan laughed, sending a chill through Juliana. Viart turned his blinded eyes toward his master. Juliana screamed. The warning was of no use to Viart, for by then Lasalle had thrust the dagger into Viart's belly. Juliana flung herself against Armand's grip, but his hand smothered her next scream. "I said don't distract your husband, girl."

Lasalle jammed the blade into the helpless man again and again in calculated rage, puncturing Viart's leather jerkin as if it were a pig's bladder. Viart reeled and screamed in short, choking yelps, his arms flapping as if fending off a swarm of bees, until he crumpled on the ground, the cries became gurgling moans and his heels ground into the ashes for the last time.

Armand de Lusignan let go of Juliana, and she collapsed against the wall. Lasalle crouched on all fours over the mutilated corpse like a forest beast feasting on a carcass, his breath coming in hard gasps, eyes wild.

A sound of revulsion was wrenched from his wife.

Armand approached his son cautiously, extracted the dagger from Viart's entrails, and wiped the blade on Lasalle's shoulder. "You show more enthusiasm than skill, son. I suppose I shall have to dispose of this for you. You may entertain your wife while I do."

Bowing to both of them, the Count of Rancon went in search of the rest of his men. Juliana crept toward the staircase.

"Juliana, wait!"

She would not wait. She held on to her skirts and aimed for the doorway, but a bloodstained apparition leapt forward and barred her way, hands gripping her fast. She struck him. "You've killed him! You've killed him!"

His hand covered her mouth. "And I would kill him a thousand times if I could. Viart and Richieu attacked Donat and Edward and took Paulette. They murdered a peasant girl and left her in Paulette's place for me to find. If I don't get you away from Armand, he will kill you just as surely, I swear it on my mother's grave!"

This was pure madness, but she would not scream; he could at least tell that, so he removed his hand. "Wh-why?"

He took her face fast between his palms as if he wanted to remember its every imperfection. "Because you are my wife."

He enunciated each word with painful care, the way he had when they first left Fontevraud. That was such a long time ago, when she thought he was just another . . .

"Oh bloody hell!" He let go of her, driving his fist into the wall, a man who had staked his life on the last losing roll of his dice. And so he had, in the convent's folly when Aliénor of Aquitaine made him marry her.

Juliana stood rooted to the ground. A part of her listened to the man soaked with the blood of the man he had murdered, the warm body of his victim nearby. And then something inside her broke and swept away her fear, as it had under the old willow at the Avre. She must have gone mad like the rest of them. "What is it I am to do?"

As usual, she did not receive a plain answer from Guérin de Lasalle. Instead, he had her by the wrist and they were plowing through Armand de Lusignan's shrubbery to the garden shed. Inside, Lasalle kicked away a pile of mice-gnawed sacking. Underneath was a trapdoor.

Don't think, don't think, don't think. . . .

Wading knee-deep in water into an ink-black tunnel, one comes to appreciate the nature of irrational fear. The torch flame cast enough light to see that the ceiling peaked above her head, allowing her to shuffle along without stooping. Juliana kept her free hand on the wall to prevent herself from slipping on the uneven bottom. Something flicked under her palm.

"Mary!" She jumped back, nearly dropping her torch. Rubbing her hand on her skirts, she raised the torch cautiously. A salamander or some such creature of the dark wiggled between the rocks. Salamanders! Before he handed her the torch and roped together a few more for her to carry, Lasalle had told her about the few rats she would encounter, but he had forgotten to mention salamanders. Of course that man would forget to tell her about salamanders!

The winding tunnel brought her to a junction with another. *Bear left; follow the smudges.* She paused below an arch of stones fitted by some ancient stonemason, allowing fear to immobilize her. In the light, old soot marks stood out against the gray walls. She took a deep breath, her torch shaking so hard that she had to hold on to it with both hands. It was going to be all right. A few steps later a faint breeze stirred the torch flame. She heard the sound of running water. The aqueduct opened onto the river, close to the place where they had skipped pebbles, he said. She lit a fresh torch and pressed on into the black tunnel.

So far, at least, Lasalle had been right: The water never reached higher than her hips. In some places, it vanished into a trickle. She inserted the torch into a hollowed-out receptacle and wrung out her skirts—and then she saw it, along the wall ahead of her. A thin, long shadow moved with the chirps of tiny birds. She gasped in fright and snatched up her torch.

Rats.

Dozens of them, all scurrying along the passage to escape the light, their hairless tails resembling writhing earthworms. After a moment of panicked flight, the rodent rear guard stopped, balancing on hind legs like so many furry acrobats. A few made tentative steps toward her.

"Shoo! Shoo now, shoo!"

She swept her torch to and fro. The rodents squeaked in alarm and vanished into the darkness. Juliana waited, listening, but all she could hear was her heart and the rushing water. The torch showered her with sparks. She could not tarry; she had only two left. He had told her it would take no more than . . . no more than . . . She could not remember. She quickly lit another torch and hurried along the passage.

The current became stronger and her heart rushed with it. She would see the light and feel the breeze, soon . . . soon. She was sobbing, forging ahead, reaching out into the darkness. . . .

Her hand struck rock.

She sat down with the shock of it. The torch smoked and sizzled. She reached for a new one and it slipped from her fingers and rolled into the darkness, swept along by the water. Her breath coming in frenzied gasps, Juliana lit her last torch from the dying one.

The passage was sealed.

Ahead of her loomed a wall built not by an ancient stonemason but by a more recent one; drips of mortar visible between the bricks. She struck her fist against it. She struck it again and again. This wall, unlike the walls of Jericho, did not yield. This could not be! She must have taken a wrong turn. *Bear left.* She could not have made a mistake. This was where the aqueduct had its mouth, by the wharf where they had skipped pebbles.

Mother of God in Heaven, he had lied to her. This was where he'd intended to have her all along. Her teeth chattered. She was burdened by the weight of saturated fabric. Her slippers were gone; her feet were bleeding. A chirping sound came from the passage behind her. From the darkness, hundreds of pairs of black eyes watched her. She screamed and waved the torch at them and they disappeared in a flash of those obscenely naked tails.

He had given her enough torches to bring her here, but not enough to lead her back. In the pitch dark, the tunnels twisted into a deadly maze. He had known. Good Lord, he had known. And he had won! Lasalle had deprived his father of the only thing Armand de Lusignan wanted from him. *No one will remember the marriage ever existed.* The torch slipped out of her hand and expired with a hiss and her world became the blackness of Hades.

"That was for disobeying my orders. You've already killed Viart. That was his punishment for allowing you to trick him."

From his position on the straw of the stall's floor, Lasalle could see the men uneasily milling outside the stable door. Earlier he had received at their hands a beating, delivered on the count's orders. On the whole, it had not added to his hatred of his father; such a thing was not possible. After that, they had left him locked in an empty stall. He knew that as soon as he acted docile enough, he would be released. "And hungry wolfhounds for Richieu, my lord?" he asked with unconcealed sarcasm, because he finally could.

Armand de Lusignan smiled and lifted the stall latch. "Something far worse. He is to accompany you to England. I told him you'll kill him if he blunders and I'll kill him if he flees." He tested the lock and slipped the key into his belt. "It just occurred to me. Wouldn't it be ironic if your engaging ways with women finally won over our dear Juliana and you've persuaded her to slip out through the old aqueduct? I had the tunnel walled. One cannot be too careful these days."

CHAPTER 60

Something moved across her eyes. She refused to open them, not wanting to face the cold, the blackness, the sensation of rodents scurrying across her legs, her arms. A shadow passed over her, the shadow of Death. Wait. How could there be a shadow in a pitch-black tunnel? It was a question for Father Osbert. The darkness yielded to light, painful on her eyelids. *I am dead and my suffering is over.*

Someone was shaking her. If it was an angel, it was an exceedingly vigorous one. A man's voice spoke and she was left alone, but the voices continued. She began to pick out the words. The angelic choirs spoke a rather common version of French. Juliana opened her eyes. This was not purgatory; it was paradise, a large chamber bright with sunlight and scented with unfamiliar spices.

She was lying under a silk canopy on a sea of pillows. An angel in a cloud of white linen appeared, wearing perfume, her bow of painted lips smiling dutifully. "I am Ziya."

"Where . . . am I?" Her voice sounded as if it had not been used for some time.

"We did not think you would wake." The girl glanced at the door nervously.

"W-we?"

"Madame Violaine and the rest of us."

"Madame Violaine?" Juliana raised her head and a sharp pain stabbed her between the eyes. She closed them and tried to think. *Good Lord, I am not dead.* And then she remembered.

Somehow Sister Eustace had escaped the tunnels to end up in a Parisian brothel. Juliana covered her face and began to laugh. It was not much of a laugh, but it was all she could do. "Tell Madame that I will make a very poor whore. You can ask my . . . my lord Lasalle. Perhaps he mentioned it to you in passing."

"He did not mention it, not even in passing. You can ask Ziya, Lady Juliana," a familiar, resonant male voice answered from behind her.

Had she had the strength, she would have bounded up like a flushed deer. She only managed to fling herself sideways before Ziya, at the sharp command in the man's voice, restrained her. Her elbow struck Ziya's eye socket, and the girl cried out and slumped to her knees. Juliana felt a flash of regret; she had not meant to hurt the girl, though she had no such scruples when it came to her other opponent. He was not as tender as the courtesan; he simply flung her back onto the pillows and held her there.

"I hate you!" she hissed with all the malevolence her puny strength allowed, squeezing her eyes shut.

"Do you? I was hoping you would get to know me better first," the man said with amused disappointment.

She opened one eye, opened it wider, and then both wider still.

"I know." The man sighed. "Infuriating, isn't it, the resemblance? Guérin is the only one with our mother's eyes. That is why few people are able to tell that Armand is his father. Few doubt that he is mine."

It was the voice of Armand de Lusignan, the same patrician features, the same thunder-blue eyes. But this was a younger man, closer to Lasalle's age. He not only released her; he proceeded to arrange the pillows for her, and when he finished, he sat back against his own bolsters.

"Do poultice that thing, Ziya, or you will lose customers. My sister-in-law and I will manage," he said to the girl, who was examining herself in her girdle mirror.

Sniffling in distress, Ziya left them with a sway of her hips. The man smiled and turned his attention from them to Juliana. "I am Geoffrey de Lusignan," he said. "Geoffrey of Parthenay, if it impresses you any better. The title belongs to my brother but he has never assumed it, just as he never calls himself Jean Armand de Lusignan."

Speechlessness could be as proper a response as anything. Juliana availed herself of it.

"Perhaps I should return when you are feeling stronger, Lady Juliana."

"N-no. I must be mad . . . I know you."

The black eyebrow shot up. "Of course you do. We met in Rivefort's chapel. You apologized for my brother."

The man seated casually across from her wore a silk *tartaire* over a very fine shirt, a waist belt with a gold buckle, and a dagger with an enameled hilt of Saracen craftsmanship. The beard was gone, the hair cut back, the cheekbones high and sharp under browned skin.

"The Templar," she said to herself in disbelief.

The Lord of Parthenay bowed slightly. "The very same. Don't let these circumstances confuse you, dear sister. Sometimes it is necessary to bend one's vows a little, don't you agree? My Order finds it regrettable, but permissible when it is necessary to protect its interests."

"The Countess de Nevers . . . your aunt said you became a monk."

Geoffrey de Lusignan laughed, the laugh an echo of Armand de Lusignan's to the last inflection. "I tried, but we Lusignans make terrible Benedictines. " 'Go to the Temple,' " my abbot said, " 'and one day you will become Grand Master.' So I took him up on it."

Coming from any other man, it would have been a vainglorious boast, but hearing it from this man, Juliana did not doubt the explanation; he was, after all, a Lusignan. Had he become her new jailer? "Your brother wanted to kill me! What do you want from me?" She sat up, but did not know she had made the other gesture until Geoffrey de Lusignan's gaze shifted to her middle, not tactfully. Dread enveloped her. "Oh God. I lost it."

"You were ill. Would that be relief or regret?"

She had no answer, but her desolation became bottomless anguish. "He wanted me to die there! I was so frightened, so frightened. . . . How could he have done such a thing, how could anyone? I hate him, I hate him!"

She did not know how long her outburst lasted, but when she again became aware of her surroundings, a steady, strong hand was stroking her hair. She was being comforted by a man who was not even supposed to look at the face of his own mother. She clung to him nevertheless, racked by sobs.

"He did not want you to die there. We used to explore the aqueduct when we were boys. Our father had the passage blocked. He expected that Guérin would try to get you away through the tunnels, and he let him do it."

Her sobs subsiding, she let go and sniffled into her sleeve. "That is a lie. The count wanted the child. He would want me safe!"

Her companion nodded. "That, too, is true."

"It can't be both! Lasalle had a reason to see me dead, not the count. How did I come to be here? Whose creature are you?"

Lasalle's older brother regarded her steadily, ignoring her accusations. "I serve God and my Order, Lady Juliana, but I also have a personal interest in Lasalle, as you so affectionately call your husband, and in you, as well."

She pushed aside the cushions and got herself to her knees. "I am nothing to you or to him. You need not bother with me. I can fend for myself. If you would order my release, I shall return to Tillières and will not breathe a word about any of you, I swear it. No one will ever know."

"They all will in a few months."

She froze, her hand to her middle. It felt fuller. "But you said—"

"That you were ill. Do you wish to get rid of it now?"

She did not know whether it was the announcement or the question that knocked her on her seat. "How can you . . . you want me to . . . ?"

"If you decide now, no harm will come to you, Madame Violaine assures me. I assured her that if she lied, I would kill her."

Shock, relief, doubt, and confusion made her dizzy. From the door, a tactful cough announced another presence. Geoffrey de Lusignan acknowledged it with a slight nod. "Madame Violaine. It seems Lady Juliana has made her decision."

"No. I did not!" She tried to stand up. Her muscles seized. She could not stand, let alone run. A sob of despair escaped her. "You want to kill it. That's all you do. You kill things! You destroy everything and anyone in your way. You are all murderers!"

Geoffrey barked an order and Madame Violaine vanished in a trail of black silks. Geoffrey de Lusignan sat back on his heels. "Listen to me. No one will harm you or your child."

She was shaking. She was trapped. "You are all liars! He never wanted this marriage! He wanted to make me an adulteress to get rid of me. He did not want this child. He told me to go to Anne to kill it." Geoffrey of Parthenay reached out for her. She struck him again and again, her strength one of frenzied desperation. Finally she began to tire, and he let her go.

"He was already married, Juliana."

PART IV

CORFE

CHAPTER 61

Corfe, England, Early Spring 1204

The fortress jutted above a promontory called the Isle of Purbeck, like a fist against the gray Dorset sky. When the fog settled, Eleanor climbed the ramparts to see the open water and to imagine the coast of Brittany beyond. Her prison was not one of ball and chain; her uncle had built at Corfe a comfortable residence and filled it with luxuries for his queen. In much smaller apartments in the keep, Eleanor's own household consisted of a steward, two maids, two waiting women who were frequently replaced, and her confessor. When in residence at Corfe, John left instructions for Eleanor's steward to keep his lady out of sight. It was the one command of her uncle's that Eleanor gladly obeyed.

Until a few months past, she was not the only prisoner at Corfe; John had confined there two dozen of hers and her brother's supporters captured at Mirebeau. The Bretons and the Poitevins had hatched a desperate plan to escape, but it was foiled and they had barricaded themselves in the keep, refusing to surrender even in the face of starvation. Eleanor had prostrated herself before John, pleading for their lives. It brought her nothing but humiliation. When the door was breached, three prisoners were still alive. One of them, she was vengefully glad to learn, was Savary de Mauléon, the bold Poitevin baron who had challenged her at Tours the day before hers and Arthur's disastrous advance on Mirebeau.

Arthur. She had not received any news of her brother in months, only dreadful rumors. Every day, she revisited their encounter in the garden at Nantes with Armand de Lusignan. The Lusignans had long been freed, but not herself or Arthur. She did not understand it. Armand de Lusignan had assured her that he would protect her.

Lies, all lies. Everyone had abandoned her. Perhaps what they said was true and Arthur was no longer alive. At night she listened to the channel winds sweeping around the keep and the guard towers with the mournful, wailing sound of souls denied consolation. Yet, in an unexpected way, the rumors and the horrific deaths of those men only served to make her more resolved to hold on to her only certainties—her life and her Plantagenet pride.

John had left a fortnight ago, traveling to London on some urgent matter; an empty treasury, rumors said. Eleanor did not regret his departure, but she did regret the departure on the king's business of Aumary de Beaudricourt, a young man who had come to Corfe as a messenger from William Marshal. Marshal was in Normandy, trying to stave off the collapse of John's forces by attempting to resupply the besieged fortress of Gaillard.

Once, she had found a few stalks of sweet woodruff, a remedy against melancholy, on her favorite bench. She had not seen who put them there, but she felt certain it was Aumary de Beaudricourt. The young man had smiled at her when others were not watching, neither bold nor ogling, a smile sad at the sight of her, as if they shared a secret loss. She had not wished to cause the young man trouble and therefore had not approached him, but bailey gossip had brought her tidbits of his own heartbreak. It appeared that both their sorrows had been caused by the same man.

The crowd in the bailey hooted with laughter. Eleanor frowned. Laughter in this place of tragedy sounded obscene. The two May mummers with their overflowing wheelbarrow who entertained the gathering made an odd pair. One was a hunchback encased in a mound of rags and strips of furs, topped by a ridiculous feathered cap. His companion, a shorter man with an enormous belly, was disguised by a thick wrapping around his head and jaw, generous swaths of some greasy stuff covering what remained visible.

The hunchback did not speak at all, confining himself to a wild pantomime that drove the onlookers into helpless wrecks of mer-

riment. The fat man wanted the wheelbarrow to be emptied of the
castoffs gathered from around the bailey. To conciliate him, his
companion wept over every one, a perfect picture of Greed. They
were good, the two of them. In a gesture of supreme sacrifice, the
hunchback tossed away a basket full of rotting fish.

The offensive items skidded to Eleanor's feet, splattering her
cloak. Eleanor glared from the soiled fabric to the perpetrator. The
hunchback cast toward her two rapid glances in succession, and
paused, mouth agape, the embodiment of a smitten lover. Then he
limped rapidly toward her.

Expecting a new diversion, the audience shouted encouragement, pummeling the man with whatever came under hand. He
gamely deflected most of it with a cooking pan that he had appro-
priated from one of the unwary kitchen knaves. One missile struck
the man on the back of his head, landing him on his belly at Eleanor's feet. The whole bailey hooted. Eleanor blushed and drew
back her hand as if to strike, but clasped her nose instead against
the smell of rotted fish. The bailey thundered with laughter.

"You may spit, if you wish," the mummer said through the
feathers, "or you may flee to the saddlery. I prefer the latter."

Under the dirt, the padding, and the smell, the distinctive,
rasping voice was just as she remembered—and the eyes. Eleanor
stared at it all, paralyzed.

"Now," he said.

She swept up her skirts and ran, with her odoriferous pursuer
behind her, to the delight of the rabble, who followed them at a
safe distance.

"You are mad!" She recovered herself as soon as they had distanced themselves enough.

"I know. Still, I am the only one who can get you out of here."

She kept three steps ahead of him. "You can't. I am watched.
They say Arthur is dead. Where would I go? Why should I
trust you?"

He lunged at her. "Because you have no choice."

The move startled her enough for a genuine shriek. The
knaves, stable hands, cooks, and men-at-arms enjoyed the humili-

ation of the haughty Pearl of Brittany and responded with catcalls in mocking imitation. Eleanor darted among the crates, casks, and chicken cages. Making imploring noises, the mummer's fat companion forced his way through the crowd with his wheelbarrow. The three of them reached the door of the saddlery.

"Inside."

Of course! They planned to hide her in the wheelbarrow. She obeyed with a wildly beating heart, her pursuer cackling like a lecher about to gain his purpose. The crowd halted in anticipation and disbelief.

"A few more screams, Your Grace. Imagine I am John." Lasalle whisked his companion inside, and began to strip him of his disguise. Under it all was a man who was not at all fat, but missing an ear. He aided Lasalle in discarding his disguise, rubbing his face clean. She noticed that his hands were shaking.

She split the air with a bloodcurdling invective she had heard from the grooms. Lasalle threw aside her cloak and replaced it with the disfiguring disguise of his companion. His companion was demolishing the interior with a great deal of noise. She was going to protest, but Lasalle secured several wrappings of the filthy cloth around her head and face. The rest of her face vanished under a layer of greasy dirt. The two men stepped back and looked at each other, then at her.

"Now," Lasalle said, and she was hauled outside, into the face of the expectant crowd. She would have panicked, only her hand was clamped by Lasalle's to the handle of the wheelbarrow, and they were racing across the bailey, where he flung something toward the crowd. It was a woman's shift, torn and stained, from which showered silver coins. Gasps of horrified, titillated disbelief became shouts of lewd levity. Their pursuers scrambled in the mud for the silver, shoving and yelling.

They were at the gate before Eleanor realized that the ruse was working—but not on the two guards who halted them at the portcullis. Her knees nearly gave, but her mad would-be savior was gesticulating wildly, pleading to be allowed to escape from an insatiable virago who was about to catch up to him. The guards, seeing the crowd pass a woman's shift above their heads, burst out laughing, ribbing each other, clearly not believing that the Pearl of Brittany had been deflowered right under their noses by the lusty hunchback. One of the guardsmen waved them to pass. They lurched forward and as they did, the guardsman's companion plunged his lance into the heaped wheelbarrow.

Eleanor's heart stopped for that instant. Had she been hidden under the pile, she would have been dead. By then, they were past the portcullis, running across the drawbridge, stumbling down the narrow approach to the gate, racing along a thicket of shrubs and saplings toward the village below. Where the shrubs thinned, Lasalle steered the wheelbarrow into them, letting it tumble down a ravine, and then pushed her after it.

They slid down the incline and Lasalle came to his feet, tearing off his disguise and disappearing into the thicket, leaving Eleanor to deal with hers. He returned wearing what one of her guards would have worn, leading two saddled coursers. He boosted her into the saddle and pressed a whip into her hand. "Use it," he said.

The coursers took the rise in great leaps; they raced along a narrow path into the open countryside and did not slow down until lather rolled off the coursers' shoulders. Lasalle reined them to a canter and they rode into a small enclosure with a half-collapsed barn hidden by encroaching brambles. Inside the barn, they were welcomed by half-light and the neighing of two horses. He had to help her dismount. Eleanor slid against the barn's roof post, gasping. "Your friend, you've left him behind."

Lasalle was stripping off the horse gear. "He is not my friend."

She tried to catch her breath. "If he is captured, he will tell John where we are."

He dropped a wineskin into her lap. "He doesn't know where we are."

After a few swallows, she could think more clearly. "Those are Lusignan horses. I recognize them."

Lasalle pulled something out of the saddlebag and threw it to her. "You have a good eye for horseflesh."

Someone had said something like that to her, a long time ago. "The Lusignans paid you, didn't they, to free me? I've heard of your reputation. They say you helped John kidnap Isabelle from under the Lusignans' noses. And now you serve them. You truly are a mercenary."

"I truly am."

She wanted to gain over this man. "Is there anything you wouldn't do for money, sir?"

"No. Put those on."

She ripped at the cords of the bundle. "These are men's clothes! Why should I wear these?"

Lasalle dragged the saddles to the fresh horses. "Because I am not contending with flapping skirts and briars."

Mindful of each sore fiber in her body, Eleanor came to her feet. If Armand de Lusignan had paid this man to accomplish her escape, escape she most likely would. Her fear was a sign of weakness. She would show the Lusignans and their hirelings that she was not someone they could use in their schemes. She threw the clothes on the ground. "I am not wearing this unsuitable garb. I could be the true Queen of England!"

"As you wish, Your Grace. You'll look suitably enough garbed wearing your crown in John's next gaol."

She folded her arms, pride battling outrage. "I will not disrobe with you here, sir. Go outside and wait until you are called."

Lasalle paused over the saddle, his eyes trailing along each curve of her. Eleanor felt her cheeks blaze as that sensation she had felt when he kissed her at Mirebeau came on her, and suddenly she wanted there to be no barrier of cloth or rank between them, only . . . His gaze returned to her face. "Put those on, Eleanor. I am not your waiting woman."

Defeated, blushing, and infuriated, she reached for her gown's laces. Lasalle resumed rubbing down their horses, ignoring her. "I can't untie them," she snapped, her helplessness nearly bringing her to tears.

He wiped the dirt from his face. She held on to her sob and turned her back to him. The laces loosened. The man did not move. She stiffened, but by then he was moving away. She caught him before he did, her hands, partly confined by her gown, clinging to his surcoat.

"No," he said, his hands on her wrists. "You are surprised that you are alive and want proof of it. It occurs after a battle, too."

"Do you feel it as well?" She did not know how those words came to her.

"Yes," he said, and his smile contained a world of understanding and a shadow of sadness, like Aumary de Beaudricourt's. "But I am no longer surprised by it and hardly ever swayed."

"Can't I allow myself to be swayed, just this once? The Count of Rancon said I had a husband chosen for me, but he lied; I know he did. And now they will marry me to someone horrid." The haughtiness had vanished, replaced by the hope and fear of a young woman, and he heard it.

"No. Not if you paid me. Not that you would have to, Your Grace." He was smiling down at her, taking the dangerous impropriety she so unexpectedly offered and diverting it effortlessly, for her sake.

"They all think I've been dishonored, anyway." Her own words shocked her, but the moment was already slipping away, as he had intended it to.

He slowly shook his head. "A ground and a cloak make for a hasty bedding. You are not a whore, Eleanor. You have the right to expect more."

She withdrew her hands, her pride reasserting itself. She did not know what had possessed her. It must have been her passionate Plantagenet blood. Lasalle returned to his interrupted task and she busied herself with her unraveled braids, not wanting the moment to pass, not yet. "Why did you kiss me, there at Mirebeau?"

"Ah. What man could claim to have kissed a girl who could become a queen and still kept his head? Besides, you are beautiful, my lady."

He replied with a perfect balance of insolence and deference, and Eleanor understood, and let him know. "You say that to all your women, sir. I've heard of your reputation."

He bowed to her formally. "I said it only to one other woman. On my word of honor."

That made her giggle. "And which one of your mistresses was that?"

He paused, his elbows on the horse's rump. "Hmm. I can't remember."

Eleanor laughed and made her way to a dark corner. She removed her gown and dressed herself in the clothes he had given her and faced him, smiling to hide her embarrassment.

He gave her a brief nod of approval. "A very handsome page, but I'd take the gown with you. You would not want to shock your vassals."

Eleanor rolled her gown into the saddlebag. "They say my great-grandmother the empress escaped her enemies in a disguise such as this."

"You see? And it made her famous."

"Is that what gave you the idea for this disguise?" She stepped aside so that he could reach the other courser. Oddly, she felt perfectly at ease with this man.

He leaned his shoulder against the horse's thigh until the gelding shifted his weight, then he rested the courser's hoof on his knee. "No. My wife did."

A sense of acute discomfort silenced Eleanor for a moment; her rescuer was, after all, a married man. "I've met her," she said quietly. She remembered the beautiful Countess de Valence, but she recalled only vaguely a tired, pale girl waiting on her. "I haven't behaved very graciously."

Lasalle released the hoof and rounded the courser's rear for the other side. "She said you were alone and afraid."

Eleanor sensed that he did not wish to discuss the matter further, yet she said, "I think she, too, was alone and afraid. Is she . . . is she waiting for you at Tillières?"

"No."

She went to sit at the back of the barn. He came to hand her his cloak, brought her bread and cheese and the wineskin, gave the horses their oat bags, and went outside to keep watch. The sun was sinking. Eleanor burrowed herself into the hay, the cloak smelling of its owner and fish. She tried to imagine what it must be like to be married to him. She had heard gossip that the marriage was not of mutual consent.

She closed her eyes. Suppose it was true and Arthur was dead? *Healthier ones have fallen to mischance.* No, it could not be true; this was pure coincidence. But the evidence was undeniable: The Lusignans were free and Arthur's whereabouts were unknown. The Bretons would have little to say about a husband for their duchess. That decision would be in the hands of the Lusignans.

The next thought made her tremble. Which one of them would they make her marry? The Count of Rancon himself? Or would it be the younger Hugh? *Your women will turn green with envy,* Armand had said of her future husband. They said the Queen of Jerusalem fell in love with Guy de Lusignan the same way grandmother Aliénor had fallen in love with grandfather Henry, at the first sight of him.

Eleanor hugged herself. What would it be like, her wedding night? Would her husband know that no man before him had touched her and that only one man had kissed her, once, as if he had the right to her body, to her soul? And she knew that she would think of him, as her husband made her his wife, and that part of her would always belong to another.

Above her, an owl swooped silently through the rafters.

CHAPTER 62

Paris

Married! That infuriating . . . ! She had always thought that nothing she could learn about that man would surprise her, but once again he had proved her wrong. Lasalle had not only

concealed his parentage; he had also perpetrated bigamy, in addition to a bevy of indiscriminate fornications. In Madame Violaine's
garden, Juliana dealt severely with several thuggish radishes. It
appeared that she had exchanged one prison for another, at the
order of another Lusignan. She did not wish to see Geoffrey of
Parthenay again after his revelation, and had made that fact ex-
plicit in a hysterical outpouring against that entire clan.

"Will I be allowed an audience, Lady Juliana?"

Geoffrey stood several paces away, the spitting image of his father, but Juliana's eyes were drawn by the pendant in the folds of
his surcoat. He held it out to her. It was a clove-pointed gold cross
set with amethysts. She clasped her hands behind her. "That depends on whose purpose you are here, sir."

"My own, but since you've made your decision, you will bear
the burden of this child and its legacy. Arrangements have to be
made for both of you. Shall we sit?" Not waiting for her objections,
Geoffrey of Parthenay escorted her to the folly, strewn with cushions. A tray with cups waited there. He handed one to Juliana and
when she took it reluctantly, he smiled and said, "I assure you that
I am not a poisoner. Would you like me to drop a sliver of uni-
corn's horn in it?"

"No. If it came to that, you'd have held my head in the
fountain."

Her companion laughed. "A practical woman. Neither I nor
my brother have designs on your life, although I could not vouch
for our father."

"I don't believe you. Your father has been—"

"You were to be killed if Guérin did not figure out how to end
your marriage in a less conclusive manner. When you fled to Pont-
de-l'Arche, our father could hardly dispose of you with so many
witnesses. He had to find other means."

"Good God, the books! Were they poisoned?"

Geoffrey shrugged. "I don't know. Neither did Guérin, I imagine, but he could not take that chance."

Juliana crossed herself. No, she'd better not venture further.
"But what about the attack on Lasalle?"

Geoffrey smiled slightly at her use of her purported husband's purported name. "Master Thibodeau is our father's devoted servant, one of the best crossbowmen one could hire. Guérin rode your mare, did he not, and haste, I imagine, precluded closer verification."

"Thibodeau! He spied on me? Oh! Does Lasalle know?"

"He does. I suppose he thought it was easier to keep an eye on Thibodeau rather than battling you over him. Unfortunately, there were circumstances Guérin could not control."

Juliana sat, sorting through the flood of questions. Should she trust this Lusignan? "But why wouldn't he disclose his marriage?"

"Because your marriage shielded him from fulfilling the obligation of his first one. Armand had them pledged while they were both children, an alliance of some import, you may come to understand. Public disclosure would have endangered a number of lives. As long as Guérin remained married to you, they were safe."

"What obligation?"

Her companion crooked up his eyebrow. "Taking the lady to bed, Lady Juliana."

"Oh." So Armand de Lusignan had almost succeeded in murdering her to compel his son to return to his lawful wife and beget a lawful heir on her. Juliana started to laugh.

"It is not all that amusing. In the opinion of some scholars, a marriage does not need to be consummated to be valid," Geoffrey said with mild reproach.

She would have none of it. "Yes, yes. The Bologna school. Saint Hugh wished to avoid making Our Lady's marriage invalid by the absence of the . . . the conjugal element."

"Well said. A position supported by Pope Alexander. A marriage is valid before such ratification, but not until then is it indissoluble. However, some believe that even if unconsummated, the first matrimonial contract supersedes a second one, even if the second one has been ratified. What does a valid marriage then make, one wonders."

You don't know what you have done, woman, Lasalle had said to her. A silence followed. Juliana squirmed. Geoffrey of Parthenay had made some study of the subject, but then, so had she, and she was not about to contest his first wife's rights to my lord Lasalle. "How did you find me?"

"The Order pays Violaine generously. She spies on spies, but this time she tried to serve too many masters. I put an end to it when I learned that our father had retrieved Guérin from her establishment before I could. The rest came from Ziya. Guérin had no other means of sending a message to our hostess that you were to be found at the mouth of the old aqueduct. I knew you would encounter that wall, and we raced to dismantle it. Armand intended to recover you at the same spot, but this time we've beaten him to it."

"We?"

"A number of acquaintances. You will meet them when they escort you to a safe place."

"And who am I running from this time?" Juliana thought she ought to ask.

Naturally, Geoffrey did not answer that one. "Lupescaire surrendered Falaise to Philip's forces and he is traveling to Paris for his reward. You may have a chance to reclaim your ward."

"Praise be to Mary! And do you know where Jourdain is?"

"No. I presume he is safe and cared for."

"I see," she said. The man surely knew of Jourdain's whereabouts, but refused to tell her. If he thought she was such a simpleton, she would leave him at it. Juliana pulled her skirts to her and stood up.

"Don't you want to know your own child's heritage?" Geoffrey asked, surprised by her.

"No. I know you are all worthy descendants of Mélusine. God willing, He will make this child a girl and none of you will care."

Geoffrey of Parthenay sat up from his pillows. "And if it is not?"

"Then I will keep him out of your family's clutches if I have to foster him to a butcher, baker, or candlestick maker!"

A few days later, Geoffrey of Parthenay accompanied Juliana to the Three Dwarfs, where she found Rosamond, her servants, and her

men—all eight of them, and none of them de Montier's men, who
had been sent, safe and sobered, back to Rivefort.

The eight waited for her in the courtyard—Joscelyn de Cantigny, Hurlain, and the rest of the Poitevins. Confused thoroughly,
Juliana slid from her saddle unassisted. Among the familiar faces
she saw one more: that of Rannulf de Brissard, maintaining an air
of dignity amidst the young men's enthusiasm.

"They are yours, Lady Juliana, here to bind themselves to their
liege lady," Geoffrey explained when the cluster parted, all bowing
and grinning.

"But I am not their liege lady," she whispered to him. "Lasalle
only kept them as John's hostages."

"Of course he did. They are all vassals of the Lord of Parthenay.
They are your husband's own men. Why do you think he did not
trade them? He knew some of their families would not be able to
raise the ransom, and that they'd likely perish in John's custody."

Juliana tripped on the threshold. "Do they know?"

"They know now, and have been sworn to keep their council."
Geoffrey motioned for the first man to step forward. "They will
give their fealty to you in your husband's stead."

"But he is not—"

Geoffrey silenced her with his finger to his lips. With Joscelyn
de Cantigny in the lead, the young men genuflected before her
one by one. She accepted the last oath, Rannulf de Brissard's, with
shaking hands. She felt like an impostor. When the old knight got
to his feet and stepped away with a short bow, Geoffrey came to
her side. "Now you will have to choose their captain."

Judging from the faces about her, that decision was of some
import. Juliana slipped her hands into her sleeves and fixed her
gaze on her toes. "I know you all to be more than capable of filling
that duty, my lords, and I am grateful for your loyalty, but I've
learned that for a number of years my . . . my lord Lasalle has
placed his trust in one of you. I know you will understand if I ask
Sir Rannulf to serve as your captain—unless he finds that position
unacceptable, that is."

The courtyard broke out in cheers. Brissard stepped forward,

waving the others to silence, half-gruff, half-embarrassed, and gave
her a very formal bow. "It will be my honor, my lady."

And so the lady Juliana acquired a guard and a guard captain,
and a semblance of liberty. None of it, of course, lasted very long.

CHAPTER 63

Dorset, England

They left the barn when the birds stirred in the trees and the
haze still clung to the ground. When they reached the coast,
the horses slid down the sandy embankment and cantered along the
beach until they came to a small horseshoe cove. A boat waited
there, an ordinary fisherman's boat with a gray-haired pilot who
asked no questions, and a nervous man with an ear missing. Eleanor
recognized him, with relief. The man offered no explanation for
how he had escaped from Corfe or how he had found them, and
Guérin de Lasalle did not ask for one.

She pretended difficulty in dismounting and Lasalle untied the
bags, picked her out of the saddle, and waded into the water. She
held on to him, not wanting to let go, not ever, but he lifted her
over the side of the boat and hauled himself in behind her to guide
her to her seat, a fishnet on top of several casks. The wind picked
up, unfurling the sail and whipping fine spray from the waves. He
was tucking his cloak about her when she caught his hand. "You
will not come?"

He finished and smiled. "Tomorrow. You'll see Brittany before
you know it." He dropped a knot of cloth into the pilot's hand and
indicated the mummer. "Cast off. If you think of straying, this man
will kill you."

The pilot applied himself to the rigging ropes and Lasalle lowered himself back into the water, helping the sloop to clear the
shallows. The sail snapped in a gust and Eleanor felt the power

of the wind carrying the boat toward the open sea, toward her freedom.

As the boat rocked away from the shore, Lasalle stood there watching them for what she thought was an unwise length of time. She closed her eyes and felt a sharp sting under her eyelids, and she knew it was neither the wind nor the salt of the sea. She opened them again, and blinked. A dark line appeared between the dunes and the sky. The rigging clanked, the boat timbers groaned. She gripped the sloop's side, her eyes straining.

Riders, about a dozen of them.

The lone man on the shore was not trying to evade them. His two coursers neighed a greeting to the new arrivals and he headed toward them. Eleanor grew as cold as if she were in a watery grave. She turned to the mummer. "Dear God. He lied to me. He is not returning."

The mummer's face answered her without words. On the shore, the man at the head of the party halted his men and rode up to Lasalle, alone. She recognized the cloak and the cap. Fear, despair, and pride welled up in her. "Turn back."

The wind swung, lifting the boat's keel half out of the water. The pilot shouted and the mummer threw himself into the rudder. "We can't. My lady, it would be a certain death!"

Eleanor of Brittany stood up. She stood up among the casks and the nets, among the smell of dead fish, pitch caulk, and seaweed, the cloak draping her like a coronation robe. "I am the Duchess of Brittany. I am the rightful Queen of England and I command you to turn back!"

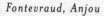

Fontevraud, Anjou

The old queen was dying.

She was dying with each piece of news brought from the north, news that reverberated through the abbey like the knelling of a bell.

The Count of Évreux had deserted his duke and was soon joined by Hugh of Gournay, Peter de Meulan, and Guy de Thouars. The barons of Maine and Anjou promised to Philip that they would acknowledge the Pearl of Brittany as her brother's sole heir if he was found to be no longer alive. That Arthur was no longer among the living became the staple of loud whispers.

After darting from fortress to fortress, unable to trust his own castellans, in early December Duke John had taken leave of his continental domains. Accompanied by his queen, he left Barfleur for England. By then, Philip's siege engines had surrounded Richard's own Château Gaillard. Sir William Marshal, sent to relieve the stronghold, failed. In early March, after an eight-month siege, Richard's "proud daughter" surrendered.

Sabine tried to withhold the worst of the news from her mistress. "The duke writes that he will return shortly to Normandy with fresh reinforcements, Your Grace." She quickly folded the message and placed it with the others.

"John has no reinforcements," Aliénor of Aquitaine said, her clouded eyes on the garden outside her chamber. "No means, no men, and no will to fight. Call Mathilde. I wish to make my profession."

Sabine caught her breath against a dizziness of heart-rending pain, like the pain she had felt on the day she had surrendered her only child to the cloister. Only her mistress was not a young widow but a woman who had lived fourscore years, outliving two husbands, a lover or two, and all her children, save one.

"Your Grace, perhaps—"

"No physician can cure age, Sabine. The young will have to fight our battles." Aliénor removed her coronet and her veil, her hair falling in a long silver braid across her shoulder. "Battles we have stirred. How do you find someone to fight for you? How do you bind them to you even after you are in your grave?"

She had asked the same question four years ago in this very place, but Sabine did not understand it any more now than she had then. The queen took her seal ring from her finger and placed it on the table. "Keep this. I don't want John to have it, even though he will finally have my Aquitaine. And sell my jewelry, all of it, and give it in alms to the poor. Lord knows we've caused them misery enough. Oh, no tears, Sabine, not you."

The dowager queen placed her hand on the head of her kneeling, weeping lady, and Sabine could feel the tremors in it. "And this casket is for our little nun when she visits my grave. She will, you know. You may leave it with Mathilde; no need to drag it about. I believe she will understand this time."

Sabine wanted to ask if the queen meant for the understanding to be visited upon the abbess or the former Sister Eustace, but her mistress was already unbraiding her hair. "Scissors, find my scissors. I will not have it said that I took the veil half-heartedly. One must not do things halfheartedly. Cut it, all of it, and let me be free."

Paris

Juliana spent the next few days in anxious anticipation of the arrival of the mercenary Lupescaire and his angelic hostage. While waiting, she sent Hurlain with letters for Jehan de Vaudreuil and Mistress Hermine, and a copy of her attested charter to de Montier. Armand de Lusignan had forwarded the document to her at the Three Dwarfs, along with an inquiry after her health. She kept her charter and threw the letter into the kitchen hearth.

A message also came from Madame Violaine, brought by the courtesan Ziya, who came accompanied by her trunks. Madame Violaine, too, inquired after the lady Juliana's health, informing her that she was depriving herself of Ziya's services in order for the girl to keep the lady Juliana company.

Since Lady Juliana could not very well toss Ziya and her trunks into the hearth, she decided to accommodate herself to her unwanted guest. Juliana's guards, on the other hand, were thoroughly confused as to the relationship between their ungarnished

liege lady and her marvelous companion. Under Rannulf de Brissard's jaundiced gaze, the Poitevins resisted with heroic efforts
Ziya's attempts to amuse herself in what must have been to the
courtesan a thoroughly dull household. It was like living with Paulette de Glanville, only in the obverse.

Paulette. The girl, Edward, and Jourdain remained in Juliana's
prayers and on her mind every waking moment. She prayed that
she would receive news, any news, and soon. That evening her
prayers were answered by a messenger from Geoffrey of Parthenay:
Lupescaire had arrived in Paris.

"Lady Juliana, are you ill?" Shielding her candle's flame, Ziya
appeared at the foot of the stairs, wrapped in her bed blanket.

Juliana shook her head and gathered her cloak about her. She
sat on a stool by the fireplace. The servant girl had banked the fire
when the cry of *couvre-feu* came, but the bricks still retained heat.
Ziya had washed off her paint, revealing underneath it a pretty but
not spectacularly beautiful young woman, somewhat older than
Mathea. The girl noted Juliana's surprise at her appearance.

"I don't like the paste; it makes my face itch. Will you tell Madame, Lady?"

Juliana pressed her fingertips to her temples. "No, of course
not. Why would I do that?"

"Oh." The girl gave her a guilty look before blurting out, "My
name is Meridel. Lord Guérin did not have me, I swear it. He only
wanted me to memorize the message for Madame. I had no choice,
you see. He asked for me. He knew me from the time he came to
Madame's with his friend Heinrich."

Juliana took hold of Meridel's shoulders. "Is Heinrich also
called Kadolt?"

The courtesan surely must have thought that the lady Juliana
had gone mad. "Yes, but he said to call him Heinrich."

Juliana shook the girl. "Do you think Heinrich would remember you?"

The girl held herself up with professional pride. "Of course he
would. They all remember Ziya."

"And do you know a man called Lupescaire?"

"No, but I've heard of him."

"Of course you have—everybody has." Juliana let go of the girl and rushed about the room, her headache vanished. "Oh, Meridel, it is so very important—do you think you can be Ziya again just for tomorrow?"

Meridel smiled, an uncertain smile, and covering her mouth with her soft, white hand, she giggled.

CHAPTER 64

Riding into the courtyard of the residence taken up by Lupescaire and his entourage, Juliana noted that the wages of faithlessness had paid off handsomely for the traitorous mercenary. The house was as large as the House of Cerberus, with a walled enclosure and a gate to keep out an army. Lupescaire had not counted many friends among the Norman barons, and he did not count many friends among the Franks.

Ziya, riding on Rosamond, had chosen from her trunks a wardrobe worthy of the challenge, and they were admitted readily. Juliana, in a servant's cloak, rode a mule behind Ziya and their hired men, all of them having slipped past their guards with Joscelyn de Cantigny's help. The sight of an intriguingly veiled Ziya descending from Rosamond drew men from around the courtyard, allowing Juliana to dismount unnoticed from her mule and walk past an unguarded door into the house, her heart racing as fast as if she were again braving the aqueduct.

Inside the antechamber, servants carted about furniture and unpacked stores. From a pile by the entrance, Juliana picked up a basket and followed several servant women. No doubt Paulette was kept imprisoned in one of the private rooms.

"Not that way, you goose—take that to the solar." An older woman with a ring of keys at her waist girdle pointed Juliana in the

opposite direction. Too frightened to argue, Juliana did as she was
told.

At the threshold she stopped dead. Around an oak table a gaggle
of women gathered to open trunks and crates to sort vessels of gold
and silver and ells of costly cloth, no doubt pillaged from churches,
fortresses, and homes.

"There you are, you silly cow." A well-dressed woman took the
basket from Juliana, following up with a sharp cuff on the side of
Juliana's head. "My lady, we've found it!"

From the group's midst, a soft voice answered, "Don't be angry,
Delphine. I knew it would be found."

With a forced smile on her lips and a deep curtsy to the speaker,
Delphine moved aside and Juliana faced a serenely beautiful young
woman, her hair held at her nape by a loop of her own wheat-
colored tresses. She wore a gown of white sindon with a girdle
embroidered with gold threads molding her hips. She took the
basket from Delphine and gave Juliana a grateful smile.

"Thank you for finding my sewing basket. We thought it was
left at Falaise—oh!"

Juliana reached out as if to an apparition. "Paulette?"

"Oh, Juliana, it is you! I am so glad. I was so afraid you would
worry about us. Oh, I am so glad!" Paulette de Glanville embraced
her, and it was difficult to tell who was crying and laughing more.
The women buzzed around them, while Paulette chattered so rapidly that Juliana could not make head or tail of any of it. She had
never seen Paulette de Glanville this animated, she noted with
shock and a great deal of relief. Whatever her ordeal, Paulette
seemed to have suffered no ill effects from it. Perhaps, miraculously,
the worst had not happened.

"Lady Juliana, Lady Juliana!"

A high, young voice, accompanied by determined tugs at her
cloak, demanded her attention. Paulette laughed and released
her. A boy stood there, wearing short boots and an embroidered
tabard.

"Edward?" Juliana reached out and the boy, who looked like he
was about to throw himself into her arms, flushed and gave her a

perfect bow instead. Another young face watched them from the
door. Edward sprang toward it, returning with a girl of about
eleven or twelve years.

He stuck out his chest. "Her name is Odeline."

Juliana curtsied slightly. "I am honored, Odeline." The girl had
dark hair and serious gray eyes, but before she could answer, Juliana sensed another pair of gray eyes on her.

Lupescaire.

With two of his men by his side, the infamous *routier* stood in the
doorway, looking much as she had remembered him from Mirebeau, unsmiling and whipcord lean. He was regarding her with
hostility precisely measured for someone of her rank and sex.

"Lady." The mercenary bowed to her. "You have deprived us of
welcoming you to our home."

What title should one grant to a baseborn man who had held
the favor of two kings? Would she insult him by granting him
none? "I was not certain I would find welcome."

"My"—Paulette touched Juliana's hand.

"Leave us, all of you," Lupescaire gestured. "Odeline, what happened to your lessons? Edward, take Lady Paulette to her room."

Hands linked, the children led Paulette away, with the rest of
the room emptying after them. When the door closed behind the
last servant, Lupescaire motioned Juliana to a seat by the fire. She
sat. "Is Ziya safe?"

"Kadolt is showing her our *routier* hospitality."

Juliana clasped her hands in her lap and decided not to mince
words. "I came to reclaim my ward and my page. You've gained
possession of them in an unlawful manner."

"At Mirebeau, you were afraid your gown would soil if it
touched me. Do you know it was the Count of Rancon who gave
her to me to deliver Falaise into Philip's hands?"

She nodded stiffly. Lupescaire was not what she had imagined.
A cutthroat he was, but not a mere butcher, as Armand de Lusignan
had styled him. "I did not mean that you had seized them. And I
did not intend to . . . to insult you. I was taken by surprise."

Lupescaire did not accept her effort at conciliation. "We're wild beasts to you, aren't we, Lady? We rob and kill because it is our nature."

"I am not here to discuss the avocation you have chosen for yourself. Paulette de Glanville is not one of your camp followers. She's gently born and you are—"

Lupescaire placed his palms flat on the table, a glint of steel in his eyes. "Avocation, eh? The only difference between your man and me is that he was born in his papa's keep into silk swaddling, and I was dropped behind a hedgerow into a pea sack."

A log in the fireplace sent sparks at Juliana's feet. No, Lupescaire was not at all what she had imagined, but that did not change who he was. "Paulette was sacrificed to a great lord's ambition. He is using you like he has used others. Let her go, please; I can pay you."

Lupescaire reached into a small casket on the table and pulled out a handful of parchments. Juliana stood up, apprehensive.

"You all think you can buy lives. Not this one. I found use for her."

"You disgraceful knave!" Her hand flew toward Lupescaire's face, but he struck it aside, pressing a handful of sheets into her fist. Juliana took a step back, battling fear and fury, but he made no further move toward her and so she smoothed out the sheets. Laboriously drawn letters sprinkled the first page, with more skill-ful renderings on the next few. "She is teaching your daughter to write."

Lupescaire took the parchments from her. "My daughter has a clerk to tutor her. Her mother is a camp follower, but I pay the clerk well. Sarlo!" The door opened and a head poked in. "Sarlo, tell Lady Paulette that the lady Juliana wishes to speak to her." The man disappeared and Lupescaire went to the door, the casket under his arm. "You can have her back, and the boy, if they wish to leave."

Juliana returned to her chair, her head throbbing with excite-ment. Keeping Paulette de Glanville would have made Lupescaire even more enemies, and Lupescaire surely had not become the man he was by being witless.

"Juliana?" Paulette ran across the room to kneel at Juliana's feet, her hands clasped. "Oh, I was so afraid, I was so afraid you wouldn't—"

Juliana silenced the girl with her fingertips. "Shhh. I am so sorry to have placed you in such terrible danger. But I did not know—sweet Mary, I didn't know. There are so many things to tell you. Everyone at Rivefort will be so happy to have you back. You can be married as soon as you wish, or you can wait as long as you wish. I know Aumary will understand."

Paulette's eyes grew larger. "Marry Aumary?"

Had the shock of her ordeal obliterated Paulette's memory? If it had, it would be God's mercy. "You were on your way to wed him when this dreadful thing happened, don't you remember? I know you love him and he worships you. Lasalle no longer owns any of us, so you see, you don't have to be afraid."

Withdrawing her hands, Paulette sat up. "Oh," she said, pallor replacing the flush on her cheeks. "I was afraid you would not approve of Jarnac."

The burning logs made the only sound in the room.

"What?" Juliana finally said, as if someone had spoken to her in a foreign tongue.

"His true name is Jarnac. He was a fisherman. I did not wish to marry Aumary, Juliana." Paulette smiled. "I taught him his letters. And now he knows them, thanks to me."

Paulette remained where she was, her hair loose, her face turned up, the face of the purest of vestals—and of a sophisticated courtesan. Some kind of perfume enveloped Paulette de Glanville, more exquisite than Ziya's or the Countess de Valence's. And the rings. Paulette de Glanville wore rings on almost every finger, nothing vulgar, just tiny sparkling gems to match the moon-shaped ones in her shell-pink earlobes. Juliana could not recall ever seeing Paulette's earlobes, let alone with earrings in them. It was as if Paulette de Glanville had kept a part of herself hidden from everyone except Lupescaire, a man who used to be a fisherman called Jarnac.

"Dear Lord."

Paulette came to her feet, sweeping back her gown's train with a gesture Isabel de Clare had no doubt taught her. "I am sorry, I must be such a disappointment to you. When they attacked us, I prayed they would kill me or dishonor me so that I would not have to marry Aumary. All my life I have done everything to please others. You asked me once what I wanted, but if I had told you, you would not have understood. I did not want a marriage to a man who would always regard me as a living saint."

Juliana stood up as well. "How can you say that? You know I would have understood."

"No, you would have said that I was mad. Not everyone can live up to your ideals, Juliana."

"Ideals? You and I have the misfortune of being given to men who have no honor and nothing to redeem it by. In my case, it was of my choice. Vaudreuil loved you. He still does, but he married Mathea because Lasalle made him. I have no marriage to go to. He is already married, Paulette. I can't change what happened to me, but you can change what has happened to you. Come with me and you will be restored to His Grace, but you must come now."

Paulette shook her head, her hair stirring like a nun's veil. "No. I suppose I am mad. But I feel more alive than I've ever felt. I don't want to give that up, not yet. Hasn't anyone ever made you feel like that, Juliana?"

For an instant, she could taste the bitter tang of a willow sprig. This was madness. She fastened her cloak's ties. "I did not come here to discuss myself. Please, call Edward."

Paulette stood there, her hands clasped as if in prayer, tears trembling on her eyelashes. "I can't. Please understand."

She did not understand it; she never would. With a bare sob, Juliana forced the door to open, Paulette's voice behind her. "Juliana, forgive me!"

She found Meridel in the courtyard with their nervous escort and Heinrich Kadolt, holding the young courtesan's hand. The mercenary released the girl's hand and took a couple of limping steps toward her. "*Meine* . . . my lady Yuliana . . ."

He did not say more because Meridel announced it all in one breath. "Lady Juliana, I am not going back to Madame. Heinrich offered to wed me."

Under the paste, Juliana could see the color in the girl's cheeks. She could have sworn that Kadolt was blushing as well, or at least his scar blazed under the wisps on his balding pate.

None of this was turning out the way she had planned—none of it.

From across the courtyard Edward was waving at her furiously, even as the girl Odeline, laughing, pulled him away without much effort. And so the lady Juliana, who had sought out the fearsome mercenary Lupescaire on a mission of mercy, returned to the Three Dwarfs short one angelic ward, a harlot whose true name was Meridel, and the tender offspring of a disemboweled highwayman. She found her losses replaced by three new arrivals: her husband's mistress, his aunt, and her father-in-law's murderous henchman, called Richieu.

CHAPTER 65

Anne's strapping guard captain had Richieu by the scruff of his neck, and the man shriveled under the Countess de Valence's vituperation and the lashes of her riding crop. "I'll have you skinned alive! I'll have you spitted and roasted, you stupid, useless rotter!"

Richieu tried to shield himself from the blows. "Lady Juliana, you're alive, miracle of miracles. I beg you to save me. He'll kill me—I swear by all saints, he will kill me." Richieu tore himself from de Querci's grasp and fell on his knees in front of Juliana. "Protect me, Lady, protect me. I have told the truth; you must believe me."

Juliana inserted herself between Anne and the object of her wrath. "Please, let him speak."

"He is in prison!" Anne threw up her hands.

Juliana looked to the others, uncomprehending, and therefore it fell to Auntie Sabine to explain it all. She did it without wasting a word. "John has Guérin clamped in the Tower for trying to free Eleanor of Brittany from Corfe."

Underneath the layers of Juliana's skirts something stirred. Precious Lord's blood, the Lusignans were all insane. "Then we will send a messenger to the Duchess of Aquitaine. She will intercede with John."

Her visitors turned to her as one. The Countess de Nevers touched the ring on the finger of her right hand. "The queen is dead, my dear. Don't you know that?"

It was a gold seal ring incised with a relief of a lady with a falcon on her wrist, the same ring Juliana had rescued at Mirebeau when the queen-duchess was still full of spirit and defiance. Juliana sat down and crossed herself. A despairing emptiness overwhelmed her. Aliénor of Aquitaine was too vast a force to encompass in a single thought, but one came to the fore: The queen-duchess was dead, and Juliana de Charnais remained trapped in her web, as were all those in this room, whether they knew it or not. The silence allowed her to form one other thought. "We have to tell the Count of Rancon."

With a plaintive moan, Richieu crossed his arms over his head. Anne slapped her whip at him. "Don't be silly, Juliana. Armand would be happy to see Guérin dead!"

Juliana took a deep breath. "No, that he would not."

The new master of the House of Cerberus welcomed them with his customary graciousness, which did not extend to his man. To Sabine the count gave a deep bow, and even though the Nevers eyes conveyed unconcealed antipathy, he kissed her hand before she could evade the courtesy. "My dear countess. *Tempus fugit.* How long has it been?"

Having paid his respects in order of age and rank, the Count of Rancon gave Anne de Valence a smile that she acknowledged with ill-concealed impatience, and then he aimed it at Juliana. Proper manners dictated a curtsy; Juliana wanted to spit in his face. He knew it and smiled as well because he knew that she would not, and turned to Richieu, who dropped to his knees with a whimper.

His master swept the room in a grand gesture. "A veritable deputation of devotion, I see. Shall we toast to the occasion that brought us all together? We are, after all, almost a family." His glance scraped Richieu. "Most of us."

The Countess de Nevers removed her riding gloves and took the edge of the nearest chair. "Let us not mince words, Lusignan. Since your mad scheme has failed, we are here to insist you exert every effort to save his neck."

Armand de Lusignan broke the seal on a small packet of parchments with his dagger's tip. "Failed? Did you fail, Richieu?"

Sweat sprang up on Richieu's brow. "No, my lord! I told them, we did not fail. We had the lady in the sloop, only she made us turn back. He never intended to return with her; he told me so. You said, my lord, to obey lord Guérin in everything. I did. Only the lady Eleanor ordered us to heave to. I had to obey her. I had to. We nearly didn't make it out alive."

Voice soft with suppressed rage, Armand de Lusignan moved toward Richieu. "And you decide to disappear, leaving me to explain to those Bretons why I did not deliver their lady to them at the appointed place."

"Mercy, my lord. There was nothing I could do. She saw him riding toward them. His old squire was leading them, the one called Aumary, and he surrendered his sword to him, just like—"

A dagger's blade flashed up and disappeared under Richieu's breastbone. A spurt of red issued from the corners of his lips, opened in half protest. Already on its knees, the lifeless body slumped to the floor.

Juliana clamped her hand over her mouth. Armand de Lusignan had killed Richieu with the same stroke Lasalle had used to dispatch Erhard of Hesse. The Countess de Nevers exclaimed and came to her feet. Anne de Valence cried out, tearing at Armand de Lusignan's arm.

"You are jealous of him, you and John. That is why you want him dead!"

Armand deflected the young woman with one hand and drove the dagger into the tabletop with the other. "Dead? I wanted him the bloody King of England!"

The words hung there.

"You are insane, Armand." The Countess de Nevers gathered her skirts with a gesture of finality. "Only the man who marries Eleanor could ever hope to wear that crown. Guérin could never marry her. The Bretons would never consent, not with Arthur vanished."

Armand wiped his bloodstained fingers on the table drapery. "Still the same scoffer? Tell her, Juliana. It's time for secrets to end. Isn't that what you wanted? Think, girl."

She did. She was being put to a test, a test that she would fail as miserably as she had failed all the others, with her pedantic clinging to the merely obvious. *There are a thousand things you don't know about me, Sister Eustace.* It was all there, so plain that she had not seen it.

"They don't have to. He is already married to her." She met Armand de Lusignan's unforgiving eyes. "They were pledged as children. It was all part of Constance of Brittany's revenge on the Plantagenets. He is the count's son."

Anne and the Countess de Nevers stood there transfixed. Then Sabine turned to face the hearth, her words a sigh. "So it's true. You and Yvetta managed after all. I have always wondered."

Anne de Valence took a stumbling step backward. "Dear God. What have I done?"

"Sullied herself with father and son, but all for Aliénor's cause." Armand de Lusignan dismissed her and picked up the parchments.

Anne did not seem to hear. "John will kill him. We have to save him."

Armand de Lusignan let the parchments slip into the flames. "The Tower is not Corfe, woman. My idiotic son cooked his own goose, to spite me. He thinks I had . . . Christ, if he were here, I'd—"

"But you can't, can you, Father? He is free of you. He bested you after all."

Only Juliana and Armand de Lusignan recognized the man at the door. A sternly handsome, formidable Templar moved across the hall, a great cross emblazoned on his surcoat, the wrath of Jehovah in his eyes. Giving the body on the floor a scant glance, he bowed to Sabine, who took the shock of recognition of her nephew's true parentage like a Nevers.

Fist to his hip, Armand de Lusignan regarded his firstborn coldly. "Geoffrey, done with your prayers already? Who are you praying for this time? Your brother's soul?"

Ignoring his sire, Geoffrey took a rolled parchment from his belt and held it out to Juliana. "Guérin's share for his mercenaries, from the Venetians. He had arranged for the Temple to hold it for you."

Mercenaries? Confused, Juliana took the parchment.

"Well, well." Armand de Lusignan folded his arms. "What do you intend to do with it, girl? Buy his life? Why bother? You wouldn't know what to do with him."

"Armand." The Countess de Nevers raised her voice. "You are a damnable—"

Juliana passed Geoffrey to face her tormentor. "You wanted to kill me. Thibodeau nearly succeeded, but your son took the quarrel instead. Your books—you sent them to poison me. You wanted to turn me over to Madame Violaine. You had Equitan murdered and Paulette abducted."

Her braid had come loose from underneath her wimple and Armand de Lusignan reached out to smooth it with the kindest touch. "Such righteous fervor, so little understanding."

She wrenched herself away with a marrow-burning desire to kill, to plunge his blue-bladed dagger into that black heart until blood splattered the chalk-white shirt. In that instant, she understood what had driven Lasalle to want to annihilate Viart. Armand de Lusignan smiled at her with open contempt and reclaimed his dagger from the tabletop. "You are a pigeon among peregrines, Sister Eustace."

"That girl is of no concern to you, Armand." The Countess de Nevers sallied to Juliana's defense. "I know why I insisted that

Yvetta not be allowed to marry you. Even as a stripling, you were a viper."

"No lands, no friends, a stripling of low degree and unwonted ambition, you called me." Armand de Lusignan's voice hardened. "And I came to you on my knees. First and last time I've begged for anything. I promised I would make Yvetta a queen. You laughed. Very well—I could not make her a queen, but I vowed I would make her firstborn son a king!" The dagger impaled the table linen. Neither wanting nor caring for a response from the Countess de Nevers, Armand addressed his firstborn, who stood there mute and untouchable. "Only he had to turn out to be the pious one. *Tiens,* some foals are throwbacks. But not the next one. And he would have been a king, but for Sister Eustace and Aliénor's scheming!"

The Countess de Nevers confronted her opponent with equal force. "What conceit. Guérin never wanted a crown. *You* did!"

"And how would he know? He's never worn one!"

Anne de Valence threw herself into the thickening acrimony. "Dear God, you have no intention of helping him."

Armand de Lusignan answered with a gesture used to dismiss fools. "I don't mind my son's cleverness, but not at my expense."

This time it was Geoffrey who moved forward. "That is not all, is it, Father? John is convinced his barons are conspiring against him. He needs Guérin to implicate Marshal, and if Guérin does not, John will have him executed. You are gambling that the barons will not stand for many more Plantagenet ploys. You are stirring up a war. A king may die. The queen is sixteen and childless."

Armand de Lusignan crooked his eyebrow at his firstborn. "Well then, let's not be hasty about returning to the *outre-mer,* Geoffrey. Think of the possibilities. Now, if we could find someone to distract you from your chastity."

The parchment seemed to burn Juliana's fingers. She held it out to Geoffrey. "I have no right to it, but for such a sum, John will release him, surely."

Geoffrey accepted it and folded the seals. "And force him to remain trapped between Scylla and Charybdis of other people's making?" He turned to Anne and the Countess de Nevers. Anne was eagerly reaching for the scroll when Geoffrey dropped it into the hearth's fire.

Juliana's heart froze. Anne cried out and threw herself at the hearth, but Geoffrey shoved her away. The seals blistered; the parchment crackled like an autumn leaf, flamed, and disappeared. Anne slipped to the floor, her fists striking the stones. "You want him dead, you bloody bastards, you want him dead!" She raised her accusing, tear-stained face to the two Lusignans. "God, I wish I were a man; I'd kill you both."

Anne loved Lasalle. It came to Juliana not so much as a revelation but as a confirmation. *No one will know this marriage ever existed.* And now no one will know that Jean Armand de Lusignan had ever existed either.

The hall became suffocating. Richieu's body drained the last of his blood into the rushes. No one paid the least notice. Juliana craved air and the assurance that outside these walls, the world had not gone mad. The voices of Armand de Lusignan, Anne de Valence, and the Countess de Nevers clashed around her. She reached the door and pushed it open. The sunlight felt like a benediction. She left the door open and went to the garden.

Sabine and Anne waited for her with their men. Anne ran to Juliana, her hair escaping from its careful arrangement. "We have tried, we both did. Good Lord, Armand won't lift a finger! What are we going to do?"

Juliana led Anne to her palfrey, trying to calm her. "First, we have to warn Sir William and Lady Isabel."

Anne shook her as if to wake her up. "But Marshal has already left for England with Isabel!"

Juliana nodded to Anne's groom. "Very well, then we will go to England."

Too distracted to notice that she was being managed, Anne allowed herself to be assisted into her saddle. "Yes, yes of course. Good Lord, I can't think. Marshal will know what to do. I shall have to make ready for us."

Anne urged on her mare, trotting out of the gate with her men.

The Countess de Nevers brought her palfrey to Juliana. "I am so sorry, my dear. For you, for Anne. Saints save us, that family is a pack of trouble." She lowered her voice. "Are you bearing up? This must be a terrible shock to you. It is to all of us. How will you explain to Sir William about Guérin?"

"I will, somehow." The answer came without hesitation and after it did, Juliana realized that she meant it.

Sabine crossed herself. "God forgive me, but perhaps it is God's will, this, for Céline."

Across the rooftops, a flock of doves reeled into the sky. *There are a thousand things you don't know about me.* Juliana gripped the reins of Sabine's palfrey. "Auntie, can you look after Anne? I have to see someone."

Her aunt by an invalid marriage looked askance at her. "'See'? Very well, but don't delay. And take a couple of my men with you. I wouldn't trust that Lusignan." Detaching two of her guards with a snap of her fingers, the Countess de Nevers ordered them to mind the lady Juliana. Thus guarded, Juliana rode out of the courtyard of the House of Cerberus and did not look back.

CHAPTER 66

Cloister of Saint-Sylvain

The sisters' necrology contained twenty-three names and the dates of internment. Juliana obtained the necrology, and entrance into Saint-Sylvain, by lying determinedly. The new gate mistress did not recognize her and dropped the volume into Juliana's hands, sighing that she was late for prayers. Holding on to her wimple, the nun hurried to the chapel and Juliana watched her, a former self, envious of the nun's simple worries.

A trapdoor underneath the choir lifted easily. Cool, dry air rushed from the opening. Juliana took a deep breath. Dark passages into the bowels of the earth did not agree with her. A dozen steps later, a shaft of light from the trapdoor revealed dusty wooden caskets filling the crypt. With her candle in one hand and the necrology in the other, Juliana wove among them, examining the numeral carved at the foot of each, searching for number fourteen. She found it at the back wall, where spiders had woven fine filaments around the coffin. It looked old, much older than the coffin of Céline de Passeis had a right to be. Surely this could not be Céline's final resting place—unless the sisters had used an old coffin for a new body?

Casting around the low chamber, Juliana counted the coffins: twenty-two. Perhaps the coffin maker had made a mistake and transposed the numerals. She counted again: twenty-two coffins. She stood under the vaulting, her heart thumping against her ribs. The sisters of Saint-Sylvain were short one body.

Calculating how long it would be until the sisters finished their progress, Juliana reckoned that she did not have much time left. She returned to number fourteen and worked the edge of the candleholder underneath the lid, where the nails had rusted through the wood. The lid came loose with a disconcerting pop. Juliana crossed herself. "Holy Mary, Mother of God." She shoved.

She had not counted on the shroud. The candle flame revealed a skeleton-thin shape sewn into a sheet. Holding her breath, she touched the cloth. The physical presence giving it its shape collapsed, crumbling into dust. She started back with an exclamation. The coffin was old, and so was the body within it. If Céline de Passeis had been laid to rest in that coffin, she would have had to have been buried for a century.

The lid replaced, the necrology under her arm, Juliana marched the length of the crypt and up the stairs with spine-tingling determination. Someone had a lot of explaining to do. She would begin with Abbess Nicola.

"Lady Juliana. Or should I say Sister Eustace? Which one are you, child?"

Atop the last step waited Abbess Nicola, standing up this time, aided by the gate mistress and a couple of walking sticks, her hip jutting to one side under her robes. Her cross gleamed in the church's dark interior. The abbess smiled a narrow smirk and nodded to the gate mistress beside her. Juliana sighed and surrendered the necrology to her. The nun disappeared from the chapel with it.

"My very question, Reverend Mother." Juliana smiled with aplomb into eyes that looked back at her with the same implacable animosity as Lupescaire's. "Or should I say Céline?"

A tiny muscle tensed underneath the dark brow. "Céline is dead."

"Perhaps to the rest of the world, but not according to your necrology, Reverend Mother."

The hostility in those eyes remained. Abbess Nicola took a few steps and sank onto a bench, sighing with relief. "I must have that thing burned one of these days, only one day is so like the others." She indicated with annoyed impatience her useless limbs. "Not a pretty sight, is it? The result of hurtling down two stories and landing on a potting shed. Broke my hips and my legs into splinters. Do you know what agony it is to have your bones grind against each other, Lady Juliana?"

"No. Were you pushed, thrown, or did you jump? After being outraged, I mean. You were outraged, weren't you, Reverend Mother?"

"Neither. I wanted him to marry me. I threatened to jump if he didn't. The balustrade crumbled. I can still see his face. He looked as if he cared, at least for that moment."

There was a sound somewhere between a choke and a wheeze coming out of Juliana. "Guérin."

The abbess arranged her sleeves with great precision. "Don't be so ridiculous. I had no use for a boy enamored of love or for his brother who wanted to be a monk. I knew them both. We were all reared under Ermengarde's tender care."

"Oh Lord," Juliana said, and loudly.

The scorn in Abbess Nicola's voice chilled the air. "I was Armand's ward, and I had loved him ever since I was a child, but he loved Yvetta. I found out about their clandestine marriage—I can read, you know. They had to separate in order to keep it a secret from her family. Why a man would become obsessed with a woman he can't have is one of life's mysteries."

"Perhaps it is because he can't have her." It was not a question.

"Unfortunately, it also blinded him to what he could have had. No wound festers or pains as sorely as one inflicted by rejection. It can lead one to commit outrageous deeds."

"Like enticing his youngest son to help you to flee? You thought Armand would come after you. Only he didn't."

Abbess Nicola licked her lips. "Oh, he did come. He knew where I would be heading too. You see, I was going to Saint-Sylvain's, not to Wales, as Guérin and those young coxcombs thought. I had a surprise for Armand. For all of them."

"Yes." Juliana's mind raced backward past the twists and turns of her impoverished imagination. "So you did. How old was Aumary and how did you keep your condition concealed?"

"The same way you do, Lady Juliana." Abbess Nicola smiled contemptuously and answered Juliana's unspoken question about the source of that information. "Violaine is a patroness of our abbey. She sometimes comes here to unburden herself to me."

That gave Juliana pause. "I see. Still, one would think that even among a flock of mistresses, one would notice one's ward in one's bed."

"Alas, no flock of mistresses. It made the whole thing simple, especially since one was sufficiently drunk, and the other wearing a particular gown and one's beloved's perfume. It was far less difficult than one thinks. All one has to do is—"

"Pretend." Juliana decided to press on. "He was born here, wasn't he, Aumary? A Lusignan family name, I believe."

"I thought it fitting. My cousin did too. She became the abbess here before my parents' death. She was much older than I was, and I made up an excuse to leave Poitou and visit her when I found out I was with child. Armand was glad to see me go. No doubt he sensed that something had changed between us, but he did not wish to know. He was busy with his latest scheme."

"Why didn't you tell him?"

"He sent an escort here to take me to my wedding to Geoffrey at Fécamp. When I arrived there, I was going to tell him, to fly off my horse and declare my love and my glorious news to the world. And then I saw them together." Abbess Nicola grasped her cross as if she wanted to crush it. "Armand and Yvetta. Those two had something I would never have. They kept it from me. They denied it to me! They stole it from me!"

Abbess Nicola's voice grew in passion. Juliana had heard the strains of it in Paulette's voice, in Anne's, in Mathea's. She thought they all had to be mad—at least a little mad—to allow themselves to become like that. Or was it she who was mad for not being able to feel that way?

The abbess took a breath to continue more composedly. "Someone with whey in their veins would not understand. I made Guérin and his friends take me away. We almost reached Saint-Sylvain, but Armand caught up with us and hauled us all to his house here, in fury at me, at Geoffrey, at Guérin. I weakened. I wanted to give him one last chance. I stood on the balustrade and threatened to jump unless he married me. Armand laughed and told me to go ahead and turned his back on me. I flung myself at him. The balustrade crumbled."

This time Abbess Nicola spoke unhurriedly, dispassionately, as if she had all the time in the world. She did, of course. But Juliana did not. "And then?"

Abbess Nicola shrugged. "They thought I was dead. They brought me here for burial. My cousin received my body. Only I wasn't dead. I suffered for months. I had a great deal to think about. I learned that Armand had sent Guérin and the others to *outre-mer* before more inquiries could be made. I knew then how much he set store by that boy. I meant to destroy him. I meant him to suffer as I did. And now God has answered my prayers. Armand has already lost Geoffrey, and he will lose his precious Guérin."

Juliana was glad for the wall at her back. "He doesn't know about Aumary?"

"Not yet. I let Guérin in on that news after he returned. I knew he would take Aumary under his wing. What a fool. He would have made a good monk except that he was broken early to lechery. I became abbess when my cousin died. I had no choice. I was dead and buried."

Before Juliana sat a still young woman, beautiful yet deformed in more than her limbs. "Guérin is the duke's prisoner. John will kill him," Juliana said, not knowing why.

With great effort, Abbess Nicola stood up and, leaning on her canes, took painful steps toward the chapel door.

"Won't he, now? Have no doubt, I would have had you locked up in that crypt till you turned to dust, but you've brought your men." She halted at the door and faced Juliana with a languid smile. "I shall pray that you and your child die in childbed. Then Armand will have only Aumary left to carry on his line."

CHAPTER 67

The City of London, Spring 1204

The Tower, foursquare and trimmed with gleaming Caen stone, dominated the north bank of the river behind a girdling of walls and defensive towers. William the Conqueror had commenced its construction to signal the finality of his claim to England. Over the years, the bastard duke's descendants had enlarged the structure and King John, not wishing to be remiss, was adding his own stamp—a ditch.

While in his capital, John did not reside in the Tower but at the fortified manor of West Minster because the queen preferred its comforts. John did, however, appreciate the security of the Tower's walls, fifteen feet thick at the foundations and rising ninety feet above the adjacent town. That day, John left his wife's bedchamber to see how one of the Tower's more recent guests fared under his regime.

"How much more do you think it will take before you confess?"

John asked, not wanting yet to resort to the usual measures their encounters entailed.

His guest-by-choice shrugged carefully. "I don't know. I am curious myself."

"I suppose Pike told you not to expect my mother to save your hide this time. Praise to all saints, she finally gave up this world for the next, wherever that may be." John probed the depths of a silver tureen with his knife. "Try some partridge. You will like the sauce; it was Richard's favorite."

His guest did not have a knife, but he did have the chain of his ankle irons, attached to the table leg. They were alone—with guards outside the chamber's door, of course. When his guest did not partake of the offering, John pointed his knife's tip at him.

"Eleanor's women tell me you didn't have her; otherwise your head would be on the gate already. Why did you desist?"

"She is not my kind."

John chortled, speared a piece of the bird bobbing in fennel sauce, and proceeded to dismember it with gusto. "Nor you your wife's. Good teeth, charming freckles, magnificent red hair. Tell me"—John ignored his napkin and licked his fingers, since this was not a public performance—"tell me, is she like that . . . ? No, I don't suppose she'd let you."

John laughed heartily. He was enjoying himself for the first time since the news of Marshal's failure to relieve Gaillard had reached him. Marshal had yet to present his case to him, but with this man in his hands John could divert attention from his own blunders. "So she found herself a lover, did she? And you are jealous, sir, jealous."

Abandoning that topic, John redirected his knife's point at his guest, who was more interested in his wine cup than the feast. For a man kept on bread and water, Guérin de Lasalle exhibited remarkable self-control—or he did not wish to disgrace himself all at once. Either way, John decided, it did not bode well for their relationship.

"Now, to our problem," the titular Duke of Normandy said. "I presume you think you are not going to tell me who put you up to it, but I know it was Marshal. He's been lukewarm in his support of me, and I am told he wasted time in relieving Gaillard. I don't believe that guff about miscalculating the tide. He's been dickering with Philip for Longueville when he should have been fighting for me. The only choice you have is a confession of Marshal's treachery, for which I'll have you dispatched promptly. I am not an unreasonable man."

Lasalle rotated the cup in his swollen fingers. The guards had hauled him from his place of confinement and, after subjecting him to a thorough scrubbing in a trough and a new set of clothes, they had marched him to the upper quarters. He was not sure if it was John's new method of extracting his confession or simply a desire not to have the royal nose offended. At that moment, more than worry about concealing his craven pleasure at the fresh air and sunlight that poured through the open shutters, he feared revealing his relief at learning that Eleanor of Brittany was alive. He had not seen her since he had caught the heart-stopping sight of her running toward him, before a blow had sent him nose-first into the shore sand.

After that, he had been blindfolded and conducted halfway across England, tied facedown on the back of a mule. Since then, he knew approximately how long he had been in the Tower by the number of times the door had opened to a short flash of torchlight for a pitcher of water and a quarter of a bread loaf to be left for him.

He had chewed the bread slowly, reflecting that in the Parisian catacombs, there were no moldy loaves to prolong the inevitable. And now John thought he could have him for a confession that would cost an honorable man his life and destroy his family.

"Marshal knows nothing. He serves you loyally, sire."

"Loyally? Hmph." John broke a piece of bread and threw it in front of his prisoner. "My mother said you would serve me loyally, Lasalle. So much for assurances. I want to know who put you up to this or I will—"

"Armand de Lusignan."

John pushed away his trencher and examined his prisoner

minutely. The more he did, the less he liked. Guérin de Lasalle was a terrifyingly clever man. And persuasive. He had seen it at Le Mans. John stood up, his whiskers stiffening. "You are a liar, Lasalle. You have a habit of trying a saint's patience, sir, and mine is all sopped up. I want that confession, damn you, and I'll have it, and after that I'll have what is left of your miserable life. Guards!"

～

Isabel de Clare opened her heart and her home on Thames Street to her unexpected visitors and listened to Anne's tumble of explanations for their arrival. Juliana did not remember the details of their journey. She did remember that the open sea had terrified her. They had traveled unusually light, just Anne and herself, her guard captain and half a dozen men, and Anne's maid.

Juliana sat in her chair, her cloak smelling of salt and seaweed, weary to the bone, the floor underneath her feet swelling upward whenever her mind drifted. She did not know how Isabel de Clare would take the news about Lasalle's parentage, but the lady Isabel did not bat an eye when Anne delivered it. Juliana kept nodding, leaving Anne in charge. Anne needed to be in charge of something.

"Gracious Heaven, aren't you surprised, Isabel?" Anne knelt by her friend's chair. "I still can't believe it. Good Lord, this is all Aliénor's fault. You were right, I should not have asked you to become involved."

Isabel patted Anne's hand. "I knew since his contretemps with de Bourgh. He grew up in Poitou and when he is not careful, you can hear it. So he is a Lusignan. We can't choose our sires."

Anne stood up and turned away, her fingers intertwined. "You are such a dear. You can forgive, but John will not. We can't stay here. We are placing you and William in danger. We only came to warn you."

Juliana took that as a signal to take their leave. Anne was right. If Lasalle implicated Sir William after all, John's retribution would be terrible. Moreover, Isabel de Clare might forgive Guérin de

Lasalle, but Sir William could be another matter. She reached for the armrest to steady herself, her hand pressed briefly to her middle. Her gown and cloak had rendered her figure shapeless and in her distress, Anne had not noticed a thing. "I am afraid I still don't have my legs back," she tried to explain.

Isabel smiled in return. "Then you must not travel until you do. William went to Pembroke with John d'Erlée and I will not have it otherwise," she said, and would not hear of it when Anne tried to object. "You are both exhausted. Tomorrow we will decide what to do. Now, off to bed and I will have something brought up for you."

Isabel de Clare called her women, who took Anne and Juliana to their rooms. Juliana was grateful for the privacy. She curled on top of the bedcovers, listening to the popping of the embers in the brazier. A scratch and a voice at the door announced a servant with a food tray. The servant turned out to be Isabel de Clare.

Juliana reached for her wimple. "I am sorry, Lady Isabel, I must have fallen asleep. I am a little tired."

Isabel de Clare placed the tray on the bed and drew aside the bed curtains. "I feel tired when I am carrying too. When is it due? Try some hot milk with honey and butter; my nurse swears by it."

Juliana considered Lasalle's usual approach when caught out— lying boldly and bluffing her way out. "How did you know?" she said instead.

"I believe it's called a woman's instinct." Isabel winked at her and held out a steaming cup, patting her own middle. "William doesn't know about this one, but he told me to make the next one a girl. He said after four boys, I've done my duty to posterity."

Juliana felt a dull pang under her heart. "I am glad for you, Lady Isabel. Sir William is sure to be pleased. But Anne is right, we are placing all of you in danger."

"It's still Isabel, remember? Now"—she set the kettle on the edge of the brazier—"tell me the rest."

Juliana sat on a chair by the brazier. "Had I taken my vows, none of this would have happened. He did not want me, and all the time I thought that he was just a no-account . . ."

Isabel remained silent. Juliana de Charnais and Guérin de Lasalle's marriage presented a problem of epic proportions, that much was true. So she asked a rather obvious question. "Do you love him, Juliana?" and watched the girl's cheeks change color, which was certainly not due to the cast of the embers.

"That would be silly of me, wouldn't it? He would make short work of me, wouldn't he? He can do it so easily, with everyone." She did not wish to relive any of it, but she owed Isabel de Clare the truth. And so she told all, even about Saint-Sylvain and Aumary de Beaudricourt, something she had not shared with either Auntie Sabine or Anne. Isabel de Clare remained attentive throughout, merely asking a question or two at times, and Juliana answered them the best she could. "I don't know how this is of any use," she said at the end. "He could be already dead."

Isabel weighed her words, but could not avoid the truth either. "I don't think John would do that. He would have him executed publicly."

I wouldn't relish being trussed up for it. Juliana crossed herself. "Like de Bec."

"I may have a way of finding out how he fares, perhaps even seeing him," Isabel said after a long silence. "Do you want me to tell him about the child?"

"Good Lord, no! Please, you mustn't. He would know that his father had won, don't you see? I think he can bear anything but that. Please, promise you won't."

"I promise," Isabel assured the girl, and taking her hand, she led Juliana to the bed and tucked her there as if she were one of her own. Drawing the bed curtains, she ordered her to rest. Juliana did not need much encouragement. For Isabel, however, the day was just beginning.

CHAPTER 68

As the orphaned heiress to one of the great fortunes in England, Wales, and Ireland, Isabel de Clare had been taken into his custody by King Henry at the age of four and had spent the next thirteen years of her life in the Tower under the watchful eyes of her appointed guardian. The Tower had become her home, and although childish curiosity had led her to explore a great deal of it, instinctive apprehension had led her to avoid certain lower regions. She had known, however, one habitué of those places, and it was that man for whom she searched among the servants of the royal household.

He was a man with graying fair hair under his cap and a jutting chin that spoke of ponderous stubbornness. He wore a brown tunic trimmed with squirrel that placed him above the servants but below the household knights. The only distinguishing thing about him was a set of keys at his belt. When Isabel moved to his side to match his step and pulled back her hood slightly, he stopped, his jaw dropping.

"Lady Isabel!"

Silencing him quickly, Isabel drew the man behind a wine cart. "Master Pike, I am in dire need of your aid. I presume you are still carrying out your usual duties?"

Pike nodded, casting a scowl about him as if he meant to challenge those who would hold otherwise. "Aye, that I am, my lady. A man with a family has to keep body and soul together. And Pike will do, my lady, Pike will do. You were the only one who called me Master."

Isabel smiled, not having the heart to tell him that she had bestowed on him that title because as a child she was afraid that if she did not appease him, he would drag her into the dark domains where he had long reigned as the king's gaoler. Now she had to tell him that she wished to see one particular occupant of those regions. When she added the name, Pike's face grew long in surprise. "Are you his friend, my lady?"

"I came on behalf of a friend. Do you think it could be arranged, Master Pike?"

The gaoler rubbed the back of his neck. "That is a pickle, my lady. The king left strict orders—"

Isabel held her cloak closer to her. "Of course." She smiled apologetically. "I should not have troubled you, Master Pike. I only thought if I could have a moment."

She turned away, but Pike spoke up quickly, his voice a worried whisper. "Only so, my lady, if you do as I say. It's not fit down there, not even for the rats."

Isabel squeezed the man's hand. "Thank you, Master Pike. You are a true friend." Pike's pallid complexion darkened visibly with a blush, and soon Isabel found herself descending into a seldom-visited part of the Tower, Master Pike's torch providing the only light.

At the end of one of the passages, at the bottom of steep steps, Pike paused. Isabel pressed to her nose a pinch of dried lavender in a piece of knotted silk. She carried it for the particularly noisome parts of London; now she found it useful in this place of foul dampness.

The lock groaned; the door opened reluctantly. Dread seizing her, Isabel stepped back at the sight of the black cavern beyond.

Pike lit another torch in a wall sconce. "You can't go in there, Lady Isabel. I'll go and grease the lock; it rusts so quickly here. Just give Pike a hail when you need me."

Isabel nodded, her palms perspiring despite the cold that crept, along with the dampness from the nearby river, through her cloak. The light illuminated her rather than the occupant of that hole, and for that Isabel was grateful. She swallowed, her hand to her stomach. Pike was right; they were both taking a great risk. The man in there knew it too, and he let her know before she could call out his name.

"Lady . . . Lady Isabel. You mustn't be here. Please, my lady, leave before—"

"Before John learns whom he has snagged?"

She could hear the effort it took him to keep his voice even. "You know."

"Since John's fête in Paris. Your animosity toward your father blinds most people to the resemblance you bear him. I suppose that's why you dress like one of your *routiers*, keep disreputable company, and assiduously cultivate your reputation." She did not know why she had launched into an elaboration, and then she realized that she wanted ordinary words to keep at bay the appalling surroundings.

When he spoke again, the lethargy was gone. "John intends to inflict harm on Sir William, but for whatever my word is worth, I swear on all that is holy that none of it will come because of me."

It took her a few moments to understand. "Is that why you think I came?"

He did not answer her at once either, as if he were as surprised by her words as she was by his. "My apology for my manners, Countess. It seemed a reasonable assumption."

"It is not," she said with some force, angry at herself for it. "William can take care of what is his. You don't have to save us all."

"No. I won't be able to save all."

Her own earlier words, handed back to her. Isabel knew he was trying to distract her. "Is that why you are here?"

"We all have to be somewhere."

She crushed the lavender between her fingers. "Don't hide behind your cleverness. I will not have it. That is one of the things Juliana dislikes about you, did you know that?"

"She is dead. I k-killed her."

"You did not, and neither did your father!" She waited in the shattering silence that ensued. And then she heard Guérin de Lasalle laugh. He laughed until the sound became a dry, labored cough. She strained her eyes into the blackness. "You don't believe me, but you must. You can see the proof yourself. There are ways of escaping. Guards can be bribed, a door left opened, a disguise employed."

"No."

"You are risking your life for no reason," Isabel commenced to argue insistently. There was nothing wrong with Guérin de Lasalle's mind, whatever the condition of the rest of him. From the dark depths came the sound of a chain sliding through an iron ring, which grew silent instantly. "My lord?" she called out. "Speak to me. This is folly."

"You must go—now." The voice rasped out from the blackness, then said, "Only one favor, Countess."

"Anything, but—"

"If there is anything left after . . . afterward, could you see to it that it is buried in . . . in someone's garden without upsetting the owner?"

At first, she did not understand. And then she did and searched for the words, but the gaoler's torch appeared around the corner.

"We must go, please." Pike pushed the door shut and secured the lock before she could protest, and when she tried, he shook his head vehemently. "No, my lady, the king could come and he'll not be pleased. He is the only one allowed to see him except for—"

"Holy Mother, he will go insane in there." Isabel picked up her skirts, anger and helplessness making her voice high and quickening her steps. "And he is sick. If John doesn't kill him, he will die in that hole."

Once they reached the upper level, she leaned against the wall. The gaoler caught up with her, alarm on his face. "My lady, I told you not to go down there. You are not well."

"I am quite well. Your wife no doubt suffered a similar affliction a few years back." Isabel found a coin in her purse and tried to press it into the man's hand. "Thank you, Master Pike. You have performed a Christian deed."

"No, no need. It is not like that." Pike waved his hand in protest. "I should have told you to make him tell the king whatever he wants to hear. They will break him, I know they will. Here now, I almost forgot."

Pike delved into his satchel to hand her a gold ring. "He had it on him. By right it's mine and I could get a pretty penny for it, but I didn't want to sell it, least not yet. There is something on the inside."

Isabel examined the lettering inside the gold circle. *Vous et nul autre.*

Master Pike tied his satchel. "Small enough for a lady's finger, I'd say. I didn't know he had any family or friends, but if you say you know of a friend, it's good enough for me."

Isabel stood on her tiptoes to kiss Pike's cheek. "Will you let me know if the king has any plans for him?" And while Master Pike blushed and stammered his assent, she pulled up her hood and hurried into the oblivious crowd. In a callous world, a little kindness was sometimes worth all the gold of bribes.

But kindness would not free Guérin de Lasalle, which was what Isabel told his current wife, skirting the rest. Isabel had planned her words carefully, the ring in her palm.

Kneeling at the prie-dieu, Juliana clasped her hands. "He was right. I should have accepted my fate. Armand wanted to make him fulfill the obligations of his first marriage to further the Lusignans' ambition. Aliénor used me to trap him into ours to prevent it. He wanted neither. I didn't want to be a nun and I wasn't even a wife."

Isabel hesitated, wanting to offer some comfort, knowing that she would be offering none, but in the end she slipped the ring into the girl's hand. "You are wrong, Juliana." But when Juliana de Charnais examined the ring and stood up quickly, crossing herself, Isabel did not anticipate that reaction at all.

"Good Lord. Of course! He fooled Armand again, completely and brilliantly. And I've been so blind and so selfish."

Isabel's confusion deepened. "Are you saying it was meant for Anne?"

Juliana shook her head. "No. Anne was Lasalle's ruse. He used her to distract Armand. And Armand doesn't even suspect. Nobody does. Geoffrey made a mistake—a natural one, but a terrible one. The mercenaries' share was intended for her. Now she has nothing and he doesn't know." Juliana faced Isabel de Clare. "We have to plead with the king; it's our only hope."

"No, not with the king." Anne de Valence stood at the door, dressed in a black gown, her bold beauty heightened by the shadows under her eyes.

Juliana moved toward her, sick at the thought of what Anne had overheard. "I am sorry, I didn't know—"

The Countess de Valence smiled a rigidly composed smile. "It's all right. So he was using me. I have used him, as well." She paused as if she did not wish to know the answer to the next question. "So he is in love with her, isn't he, that whore in Diceto's stews?"

And Juliana de Charnais answered in as steady a voice as she could to tell a perfectly convincing lie. "Yes. Yes, he is."

CHAPTER 69

Despite Isabel de Clare's insistent hospitality, Anne and Juliana set up their own quarters the very next day. Ever mindful of his mistress's safety, Peter de Querci found them lodging within the town walls with a passage that connected the house to its neighbor. De Querci also paid a number of street beggars to warn him of anything unusual in the neighborhood. Anne spent the hours trying the patience of her guard captain. Juliana did not wish to be a witness to Anne's outbursts and so she spent her days at prayer in a small, blessedly quiet church nearby.

When she returned to her lodging that day, she was told that the Countess de Valence had gone out to attend to certain affairs. During Anne's absence, Juliana was visited by a chained trunk guarded by four men.

She had expected Rannulf de Brissard, but instead there was Vaudreuil and a man she did not know, along with Joscelyn de Cantigny and Master Thibodeau. Juliana saw to it that the last two were looked after, then turned her attention to her mysterious visitor. While she tried to place that nose and those cheekbones, he gave her a smart bow.

"I've heard about you, Lady Juliana. From my brother."

Ralph of Exoudun, the Count of Eu. So this was the man whose property John Plantagenet had so ill-advisedly seized, thereby unleashing the Lusignans' fury. The Count of Eu looked like the rest of them: tall, solidly hewn, dark haired, dark complexioned, about the same age as Lasalle. Confused, Juliana turned to Vaudreuil.

Vaudreuil answered her wordless query. "He knows about Guérin. I had to tell him."

"Are you not in danger yourself, my lord?" Juliana asked the Count of Eu, still not certain about the reason for his presence.

He patted his thick cloak to the sound of chain links. "John was so anxious to get rid of us he even granted us safe conduct to our English estates." He grinned. "Of course, I wear my mail. My brother, the Count of La Marche, is here as well. We don't want to give John the idea that he can take us one by one. This time cousin Armand is gambling with all of our lives. Uncle Geoffrey is in Poitou, making John's seneschal anxious. John took the Angoulême girl from us and lost Normandy—now to keep Poitou, he needs us."

Juliana cast a questioning glance at Vaudreuil, who gave her a what-do-you-expect-from-the-Lusignans shrug, but the Count of Eu was leaving them with a flurry of his cloak and a dismissive wave of his arm. "I am delighted to have made your acquaintance, Lady Juliana. Don't fret. Hugh and I will mount our attack on the Tower tomorrow."

And before she could add a word, Ralph of Exoudun was spurring his horse out of the courtyard. Juliana closed the door and leaned against it. "This is all my fault. I should have let you search for him."

Vaudreuil ran his fingers through his hair. It had been recently cut, and despite several days' stubble and the marks of travel, he appeared neatly dressed, and somehow contented. "Ah, I don't suppose you had noticed that I did not need much persuasion." He came to the fireplace to warm his hands and said, wonder in his voice, "She is carrying, you know. I am going to have a son. Or maybe a daughter," he amended when Juliana looked up at him.

A dull pang went through her, but she smiled back. "Not an

unexpected consequence of marriage, I am told. I am glad. Most people want someone for their own, don't they?" She hesitated. "Even Paulette."

"I've heard. Is she . . . is she truly happy?"

"Oh, ecstatically," Juliana assured him with such conviction that Vaudreuil burst out laughing.

"Do leave a man some pride, Lady!"

Abashed, Juliana folded her hands into her sleeves. "I am sorry, I am not good at these things. Do you think that Ralph and Hugh will succeed?"

Growing serious, Vaudreuil frowned. "Sometimes I think that Lusignan luck will carry them through anything; sometimes I think this time it will run out. I should go with Ralph."

He said it as if he anticipated something from her. She realized it was her consent. She was, after all, this man's liege lady. She nodded and remained standing at the window long after Vaudreuil rode out of the courtyard. "Master Thibodeau," she then called out, "you may come in."

The little man shuffled in with an armful of volumes and bowed to her in spades. "I brought the accounts, my lady. They didn't want me to burden them, but I said, oh no, Lady Juliana will be not pleased if I do not discharge my duty to her."

Juliana picked up the tongs and poked at the fire. "Was not the Count of Rancon pleased about the way you've discharged your last duty to him, Master Thibodeau?"

Master Thibodeau pressed his stubby fingers to his heart. "My lady, I don't know what I am being accused of!"

She stepped toward the door. "Don't you? Shall I call Peter de Querci and de Cantigny? It will not take them long to refresh your memory."

The little man intercepted her, his belly quivering, his cheeks the color of dough. "I had no choice, my lady. No one defies my lord Armand—no one! He would kill me if I did not do as I was told. I beg of you, have mercy. I will do anything you command."

"How much do you think Tillières is worth?" Master Thibodeau's jaw fell open. "How much?" Juliana raised her voice. "King

Philip is forcing John's supporters in Normandy to choose between England and their continental lands. There must be a market around here for a Norman viscounty in exchange for an
English fief."

Master Thibodeau wiped his palms on his girth. "Yes, yes there
must be."

"Then find someone who wants to trade and make sure it is a
fief a king with an empty purse would covet."

Master Thibodeau's expression changed from fear to shrewd-
ness. "You are going to trade Tillières, my lady? But I thought you
said you would never—"

"So I did. Take the books and go; you don't have much time."

The look of utter devotion returned to Master Thibodeau's
countenance. He bowed and, mumbling with relief, reached for
her hand. She jerked it away. Bowing with each step, Master Thibodeau drew toward the door.

She turned her back to him. "If you breathe a word of this to
anyone, I will have Sir Joscelyn kill you, do you understand, Master
Thibodeau?"

~✦~

"He is a what!"

"Shh. Keep your voice down, William, you'll wake the children."
Isabel de Clare closed the door to the nursery. From the hallway's
floor, she collected a toy wagon, a hobbyhorse, and the remains of
several wooden swords and walked on ahead of her just-returned
spouse.

She did not have much time to prepare him for both pieces of
her news, so she came out with the first right after her husband bestowed on her the kiss of someone who had not had the opportunity
to kiss his wife for a long while, and who had not done anything
about it. That, she anticipated, would give her an advantage.

"A Lusignan, I said. He is Armand's son. And he is in trouble.
John wants Guérin to accuse you of a plot to replace him with Eleanor of Brittany."

"What plot?" Marshal's voice threatened to climb to a thunderous level. During the long ride from Pembroke, he had not looked forward to facing John; he had looked forward to a long soak, a good night's sleep, and a fresh morning, when he would make love to his wife while she protested unconvincingly about the impropriety of it. This was not on the agenda.

"Shh. My point precisely." His wife hushed him. "But you will have to hurry and convince John to release him. I wanted to arrange for his escape, but he won't."

"Arrange for his escape?" Good Lord, he'd been in Wales to look to Pembroke's defenses should John's anger over Château Gaillard become more than anger, and now he had returned to find his wife in the middle of a raging bonfire of political intrigues, kindled by those infernal Lusignans. And Lasalle being one of them!

"Don't worry, William, I said he won't do it." Isabel steered her husband into her chamber.

"And why not? Christ Almighty, if he is a Lusignan, he ought to have more lives than a cat!" Marshal slammed the door shut on a parade of servants with steaming water buckets, bath linens, and their master's fresh clothes.

"Because John would use his escape as a proof of your guilt, don't you see?" Isabel commenced on her husband's buckles and straps. "You have to help him, William."

"Saints' bones, Isabel, you've turned into a schemer. You and that flighty Anne. I can't believe it. A Lusignan!" Marshal shook his finger at his wife. His wife was not deterred.

"We can't pick our sires. You said you would rather have him watch your back than anyone else. That has not changed. He is not responsible for your bad blood with the Lusignans. He was not even born." She buried her face against the fabric of his shirt, which smelled of sweat, horses, and the wildness of Wales. "William, you have to help."

Marshal pushed his wife away, leaving her to stand there, her hands clasped. He sat in the nearest chair, his elbows on his knees, his temper receding. "The bloody fool. John wants me to wage war on Philip, but I owe Longueville to him. I said I would not turn on any liege. And now John will have me, thanks to the Lusignans."

Isabel came to her husband and knelt by him. "John is king because of you. What would have happened if you had chosen to support Arthur and he had died? Eleanor would have inherited this kingdom, her husband would have ruled it, and you would have supported him, would you not?"

Marshal nodded with a troubled frown. "Of course."

"Why would you support him, William?"

"Because I'd rather not see this land plunged into another war. We had enough of it under Stephen," William Marshal snapped, not happy with the turn of the conversation.

Isabel took her husband's hand, large and scarred by years of wielding lance and sword, and kissed it. "If Guérin de Lasalle had his father's ambition, you would have sworn fealty to a Lusignan."

Marshal hurled himself to his feet despite the stiffness of his joints. "What? He is married to Eleanor? Christ Almighty, is there no end to this? *Ma foi,* I would not!"

"You would, William. You would because you care more for justice than your pride or your personal feelings. You would do it," Isabel said quietly.

The words made Marshal face his wife. The seventeen-year-old beauty he had married had grown into a beautiful and astute woman. "Lizzie—"

"What would have happened to you if a king had not taken pity on you and spared your life when your own father would have thrown it away?"

That was a tack William Marshal had not expected. He tried to maintain his ire. "Stephen spared me because he was soft. He drenched England in blood for nineteen years."

Isabel smiled and approached her husband despite his words. "He had also spared the life of a boy who grew up and steered this realm into hands he thought more capable, only they are not. We all owe our lives to someone. You are the Earl of Pembroke because of me. The future of this realm is in your hands again, William Marshal." And with those words, Isabel lifted up her face to her husband and he saw the simple and awful truth of it.

"Christ," Marshal said without conviction, "I had no idea you'd be such a costly proposition, my lady."

"True," Isabel de Clare whispered coyly and stood on her tiptoes to kiss her husband's bristly cheek. "Would you like to see what sort of a bargain you've made yourself, my lord?"

CHAPTER 70

Juliana and Joscelyn de Cantigny rode along the river floating with jetsam, past the free-floating fishnets tied to wooden kiddles. As they approached the Tower, its stones, which were said to be mortared with the blood of dragons, turned out to be dirty gray in color. Seagulls and ravens circled above the turrets. In the new outer bailey, the king's men milled about the forges, stables, cattle pens, and poultry coops, giving the place the impression of a fortress under siege.

Juliana had prepared herself for fruitless waiting, but she was allowed into the inner ward as soon as she announced herself. She left de Cantigny behind with the horses and followed one of John's household knights up a staircase into the hall occupying the upper story.

Despite the presence of John's barons, retainers, and servants, the expanse of the hall and the height of the walls to the massive roof timbers gave the great chamber an intimidating appearance. Her charter in hand, she halted. She should have prepared her words better; she should have sought guidance; perhaps she should have—

"My dear Lady Juliana. We heard you were in London. Why have you not presented yourself? My, you do look distressed. A chair for the lady Juliana!"

John was examining her as if he were a tomcat who had chanced upon an unattended cream bowl. The young men of John's personal entourage smiled knowingly, whispering and nudging each other. Several older barons remained to the side, blank faced.

Juliana avoided being cornered into the chair by getting to her knees, praying that her words would do her intentions justice. "I do not want to draw you from your duties for more than a moment, sire. I came to beg you to spare the life of my . . . my lord Lasalle. He is an impulsive and reckless man who was ill-advised in his actions. I beg of you, Your Grace, spare his life. He served your brother, your mother, and yourself bravely and well."

Reminding John that Lasalle had served his brother and mother was perhaps not the wisest strategy, but she could say little else in this hall of men who had done likewise. She held out her charter, trying to keep her hands from shaking. "Have his lands forfeit but not his . . . his life, sire. I have exchanged Tillières for estates in this land. They are prosperous and will bring you steady dues."

When she had finished, she did not know whether she had broken some rule about speaking to a king, or whether she had been too bold or not bold enough. John unrolled the charters, his frown giving way to a smile. He examined the seals and helped her to her feet to kiss her hand. "Very well said, Lady Juliana. We are touched by your wifely devotion, are we not, my lords?"

"Very touched, sire," called out several of the younger men, accompanied by sycophantic noises. Others remained silent.

"There, you see, Lady Juliana?" John's fingers caressed her wrist. "We understand. Be assured that as soon as you are a widow, we will arrange for you a more suitable marriage. As for this mesne," he tapped the parchment against her shoulder, "we will keep custody of it until we are ready to grant it to your new husband."

And with that, the king called for his dogs and strode off, whistling. The men filed after him. Juliana heard nothing until one of the Norman barons, passing by her, lowered his voice into a warning. "Leave this place now, Lady, with whatever you have left."

"The Lusignan luck finally ran out." Vaudreuil, who had brought them the latest lack of news, sat on the bench by the fire, his head in his hands.

Anne heard him out, offered an obscene oath involving the

King of England's marital bed, and slammed the door behind her.
Juliana remained sitting where she was, her mending on her lap.
She, too, had something to tell Vaudreuil.

"I traded Tillières for an English barony," she said, and when
Vaudreuil's head went up, she hurried on. "John holds my char-
ter for it, but I am certain the new lord will respect your rights to
Belvoir."

Vaudreuil came to his feet. "You did what?"

"I thought it would free him; I truly did. Perhaps I should have
given him the coffer, but I thought it would be enough."

"For John? *Par Dieu,* woman, how could you be so daft?" Vaudreuil lashed out so hard that the girl cringed, but he did not
spare her. "Guérin safeguarded Rivefort and Tillières for you—he
always safeguarded it for you, and you just give it up?"

Juliana could barely see the stitches, but her defense was un-
dershot with stubbornness. "It's only a pile of rocks. It is not as
if . . . as if it had a mind, a heart, and a soul, is it?"

"Juliana—"

"He is there because I kept him to this marriage."

Vaudreuil kicked the fire iron. "He is there because of himself,
but most of all, he is there because of Armand. That vulture ought
to be entertained. Doesn't he know that this is his last gamble with
his son's life?"

The needle went into her thumb but she did not notice the
pain. *My father couldn't win at games of chance either.* A sense of panic
and exhilaration seized her. "Armand is in London? Where does
he reside? I have to find him."

"Juliana, you can't—"

"He can't afford to gamble, not this time. My cloak and my
horse, please—or shall I call Joscelyn, sir?"

Her ultimatum, accompanied by her vehemence, had their effect. Vaudreuil gave her a grand bow. "You are a most challenging
woman, Lady Juliana."

~❦~

They dismounted in the bailey of a fortified residence, to be
greeted by the man they sought. "Lady Juliana," Armand de Lusi-

gnan said, "what a pleasant surprise. And dressed in widow's weeds already. You were always such a practical child."

Indicating to Vaudreuil to stay put, Juliana lowered herself from the saddle and smiled at her splendid enemy. "And you, my lord? You must be Saturn, devouring your own children."

She walked uninvited past Armand de Lusignan into his residence and gave the place a brief inspection. Armand de Lusignan followed her with brow-creasing curiosity, she noted with satisfaction. She untied her cloak and sat down. "Contrary to your fondest hopes, sir, your son has not denounced Sir William and he never will. Your schemes are failing. Save him before it is too late."

Armand de Lusignan took her on sufferance. "I am disappointed by the news, but my son chose his own demise. Fortunately, he left behind a little gift for me in your belly. How fares our little viper?"

She folded her hands with the gesture used by Abbess Mathilde when dealing with difficult novices. "My mother died in childbirth, did you know that? You seem to know so many things."

There was a hair's-breadth fissure in Armand de Lusignan's self-control before he crooked his eyebrow at her. "A dreadful tragedy, Lady Juliana."

"It was. She bled for three days. The child died with her."

Armand de Lusignan's smile froze. "What is your point?"

"If I die, you will not care. But if the child dies as well as its father, you will have nothing. You are no longer playing a game. You are gambling. And you are very bad at that, just as your son is."

Armand de Lusignan hooked his hands behind his back. "I have gambled my whole life."

"Not without being very certain of the outcome. You taught him that winning is the purpose, but he figured out he can vanquish you by losing. No one can counter stakes like that. You are not the master here. God is. If you stake your hand on this child, you could lose everything."

"I've broken bread with the Devil, girl. What makes you think I would not dare God?"

"How did Yvetta die?" The question came to her as if someone else had spoken, as if a vengeful presence had entered the hall.

The answer came without hesitation. "She bled for three days. The child died with her."

"Oh! I thought . . . I thought she died of a broken heart."

"It was not my child. She died giving birth to Guérin de Lasalle's child. Did you think that I was the only man Yvetta de Nevers ever loved? That she had denied herself to the man she took as her bigamous husband? I suppose at first she did. But she came to pity him or to love him—which, I don't know. He was a lesser man than I, but he was there and I was not and so she forsook me. Does that please you?"

She did not know if this was another Lusignan lie or truth so plain that most men would have shrunk from it. "No. Other people's pain does not please me."

"A pity. One should find diversion where one can."

She was not going to allow him to trap her into playing by his rules. "You have corrupted him. He hates you for that."

"All innocence longs to be corrupted—look at your spotless Glanville girl. I have shown him corruption; the rest is his doing. That's why he hates me. Return to your lodging and stay there, Juliana. I will not have you meddle."

She was defeated and dismissed with Lusignan thoroughness. She would go, but not silently. "Why are you here, my lord?"

"Why, to find out whether a king or a count is a better gambler."

Juliana woke up before dawn after a night shot with vivid and violent nightmares. Outside the shuttered windows, the rain poured down as if heavenly sluices had opened up. She lit a candle and put on her gown. The coin chest sat next to her bed, wrapped with padlocked straps. *This is blood money,* she had once said to the man who brought it to her. And the answer, simple and terrible, came to her.

She opened the door, called out, and waited. The man who came to stand in front of her in a rabbit-lined robe and nightcap was a soft and undistinguished little man. A man she could buy.

"Tell me, Master Thibodeau, how did you kill the lady Yvetta's first husband?"

"My lady!"

"Tell me, do you often miss your target or are you as good as they say? Did he die instantly, or did you leave him to rot from a poisoned wound?"

The look in the lady Juliana's eyes warned Master Thibodeau not to try evasion. "I rarely miss, my lady. It is a knack—a gift, some might say. It is a swift and painless death, I assure you." Master Thibodeau shifted uneasily under her gaze. "And what person should I remove for you?"

Juliana looked into the hearth, the fire long dead, and told him. *One day, you will,* a great queen once said to a novice.

CHAPTER 71

A horseman skidded to a halt in the courtyard below. It was Vaudreuil with the news that John had granted Hugh and Ralph de Lusignan a hearing. Vaudreuil insisted that only Juliana accompany him to the Tower, since the sight of the mistress John and his prisoner had shared might further inflame the king's anger. Anne embraced Juliana without a word and kissed her cheeks, her lips cold and as pale as her freshly washed face.

The cheek-by-jowl throng was filling the great hall by the time they arrived. Juliana was searching for a familiar face when the king's household knights charged out of nowhere, shoving and pushing the crowd until it separated into two ranks along the length of the hall. When she recovered her bearing, she was on one side and Vaudreuil was on the other, looking about frantically for her. She tried to wave to him, but could not catch his eye. She could not move either, back nor fore, but she could see and hear.

Wearing a white mantle topped by a golden chain with a clasp of three lions, and surrounded by lords secular and spiritual, the King of England arrayed himself on a draped chair on an elevated dais to give him advantage over the company. So this was not going to be a private audience for the Lusignans. But there were three, not two, Lusignans before the king.

That was Armand de Lusignan facing the King of England, the Counts of Eu and La Marche by his side.

The three Lusignans presented themselves in surcoats of blue samite slashed with silver chevrons, swords at their sides. Beyond the perfectly administered bows, there was nothing supplicant about them. Across the hall, Juliana saw Vaudreuil cross himself; so did his neighbors. She would have as well, only she was wedged between immobile bodies.

Without waiting for an invitation, Armand de Lusignan addressed the king-duke in a voice that rang as clear as a chapel bell. "Your Grace, we have come before you to have you order the release of your prisoner, a man known as Guérin de Lasalle, the Viscount of Tillières."

Had Juliana not been propped up by her neighbors, her knees would have given out. The crowd hummed with excitement. John sat up. "You have the nerve, showing yourselves in England. Am I to take it, then, that you were behind this? It was you who sought to remove my niece from our protection? I thought Lasalle lied. It is rather difficult to tell where truth ends and lies begin with the former Viscount of Tillières."

Armand took a step forward, his voice constrained. "Former?"

"Former! Traitors cost me Normandy, at least for a while; hence he can't be my viscount, now, can he?" John's tone dipped into sarcasm. "Never mind. You will all witness how a king deals with traitors."

The gasps and whispers did not distract the Count of Rancon, and when he advanced another step, he had everyone's eyes and ears. "We had openly abjured our oaths to you, sire. Our actions, therefore, cannot be declared traitorous."

Dear Lord. Armand de Lusignan was gambling after all. He was gambling for his son's life.

John's expression transformed from smug satisfaction to outraged disbelief. "Yours might not be, Count, but Lasalle's surely are!"

"You are in error, sire. He is a Lusignan."

The hall went grave silent.

"He is a what?"

"A Lusignan. Jean Armand de Lusignan, *sieur* of Parthenay. He is my son."

And there it was, for all the world to see.

Several voices sputtered into nervous laughter. John's counselors bunched together, dismayed and disturbed in their official robes. Good God, this was not in the plan. She had to do something, she had to . . . The King of England charged from the dais toward the Count of Rancon. "That is a lie. I know you Lusignans. You are as faithless as you are lawless, born and bred to treachery!"

Instead of retreating, Armand de Lusignan swung a roll of parchment toward John like the point of a lance. "My marriage to Yvetta de Nevers and my son's baptism, witnessed and under the seal of the Bishop of Évreux."

John tore the document from Armand's hand and Juliana thought that he would tear it apart. Instead, he threw it to the Bishop of Norwich, and while the king paced stormily about, the good bishop, as puzzled as anyone, examined the roll before nodding and passing it to the nearest clerk. Another perusal and another assent followed.

Bouncing on the balls of his feet before his vassals, who topped him by a good head, John's voice squeaked. "This is a scurrilous trick of the basest sort. You've put him up to it. You've humiliated me—you think you've fooled me!"

"Your Grace"—Bishop Hubert leaned toward the king—"if these are the true circumstances, one should consider . . ." Hubert commenced whispering into John's ear while the nearest prelate claimed the other.

"Enough!" John shoved away his advisers. "I've heard enough. Very well, I shall be magnanimous. You can have him back for a pledge of support against Philip!"

"We will not take the field against Philip. He has our homage and fealty for our continental lands," Hugh of Lusignan said curtly.

"Then abjure it, damn you. You cast your loyalty aside easily enough when it suits you!"

The three Lusignans did not part ranks. "No. We will pledge to keep Poitou neutral," Armand de Lusignan replied this time.

John threw himself into his throne. "That is no pledge at all, Count. You'll figure how to work against me. You did, even in my gaol. Pledge yourselves or you will take back that misbegotten son of yours in four sacks!"

One could have heard a mouse sneeze. Juliana's mouth was parched, her knees shook, her back ached as if she carried a quarry stone. It could not end like this.

His hand on his sword's hilt, Armand the Lusignan moved toward the dais. He spoke for himself and wanted all to know it, but what he said was intended for everyone's ears, delivered in a voice Juliana had heard before, clear and low, like the hiss of a serpent. "Do not threaten me, John Softsword. You harm my son and I swear that I will raise such a rebellion against you in Poitou and Aquitaine that it will make your father's and your brother's wars with us seem like a child's quarrel. When I am done there, you will be the duke of nothing. And by the time I am truly finished, you will be the king of nothing and Isabelle will be sleeping in a Lusignan bed."

If the silence that had followed the King of England's threat was ominous, what followed the Count of Rancon's words was sepulchral. John staggered, his eyes bulging. His advisers surrounded him, exclaiming, denouncing, offering aid, causing confusion. Behind the line of guards, the hall broke into pandemonium.

Juliana saw Vaudreuil fight his way toward her. She tried to reach him, but she was trapped, being carried to a place of execution. She cried out. No one heeded or yielded. The voices grew louder and louder.

"Your Grace!"

"Sire!"

"The queen! Stand aside!"

"John? Where are you, John?"

From a side door came a small voice. The crowd parted like the sea before Moses and from it emerged the Queen of England. She wore a gown as pure as cherubims' wings, a gown that had surely by accident slipped from her shoulder due to a careless maid. The gold flood of her hair, unattended as well, reached to her knees. Tears darkened her eyelashes; her madder-red lips quivered. The crowd watched, dazzled. The queen held out her arms. In them was an infant.

No. Not an infant. A rabbit. An enormous, fat, gray rabbit with a white ribbon and a silver bell under its chins. A very placid rabbit.

"They killed her. Your dogs, John. Philomena is dead. She . . . she died of fright."

The queen's appearance and her distressing news supplanted all matters of state. John rushed to his consort. "Isabelle! Poor Philomena. And such a long life she's had. But let us have you retire, shall we? And we'll find Philomena a proper resting place. Would you like that?"

The Queen of England sniffled and clutched the furry carcass to her bosom, a bosom on which a crucifix set with pearls bobbed as if riding the crest of raging waves. "How can I part with Philomena when you will be leaving me as well? Oh, John, I can't bear it."

"What? Leaving you?"

"Yes, John. You'll go and fight those horrid Lusignans. They will attack my Angoulême; you know they will. And you will go and defend it for me, and this time you won't take me with you; I know you won't. You would never put me in danger of being captured by them, like Belle-mère nearly was at Mirebeau."

Mouths opened. All eyes went to John Plantagenet.

"Isabelle—"

The queen sniffled. "Very well. I will go. You can go too, and wage your silly war over one man. I will stay here with Sir Theobald, Sir Ivain, and Sir Umbert." And reaching to sweep up her train, the queen, with a flutter of her eyelashes, indicated the three stalwarts standing closest to her person.

John of England capitulated like Paris before Helen. "For Christ's sake, Isabelle, if it means so much to you, I'll have the knave released." He stabbed his finger in the direction of the Lusignans. "Tomorrow you can take him and go, and don't let me set my eyes on you again. You stand against me in Poitou and your English fiefs are forfeit!"

"No." Armand de Lusignan stood apart. "We don't take the bare promise of a Plantagenet. Release him now."

The hall swirled about Juliana. *Thibodeau!* What had she done?

John's face turned ashen, froth on his lips. "Do you dare to question the word of a king, Lusignan?"

Those who stood proximate drew back. Everyone knew that Armand de Lusignan's next words would seal not only his fate, but his kin's. But instead, another voice rang out.

"No. The word of a king is as the Rock Everlasting. On that I pledge my honor."

In the wide-open doorway stood the Earl of Pembroke and his countess. How long they had been there no one knew, but they came alone. With his wife on his arm, William Marshal walked toward the dais, a single red lion rampant on his tunic, the symbol of his service to three kings. The crowd parted before them. Everyone had heard the rumors surrounding Marshal's fall from favor and no one expected Marshal to appear so boldly. But now certain voices, and soon more, expressed their approbation, relief, and admiration.

Marshal did not acknowledge any of them. He paused next to the Lusignans and bowed to his king.

"Marshal." John forced a shallow smile. "We've missed you. Have you come to prefer the ramparts of Pembroke and your friends to our company?"

The allusion to some dark conspiracy was there, but before Marshal could answer, Isabelle d'Angoulême stood on her tiptoes and whispered into her husband's ear. John's expression altered slightly. "The queen"—John Plantagenet swallowed spittle and tried again—"the queen informs me that she has missed as well the lady de Clare's good company and wise counsel."

"We all profit from good company and wise counsel, sire. Especially those who would be great. It is what makes them so," Marshal answered steadily.

The king's smile remained as calculated as his words. "Then we are glad to have you back to advise us, Marshal. As you say, a king's word is his sacred pledge." The irony of it escaped no one, especially John, and he laughed and gestured to one of his knights. "Tell Pike to bring up the man. Time to clean the cellars."

Juliana swayed. *Thibodeau!* No, surely it could not be? Surely Thibodeau needed more time—a few days, he said.

Excited, joyful voices called out to Marshal openly and noisily. John, his smile strained, embraced Marshal with fraternal osculations. Isabel de Clare offered her curtsy to the queen, who was thereafter escorted by her husband to their private chamber. When the doors closed behind them, the cheering crowd engulfed the earl and his countess.

Dear God, it could not come to this, to a few precious, irredeemable moments. Sobbing, Juliana fought to reach the Lusignans, who were making their own way to the hall's entrance. A strong hand extricated her from the current—Vaudreuil!

"Thibodeau! I have to find Thibodeau!"

Over the noise Vaudreuil heard the terror choking the girl's voice. "Why?"

"I thought Armand lied! I paid Thibodeau to . . . to . . . He was the bowman at Rivefort. Dear God, we have to stop him!"

Vaudreuil grasped her words with a soldier's instant comprehension and, hooking her under the arm, he tore them through the crowd.

"Christ, woman, *Jesu* bleeding Christ!"

Outside in the bailey, the rain had left muddy pools around which the servants and retainers stepped and skipped. Juliana and Vaudreuil desperately searched the faces, the window slits, the parapets, the high-piled barge goods. A hope, a crow's hope, seized her that Thibodeau's fear was greater than his greed.

Across the bailey, the Lusignans and a small group of the curious gathered at a low-browed door. With the sound of grating metal, it began to swing open. She caught at Vaudreuil's cloak. Vaudreuil followed her gaze. A straw-haired man with a ring of keys in his hand stepped out, followed by one of John's guards. Behind them a tall, lanky figure in filthy rags, tangled hair, and matted beard limped into the daylight, moving in his irons like an old man.

"Holy Mother of God. Stay put!" She was shoved into a doorway with Vaudreuil's cloak at her feet. Vaudreuil was racing across the bailey.

Pale English sun pierced the clouds. And in the sunlight she heard the sound, the sharp and distinct sound delivering swift and painless death. And she saw Jehan de Vaudreuil hurl himself across the remaining few feet that separated him from the man he had sworn to protect with his life, and the two went down, and the air smelled of spring and of dead, rotting things.

CHAPTER 72

Longueville, Normandy, Summer 1204

I t was a boy.

Isabel de Clare kissed the strawberry patch of her fifth, well-fed son, and returned him to his cradle, draping fine linen over it. "With four brothers, Anselm will have nothing to inherit. He will be like his father, with only his name to take into the world. A man ought to be proud of his name."

She nodded to her women, who curtsied and filed out of the nursery. Her guest, standing at the window, turned to it. "Was I called for that lesson, Lady Isabel?"

"I can't help myself. I've always believed that children need to be properly instructed. It makes them easier to live with when they grow up."

Guérin de Lasalle kept his smile hidden from her, but she knew that he smiled. She took that as a good sign. She joined him by the window. In the bailey below, the Countess de Valence was returning from one of her long rides.

"And I am not easy to live with," he said, watching his mistress.

"So my guard captain informs me, now that you are well enough. But you can still learn."

Their relationship was an odd one, she had to admit. She was not his lover, yet she knew him in some ways better than his mistresses or his wife. That, ironically, gave her a certain advantage. That, and his steadfast loyalty to her husband—and to her.

"I am too old to learn," he said, his eyes fixed on the sea in the hazy distance, stretching to the shores of England. They had left that country some months ago under rather extraordinary circumstances.

"You and I are almost the same age. Are you telling me that you've acquired the sum of knowledge? In Paris, you were afraid that I would expose you. I told you that many of your lessons were wrong ones."

"You are referring to my whoring," he said, not looking at her.

Isabel de Clare dropped her hand to her bosom in pretended shock. "I was referring to your flute playing, sir."

He caught her gesture out of the corner of his eye and smiled again, still watching his mistress. In his cradle, Anselm began to fuss. Isabel went to him and he quieted down. She picked up her flute from the table, the one she had given to Guérin de Lasalle in Paris. Aumary de Beaudricourt had returned it to her and she had pieced together its story from the young man and from Juliana de Charnais. Isabel had not believed the accusations leveled against the former Viscount of Tillières, but she could offer little comfort to Aumary. She held out the flute. "Play something for me. Anselm likes it."

Lasalle abandoned the window and came to her. "What you are saying, my lady, is that my playing puts children to sleep."

"Far better than keeping them awake," she assured him, and he smiled openly and reached for the flute.

It was a ruse and he fell for it. Isabel de Clare took hold of his hand before he could pull away. "Squeeze hard. As hard as you can."

He withdrew his hand. "No. It makes no difference."

"It does make a difference. Give yourself time, my lord. William would be the first to tell you that."

Inducing Guérin de Lasalle to take up the flute served the twin purpose of distracting him and of restoring most of his hand's mobility. That she had succeeded to the degree she had was due largely to Master Pike, who had acquired as much skill in setting bones as in breaking them.

He picked up his cloak and bowed formally.

"I have not given you leave yet," Isabel said quietly in deference to Anselm. Returning to her embroidery frame, she sat and gestured to a chair. "You once had asked a favor of me and I would have granted it to you. Now you are under an obligation to me. You will hear out my lesson."

He remained standing. "I hate lessons."

"I know. You also hate to take your medicine, turnips, or have someone touch you unless you are in command. All consequences of your upbringing, I imagine," Isabel said, inspecting the last row of her stitches. They looked a little askew.

Guérin de Lasalle winced visibly, ignoring the chair. "I believe one of your lessons was to disabuse me of my omnipotence, Countess."

"It was. That is the point. You can't continue to live a lie. You came perilously close to losing your life and taking a number of people with you, including my husband."

"I was born a lie."

She threaded her needle. "True. But you have also managed to confuse us as well. Most of all, you have Juliana confused." Isabel broached a subject unmentioned since their departure from England. Lady Juliana's name had not passed Guérin de Lasalle's lips, at least not while he was in full possession of his senses. "In fact, as much as she has you confused, I suspect."

He drew in the corner of his mouth like Willie, her eldest, did when she chastised him for some act of juvenile thoughtlessness.

She waited, and when Guérin de Lasalle offered nothing in return, Isabel gave her attention to her stitches. This time they were perfect, and she found that encouraging. "Venus herself would not have succumbed, my lord, trust me. It takes time for the girl, longer for some than others. It took me months and I was very much in love with William. I was not driven by desperation; he did not call me bone and gristle before half of Paris, and did not entertain mistresses under my roof. And I had not convinced myself that William lusted solely after my fiefs or my virginity, or pined after a past paramour."

The lesson was not a very palatable one, but she meant for him to swallow it.

He did not avoid her eyes. "I forced her."

Isabel remembered that she liked this man, who insisted on calling himself Guérin de Lasalle, for the unexpected flashes of brutal honesty. She pulled at the gold thread with great care. "I don't have all the answers. I am trying to protect those I love, just as you are. You must right what you have done wrong."

"What I have done can't be righted."

"Perhaps not in the way you want. You cannot free Eleanor of Brittany without endangering lives—hers, William's, mine, my children's. That is a truth you will have to learn to live with. As for the rest, you know what you ought to do."

"What I should have done four years ago."

Isabel wove the needle through the fabric and clasped her hands in her lap. "You can't run away; none of us can. I promised Juliana that I would not tell you what I am about to, but I have concluded that more harm would be done by concealing than divulging. You can consider that my last lesson."

Guérin de Lasalle gave her a squint of cautious relief and leaned against the wall, crossing his arms in an obedient anticipation of another earwigging. This time it was Isabel who tried to hide her smile. He reminded her so much of her Willie that she almost forgot she was dealing with a man of a formidable pedigree, a man who, but for a righteously determined red-haired young woman, could have been the King of England.

"We can't find her."

That took him by surprise. He elbowed himself from the wall, but before he could ask the obvious question, Isabel answered it. "She is not at Rivefort. She traded Tillières to John for some estates in Wessex, hoping to save your life. John took her charter and left her with nothing. No one has seen her since your release."

He was at her embroidery frame, startling her not inconsiderably. "She did what? The stupid, silly chit! Why didn't somebody tell me?"

"Because when I brought you to Longueville, you were in no condition to do anything about it. Besides, we did not know what you would do. She, like you, is running away from those she thinks she has harmed. She is also running away from those she fears would harm your child."

Guérin de Lasalle gripped the frame so hard that Isabel de Clare feared he would render it into kindling. "Ch-child?"

"As you said, my lord, you forced her. Unless you believe it is not yours."

He released the frame and struck the wall with his fist, adding a pithy, pungent oath, and Isabel de Clare was certain that if he were in someone else's abode, Guérin de Lasalle would have thrown every stick of furniture out the window and possibly a body or two with it. In Anselm's nursery my lord Lasalle restrained himself with supreme effort.

"Of course it's mine. She didn't think she could . . . and I sent her into that aqueduct and she didn't tell me?"

"She couldn't tell you. She didn't know what you would do if you found out your father had what he wanted. Your father can't find her; neither can any of my people. I would fear foul play, but I think there must be a refuge she has learned of, so well hidden that we cannot find it. I think you know where it is. She did find out about Céline and Aumary."

"She *what*?"

"In some ways, she is very clever, you know." Isabel smiled, teasing into place an errant thread.

Guérin de Lasalle groaned and slid to the floor after all. "Sister Scholastica with the nose of a ferret. Bloody hell. What in Christ's name should I do?"

Isabel ran her fingers over her silk peacocks and golden prim-roses. "Stop living a lie. Tell her the truth even if she throws a chamber pot at your head. Or do you wish your father to find them first?"

Lasalle stretched his arm, balling up his fist. "You are a very clever woman, Countess."

"I know that the mention of your father and your wife in the same breath would drag you from Death's door. In fact, it did."

He dropped his head back against the wall and closed his eyes. After a while, he said, "Can I impose on you to borrow a nag? I promise not to lame it."

"No need to borrow one. Your father left you half a dozen horses in our pastures and enough silver to pave the market square."

Guérin de Lasalle got to his feet. "Of course he did. And a couple of angels to watch over me. You can keep them all for one of your horses."

"The horse is yours, and the sword. It's William's old one."

He looked toward the window. "I have to tell Anne."

Isabel nodded. He opened the door and this time she did not stop him. He paused on the threshold anyway, and said very quietly, like Willie did when, after chastising him, she gave him a cake anyway, "Thank you."

And she realized that she missed him, the way she missed her William in the first painful heartbeats when he rode out under the portcullis.

"And so it ends where it all began." Anne ran her finger along the stall rail, having sent the stableboys packing. He was tying his cloak behind the cantle. She noticed that the traces took him longer than usual, but she did not offer to help.

"An appropriate ending, all considered."

Anne tamped down an ache she had told herself a long time ago she would never allow herself to feel. "Yes, perhaps it is. You and I are like tinder and fire. Blazing flame, but little consolation."

He backed the horse out of the stall. "Well, we did get singed on occasions."

She smiled; he still could make her smile. "You were right, I should never have used Juliana against you, but when you went to my sister, I felt so humiliated. And jealous. And angry. That's why you did it, isn't it? To let me know what a cur you are so that I would give up the idea of talking you into wedlock. And then you came to Dreux with Juliana. I can still see her, so hopelessly out of place and putting such a brave face on it. I wanted revenge, only you did not care about Armand. That made it worse."

Lasalle went around the horse's rump. "You were entitled."

He was still not giving her truthful answers. "I've always preferred him to you. Did you ever suspect?"

"Every time you shrieked his name in my ear."

Anne clasped her hand over her mouth. "I did not! How could you? I did not." His expression did not help her, and she felt the familiar surge of aggravation and attraction she experienced every time she came near this man. "Good Lord. Did I?"

He winked at her and she struck at him as he led the rounsey past her. He did not bother to fend her off and she followed him into the bailey, where he paused to tighten the saddle girth. He turned to her there and kissed her hand. "Anne, you are an admirably audacious woman, but John is the Duke of Aquitaine and your liege. Find a man with good stamina and marry him before John picks someone old and jealous for you."

She touched his cheek. "I was considering Armand. What do you think of that?" She was aiming to draw some reaction from him; which one, she did not know.

He gave her a crooked smile. "You'd be the most beautiful stepmother a son has ever swived."

Anne took her hand away. "Good Lord, you are a cur. But you would still settle for a friend?"

"Yes."

She wondered when she would begin to cry. Perhaps later, in her own bed, which she had occupied alone since their arrival at Longueville. She watched him mount up and she came to his side. "You meant what you said to Isabelle at Angoulême, didn't you?"

He gathered the reins and the rounsey lifted its head, ears flicking. "My dear countess, are you telling me you'd believe a lying cur?"

❦

Lasalle ambushed the two men who had followed him out of Longueville, killing the first without much difficulty because the man did not think that he would do it. The second one took longer because Lasalle had dropped the sword, and so he had to smash the man's skull with a rock.

In a cold sweat and nauseous, he fell to his knees, nursing his throbbing hand. After a while the pain eased, the pounding in his ears ceased, and the alarmed skirr of birds above his head receded. He wrapped his hand with a strip from one of the dead men's shirts, stripped the bodies of anything that would identify them, and weighted them down under the trunk of a tree the river had wedged into the bank.

He sold one of the horses along with the men's belongings in the next town, keeping the other as his packhorse. He had coins in his belt, and although his hand still ached, he felt a familiar stirring in his blood. He set his spurs to the rounsey's flanks, wondering if the child would have red hair. And he had absolutely no idea what he would say to its mother when he found her.

CHAPTER 73

Fécamp, Normandy

The Benedictine brothers at the great Abbey Church of the Trinity venerated a fragment of a fig tree in which Joseph of Arimathea had preserved a few drops of the Precious Blood. The magnificent abbey and its relic had become the first destination

for English pilgrims traveling along the route of Saint-Jacques-de
Campostelle.

The permanent residents of Fécamp made their fortunes from
the purses of the pilgrims and from nets glistening with cod. Between the cliffs sheltering the town, the slate-green sea lapped at
a white ribbon of beach, above which the cliffs unfurled like the
sails of a ship. Above them, a patchwork of woodlands and fields
spread inland, and gulls flocked over the furrows.

Juliana liked to climb to the top of the cliffs to watch the fog
drift in from the sea and to wait for the dawn to become morning.
She often thought that she could see the coast of England before
her sight blurred and the sea and the sky merged. She then followed the path to the beach and to an old cottage within sight of
the fishermen's colony.

Whenever she went to town, she carefully avoided meeting by
chance a young woman called Gwenllian and her doting old nurse,
called Philomena. Sometimes they or a servant girl minded a little
boy with round brown eyes alive with mischief, whom they called
Jourdain.

Gwenllian lived in far greater comfort than Juliana did, above
Fécamp in a half-timbered manor called Seneterre, hidden behind tentacles of ivy and watched over by a tower dating to the
times when the Normans were a menace and not merchants in the
town. Gwenllian had several servants to wait on her and four of
Philomena's grandsons and their widowed father to guard her
from unwanted advances. Some of Fécamp's men would have very
much liked to advance, Juliana had observed, but Gwenllian did
not appear to favor any particular one.

As life went, Juliana's was endurable, even though her cottage
leaned to one side and when north gales swept the coast, sand and
rain poured in through many a crack. She had made over the
fireplace into an oven—a small one, to be sure—but every week
she would turn out two dozen palm-size pies. She would pack them
in a hay-lined basket and offer them to the fishermen before they
set out. After a diet of cod, the men appreciated her pigeon pies.
In return, she received two or three pennies and a fish.

The fish, with the yield of her struggling patch of a garden and the leftover crust, provided her with a sumptuous meal. She gave one penny to her skillful supplier of pigeons, an eight-year-old urchin called Wink, who pinched them from the abbey's dovecotes. The rest of the pennies were spoken for as well. That day she returned later than usual to sweep the oven ashes into an old bowl. With the bowl in hand, she reached the door at the very instant an unannounced visitor crossed the threshold, ducking low to enter.

He was alive, very much so, down to the glint in his eyes, the flash of that earring, the stubble along his jaw, and someone's well-worn gambeson.

They stood at arm's length from each other, and for some reason it took him a spell before he moved, reaching out to touch her sleeve as if inspecting a statue. She stood there like one too, and if he had wanted to wring the life out of her, she would not have fought him. Her eyelids fluttered, her chin went up, and for a moment, an absurd moment, she thought he would—

"You smell of fish."

Her ludicrous illusions and self-delusions cracked and shattered in that hollow where her heart had plummeted. And then she gathered up her half-snared heart and mended it with hoops of stone-cold sobriety.

"Yes. Yes, I do, don't I?" She pushed a stray hair under her head rail. Her hands were shaking. "I am glad you are well, my lord. The lady Isabel is very kind, is she not? And Sir William. Sir William too. Very kind. They are both very kind. Well now, I know you wish to go on, and I must too. They are expecting me. The fishermen. God . . . God be with you."

She untied her apron to hide under it the small garments she kept in her spare basket, praying that he would not notice. He did not. She threw her cloak about her and, executing a self-conscious curtsy, made it to the door, the basket under her arm. She hurried past a dun packhorse and the black rounsey that had brought him to her doorstep, and once hidden by the tall grass, she ran down the path toward the town, her stomach knotted with terror.

꩜

A dozen horsemen, their approach muffled by sand and the wind, barred her way. Above their lance pennants snapped an azure banner charged with silver chevrons. She dropped her basket and turned to run. The horsemen closed her path. A black-legged, dappel-gray courser loomed before her.

"Dear Lady Juliana. Always in such a hurry. Do you mind if we accompany you?"

Snorting muzzles and foaming horse bits surrounded her. "I . . . there is no reason for you to accompany me, my lord. There is nothing—"

Armand de Lusignan leaned forward. He pointed his chin toward the contents of the basket. "Nothing? I've searched for you for months, girl. I knew my son would find you, but he had disposed of his keepers and gave me the slip. Do not hold us in suspense. The first grandchild always stirs such expectations."

She stooped for her basket and pressed it to her. "It's a girl. Only a girl. She can do you no harm and neither can I. We ask for nothing, only to be left in peace."

Armand de Lusignan sat back. "A girl," he said.

His men waited in tense anticipation, unsure whether they should withdraw or draw their swords on her for displeasing their lord.

"And where, pray tell, are you hiding my granddaughter?"

Eyeing the men, Juliana gulped. "The wet nurse keeps her. I have no milk for her. I can't keep the cottage warm. You see, you have no reason to be concerned. It is just a girl. I have failed you. You have no more use for me. Or her. For any of us."

"What sort of a fool do you think me to be, girl?"

The question was not a rhetorical one. She was a pigeon among peregrines. Armand de Lusignan had gambled and won. The basket slipped from her fingers. Fear claimed her, not for herself, but for the child she could not protect and would never see grow up. And she was equally afraid for a young woman who was in grave peril from a man she had never met, and suddenly death seemed like an indecent liberation. She untied her cloak and let it drop. She did not want them to touch her so she folded back the much-mended edge of her gown to uncover her neck, bone-thin like the rest of her. Surely it would be enough for a single stroke? Surely they could not miss? She only prayed that if they stripped her body, no one would bother to search the seams and find an inscribed gold ring.

"I wish to say my prayer before . . . before . . ." She searched from one face to the other, wondering which one of them would deliver the blow.

The men watched her, silent, impassive. She knelt, crossed herself, and clasped her hands. "*Sancta Maria, mater Dei, ora pro nobis . . .*"

The words were only sounds on her tongue. She could hear the horsemen part and withdraw and the sound of someone dismounting. So Armand de Lusignan had chosen to behead her himself. She finished her prayer, crossed herself, and bowed her head and waited for the Hereafter. And waited . . . and waited. Armand de Lusignan knew how to prolong someone's agony for his amusement. That earthly and annoyed thought flashed through her still attached head. "I have commended my soul to God, sir. You may have my body!"

"Now that would be a miracle," said a voice in front of her, hoarse and harsh with sarcasm.

She sprang to her feet with the sound of ripping cloth. The tear revealed the tattered, sooty edge of her shift to the entire world. Only the entire world was Guérin de Lasalle, sitting there on a piece of bleached driftwood, his elbows on his knees.

Humiliation supplanted her resignation to martyrdom. "Oooh, look what you've done!"

"What in blazing fires of Hell do you think you are doing here, mouse?"

"I . . . I live here. This is my home. We . . . I manage."

They were alone. Armand de Lusignan had gathered his men a short distance away, where they dismounted. Alarm and confusion swept over her, but Lasalle did not give her a chance to ponder the meaning of it all.

"Manage?" He came to his feet to lean to her nose tip. "You live in a hovel and reek of penury, Lady Juliana!"

"There is no disgrace in poverty. Our Lord was poor. I sell pigeon pies. I am not helpless, you know!"

"Helpless? You are a gale of wreck and devastation, woman. Do you know what your customers call your pigeon pies? Do you?"

She set her teeth to her lip—a habit she never could banish, not around Guérin de Lasalle, especially when he was in a state of unreason—and she chose not to answer.

He threw up his hands. "Lusignan pies. Lusignan pies, for Christ's sake!"

"That is not my fault. No one but Fulbeck knows me. They think it amusing. I had nothing to do with Mirebeau."

"You had everything to do with Mirebeau, you silly chit. I could—"

"Enough!" Armand de Lusignan charged toward them. Juliana yielded ground immediately, but became the target nevertheless, at least of his accusing finger.

"I am running out of patience with you, girl, and out of men with my son. He's killed two more, not very adeptly, mind you; not with that hand of his. I want him in Parthenay befuddled by domesticity before he gets himself skewered in the next tavern row!"

"He is not my husband!"

Lasalle spat at Armand de Lusignan's feet. "Ha! You forget none are burning for this wedlock."

"You are not that good a liar, son. Go and stay with my men while I have a word with our Juliana. Go or I will have you bound and gagged."

Lasalle gave his father so venomous a glare that Juliana's heart shrank, but it came accompanied by a bow of contrived submission. "Then by all means, say your peace, if she can stomach it."

The count's men fell back, one of them holding out to Lasalle the reins of his horses with due caution. Her remaining adversary came nearer with a dry smile. "If you seek to annul your marriage, Eleanor of Brittany's name will be revealed. No one has seen Arthur lately and I don't expect him to be seen henceforward. What do you think John will do when he finds out his niece and heir presumptive is wed to a Lusignan? On second thought, she is no longer of use to me. Shall I make the announcement for you? John will kill her and your marriage will stand unquestioned and indissoluble. Would that ease your conscience, Juliana?"

She would have struck him if he had not anticipated it, his hand crushing her wrist. "Such passion. Will it be enough to protect your daughter from vanishing one day?"

"You are a dem—"

His hand covered her mouth. She threw herself at him, trying to bite, to maim.

Their struggle drew the men's attention, but they made no move until their lord's full-size opponent dropped the reins of his horses. Armand de Lusignan shoved her aside and halted his men with an upraised hand. He swung into the saddle of his courser before his son reached him. The dappel-gray volted on a tight rein, keeping its rider out of harm's way.

"Ah, the uxorious husband." Armand drew a leather folio from his saddlebag and dropped it at Lasalle's feet. "Geoffrey formally relinquished his titles. Whether you like it or not, you are the Lord of Parthenay and of the rest. There is a surprise there for the lady Juliana. I am sure she has one for you, as well. She has agreed to come to Parthenay and to behave like a good wife."

Circling around them, Armand de Lusignan indicated his company. "I am leaving you my men. Try not to take out on them your murderous indignation that you are not dead yet, son. I am not entirely happy with the turn of events either, my loves, but life is full of small disappointments."

CHAPTER 74

I did not agree to any such thing, I swear, sir. I have another plan, but I must leave, now, and I know that you also don't wish to stay." She did not want to give Lasalle a chance to embark on one of their bruising conversations, but her putative husband's attention was on the departing rider.

"Next time I will kill him," he said to no one in particular.

"My lord—"

"Sit down, Juliana."

She did. He picked up the folio and shoved it into his gambeson, uncinched his sword, and sat across from her. "I said, what are you doing here, mouse?"

"I live here, thanks to Fulbeck." He squinted at her impatiently. "Fulbeck guarded the prisoners at Mirebeau." Lusignan prisoners, she meant to say. "He is a fisherman. He was one, with Lupescaire, before . . . He recognized me at Le Havre, but he has no love for the Lusignans and took pity on me. I was rather . . . ill and he brought me here, to his wife. I remembered the Countess de Nevers saying that your mother was in possession of a small fief at Fécamp and I knew then that's where you sent them."

She slid her fingers along the seam of her sleeve. A gold ring popped free. She handed it to him. He rolled it in his palm. "You had it all this time and you've never sold it? I thought you were a practical creature, Juliana."

"I would not sell what does not belong to me. I had a few coins for . . . for what I needed. I so wanted to give it to her, but I was afraid that I might be watched after all. I have done so many sinful things, but I've kept your secret. No one knows, at least not because of me."

"What secret?"

"That you love her." Among the dunes, the horses snorted and shifted, the men talked in subdued voices, none bold enough to interfere. *Dear God, make him leave and go where his heart belongs so that I can return to my fish stew that tastes of sand and penury.* "You do, don't you?"

He watched her, a bundle of wash-broken linen and disobedient twists of short, very red hair. And across the dunes he could hear a dead queen-duchess laughing. At him.

He pushed the ring onto his little finger and held out his hand to her. She looked up at him with that mixture of perplexity and apprehension she always wore if she looked at him at all, so he lifted her to her feet and onto his packhorse. "You do have the most galling habit of poking your nose down the wrong holes, Lady. If you think of running, I'll tie you to the tail."

The men kept their heads down, except for one who bravely stepped forward and bowed promptly. "My lord, I am Henri de Blaye, your man and vassal. What is your command?"

"Take them all to Fécamp and stay there."

They cantered along a stretch of sand, where retreating waves left seaweed and white froth under the horses' hooves. Lasalle headed unhesitatingly into the water to round a cliff rising precipitously from the sea. Beyond it, the beach curved ahead of them.

In the middle of it, several children and their older siblings cavorted through the tidal pools in the company of their dogs and an old donkey. The wind carried the children's laughter to them, and so they approached before the dogs noticed and charged at them with deep-throated baying. Shading her eyes, one of the older girls skipped like a spring kid and ran toward them, her skirts high, her hair a dark stream behind her.

"Guériiiin!" Besotted with joy, Gwenllian ran and laughed, leaving the rest of her company behind.

Lasalle dismounted, dropping the rounsey's reins. "Gwen, you'll break your neck!"

Gwenllian knocked him backward, covering his face with fervent kisses between a torrent of questions in Welsh and much-improved French, while he tried to fend her off with halfhearted reprimands. Juliana shifted in her uncomfortable saddle. Her presence could add nothing to that reunion, so she nudged the horse toward the dunes. He would give Gwenllian her ring and tell her what needed to be said, in private, and Juliana prayed that she had atoned at least a little for her many sins.

"Juliana, wait!"

Running up to the packhorse, Gwenllian took hold of the reins. "Thank you for bringing him back to me. We've been separated for so long."

"You won't have to be any longer." Juliana wanted very much to reassure the girl. "You can come to Parthenay and sit at the high table; many a lord's mistress does, and who's to gainsay him? I didn't know that he loves you, that he truly does. I don't know much about such things. I was to be a nun, you see, but I was not a very good one, but I shall be a much better one now."

Gwenllian listened to her with increasing puzzlement, casting glances in Lasalle's direction. With no help from that quarter, Gwenllian let go of the reins and brushed away her hair. And Juliana saw that the girl was not merely comely; she was as seductive as a Nereid, but with an earthbound vitality that went as deep as tree roots.

"He didn't tell you? I am not Guérin's mistress. I am his sister."

The roar in Juliana's ears drowned the sound of the sea.

"Half sister, in truth." Gwenllian was smiling up at her. "My father took me to Wales after our mother died giving birth to me. He was afraid of what Armand would do. I grew up there. Guérin brought me back when the fighting turned bad."

"Your f-father?" Juliana clung to the saddle. "The countess Sabine said he died in Wales and Armand said the child . . . the child had died too."

Gwenllian shrugged, her smile clouding. "I lived. My father died in an ambush on his return journey after he left me with our mother's nurse. Juliana, you look very pale."

❧

People were arguing, two angry voices. The female one was winning. The sound of a slamming door confirmed it, but the man was not free of his challenger. "Guériiiin! Guérin. Don't you dare to walk away!"

Juliana stirred, her head thick.

"Ah, you are awake. I told those two they'd wake up the dead."

Between the meticulous folds of a white wimple, a softly wrinkled face was smiling at her. The slightly stooped matron she had watched from afar at the market stood by her bedside, a bundle of keys at her girdle, a spindle under her arm. A boy clung to her skirts, thumb in his mouth, brown eyed and fair haired.

Juliana tried to sit up. "Jourdain?"

The nurse reached down and tussled the child's hair. "Run along now, bug, and play with the others."

The boy scampered out the door without as much as a backward glance. The woman smoothed Juliana's pillow and handed her a cup. "Are you feeling better, love?"

Juliana swallowed half the cup before she handed it back. "Thank you, Mistress—"

"Philomena, my dear, just Philomena." The nurse patted Juliana's hand.

The wine revived Juliana, along with her fear. Despite her light-headedness, she threw the covers aside and climbed from the mattress. In the tidy, whitewashed room, her gown's appearance embarrassed her. Through the open door she could see the kitchen, as neat as its mistress, copper pots gleaming above the fireplace, one of them bubbling merrily over the fire. From there, she could see another door, no doubt the one through which Lasalle had made his escape.

"Hungry you must be, and no wonder. A gust of wind could blow you away." Philomena bustled into the kitchen, and seizing a ladle, she attacked the pot. "Ham hock and peas, there is nothing like it, I say. I have plum cakes rising too."

After months of penury, she found herself in a residence brimming with bounty, a bounty that was not hers and that she dared not sample lest she abandon her resolve for a bowl of hocks and peas, plum cakes, and a feather bed. Juliana summoned a smile. "May I borrow a cloak? I seem to have left mine somewhere. I need to . . . ."

"Of course, child." Philomena nodded at a cloak on the wall peg. "It's behind the woodshed. I will have something ready for you."

"That would be lovely, thank you." Juliana kept her smile and with the cloak about her, she ran out the door. She had to reach Fulbeck's cottage before Armand de Lusignan did.

She had just passed the privy when he caught her because her attention was claimed by the sight of Jourdain running down the path in the opposite direction, as if his shirttails were on fire. Lasalle set her on the ground with a click of her teeth. "Now look what you have done. You ran him off much like Rivefort's husbands ran off his father."

Juliana followed the child's flight with a sunburst of recognition. "He is Petit Jacques's! Oh, Ravenissa got rid of a mouth to feed. But how did you know?"

"Every time she shrieked his name in my ear."

She did not understand and then she did; a hot flush claimed her. She hid her hands in her sleeves. "But why did you hide him? If Armand thought Jourdain was yours, he would not have harmed him."

"If you don't consider as such bringing up a child in his own image."

In Armand de Lusignan's own image. That lump in her chest threatened to overwhelm her, but he did not give it a chance to do so. "Where are you heading this time, mouse?"

"My . . . my plan. To counter your father's. But I have to return to Fécamp."

"A plan? More likely a plot. Are we fresh out of all the current ones?"

The question was as testy as the questioner. He stabbed his finger in the direction of the garden. She bowed her head and led the way to a bench in the rose arbor, where, with a crook of his finger, he made her deposit herself. He leaned against the post and crossed his arms. "Well?"

She had to make him understand. "I plan no plots, my lord, only to emancipate you from your father's, but I must be allowed

to leave, please. Had I known this marriage would cause such misery to so many, I would have taken my vows, and willingly."

"Misery?"

"All those dead . . . and Paulette. Not dead—no, oh dear. But
there is Mathea, Lord help her bear her loss. How can I even
begin to atone for that?"

Lasalle impatiently booted away a snail. "What loss?"

She crossed herself, sick at the thought. "I thought you knew.
It was my doing. Vaudreuil is . . . he is dead."

"You are all wreck and devastation, Lady Juliana, but you can't
bear the blame for the Chevalier de Vaudreuil's demise. Not unless you intend to try again."

"That is a lie. The quarrel felled him!"

"Thank you for the confidence. I was there, as you will recall.
Of course it did. Jehan wore a double mail and a flat iron nailed
to a piece of English oak, a precaution against John's plots. Why
do you think he moved like a lumbering ox?" Lasalle grimaced,
rotating his shoulder carefully. "The quarrel knocked him off his
feet and me with him. Damn near broke my collarbone. Jehan
returned to Belvoir as soon as we crossed, being able to cope with
Thibodeau's quarrels but not with Anne's salves and sauciness."

She heard him over the loud thump of her heart. "Oh, I am so
glad. God is truly merciful. And I meant to . . . I only meant to save
you from—"

"Our marriage?

Juliana cringed. He knew. Vaudreuil must have told him—or
Lady Isabel—and still he would make a jest of it.

"I wouldn't flagellate myself over the Lady Fair, either. I've
heard she smiled at Philip and he made Lupescaire the seneschal
of Gascony. From all reports, she does not allow him to stray far
from her apron strings. Not that he would, I imagine."

Juliana kept her gaze on her toes. She did not wish to think
what made Paulette prefer Lupescaire to her other suitors, but she
did note the irony of a dowerless girl becoming a great lady because of a man raised up from the dust.

"When were you going to tell me?"

She could not dodge him this time, even though her heart missed a couple of heartbeats. "Not ever."

"We have a child, for Christ's sake!"

She stood up. She had to make her escape; she had to keep ahead of Armand de Lusignan. "That alters nothing. You were pledged. I can't pretend to this marriage."

"Is that the plan?"

"Y-yes. There are sisters in a house attached to the abbey; they will take us both if I have a small dowry. I had hoped for a few more pennies, but with Armand finding us, I can't wait any longer." She kept her eyes on the ground at her feet, trying desperately to reassure him. "You were right. A year hence no one will remember this marriage. The bishops would not grant dissolution to Guérin de Lasalle, but they will surely grant it to the Lord of Parthenay. Eleanor and I will vanish from this world."

"What Eleanor?"

The tone made her flinch. "I had her christened Eleanor. For your Eleanor, not mine. I thought I should."

"A girl!"

"Yes, but we don't mean to be trouble. Please, I must go before your father finds her." She dropped a curtsy, not a very deep one because her knees would not allow it, and took two steps. His arm barred her way.

"I want to see her. Go and put on one of Gwenllian's frocks."

She did not move. He let her go. "I know you don't trust me. I'll ask Gwen to come, if you want."

Juliana shook her head. She did not want any more family entanglements.

CHAPTER 75

Nurse Flotte, the wife of the former mercenary Fulbeck, was a robust, frightfully clean woman who displayed infinite patience with her fosterlings and her own ever growing brood. With everyone else, she was not hesitant to give her advice when she judged it necessary, which was often. She greeted their arrival with suspicion, keeping the little Fulbecks behind her skirts.

"Hmmph, it's him, is it? Leaving a girl in trouble while he goes gallivanting about." She measured her adversary from head to foot. "Well, you, come and see your daughter."

Juliana beat them all across the kitchen's threshold to reach a swaddled bundle in the cradle by the hearth. She faced Lasalle. "You needn't concern yourself, my lord. No one will notice her. Or me. She is small. Very small. Inconsequential."

Juliana's protestations caused Nurse Flotte's finger to wag in Lasalle's direction. "And a blessing, too. The Lord nearly took her and the little one. Well, she can have you, but she won't have any more of yours or any other man's, trust my words, and that's her only good fortune."

"Goodwife!" Juliana wanted to stem the nurse's loose-lipped indignation, but the occupant of the swaddling awoke at that very moment. Eleanor of Fécamp hiccuped and let out an ear-splitting caterwaul.

Her father's reply was a black frown, and he turned on his heel and left them all standing there. Juliana thrust the howling infant to her nurse and ran after him. By that time, the courtyard was full of men—Henri de Blaye's men. Without a word, Lasalle got Juliana into the saddle of her rounsey and mounted up as well.

"If Armand de Lusignan comes here, kill him," he ordered de Blaye.

❧

At Seneterre, the supper served in the pitched-roof hall was fune-real, which was not a comment on Philomena's pudding. In sight of the empty chair at the head of the table, Juliana poked at her trencher while Gwenllian silently finished hers. Philomena looked into the hall, and seeing the gloom inside match the dusk outside, she lit the candles, then dismissed the serving girl and came to Juliana.

"I have a bath waiting for you—it will ease the day—and some wine to soothe the spirit. If you won't eat, you must sleep, child."

Juliana nodded and took herself from the table to the bed-chamber. A sheet-lined tub waited for her there, filled with steaming water and the scent of chamomile. It wrenched at her memory like a suddenly tender tooth.

"Juliana?" Gwenllian stood at the door, a ewer and a cup in hand.

Juliana quickly turned her back, slipped out of her borrowed gown, and immersed herself in the water, inhaling at the sensation of pure, sharp pleasure. *Make no provision for the flesh in its concupiscence.*

Gwenllian came to her to hand her the cup. "It's raisin wine. Drink it before Guérin finds it. What do you think we should do?"

Good Lord, raisin wine. Juliana set down the empty cup and slid deeper into the tub. A shiver went through her. Gwenllian sprinkled a handful of lavender florets into the stream. Juliana half-expected her to offer an incantation. She suspected that Gwenllian had an answer to her own question, and not wanting to hear it, she dedicated herself to scrubbing her skin, yet she climbed out as soon as she was done, before she took any more pleasure in the seductive warmth. "May I borrow a shift to sleep in? The sisters at Fontevraud—"

Gwenllian held out a shift to her. "You are not at Fontevraud. You have a husband and a child."

That was an admonition as pointed as Abbess Mathilde's. Juliana accepted the shift, but not the admonition. "I have a child, but not a husband. I never did."

"What makes a marriage?"

"Gratian says consent, consummation, and affection, although there are differences of opinion, especially on the second point," Juliana quickly enumerated, feeling herself on a safer ground. She was wrong.

"Then your learned scholars granted you two of the three. I believe you are meant to find the third for yourself."

"One cannot find what does not exist, don't any of you see? And even if . . . Aliénor said it can destroy you. Why would I ever risk myself as foolishly as—"

"Our mother did?" Gwenllian concluded with a sweet smile.

"Yes. No! I am sorry, I didn't mean to offend."

"None taken. I am a bastard but I have a home here, and I can have any man I want. Geoffrey found his family with the Temple. But he, he has nothing, Juliana."

Juliana reached for her gown. "He has Anne and his other women, and more lands and wealth than most men."

Gwenllian took Juliana's hand, her fingertips following the lines on her palm as if to divine a pattern. *They say she is a witch.* Sensing her unease, Gwenllian let go of Juliana's hand, although her voice remained soft and insistent. "What do you think he will do next?"

Next time I will kill him. "Dear Lord. He will try again."

The girl nodded. "I am afraid for him, Juliana. We have to keep Guérin here as long as we can. Take your courage from the cup if you need to, but you have to try. You've done it before, for your Tillières."

Juliana crossed herself. "I will not lend myself to such a thing! He puts so much by you—you suade him."

Gwenllian filled Juliana's cup. "I am not the one for such suasion."

No, it would not come to that. She only had to delay him, to distract him, only for a while. Besides, even if it happened, it would not take very long. It did not the last time. Or did it? She could not remember. She did remember that she had drunk enough raisin wine to conceive Eleanor as a consequence of her inebriated wantonness. Oh blessed Mother Mary. Very well, even if she took

courage from the cup this time there would not be those consequences. Flotte told her that when she first held out Eleanor to
her. She was now as barren as Anne. No other children of her own
would she ever hold, not his or any other man's.

Did she still have a duty, a wife's duty, to keep her husband
from imperiling his soul, even though she was not a wife, not truly?
What makes a marriage? Juliana took the cup and drank its contents
so fast she wheezed. Gwenllian held out a full one. The effects of
the wine spread through her veins. Very well, she had done it before. God was her witness that she acted only with the purest of
intentions. Through a haze of wine and scented vapor, Gwenllian
was smiling the smile of the sprite Mélusine.

In the dark, cold stairwell of the keep, she made herself swallow
the last of the wine. She left the cup and the lantern outside the
door, smoothed her gown, and assured herself that her wimple
was properly fixed. She pushed open the door. The square room
smelled of dust and seal wax. Several candles on an old table in
the middle of it dripped wax onto the floor, their light illuminat-
ing a stack of parchments and a simple curtained bed. She was
going to make a grand entrance, a dramatic announcement. . . .

She hiccupped.

The man leaning his hip against the table and reading a sheet
with squint-eyed concentration looked up. Surely it was the uncharacteristically clean shirt, no doubt belonging to one of Philomena's grandsons, that made her notice the neglected lacing of
it? The very green eyes narrowed at her over the parchment. He
lowered it.

"Lady Juliana, you are drunk."

"Gwe-llian . . . Gwenllian made me." She corrected herself and
navigated with care to the nearest piece of furniture. "It tashtesh
like Hermine's."

"Did you bring me some too?"

She paid him back with a suspicious frown. She was there on
a serious matter, she told him. He smiled at that, as well, and got

her into the chair. When her bottom touched it, she jumped up, sobering. "Oh!" Reaching behind, she found a pile of sodden clothes.

"Ah." He took them from her. "I went swimming at the cliff pool. I'll go and hang them to dry since it offends your sense of tidiness."

He went, but alarmingly, the fog in her head was lifting. She did not want it to. There had to be a flagon about. There was, next to all the parchments. She reached for it, her gaze falling on the parchments. She picked up a sheet and blew the fine grains of sand from it.

Stubborn strokes of unambiguous Latin covered each sheet. It was a will, not signed, but she knew whose it was, leaving a wealth of estates to her and appointing for her and for Eleanor a guardian—Sir William Marshal, the Earl of Pembroke. The other sheet was her charter to Tillières. Juliana jumped back as if struck through the heart, dropping the parchment and knocking the others to the floor.

"Juliana?"

She was on her knees, gathering up the sheets as fast as she could, crumpling several in her haste. He knelt next to her without hurry, helping her to collect the rest. A silver earring shone through the thickness of his hair, which curled here and there and almost concealed a scar from a wound that properly should have killed him. It was as if they had returned to that chamber at Fontevraud. . . .

"I didn't know there was so much scribbling to all of this. We will need witnesses, but it can wait till morning."

An understanding came to her, unimpeded by wine. "You are returning to *outre-mer*."

He stood up and she did as well, sudden sobriety and an empty stomach dizzying her.

"Marshal is the best I can do. Thibodeau traded Tillières for one of Ralph's manors in England; that's how Armand got your charter. You still hold Tillières of Philip and if you stay away from Poitou, you and Eleanor will be safe from John and my kin. I am

leaving Seneterre to Gwenllian; I didn't think you would mind.
Aumary is back with Marshal . . . and d'Erlée."

"I see." She was a practical creature, and she was going to em-
ploy persuasion. That creature, however, had been supplanted by
an entirely different one. "You'll never think of anything else but
besting your father, will you, my lord? You would just as soon die
in a pit somewhere, but victorious in the end. You frighten me.
You . . . you terrify me. You frighten most of us, don't you ever see?
I came here—oh God, I don't know why I came here. To try to
seduce you. To curb you. Only I can't. No one can. Gwenllian
thought we could, for your soul's sake, for hers, for mine, for Eleanor of Brittany's sake, but I can't."

She spread her hands toward Heaven, the only thing she had
left to beseech, knowing that she must appear like a madwoman
in her ill-fitting gown and stripped emotions. "You would only
come up with something else, I don't know what—perhaps the
Apocalypse. Can't you allow us a victory once in a while, a small
one for us lesser mortals so that we don't have to fail so miserably
when we strive to do what is right and just? Oh God, I wish Eleanor
and I had died!"

The open door was a black blur and she ran toward it and the
precipitous steps and the void beyond.

He grabbed her around her waist before she reached it. She
fought him, shrieking at the top of her lungs. They came down in
the middle of the floor in a snarl of her skirts. "Juliana. *Juliana!*" He
could have struck her, but it was his voice, for a moment so much
like his father's, that silenced her instantly. "Isabel . . . Isabel said you
might throw a chamber pot at my head, not my entire existence."

"A chamber p-pot?"

"For not telling you the truth. That I want you. Bone and gristle. Don't ask me why. Maybe it is the hair."

Her hair. She had lost her wimple. Her unruly, short-shorn
nun's hair. She had cut it with her own hand after Eleanor was
born so that the sisters would not have to.

"See? The way you do that. The way you hide your nose and
your smile when you are not hiding your hands. The way you be-

rate me with a glance. Maybe Armand was right, it was your maidenhead. Aliénor knew it too, the scheming old witch."

"Good God. Aliénor knew about you. She lied to me!"

He had her on her feet. "Is that all? I bare my soul if you think I such possess, and you still can't say my name. Is that what you came to tell me, Juliana? Or is it Sister Eustace?"

He had asked her as much during their encounter before Paulette's abduction, a question compelled by anger, frustration, and derision. Her answer had been aimed to drive him away and it did, bringing on such devastation. This time she had to keep him. Not forever—she could never do that, could she? Between her shoulder blades, her shift clung damp. *Which one are you, child?* "I don't know your name, my lord. I can't know it before you know it yourself."

And there it was. A reply uncalculated, yet more perilous than all the lies laid end to end.

"That makes two of us." And he paused, the hesitation of one at the threshold of the unknown, and then he bowed to her.

"I was christened Jean Armand de Lusignan, Lord of Parthenay, seigneur of Couhé, Saint-Cyprien, Luçon, Gençay, Châtellerault, Vivonne, Cantigny, and sundry fiefs too petty to mention. Whom do I have the honor to address?"

Something in the room crackled, perhaps the very air. She curtsied as best as she could and answered, faltering, at least at the beginning. "Juliana de Charnais, Viscountess of Tillières, wedded wife of . . . of the Lord of Parthenay."

CHAPTER 76

After sailing through the air, she landed on the mattress, her bigamous, long-absent husband next to her. "Oooh, you are—"

"I know. Mad, but I swear I have not been with a woman since we made Eleanor. Fortunately, water runs rather cold in the middle of the night."

"But what about that woman at Diceto's?" Juliana recovered enough to remind him.

"What woman? Mine was Mistress Avre. I must have swallowed half the tadpoles."

He laughed, distracting her from the fact that her gown had dropped to the floor and that her shift was about to join it. She crossed her arms over her breasts to prevent it. This was too sudden, too impassioned, born out of the events of the day, out of emotions spilled forth when words were uttered that had no import at all.

He stopped, stone cold. "Juliana?"

It was a question, not a claim. For the first time, he wanted her consent. He was close, so very near. She could see only the angle of his cheekbone, the black brush of his eyelashes. Fear surged up in her, and yet, and yet . . . Her chin came up, ever so slightly, for her lips to touch his. *Let him kiss me with the kiss of his mouth, let him become the spring in me. . . .*

She anticipated the bitter taste of willow bark. It was not there. He could tell that something had surprised her, but he was making no demand in return. It emboldened her. Her fingers slipped to the ledge of his collarbone. Under her touch, the skin was hot, damp. She should withdraw, she should abandon this foolishness, this madness, she should keep her mind firmly fixed on . . . firmly fixed . . .

He propped himself on his elbow over her, his fingertips on her brow, the bridge of her nose, her lips. "I am sorry for what it cost you to bear Eleanor, but I am glad. If I had to hear Armand cackle over another grandchild, I would truly kill him. Juliana?"

"G-Guérin, just don't quote Horace."

Honor, like love, comes in many guises. And one day, love and passion simply vanish.

She wanted to ask the man next to her if it was true or if she was silly or credulous, but his eyes were closed, each breath steady. She watched him because she could without being made self-conscious, and waited for the passage of time to erode the last of the candles and bring the dawn.

At the third cock's crow, she climbed cautiously from the bed, found her shift, and went to close the shutters to the encroaching light. The click of the latch sent him upright with a sharp gasp. She looked back. "Guérin?"

He dropped to the pillows. "God, I thought it was all a dream." He closed his eyes and shuddered, yet when he opened them she still stood there with the light transforming her shift into nothing more than a cobweb to modesty. She did not know it, which made her standing there even more beguiling. But he did not want her standing there; he wanted her . . .

She let the shutters be and scurried to him, climbing under the covers and curling herself into his warmth. He drew her closer, pressing her hand against his heart. They lay quietly in the brightening light until she stirred.

"I miss Richard's cross." She sighed.

"You do?" His drowsy voice sounded sheepish, and when she looked up at him, he grimaced guiltily and pointed his chin to the height of the bedpost. Something there coruscated in the folds of the fabric.

"I forgot it was there. Geoffrey brought it to Gwenllian before he returned to *outre-mer*, informing her of my imminent demise. I'll take it down if it—"

"Don't move." She held him, and he did not. Above them the amethysts sparkled and danced, as if to sign that God did not mind this lapse of piety.

"We were all conceived and born in this bed," he said after a while. "Gwenllian inherited that irascible streak from our mother. She had three husbands you know, two at the same time."

They remained with their own thoughts, and then he reached over and twisted the gold ring from his little finger and placed it on the tip of her ring finger. "It's our mother's ring. Gwenllian gave it to me when I brought her from Wales. I guess Pike kept it, huh? It was meant for you, Juliana. Do you think you can believe me?"

Vous et nul autre. She slipped her finger into the circle until it passed her knuckle. "Hmmm. I think I can."

The hard pillow of his muscles relaxed under her cheek, but his voice was puzzled, as if she harbored some feminine secret he could never divine. "Truly? You can? How?"

She kept her voice solemn. "Because this one fits me a little better than the first one."

She heard his heart thump and he whooped with laughter, toppling her under him. "Ah, headway!"

Later, much later that day, they rode without company to Fécamp. During the previous night, de Blaye's men kept away not only any intruders but also Master Fulbeck, who was at last reunited with his family on Lasalle's orders.

They took Eleanor to the garden. Juliana set the basket on a carpet of grass dotted with dandelions and unwrapped the swaddling. Eleanor wriggled her toes and found them all to be delicious. Laughing, Juliana picked up her daughter, still not believing that this lively, demanding creature came of her. Eleanor's face wrinkled in anticipation of a good howl. Her father rescued her, raising her high into the breeze. Juliana watched with heart-pounding apprehension while he examined the child minutely, but without any pretended paternal affection.

"She is not that small. Look at those feet. She'll take getting used to though, especially since she is a screamer. You are in charge of the napkins. Isabel de Clare says I am better with flutes. Good God, I've left it at Longueville."

Juliana took the babe from him, smiling at his expression of feigned regret. "She is not a hound, my—oh, I don't know what to call you. We both have other names. I've always thought of you as Lasalle."

The bearer of that name went supine. "You can call me cur for all I care. Until Parthenay, I would heel only to your Jean Armand as yet."

Trying to swaddle Eleanor, Juliana thought about it. The babe wriggled, wiggled, and fussed. Lasalle lifted his head. "I'd leave her."

"But babies must be swaddled," Juliana protested.

Lasalle harrumphed and dropped his head against the grass, eyes closed. "You seem to speak from vast experience, Sister Eustace."

She giggled and threw a handful of grass on his face. He had expected it and retaliated, knocking her wimple askew and scooping her up before she could rally. That left as her only defense a pretended squeak of pain, which dissolved into laughter when he dropped her like a hot chestnut. He growled at her in mock retaliation and Juliana reached for her wimple and covered her mouth, abashed. "I am sorry, I mustn't."

He settled himself on his side, his chin in his palm. "You were louder last night."

She touched her flaming cheeks, surely the consequences of the tussle. "I wasn't . . . was I?"

He picked a dandelion as gold as a ducat and dabbed the tip of her nose with it. "As long as I don't hear Armand's name at a crucial moment, you can holler to high heaven, mouse."

The pause that ensued was uncomfortable. Juliana cleared her throat. "Anne?"

"A beautiful and passionate woman, Lady Juliana, but it's hard to swallow being taken for one's father, or any other man, one too many times. Maybe that's the reason I wanted you. At least I wouldn't hear any other name, if not exactly my own, whatever that may be."

She grabbed his arm. "I have a thousand questions."

He rolled on his back. "As long as you don't ask them all tonight."

She ventured closer to him, wanting to kiss him. "When will we leave?"

He reached his arm around her. "As soon as you care. We'll pick up supplies and what men we need at Rivefort, if you let me use your fat knights. We could use Thibodeau to make sense of all the fiefs and titles. Only if I catch him, I don't know whether to hang him or hire him. What do you think?"

She held on to her knees to prevent herself from toppling over in laughter, and this time he waited, his face serious. "Juliana? Am I trying too much?"

She propped herself at his level, her lips hovering above his. "You don't have to, no more than you did last night."

He was looking up at her the way he had under the willow branches at the Avre, but he could find no fear or desperation in the wide, dark eyes, nor in the trembling, shy kiss she gave him. And Jean Armand de Lusignan closed his eyes and smiled.

They packed and provisioned for the return to Tillières, having recruited a wet nurse from the next village, personally selected by Flotte. Mistress Philomena cried, as did Nurse Flotte, who at the last moment insisted that perhaps she should venture among the faithless Poitevins for Eleanor's sake, to the great dismay of her husband. When Gwenllian appeared at the garden gate, Jourdain in hand, Juliana made excuses about the carts and servants, leaving Lasalle and his sister alone.

He kissed her hand. "You won't come, then?"

"No. You two need to be together, alone. At least for a time. This is your proper wedding journey, you know."

Lasalle looked back at the caravan. "Seems like the first one. Perhaps you should come along. Juliana may need a woman's advice."

Gwenllian's eyes lit up. "Send for Anne. She can tell her more about you than I."

"Christ, she already did. Besides, she may be our stepmother."

Jourdain tore himself from Gwenllian's hand and went in pursuit of the dogs. She did not seem to notice. "Fascinating," she said.

Her brother gave her a squint. "Gwen, are you plotting again?"

"Of course I am. Go and enjoy my last one. I shall come to Parthenay when the time is right," she said, and stood on her tiptoes to kiss his cheek. Then she watched him join his wife and help her into the saddle.

When the carts rolled out of the courtyard, she took her cloak and walked along the path to the cliff, climbing the steep incline. Partway up the side, she rested to watch the carts and the riders take the slash of a road that led inland. She did not hear him over the wind until his horse snorted and his voice gave him away.

"You look pensive, Mistress. Is it painful to watch your lover ride away with his wife?"

She faced him without hurry, her hood concealing her. He was alone with only his name and his reputation to grant him passage. She nodded toward the caravan. "Was it painful for you to watch your rival ride away with your wife?"

She caught him speechless on the first try, and so his offense fell short of what she had expected, but it did get him out of the saddle, his riding crop swinging from his wrist. She ignored him, glancing toward the keep. "After Yvetta died, you never come to Seneterre. Your son talks about you only lately, and only to his wife. I've long wondered what sort of a man you truly are, Armand de Lusignan."

He took a deliberate step toward her. "You wonder a little more and I'll have you burned for sorcery."

She turned her cheek against the wind. "Isn't your son's mistress waiting for you at Pont-de-l'Arche?"

He grabbed her arm. The girl stood fast, her face pale in the cave of the hood. He could see the gleam of her eyes, unafraid. She could not have been more than . . .

"God's blood, who do you think you—"

Something flashed toward him. A knife's blade pressed underneath his ear, about where his son's scar commenced. The edge dwelled there long enough for him to register it fully. "Will you give your life for that answer, my lord?"

She thought that he would at least try to save himself. He did not. In the midnight-blue eyes of this merciless man flickered the gratitude of a dying felon delivered by a coup de grâce.

He closed his eyes and felt the sharp sting of broken vessels—and nothing more. He opened his eyes. The girl's cloak lay on the ground, her loose, shining black hair braided at her brow in a fashion that he had seen once only. And despite the different color of the eyes, he recognized in that face an unmistakable resemblance, and on the lips a smile, a ghost of a daring smile that he had first encountered years ago, a smile that took his heart, his reason, and his life away.

"I was wondering what my mother meant when, on her deathbed, she called you Mélusine's spawn."

He would not have noticed if he were struck by lightning and therefore the great, omnipotent Armand de Lusignan did not notice another rider on a higher point of the cliff.

The young man was not looking at the two of them, either. Wearing the colors of the Earl of Pembroke and holding the reins in one hand and a simple wooden flute in the other, he watched the departing train of the count's son with hate in his eyes.

AUTHOR'S BIBLIOGRAPHIC NOTE

Virtually no original sources were harmed in the research for this novel because the secondary ones have provided a wide path for my imagination to tread. Nevertheless, *The Sixth Surrender* follows the characters in chronological order through the twists and turns of events in England and France between 1200 and 1204.

With few exceptions, I opted for the older narrative histories to light the spark, rather than the latest scholarship, which tends to leave out the stuff of interest to novelists. I drew heavily on the premier account of this turbulent period, the original 1913 Manchester University Press edition of *The Loss of Normandy, 1189–1204*, by Sir Maurice Powicke. There was a Lady Juliana of Tillières, and there were a couple of Guérins.

Equally rich in detail is Kate Norgate's *John Lackland* (Macmillan and Co., 1902). Of more recent vintage and still indispensable among the books of Eleanor is Amy Kelly's *Eleanor of Aquitaine and the Four Kings* (Harvard University Press, 1950).

William Marshal has received attention in a number of fictional treatments and is the subject of Sidney Painter's *William Marshal: Knight-Errant, Baron, and Regent of England* (Barnes & Noble Books, 1995) and Georges Duby's *William Marshal: The Flower of Chivalry* (Pantheon Books, 1985). Two good sources on King John are W. L. Warren's *King John* (W. W. Norton & Company, 1961) and Ralph V. Turner's *King John* (Longman Publishing Group, 1994).

The Government of Philip Augustus: Foundations of French Royal Power in the Middle Ages (University of California Press, 1986), by John W. Baldwin, provides a scholarly grounding on the rise of medieval France.

For a discussion of what does a marriage make and the role of the naughty bits in medieval history aimed at the academic reader, see the encyclopedic *Law, Sex, and Christian Society in Medieval Europe* (University of Chicago Press, 1987), by James A. Brundage, and the more digestible *Eunuchs for the Kingdom of Heaven: Women, Sexuality, and the Catholic Church* (Doubleday, 1990), by Uta Ranke-Heinemann. The roles of women religious during this time is explored concisely by Penelope D. Johnson in *Equal in Monastic Profession: Religious Women in Medieval France* (University of Chicago Press, 1991). A little jewel of a book on the mundanity of medieval life is *Daily Living in the Twelfth Century, Based on the Observations of Alexander Neckham in London and Paris* (University of Wisconsin Press, 1952), by Urban Tigner Holmes Jr.

References to the Lusignans and their tangling with the Plantagenets are scattered throughout several of the above sources. The Lusignans' origins and their activities in Poitou and their confusing genealogical lineages are dealt with in detail in a number of accessible scholarly articles. In my genealogy, I picked Hugh Jr. as the jilted betrothed of Isabelle d'Angoulême. Of particular interest to the academics are the Lusignans' activities as the kings of Cyprus— the next place for the further adventures of Juliana and Lasalle.

When faced with a choice of historically correct versus contemporary terminology (e.g., the use of the term *Plantagenets*), I chose the contemporary terminology wherever possible for the sake of narrative shorthand. When it came to names and their spellings, I took artistic license and chose those that looked nifty. Mea culpa for all sins of omission and commission.

ACKNOWLEDGMENTS

With gratitude to my clever, long-suffering friends Martha Ellis, Dr. Cheryl J. Foote, and Rick Reichman. Particular thanks to Martha Hoffman, of Judith Ehrlich Literary Management; Denise Roy, of Plume; and Parris Afton Bonds, a true storyteller. Last but not least to my mother, who encouraged my dreams, and to my husband, who made them real.

Hana Samek Norton
Albuquerque, NM
July 2009